CRITICS ARE RAVING ABOUT *SEAN*, LEIGH GREENWOOD'S LATEST IN *THE COWBOYS* SERIES!

"*Sean* is like a vivid canvas, painted with vast landscapes, brushed with ugly shanties, then splattered with the mud and filth of a mining town. The author molds characters like a potter, then breathes life into them as tensions and conflict build. Every Western lover and romance enthusiast should include Leigh Greenwood's books in their collections—they are classics."

—*Rendezvous*

"Sean and Pearl are as tough as their surroundings, but both hide a heart of gold. This book rivals the best this author has written so far, and readers will want to make space on their keeper shelves for *Sean*. While you're at it, you might want to save room for the other *Cowboys* as well! . . . *Sean* is Western romance at its finest! Leigh Greenwood continues to be a shinning star of the genre!"

—*Literary Times*

"*The Cowboys* series is still riding high in the saddle! Leigh Greenwood has the ability to bring together unique plot lines which suit the characters and personalities already established in the series' early books, he makes it look easy! It's not! What it is, is captivating to this reviewer, who anxiously awaits the next *Cowboy*."

—*Heartland Critiques*

SEAN'S SEDUCTION

"What are you worried about?" Sean asked.

The question startled her. How much could he guess? "Nothing. Why do you ask?"

"Your body's tense. Does the first time with a man make you nervous?"

She was disappointed his thoughts hadn't changed. Why? What did she want him to think?

She sidestepped his question. "Do you always romance a woman by taking her dancing, eating supper in her bedroom?"

He held her a little tighter. "It's the first time."

"Why now?"

"It feels right."

Then he kissed her. A light peck on the forehead, but the kiss rocked Pearl as nothing else had in more than ten years.

The Cowboys

Sean

Leigh Greenwood

LEISURE BOOKS   NEW YORK CITY

To my son, Chris.
If he had red hair, the book could have been about him.

A LEISURE BOOK®

April 1999

Published by

Dorchester Publishing Co., Inc.
276 Fifth Avenue
New York, NY 10001

ISBN 0-8439-4490-0

The name "Leisure Books" and the stylized "L" with design are trademarks of Dorchester Publishing Co., Inc.

Printed in the United States of America.

Prologue

May 13, 1861
San Antonio, Texas

Sean O'Ryan stood perfectly still, his eyes respectfully lowered, but it was hard not to stare. He'd never seen a woman dressed like his aunt. He could hardly take his eyes from her ruby lips or her nearly black eyes that seemed to be surrounded by a dark green color. Her dress of rich red fabric rustled noisily every time she moved. A profusion of ruffles and buttons decorated the front of her dress. A funny little hat of flowers and feathers rested precariously on her abundant raven's-wing hair without benefit of a strap under her chin. Sean wanted to ask how it stayed on, but he was afraid if he made a sound, his aunt wouldn't take him.

"You sure this is my nephew?" Kathleen Kelly asked. She moved restlessly to and fro, impatient to be gone. "He looks too big to be just nine."

"The records say he's Sean O'Ryan, son of Shamus and Gwenda Kelly O'Ryan," said Mrs. Grasty. She ran the orphanage where Sean stayed. It baffled him that she looked almost as angry at his aunt as she was with him when he got into trouble.

"What would I do with a nine-year-old boy?"

"Bring him up properly like any decent woman."

But Mrs. Grasty had told Sean his aunt wasn't decent, that she was a dancer, that she painted her face to attract men. Sean didn't see anything wrong with that. He thought she looked a lot prettier than Mrs. Grasty.

"He needs a home," Mrs. Grasty said. "He needs to learn responsibility."

"I'm too busy to have a home. I live in hotels. Why can't he stay here? As big as he is, some farmer's bound to adopt him."

"He's been thrown out of two homes and one orphanage already."

"Well, if you can't handle him, how do you expect me to?" Kathleen pulled on long black gloves and tossed something that looked like a tangle of furry animals over her shoulder.

"I see you refused to take him nine years ago," Mrs. Grasty said, her tone more severe than Sean had ever heard it.

"He was a baby," Kathleen said. "What could I do with a baby?" She peered at him again, made a face. "Are you sure he's my nephew?"

"Positive."

"Well, I can't take him, no matter who he is," she said with an air of finality. "There's a war coming. I gotta head West."

"Take me with you," Sean cried. Being quiet wasn't working. "I can ride and shoot."

"Don't lie," Mrs. Grasty ordered.

This was no time to be shackled by the truth. His only chance to escape Mrs. Grasty was about to walk out the door. "I can fight Indians, too."

"I'm going to San Francisco," his aunt said. "They don't have Indians there."

Nor did they need little boys who could shoot or ride horses. She didn't need him at all. She didn't want him. Nobody did.

May 13, 1861
St. Louis, Missouri

Agnes Satterwaite stared at her father, wondering if she'd ever loved him. If she had, she'd stopped today. No matter what happened, he'd never hit her again.

"Don't leave this room," her father said. "And if I find Rock Gregson hanging around when I get back, I'll teach him what happens to men who try to ruin decent girls."

"He's not trying to ruin me," Agnes said, willing to try once more to make her father understand. "He wants to marry me."

"Men like him don't marry their women," her father yelled at her. "They turn them into whores, then leave them for somebody else."

"Rock isn't like that. He loves me. He says we can live on the riverboat in a room all our own. He's offered to buy me any dress I want for a wedding present."

"Is that all you can think about—fancy clothes and ruining yourself for some gambler?"

"He's not a gambler. He works for the riverboat company. Besides, being the wife of a gambler couldn't be worse than working on that farm until I'm so worn out and ugly nobody will have me."

"It'll keep you pure and virtuous for when you get a husband."

"When will that be?"

"When you're older. Fourteen's too young to be thinking about getting married."

"Mama was fourteen when she married you, fifteen when I was born." And twenty-seven when she was laid in her grave.

"It was a mistake to bring you to St. Louis. It's turned your head. You'll marry a decent man one day, and—"

"How? You won't let Benton get down from his wagon when he comes. And you told Orvis you'd shoot him if he ever set foot on the place again."

"I won't have them nosing around you like you was in heat!" he shouted. "It's a sin."

"Ma said it's natural for a man to want to be with a woman. She said—"

"Don't argue with me, girl. You'll do as I say."

"Mama told me not to let you keep me on that farm. She said you'd work the life out of me like you did her. She said—"

"I loved your ma."

"Is that why you hit her?"

"I had to. She wouldn't mind sometimes. She wanted things no decent woman wants."

"She only wanted to laugh, to have pretty things."

"A good woman doesn't want anything but her husband and her children."

"I'm not going to be like Mama, Papa. I'm going with Rock. He loves me. He'll—"

"I'll kill you before I let that man have you."

He lunged for Agnes, but she was ready. She hit him as hard as she could with the washbasin. Stunned, he dropped to his knees.

She grabbed her coat and ran to the door. "I'm leaving, and you can't stop me. When I come back, you'll see—"

"If you go with that man, don't ever come back. I won't have a whore for a daughter."

"Papa!"

"Whore!"

She ran from the room, the horrible word still ringing in her ears.

Chapter One

Colorado gold fields, 1876

"Sit still and be quiet, or I'll wrap this bandage over your mouth," Sean O'Ryan admonished Pete Jernigan. "I can't get it tight with you squirming." Pete had been shot during a gold shipment robbery, and Sean had gotten stuck with patching him up.

"You've got to see her," Pete said, trying to turn so he could see his friend. "She's absolutely beautiful. Every man who sees her falls in love with her."

"I won't."

"Even you'll agree Pearl's gorgeous," Pete said earnestly. "She's perfection."

"You think about her perfection. I don't have time, not with having your work to do and mine as well." Pete had taken care of their tent, buying supplies, and seeing about the laundry until he got shot.

Sean and Pete had been in the gold fields nearly

two months, plenty of time to stake their claim and set up their tent in the ramshackle settlement that served as home to the men who searched for gold in the nearby hills and streams. Tents, log houses, huts of sticks and brush, even caves hollowed out of the hillsides served as shelter for men who poured all their energy into the pursuit of the yellow metal. It represented a dream so powerful that it drove them to leave homes and families—even to abandon wives and children—to travel a thousand miles into a wilderness, toil endless hours at backbreaking work, and live worse than barnyard animals. All for the hope of the riches represented by those tiny flecks of gold.

Sean had come for the dream, too, but he had no family to leave behind.

"If you didn't spend every daylight hour at the diggings, you'd have enough time," Pete said.

"I don't intend to stay here any longer than I have to. I mean to have my own ranch by fall."

"I know," Pete said, rolling his eyes at Sean's oft-stated goal. "You want a ranch like Jake's and a wife like Isabelle."

"What's wrong with that?"

"Look, being adopted by Jake and Isabelle was the best thing that ever happened to us. I'm just as grateful to them as you are, but I don't want to be just like them."

"Why not? They're good people. Besides, I like ranching. I'm good at it, too."

"I know. Jake told everybody it would take two men to replace you. But we agreed it was time to make our own way. That's why we're working like demons for this gold."

"*I'm* working like a demon," Sean said. "You're getting yourself shot."

"I'm not in such a hurry to leave," Pete said, ignoring Sean's jibe. "I don't have a ranch to buy or a wife to find. I mean to enjoy myself before I get married."

"I'm not looking for a wife out here. Sit still so I can finish this bandage. I want to leave for Twisted Gulch before dark. Damn, I hate that place. There's not a person in the whole town who cares for anything but your money."

"You'd like it better if you'd go to the Silken Lady," Pete said, reverting to his favorite subject. "Pearl serves the best food, real whiskey, and has the prettiest girls. Not that you'll notice them with Pearl around."

Movement outside their tent caught Sean's attention. He turned to see the washerwoman drive her wagon into camp.

"I forgot to tell you she was coming tonight," Pete said. "You'll have to sort the clothes before she gets here."

Sean secured the last pin in the bandage. "You and I have been friends and partners for ten years. I'll fix your bandages, cook your food, and do your work at the mine, but I'll be damned if I'll sort your clothes."

"You too good?" Pete asked, firing up.

"No. Too ornery."

"That's God's honest truth. All the more reason to go see Pearl. She'll—"

"Stop!" Sean shouted as he began gathering up dirty clothes. "I give up. I'll sort your clothes, tuck you into bed, do practically anything if you promise not to mention that woman's name again."

"I don't understand why you're so set against her," Pete said. "I'm the one who got rolled by that little tramp in Ogallala. I'm the one who should hate women, not you."

"Not all women. Just women of that type. Why can't you put your clothes in a heap like a normal person?"

"Pearl's different."

"You've got stuff scattered from one end of the tent to the other."

"You'd know that if you met her."

"I'm not crawling under your cot. Let them rot."

"And wait until you hear her sing."

"When you get set up in that fancy hotel you're always talking about, you can hire a maid to find the clothes you drop down cracks."

"Your laundry ready?"

The washerwoman stood before the tent. Sean hadn't heard her come up.

"It's not sorted." He came out of the tent into the daylight. The woman's expression changed abruptly. Sean wondered if his size had frightened her. He was so big that he intimidated some people. He dropped the clothes on the ground. "There's more inside. I'll get them." When he returned, the woman had begun to sort the clothes into two baskets. "Pete'll do that for you," Sean said.

Pete emerged from the tent to drop more clothes onto the pile. She looked at his tightly bandaged shoulder. "Looks like I'd better do it myself if I want it done."

"Good. He can help me fix dinner."

"Why don't you go back to town with her?" Pete suggested. "You can eat at the Silken Lady."

Leigh Greenwood

"If I didn't know better, I'd swear you wanted me to marry that woman."

"Pearl doesn't want to get married."

"It's a good thing. Women like her aren't likely to make good wives or mothers."

"Half the men in Twisted Gulch would marry Pearl if they had the chance."

"They may not mind spending their gold on her, but I bet you won't see anybody offering to take her back East."

"Pearl's different," Pete insisted. "She's older, too."

"Then nobody'll marry her. She probably paints herself to look younger."

"That's all you men think about, isn't it?" the washerwoman asked. "You can't pay enough attention to a woman when she's young and pretty. But when she starts to lose her looks, you forget she's alive."

"Decent men care about more than looks," Sean said. "There's—"

"Men are all alike. I ought to know."

"You saying you were pretty once?" Pete asked.

"Not as pretty as Pearl Belladonna, but I used to be accounted a good-looking woman."

Sean didn't see any beauty in her ravaged face. He didn't want to be rude—Isabelle had taught all her boys to be polite to women, regardless of their station—but he wished she'd stop staring at him, finish sorting the laundry, and leave. He wanted to wash and get into some clean clothes before he started dinner.

The washerwoman had come a few steps closer and was staring at him again. If he hadn't known she'd

18

never set eyes on him before, he'd swear she was looking for something she recognized.

"What's your name?" she asked.

"Why do you want to know?" He had no objection to telling anybody his name, but why should she want to know?

"He said it was O'Ryan," she said, pointing to Pete.

"There are a lot of O'Ryans about," Sean said. He could detect an Irish lilt to her voice. Maybe she was looking for relatives. She looked as though life had used her harshly, but she had to be making good money. Miners paid dearly for the luxury of clean clothes.

She was peering at him again, even harder this time.

"You look the spitting image of somebody I once knew. His name was Shamus."

Sean's impatience turned to sharpened interest. Shamus was his father's name. Both his parents had died when he was an infant. "Why would you be caring about a man named Shamus?"

"That was my sister's husband's name."

"Shamus is a popular name in Ireland."

"You look enough like Gwenda's Shamus to be his son."

Something inside Sean squeezed hard. Gwenda was his mother's name. If this woman was her sister, she was his Aunt Kathleen, the woman who'd condemned him to fourteen years in orphanages and foster homes. He looked at her carefully, but he couldn't see any resemblance to the painted beauty who'd turned her back on him sixteen years earlier.

"So you're Kathleen Kelly," he said, coldly polite.

"Do you remember the last time we met?"

Her gaze didn't falter. "I remember."

She still had a dancer's lithe figure, but years of cosmetics, bad diet, liquor, and late nights showed in her face.

"Are you really Gwenda's boy?" She came closer, reached out, tried to touch him.

Sean backed away. "My parents were Shamus and Gwenda O'Ryan. They were married just before they left for America. They died in Boston and I was sent to Galveston to their only relative in this country. Her name was Kathleen Kelly. She refused to take me because she said it would interfere with her career as a dancer."

"I was good," Kathleen said proudly. "Everyone said so."

"Maybe." He paused a moment to let some of the anger leave his body. "You don't look like the woman I remember."

"Women in my profession don't age well."

"Pearl is beautiful," Pete said.

"Wait until she's forty-two," Kathleen said.

"She'll still be beautiful," Pete insisted.

Ignoring Pete, Kathleen spoke to Sean. "We should get to know each other. That's the way families do."

He'd thought as much. But when he was a helpless baby or a troublesome boy, she didn't have time for him. Now that he was supposed to have some gold hidden away, it was another story. "I want nothing to do with any woman of your type," Sean said. "None of you know the first thing about being a *real* woman—working, caring, sacrificing for the people you love. All you care about is men and drinking and

20

having a good time. Where are all those men now?''

He could feel the anger building in him again, and he consciously cut it off. He didn't want to dredge up past hurt and bitterness. He didn't want to remember how he'd felt, knowing his only relative in America had turned her back on him. He just wanted her to leave so he could forget her all over again.

"If you're through sorting," he told her brusquely, "I'll load your baskets into the wagon."

"You'll need me one day."

"I needed you twenty-four years ago. I'll never need you again."

"If you take up with Pearl Belladonna, you'll need more help than the likes of me can give."

"I'm not taking up with Pearl. I don't intend to set foot in her place."

Pearl Belladonna belted out the last note of her song, kicked her leg as high as she could, and landed in a split. She struggled to keep the smile on her face as a sharp pain shot through her thigh. Damn! She was going to have to give up all this fancy stuff. It was hard enough to make a living singing and dancing. But hitting the floor with one leg pointed north and the other south was getting to be too tough on her body. The way her muscles were screaming, she'd be lucky to walk off the stage without limping.

But the drunken shouts, ear-piercing whistles, and thunderous foot-stomping reminded her of why she put herself though this three to five times a night. The miners loved her. Every night, while they waited for her to perform, they filled her saloon, drinking and gambling, adding steadily to her secret savings account in a Denver bank. The day would come when she couldn't dance anymore, when the sight of her leg tightly encased in a mesh stocking wouldn't send men into a frenzy of shouting and stomping. When that day came, she meant to have enough money to slip into a respectable old age.

She had been dirt-poor, and she hadn't liked it one bit.

Pearl rose to her feet with a grace practiced and perfected over ten years. She gave her audience a saucy smile, a double bump-and-grind with her hips, a final glimpse of her shapely leg, and headed off the stage, making sure to swing her hips seductively each step of the way.

The men shouted, whistled even louder, and surrounded her the minute she reached the floor from the stage she had had constructed at one end of the long, narrow saloon. She had done her best to make the saloon look bright and cheerful. The facade had been painted blue and trimmed in brown. Inside, she'd covered the rough lumber walls with canvas to make the room brighter and keep out drafts. But the focus of the saloon was the huge walnut bar she'd paid to have brought out from Denver. The large mirrors and rows of sparkling clean glasses gave the place a distinctive touch of class. The cost had been significant, but so far the rewards had been greater.

"How about a dance?" a tall, gangly young man named Dusty Logan asked.

"I got a pitcher of beer waiting for the two of us," Paul Higgins, a respected local merchant, said.

"How about a little cuddle?" asked another.

"Come on, Pearl," Dusty begged. "You danced with Ossie."

"I'm old enough to be your big sister. Go ask one

of the girls." Pearl signaled the bartender to make up her special drink.

"Hell, you're not old," Dusty protested. "You got more energy than any two of your girls. You're prettier than all of them put together."

Pearl laughed and pinched Dusty's cheek. "You're a sweet boy, Dusty, but you're a terrible liar. This place is full of mirrors. I *know* what I look like."

"How about coming out back with me?" asked a crusty miner who'd been trying to get into Pearl's bed from the moment he saw her.

"Have you been drinking that rotgut they serve at the Red Rooster?"

"I haven't set foot in the place since I discovered you."

"Then you've been dreaming. Try working your mine a little harder. You'll have more gold and fewer unanswered prayers."

"Can't I buy you a drink?" he asked.

"I'd drink your beer," Pearl said, giving him a playful punch in his rock-hard stomach, "if I thought you weren't using it for an invitation somewhere else."

"I'm man enough," he said proudly.

"You'd scare a poor little girl like me to death," Pearl said. "You wouldn't want that, would you?"

"Hell, yes," the miner said, and all the men except Dusty clapped him on the back and laughed.

"I'm mighty particular when it comes to choosing a man."

"Who're you going to choose?" Dusty asked.

Pearl grinned and sidled up to Dusty, hand on hip, breasts jutted out, a smile on her lips. "You hoping it might be you?" A quick shift in weight, and her hip bumped into his, knocking him slightly off balance. The men around her hooted.

"Yeah," Dusty said, striving to ignore the flush of embarrassment tinging his cheeks. "I'm young and strong. I can keep going all night."

"That's what she wants you to do," Paul said, "keep going until you get back to your claim."

Pearl sidled a little closer, letting Dusty get a whiff of her perfume. "You're cute," she said in a sultry voice brought to perfection by years of practice. "I might give you a thought or two."

"Give him all the *thoughts* you want," Paul said, "as long as you give me your time."

Pearl laughed. "If you men worked as hard on your claims as you do trying to get into my bed, you'd all be rich."

"Getting into your bed would be as rich as I'd ever want to be," Dusty said.

"Richer than you deserve," Paul said.

"You boys go talk to the girls," Pearl said. "I've got to catch my breath. Play a fast polka," she called to the piano player. "Something to take the starch out of them so they can sleep good tonight."

"Hell, who wants to sleep?" a particularly ugly miner asked.

"Nobody could with your face giving them nightmares," his partner said.

Pearl lifted the bar gate and moved inside, safe for a time from wandering hands but still able to keep an eye on everything that happened. She looked into one of the mirrors that were part of the bar and gave herself a critical glance. "I'd better fix my face before you boys decide I look uglier than an old maid aunt."

Pearl grinned at the chorus of dissent that erupted

around her. Her looks were holding up pretty well for a woman of twenty-nine. That was fortunate. You had to look good in this business to stay on top.

For herself, Pearl wouldn't have minded being a little less pretty. When she was younger, she'd thought her looks were a passport from the mind-numbing labor on her parents' farm. Now that she knew better, she needed them to ensure her future.

She used the mirror to pin a few curls into place. A closer look revealed some blond roots. It was about time to dye her hair again. Blond was okay for her girls, but the men expected fire from her, fire that matched the bright red curls piled atop her head. Another lie, she thought to herself. But it was hardly noticeable in the middle of so many others.

"The boys seem a little tense tonight," she said to Calico Tom as he handed her a special mixture of honey-sweetened tea laced with a dash of expensive bourbon.

Calico Tom, who stood by the bar every night as long as Pearl was in the saloon, was a tall, thin Chinaman she had nursed back to health just after she bought her first saloon. Despite being past fifty, he had appointed himself her guardian.

"They mad somebody steal gold," Calico Tom said.

"They ought to keep it in their camp or take it with them when they leave."

"Too much gold bring thieves. Somebody die in camp every week."

"Why do they do it? Hardly any of them find enough gold to make it worth the risk."

"They hope get rich. Go home big man."

Pearl could understand that. She'd felt the same

25

way when she fell for Rock Gregson's handsome face and smooth line. She'd been so anxious to leave the abject poverty of her Missouri home she'd been more than willing to believe him when he said they'd get married in the very next town. It had taken her nearly five months to get it through her thick head that Rock would say anything you wanted him to say. Then do what *he* wanted.

She'd been left on her own, disgraced, desperate, unable to go home. Being young and pretty, success had come quickly. She soon discovered an endless string of handsome men eager to help her enjoy her good fortune. But Pearl was looking for something more than a Good-time Charlie. When she thought she'd found it in a young cowboy, she married him. When he was killed in a gunfight, Pearl swore off men. It hadn't been an easy vow to keep, but after years of seeing little beyond the dregs of humanity, she found temptation easier to resist.

"Man come see you," Calico Tom said.

"Who?"

"He not say."

"What does he want?"

"He say he have business proposition that make you rich. He say he come back later."

That intrigued Pearl. She'd be interested in anything that would allow her to retire sooner. "What did he look like?"

"Big man. Fancy clothes. He dress like dude, but he been around."

"Haven't they all."

"You want me throw him out?"

"I'll see him, but his idea had better be a good one. I can't afford to take time away from my customers."

26

"They want nobody else," Calico Tom said of the men who kept watching to see when Pearl would come out from behind the bar. "You goddess."

If so, she was a goddess with clay feet. There were two kinds of women in the gold camps and the towns that grew up around them. There were the good women—the wives, mothers, sisters, and daughters—but there were so few of them that a man would sometimes travel fifty miles just to sit and stare.

Then there were the *other* women, women whose fall from grace was determined by one thing only. Chastity. Whether the fall was real or only suspected, the brand was irrevocable. Men were just as thirsty for a look at these women, but with them they could touch, dance, tease, carouse. No nagging, no limits. The men made the rules, and the women played along.

Pearl was one of those women. Because she was prettier than most, had a little talent, was always ready with a friendly smile, and owned a saloon where the liquor was decent, she was the most popular. But she was one of the *other* women, and she was never allowed to forget it.

She resented that. She wanted all the things decent women wanted—she was willing to work hard and ask little—but it seemed she would be forced to spend the rest of her life paying for the mistake of a foolish, desperate, fourteen-year-old girl.

Pearl took the last swallow of her drink and heaved herself away from the bar. Time to stop worrying about what couldn't be changed and get back to work. She put her hand out to raise the bar and froze. Rock Gregson had just walked into the saloon. Pearl hadn't seen him in several years, but she recognized him instantly. Barely changed, he looked as handsome and worthless as ever.

"That man," Calico Tom said.

Pearl knew Rock was the one Calico Tom meant. Every time she moved to a new mining town, she hoped she'd never see him again. But they both depended on miners for a living. She'd been in Twisted Gulch over a year. Rock was long overdue.

"You want see him?" Calico Tom asked, watching her closely.

"No, but I will." Her mood turned stormy at the memory of what this man had done to her. He'd taken her innocence—mind, body, and soul—then betrayed her. Now he smiled at her as though they were the best of friends.

She opened the bar and pushed her way into the crowd. She took her time crossing the saloon, stopping several times to joke with the men, exchange a few wisecracks, enjoy a little innuendo. She wanted Rock to see that these men adored her, that she didn't need him.

When she finally reached him, she experienced a stab of envy as she looked him over from head to foot. He actually looked better than ever. It wasn't fair that men got better-looking with age. He ought to have lines, crow's feet, aching muscles. She'd bet he slept well at night, too.

She faced him squarely. She wasn't the fourteen-year-old innocent she'd been when he found her. After fifteen years on her own, she knew what was behind those good looks, that broad grin, that air of confidence. Rock was a crook, a liar, and a cheat. He always had been. He'd never be anything else.

"Hello, Pearl."

Damn! His voice was just as sexy as always. Somebody ought to shoot him to keep still more women from making fools of themselves.

"What do you want?" Pearl asked.

"Who says I want anything?"

"Okay, what are you going to give me?"

Rock laughed easily, just as if he had a clean conscience.

"You always were ready with the joke."

"That must have been some other girl. I was the serious one who talked about marriage, you settling down and getting a decent job. I don't blame you for not remembering. After so many women, it must be hard to single out any particular one."

"You never did like to share."

"Now you're remembering. While you're at it, remember I don't like liars."

"This man bothering you?" Paul asked.

Pearl had been concentrating so on Rock, she hadn't realized several of the men had gathered around her.

"No," Pearl said. "He's just somebody I used to know."

"I've come to talk over old times," Rock said. "And do a little business."

"Talk fast," Dusty said. "Pearl owes me a dance."

"We've got no business to discuss," Pearl said.

"You haven't heard my proposition yet," Rock said.

"She says she's got nothing to say," Paul said.

Rock continued to smile, his good mood apparently unimpaired. But she could tell from the way his eyes changed from bright to dull that he was mad. When Rock got mad, there was always trouble.

He reached into his pocket and drew out a gold coin. "Have a round of drinks on me. Pearl and I are going to her office." He held out the coin, but no one took it.

"Go ahead," Pearl said. "You might as well drink on his money. I won't be long."

Paul and Dusty seemed reluctant to leave her, but another of the men grabbed the coin. "Free drinks for everybody!" he shouted.

"Come on back, Rock. Say what you have to say and get out. I don't need stray dogs messing up the place."

"Always a kidder," Rock said as he followed her. He didn't sound amused.

Pearl's office was really a storeroom. She'd pushed into a corner the battered desk she used to pay bills, transact business, and reply to her correspondence. She kept her best whiskey in the desk drawers. She opened the door for Rock, then followed him in. "Okay, what do you want?" she asked as she closed the door behind her.

"Don't be in such a hurry," Rock said. "We haven't seen each other in a long time."

"It hasn't been long enough." Pearl crossed to her desk, then turned to face him. "Talk. I've got to be back outside in ten minutes."

"Looks like you're doing pretty good here."

Pearl didn't know what purpose Rock had in complimenting her, but she was certain it wasn't to her advantage. "I'm barely keeping my head above water. I give them real whiskey." She had no intention of letting him know the extent of her success.

"I'd say you were doing better than that."

"I just hope the gold holds out for another year. I don't have the money to set up again."

"I'd say you do."

"I don't. But if I did, you wouldn't get any of it."

Rock laughed again. She'd forgotten how easily he laughed, how little it made her feel like joining him. "Not a very generous attitude."

Pearl started to feel nervous. "I don't want anything to do with your schemes. I run a clean operation here."

"I'm not going to suggest anything illegal."

"Don't try to tell me you're going straight."

Rock laughed again. She wished he wouldn't.

"I'm looking for somewhere to set up, and your place is perfect."

"I don't need professional gamblers. My customers spend most of their time dancing with the girls or playing low-stakes games among themselves. If you're looking for heavy plungers, head down to Bailey's Emporium."

"You've got class, Pearl. We could attract the biggest gamblers in town. You and your girls could ply them with whiskey, get them to the table. I could do the rest."

"What percentage of your winnings would I get?"

"The extra money from liquor ought to be enough."

"In other words, I take the risks, shoulder the expense, and you take the cash." After everything Rock had done to her, he kept floating back, expecting her to take up right where they'd left off. He had to be crazy. "Get out, Rock. I wouldn't help you rob your victims years ago, and I'm not going to now."

"I'm just offering your customers a little fun."

"I don't see how you can call being robbed blind fun."

"It's all in one's viewpoint. Just call it a man paying for his pleasure."

"No matter what you call it, I won't do it. And there's no need to get angry. I see it in your eyes. I haven't forgotten you even if you can barely remember me."

"I remember you very well, Pearl. You were the best-looking woman I ever had."

"Shame you couldn't remember that then."

"I remembered it. I just couldn't see limiting myself to one when there were so many to be enjoyed."

"Get out, Rock. And don't come back."

"I'm not asking much."

"I'm not turning my place into a gyp joint for you. I've got a reputation to uphold."

Rock sneered. "What kind of reputation does a woman like you have beyond sleeping with any man who has the price?"

His remark made Pearl so furious that she was tempted to reach for the gun in her desk. If she'd ever had that reputation, he'd been the one to give it to her. "If I were a man, I'd make you pay for that."

"You'd better think about my offer. I really think you ought to say yes."

"What you think doesn't mean a damned thing to me." She marched over to the door and opened it. "Now get out."

Rock didn't move. "You've got a nice little business here, but you never know when things might change."

Pearl bridled. "Are you saying, if I don't let you fleece my customers, you'll ruin me?"

"It would be a shame if that happened."

"As long as I deliver the best entertainment in town, sell the best whiskey, and have the prettiest girls, I'll have the most business. You try to do anything to change that, and the boys will run you out of town so fast, you won't have time to pack your underwear."

"Things don't have to be like this. We could—"

"Calico Tom!" Pearl called out as she stepped through the doorway. "This gentleman is ready to leave, but he can't find his way to the door."

Calico Tom and Paul had been standing just outside the office door. They plucked Rock from the office like lint from a dress coat.

"I can't say it was nice to see you again," Pearl said. "And if you think about dropping in again before you leave town, don't."

The look Rock gave Pearl caused her courage to falter. "I'm not leaving until I get what I came for," he said.

Calico Tom propelled Rock toward the door.

"What did he come for?" Paul asked.

"Trouble," Pearl replied. "That's what he always brings."

Chapter Two

Laughter and music from two dozen brightly lighted saloons spilled into the street and echoed off the high mountain walls that squeezed the raucous town of Twisted Gulch into a narrow gorge that until a few years ago had been known only to the Indians and the elk. All the saloons competed for customers, but Pearl Belladonna's Silken Lady was the most popular. Everybody knew that wasn't her real name, but then, half the men in Twisted Gulch had shed their Christian names when they crossed the Missouri River, just as anxious as Pearl to leave some part of their past behind. Here and now was all that counted.

For some of them, their name was all they had left.

Sean O'Ryan paused in front of the Silken Lady. Instinct told him to avoid this place, to eat somewhere else and hurry back to camp. But he was restless tonight. Bored. He hadn't been with a woman in months. After a shave, haircut, and a bath, he felt human for the first time in weeks. Since he was already in town, he couldn't see any reason not to have a little fun. Besides, the Silken Lady was reputed to serve real whiskey, not the kind concocted in the back room from pepper, tobacco juice, and strychnine.

After listening to Pete talk about her for weeks, Sean was curious about Pearl. He didn't think any saloon dancer could be as perfect as Pete insisted, but he was tired of looking at rocks, donkeys, and ugly men. He was tired of working himself to exhaustion each day, of going to bed with this gnawing need for feminine company. A pretty woman, no matter what her character, would be a welcome change.

Pete said she had red hair and blue eyes. Same as his. Maybe she was Irish, too.

Sean wasn't a monk, but he had no intention of becoming infatuated like Pete. The other miners at the camp were just as bad. They talked about Pearl as if she was the pinnacle of womanhood. Sean knew better. Women like Pearl were strictly for having a little bit of fun.

Sean pushed open the swinging doors and stepped into the saloon. A sudden rush of men toward the stage warned him Pearl was about to perform. He moved to one of the empty chairs farthest away from the little platform that served as Pearl's pedestal.

Pearl appeared on the third measure of the piano introduction. Sean leaned forward, half rising out of his chair. Pete hadn't exaggerated. Pearl Belladonna was stunning. Her face reflected none of the life she'd lived for at least a decade. Her tall, stately body was lush enough to cause a riot, but his attention was drawn to her hair. Sean had been teased about his red hair all his life, but it couldn't hold a candle to the fiery tresses that framed Pearl's face and cascaded down her back. Neither did she have the freckles and pale skin that were the curse of every true Irish redhead. Pearl's complexion was as flawless as her namesake. She looked as pure and honest as Isabelle.

Sean forced himself to settle back, to breathe slowly, to relax. She might be so beautiful that she took his breath away, but he could never let himself forget that Pearl Belladonna was one of the *other* women.

The roar from the men drowned out the first words of her song. A bit of exposed leg caused whistles to drown out more. The abundant high spirits of the place drew him in like an aphrodisiac. It had been a long time since he'd let himself have a little fun. He loved music, and Pearl had a nice voice, low and husky. Occasional high notes lifted her voice into a range that sounded as though it had been designed by Mother Nature for lullabies. That was a terrible waste. Women like Pearl Belladonna didn't have babies.

She did one of her kicks and was rewarded by more whistles and shouts.

A couple of men down front were causing a disturbance. One stood up and shouted something rude at Pearl. The men on either side jerked him back down. The second rowdy came to the aid of the first.

Sean knew immediately that they weren't miners. It looked to him as if they had come to the Silken Lady just to cause trouble. When one of them broke a chair over the head of the man trying to force him back down into his seat, Sean was sure of it.

Sean didn't move. Pearl's regular customers could take care of the ruffians. There seemed to be enough of them. But it was getting too noisy to hear Pearl's song, and he hadn't had a good fight in weeks. Not since that Welshman tried to jump his claim.

Sean ducked. A chair sailed by his head, crashed against the wall, and broke into pieces. It was going to be expensive if things didn't calm down soon. A girl came to take his order. She had the bright, untroubled look of youthful innocence—long flaxen tresses, warm brown eyes—exactly the look Sean had always expected in the woman he would one day marry. She was truly beautiful. Sean didn't understand why Pete had never mentioned her.

"Is it like this often?" he shouted above the din.

"I don't understand it," she said as she moved to keep from being knocked over by two men who tumbled toward her. "We never have fights."

He ordered a beer and dinner to follow. Pearl was still singing, but she looked angry. When she reached over and threw one of the fake flower arrangements into the crowd, he knew he could forget the rest of the song. One man stumbled across the room, knocking the waitress into Sean's lap.

"Come back when I've finished my dinner, and we can go up to your room," Sean said, grinning. He was amused by her shocked expression as she jumped up and ran away.

The fighting was getting worse. It was bound to delay his dinner. Two more men jumped to their feet and attacked men next to them. This had to be a deliberate attempt to stop Pearl's show.

When two more came in from the street, each with a stick in his hands, Sean realized this was more than an attempt to disrupt a single performance. Somebody was trying to break up Pearl's saloon. He didn't know Pearl, but he didn't like to see anybody take advantage of a woman. It went squarely against his sense of fair play and his beliefs about how a man should treat a woman—*any* woman.

Suddenly all restraint and lack of interest left him. The smell of battle was in his nostrils, and he couldn't resist. He leapt to his feet and waded into the middle of the fray.

At six inches over six feet and more than two hundred and fifty pounds, Sean was the biggest man in the room. He moved people out of his way like a train plowing though a snowdrift. He came up behind the two men with sticks as they began hitting Pearl's customers. He grabbed them by their collars and banged their heads together until they sank to the floor.

Next Sean waded into the free-for-all that was rapidly reducing Pearl's tables and chairs to kindling. He picked up one of the bully boys and threw him against the wall. The second had picked up a chair to throw at the huge, expensive mirror that covered the back of Pearl's bar. Sean picked up the surprised bruiser by the seat of his pants and the back of his shirt, lifted him over his head, and threw him through the swinging doors into the street. He then pushed his way to the front and the two men who'd started the trouble. A man dressed like a conservative businessman had one of them down and was beating his head against the floor. A skinny youngster was struggling with the other. Sean gripped the back of the man's collar and lifted him off the ground.

"Let me know when you're through pounding his innards," Sean said to the young man.

The skinny fella laid into him until Pearl shoved him aside and punched the ruffian with unfeminine vigor.

"I think you can stop now," Sean said when the man's eyes glazed over. He dropped the man to the floor, where he lay unmoving. "Any idea who's behind this?"

"Probably one of the saloons down the street," Pearl said. "Trying to close me down because I'm taking away their business."

"Then they're real serious about it. This was planned. Two of them came in with cudgels."

"Just some local bums working for a few dollars. They won't come back."

"You sure you don't have some enemies?"

Pearl shook her head. She was trying to put on a brave front, but he saw the haunted look in her eyes. She kept glancing around, as if she was looking for somebody she was afraid to see. It didn't surprise him. Women like her always had a past, and somewhere in that past were usually enough rotten characters to fill a county jail.

"Everybody loves Pearl," said the businessman who was sitting on the man he had down.

"Somebody's got a funny way of showing it." The saloon hadn't suffered much damage, but it was going to cost a lot to replace the furniture. "Okay, fellas, dig down and see how much money you can find."

"What for?" somebody asked.

"To pay for all this furniture you helped break up."

"It was those men," the businessman said, pointing to the still bodies of the assailants.

"Empty their pockets and see what you can find," Sean said. "If it's not enough, you'll have to make up the difference." He reached into his pocket, pulled out a coin, and put it on the bar. "Make sure every one of you matches it.'' He turned to leave.

''Wait!''

He turned at the sound of Pearl's voice. She acted strong and determined, but he sensed a vulnerability behind her bravado.

''Who are you?'' she asked.

''Sean O'Ryan.''

''Well, Sean O'Ryan, you've got to let me to thank you for saving my place.''

''Thank these men,'' he said, gesturing to her hard-breathing regulars.

''I found fifty dollars,'' called out one of the men going through the assailants' pockets.

''This one's got fifty dollars, too.''

It turned out that each of the men had apparently been paid handsomely.

Pearl picked up Sean's gold coin and handed it back to him. ''I won't need this, but I thank you for offering.''

Sean didn't want to take it. He had the distinct feeling that if he touched anything that had been in Pearl Belladonna's hands, strange things would start happening to him. He didn't believe in gremlins or little people. He didn't quite believe in magic, either, but he wasn't so sure about that. A lot of things happened that people couldn't explain. ''You might need it,'' he said.

''I won't.''

She held the gold out to him, her posture straight, the pride behind the gesture undermined by the shock that still lurked in her eyes.

Sean held out his hand. He told himself he was imagining the warmth, the slight tremor that raced though him when the coin hit his palm. It had to be a result of the excitement and his exertion.

"The boys found nearly three hundred and fifty dollars," the businessman said, handing a fistful of money to Pearl. "That ought to cover it."

"Okay, everybody, have a drink while the girls get this cleared away," Pearl said.

As the men moved toward the bar, Sean turned to leave. He'd get something to eat at one of the other saloons. He was halfway across the street when he heard his name. Pearl. He'd recognize her voice anywhere.

"You can't run away before I get a chance to thank you."

"You already did."

"Aren't you going to give me a chance to show my appreciation?"

She was standing on the steps that led down from the boardwalk into the dusty street. She had an impudent smile on her face, her body positioned so her figure showed to its best advantage. Sean wondered what she was offering.

"No need," he called back.

"At least let me offer you a drink."

"You're a fool if you turn down an invitation like that," a passerby told him. "Half the men in Twisted Gulch would give a month's diggings to be in your shoes."

Sean recrossed the street. "If you really want to thank me, you can give me supper," he said. "I haven't eaten since morning, and I'm starved."

Pearl looked him up and down. "I'm not sure I have enough food in the place to feed a man as big as you."

She was flirting with him, smiling through sky-blue

eyes, undulating her body ever so slightly but more than enough to remind Sean that his need for a woman hadn't been satisfied in a long time. She used too much greasepaint and wore clothes that accentuated every curve of her body in a way guaranteed to put a man into a sweat inside of a minute, but she was genuinely a beautiful woman.

"You considering eating me?"

"Huh?" Sean said, coming out of his trance.

"You were inspecting me closely enough."

Sean felt heat creep up his neck from under his collar. He turned red at the slightest provocation. It made him mad, but there was nothing he could do about it. "I just wanted to see if I could tell how much of you was real."

The welcome faded from her eyes. He hadn't meant to be so rude. It must have been the embarrassment that made him say such a thing.

"It's all real, buster," Pearl snapped, giving her body a twist that exposed enough of her cleavage to make him certain everything he couldn't see belonged to her as well. "Now if you want that supper, come on inside, but I'm not part of the menu."

"I wasn't asking," Sean said.

"The hell you weren't," Pearl said. "I've seen enough men to know that look when I see it."

"You may have been around half the men in the world, but you've never been around me."

"All men are alike, especially miners." Pearl spun on her heel. "Come on if you're coming."

Sean didn't like being lumped with *all men*. He was certain she deliberately exaggerated the sway of her hips just to taunt him. What really upset him was that it worked. There was something about Pearl that unleashed the primitive lust in men, but he was determined not to succumb.

Inside, Pearl turned to face him, assuming a stance that accentuated the shape of her body. Only this time she wasn't being coy. Intensity blazed in her eyes. Her whole being challenged him to ignore her, to pretend he was unaffected by her. She was sultry sexuality stripped of any pretense.

Despite himself, he responded to her, wanted to reach out and touch her. The creamy skin of her shoulders and the upper part of her breasts owed nothing to cosmetics. There was a fullness to her he saw only in mature women. No bird-thin legs or twig-like figure. Mother Nature had rounded off every angle, padded every bone, molded the whole into proportions so perfect not even Sean's prejudice could shield him from the force of her attraction.

He felt his body begin to swell. He turned to the nearest table and sat down. He'd leave Twisted Gulch without a morsel of food before he let Pearl see the effect she had on his body.

"I'd like some steak and potatoes," he said.

"Anything else?"

"Bread, hot coffee, and a big slice of whatever pie you're serving."

She regarded him with a look that was nearly angry. "I've never seen you before. What made you come in here tonight?"

"I was hungry."

"There are other places to eat."

"I've been hearing about you ever since I got here. I figured you were past your prime, but my partner insisted that despite your age, you were still the best-looking woman in town. I had to come see for my-self.''

If the fire in her eyes was any indication, he'd made her fighting mad.

''Some of us *old* gals manage to keep on breathing.''

Sean had no desire to get into a fight. He only wanted to eat his dinner and leave. ''Are you going to feed me, or do I have to go to the Naked Dragon?''

She studied him with a speculative gaze, then shrugged. ''I'll have your dinner brought to you as soon as it's ready.'' She turned and signaled to the bartender. ''Bring this man a beer.'' She turned back and gave him the once over. ''Better make it whiskey. He's here against his better judgment. He needs some-thing to help him relax and enjoy the show.'' She rolled a shoulder at him. ''Maybe you'd like one of the *young* girls better. I'll send one over.''

He watched Pearl as she worked her way through the crowd. Men flocked around her, eager for her to notice them for a moment. They ought to be saving their money to send back to their mothers, fiancées, daughters—women they'd made promises to, women waiting anxiously for their return.

But he knew these men spent their time and money on women like Pearl because they were the only women around here, the kind of women who didn't expect anything more than momentary attention. These women probably didn't want more than a little fun, certainly not the loyalty or love other women wanted and needed.

The young woman who'd already taken his order wended her way through the crowd, then set a pitcher of beer and a glass of whiskey down on the table.

"Pearl says I wasn't to pay attention to anybody but you for the next hour," she said with a bright smile.

It shocked Sean to discover that despite her obvious beauty, he wasn't interested in this young woman. The surprise was even greater when he realized that next to Pearl, every woman in the room paled. And it wasn't just physical beauty. Pearl had a vitality, a kind of incandescent quality that, despite the paint and the poses and the blatant sexuality, overshadowed every other woman in the saloon. She made men smile because she smiled, laugh because she laughed.

Sean gestured to the men who were preparing to settle down. "You'd better serve them before the show starts."

"You sure?" The girl looked a little apprehensively in Pearl's direction. She also looked a little miffed that he would send her away.

"As soon as I eat, I'm headed back to the mining camp. You ought to pay attention to the men who're staying."

He smiled inwardly when she hunched a shoulder and flounced away. He hadn't meant to prick her vanity. He just wanted to eat his food and get back to the camp.

But as he listened to Pearl sing and watched her dance, he forgot about his food and going back to camp. She was performing for him. No doubt about it. Every time she sang a suggestive lyric, she looked in his direction and winked. Each time she swiveled her hips, she tossed him a saucy smile.

When she did her final high kick and landed in a split, he jumped to his feet and applauded with everybody else. Pearl put on a good show. So good he hadn't realized his food had arrived.

When he tasted it, it was as good as he'd heard it was. Pearl definitely knew how to run a saloon.

Pearl retreated to her place behind the bar. She refused to step one foot toward where Sean O'Ryan sat eating his dinner as if he hadn't had anything but charred bear steaks to eat for a month. She had the satisfaction of knowing he wasn't immune to her charms. She hadn't missed his enthusiastic applause at the end of her dance, but that didn't rid her of the irritation burning in the pit of her stomach. He hadn't actually said it, but she knew what he thought of her, of women like her. The adoration of the other men usually allowed her to forget it. Something about Sean thrust it in her face.

No woman, regardless of what she had done, wanted to be looked down on. Pearl told herself she was just as good as any woman. She believed it as long as she didn't come across a man like Sean O'Ryan.

It gave her great satisfaction to see that no matter what he thought of her *type* of woman, he wasn't immune to *her*. When he stood and applauded her as enthusiastically and honestly as any other man in the room, her anger died down.

"What did you two talk about?" she asked Ophelia, the girl she'd sent to keep Sean company.

"Nothing," Ophelia said, pouting. "He told me he was leaving as soon as he finished eating."

Pearl cast a glance in Sean's direction. He was giving his entire attention to his food. "Make sure he doesn't want anything else."

"He already told me he doesn't."

Ophelia was obviously feeling put out by her dismissal. "Ask him anyway. I don't want him saying I wasn't sufficiently grateful."

"He sure is big," Ophelia said, forgetting her annoyance for the moment. "Good-looking, too."

"Stay clear of Irishmen with red hair," Pearl warned. "Every one I ever met had a temper worse than the Devil, a roving eye, and wandering hands."

"I wouldn't mind his hands doing a bit of wandering on me."

"I imagine most of the women he meets feel the same way," Pearl said, disgusted at how easily Ophelia was taken in by a handsome face and a big, young, powerful body. "He probably has some dewy-eyed girl back East waiting for him. You make sure he doesn't want anything else, but don't do anything to keep him here."

Pearl moved around among the customers, teasing, joking, keeping everyone's gaze and attention on her. But her thoughts were on something quite different. Rock had said he'd try to ruin her, but she hadn't expected anything so soon. She was worried about what he'd do next. Rock wasn't one to give up or to take defeat lightly. Who'd protect her when he tried again? She was certain Sean O'Ryan wouldn't be back.

Did she want him back? She wasn't certain. He confused her. He had come to her aid for no reason whatsoever. He'd been reluctant to accept anything in the way of thanks, even something as paltry as a meal. All the men she'd ever known had taken anything they could get. She couldn't put her finger on what was so different, but she'd never met anybody quite like him. When he stood up, dropped a coin on the table, tipped his hat in a parting salutation, and left the saloon, she felt as though the energy had suddenly gone out of her body.

She worked her way back to Calico Tom. "Do you know anything about that man?"

"He never come here. You think he come back?"

"I hope not."

Calico Tom looked surprised.

"I can't afford to feed him. He eats enough for two men."

"He big like two men."

"Yes, he is."

She hoped Calico Tom had missed the sigh in her voice. As much as Sean irritated her, he made her think how nice it would be to have someone big and strong to depend on. After having to take care of herself for so long, the desire to depend on someone else, even for a short time, was inescapable. She was certain that once Sean O'Ryan decided a woman was worth defending, she'd be safe from danger for the rest of her life.

Pearl told herself to put thoughts like that out of her mind. She'd given up all chance of a future like that when she ran off with Rock Gregson. She'd lost her one chance at redemption when her young husband was killed.

"Give me my drink," she said to the bartender, determined to put all such maudlin thoughts out of her mind. "I've got to wet down the pipes. It's about time to sing again."

But for the first time in a long time, she didn't feel like singing.

"We couldn't stop him," the man said to Rock. "He's as big as two men and as strong as four."

"There were six of you," Rock said.

"Those miners are mighty protective of Pearl," another man said. "Unless you catch her when she's closed, it'll take a dozen men to do any real damage to that place."

"I have a better way. I won't need you anymore."

"How about our money?" the first man asked.

"I paid you half," Rock said. "I don't owe you any more."

"He took our money," the man complained.

"Then get it back from him."

"And get my head broken? You've got to be crazy. You try it."

"I've got a better way into that man's pockets," Rock said, "a much better way."

Chapter Three

Three days later Pearl was at the bar, Calico Tom at her side, when Rock entered the saloon, his features wreathed in that familiar smile. She experienced a flash of anger. She knew he had been responsible for the attack. She'd been hoping he'd given up, but she wasn't really surprised to see him. His presence meant he had come up with another way for her to help him. Or another way to coerce her.

"That man again," Calico Tom said. "I get rid of him quick."

Pearl put out a hand to stop him. "I'll talk with him."

Pearl was determined that Rock wasn't going to see how he affected her. She walked to meet him with all the swaggering confidence she could muster. The admiration of the men who begged her for a few minutes' attention bolstered her self-confidence. A woman desired by many men was never without power.

"What do you want?" she asked, going straight to the point.

"You didn't tell me you knew Sean O'Ryan."

"I don't," she said. "You just happened to pick the first time he came here. Seems he doesn't like to see bullies break up a lady's place."

Rock's expression combined mockery and scorn. "You and I both know what you are, Pearl. And it certainly ain't no lady."

"I'm not letting you move in here, Rock," she said, her voice as cold as the ice in her heart. "Now get out before I throw you out."

"I've got a new deal for you."

"I'm not interested."

"I'm not asking to move in except for one game. I have just one pigeon to pluck."

"Who could have so much money?" Pearl asked, certain Rock wanted far more than he'd said.

"Your miner."

"Which miner? Dozens come in here."

"O'Ryan."

"Him!" Pearl laughed scornfully. "He's as big as a mountain, but he's too clean to have done any work."

"He's taken out more gold than any man at the diggings."

"If so, he lost it in the robbery."

"He didn't send it out. It's still up there."

"If he's that close with his money, how do you expect to get him into a game?"

"He plays all the time at the camp. Everybody says he's the best."

"Aren't you afraid he'll beat you?" That was a stupid question. "Of course not. You'll cheat."

Rock just smiled.

"I won't have cheating here, not even for one game."

"Not even for Elise?"

Pearl froze. She had to be mistaken. He couldn't possibly know. She smiled, hoping he hadn't noticed her moment of panic.

"Who's Elise? Your latest conquest?"

"She's a little young for that. But if she turns out to be as pretty as her mother . . ."

How could he have found out? She'd been certain nobody besides Calico Tom knew. She had to bluff, pretend she didn't know what he was talking about.

"I'm not helping you rob this man, especially not after he defended me."

"I don't know where you're hiding her, but if you don't help me, I'll find out."

"I don't know what you're trying to pull, but—"

"Why isn't your daughter with you, Pearl? What kind of mother are you?"

He knew! The bastard knew she had a daughter! All these years she'd gone to great lengths to keep her two worlds separate. How had he found out?

"I kill him," Calico Tom offered. "He no cause trouble if neck broken."

She wanted to throw Rock out, but she didn't dare before she knew what he was threatening to do. What he might already have done. "No, I'll take care of it. Come into my office, Rock."

She refused to give in to the fear that threatened to

overwhelm her. She would not lose control. She didn't dare show any weakness. Rock would pounce on it. He had no conscience, no reluctance to use any method to get his way. She had worked for years to provide for her daughter, to shield her from the tawdry world she inhabited. She didn't mean to give up now.

"Why didn't you tell me you had a daughter?" Rock asked after she closed the office door.

There was no point in pretending any longer. "I didn't figure you'd be interested."

"Is she my daughter?"

"No."

"How old is she?"

"Twelve. She was born a little more than a year after I quit the riverboats."

"Who is her father?"

"A cowboy I met after I left you."

"Where is your lover now?"

"Dead."

He had died in a gunfight defending a reputation Pearl no longer had. Pearl had sworn on his grave that his daughter would be reared as a *real* lady. Better to think herself an orphan than know herself to be the daughter of a woman men wanted for the night and wanted to forget the next morning.

"Why isn't your daughter with you?" Rock asked.

"She has to go to school."

"I'll bet you could teach her more than any schoolmistress."

"She's going to a proper school. She's going to be a lady."

"With you for a mother?"

He never let up.

"Do you visit her? Does she know what kind of woman you are?"

Pearl had no intention of letting him know how much she loved her daughter, how much she missed her. "I'm not very maternal," Pearl said. "Tending babies was never my style."

"Are you going to tell her what you do?"

Pearl shrugged. "She isn't the type to go into the business."

"You weren't either, but you learned."

"I doubt she can. She'll probably marry some farmer and raise a houseful of kids."

"You'd let her do that?"

"It's better than having her around here."

"I don't believe you."

He *had* to believe her. She had to convince him. "Would you want your daughter hanging on your arm, spouting proverbs and quoting the Bible at you all the time?"

"Why did you let something like that happen?"

Pearl shrugged again, trying to look as if she didn't care. "I wanted her to be educated. I didn't know she'd end up as bad as a nun."

He considered her with a smiling, speculative gaze. Pearl hated it when he smiled. That meant he had something truly diabolical up his sleeve. Coldness went all though her.

"I figure you don't want this girl to know what kind of mother she has. I agree. I'll even help you."

Pearl forced herself to laugh. "As long as I help you with Sean."

"All I ask is that you get him into the saloon, get a few drinks in him."

"He doesn't like me, Rock, or my kind of woman.

He hasn't set foot in the place since you tried to break it up.''

''I have faith in your ability to get him back. I've never seen a man you couldn't wrap around your finger.''

''I couldn't wrap you.''

''But you did. I never planned to run off with a farm girl from Missouri.''

''It didn't take you long to correct that mistake.''

''You kept nagging me to marry you. You know what's funny? I probably would have if you hadn't run off.''

Pearl felt a shiver of disgust run through her at the thought of being Rock's wife. Running off with him had been a huge mistake, but marrying him would have been much worse.

''I'm not special to Sean O'Ryan. You'll have to find someone else.''

Rock smiled again, and his eyes got harder. ''I don't know where you've hidden this girl, but I'm going to find out. If you don't help me, I'll take great pleasure in showing her exactly what kind of woman she has for a mother. They'll probably throw her out of your fancy school.''

Pearl had suspected that was what Rock meant to do from the moment he mentioned Elise's name, but hearing it was still a shock. Pearl had already made up her mind what she was going to do. Sean O'Ryan was a grown man. He could take care of himself. If he didn't know enough not to get into a card game with the likes of Rock Gregson, it was time he found out. No matter whom she had to sacrifice, Pearl was determined Elise would grow up, marry, and have a family without the taint of having one of *those women* for her mother.

Pearl forced herself to remain calm. "I don't imagine she'd like that. And I wouldn't like having her around."

"She might be a help."

"No." Pearl made a disgusted face. "She's afraid of men. I really don't want her anywhere near Twisted Gulch. My having a daughter wouldn't be good for business. Are you sure all you want me to do is get this O'Ryan fella into the saloon and give him a few drinks?"

"Sure."

"You don't expect me to help you rob him?"

"It's not robbery to beat a man at cards."

"Stop fencing. All you want me to do is get him inside the saloon?"

"Right."

"And you'll stop looking for my daughter."

"Sure."

"I know you, Rock. You're a rotten bastard. But you'd better know something about me. You do anything to hurt my business, and I'll set Calico Tom on you."

Rock laughed, but she had the pleasure of seeing it wasn't as easy for him this time as he pretended. "I mean it, Rock. I didn't go to all the expense of setting up here to let you ruin it for me. Now get out. I'll send someone to tell you when your pigeon is ready to be plucked."

Pearl left the room without looking to see how Rock reacted to her threat. She didn't know how much he believed, but it was crucial that he not guess she would sacrifice anything, *anybody,* for her daughter.

"What are you going to do to make him stay?" Ophelia asked. "I did my best, and he hardly looked at me. I don't think he likes women."

Pearl smiled. Ophelia would never understand that sometimes other things counted more than youth. "I'll flirt with him. Tease him. He's out there on that mountain for weeks without seeing a woman. He's got to be susceptible."

"Yeah, to food."

"All men like to feel they're attractive, that women can't resist them. They'll believe anything I say as long as I smile and stare adoringly up into their eyes while I say it."

"I don't think he's going to fall for that. You don't like him."

"Showing that was a serious mistake. It'll make things harder, but I'll manage."

"Why do you care about him?" Ophelia asked, puzzled. "You've got dozens of men after you."

"I don't know," Pearl said, hoping no one would ever learn why she was doing this. "Let's just say it's a challenge."

"You're upset he didn't fall all over you like the other men," Ophelia said, pleased to have found a weakness in Pearl. "He's hurt your pride."

"You might say that." It wasn't flattering, but it was better than the truth. "Make sure you keep the beer coming. No matter how stiff or prudish a man is, he gets real friendly once he gets a few drinks under his belt."

She'd have to pretend to like him. She was a good

actress, but it was hard to make doe eyes at a man when he thought a woman like her couldn't possibly interest him. Well, Pearl Belladonna had every intention of showing him just how wrong he was.

Two voices had been arguing inside Sean's head all day. One told him he ought to have dinner in some other saloon, that on no account should he set foot in the Silken Lady. The other voice argued that Pearl's place had the best food in Twisted Gulch, the best entertainment, the best-looking women. It insisted he wasn't fool enough to fall for one of them, that there was no reason to take second best when he could afford the best.

Still of two minds, he'd made his way to the Silken Lady.

The saloon was unlike any other place in Twisted Gulch. Some saloons were deathly quiet, with serious gambling going on at every table. Some were noisy, with loud women and crude men showing the worst of their natures. The Silken Lady rang with the songs and shouts of men and women enjoying themselves. Pearl insisted on just enough good behavior to keep the place from turning into a carnival. She also swept her floors and washed the tables. Pearl and her girls must have used a quart of perfume a night. You could smell them before you reached the door. Even the men tended to get a bath and put on clean clothes before they entered the saloon.

Sean had just walked in and settled at a small table in the far corner. Up front Pearl was beginning a silly song, one of the customers accompanying her on the banjo, another trying with limited success to sing harmony. Men were eating, drinking, gambling among themselves, all with the same sense of fun that seemed to radiate from Pearl. Sean could readily understand why so many men crowded into her place every night. You couldn't be around Pearl Belladonna very long without smiling.

"What can I do you for, handsome?" The girl winked suggestively. "You up for a bit of fun?"

It was the same girl again—Ophelia, Sean thought he'd heard somebody say. He wondered if she knew she was named for Hamlet's girlfriend, a weak-minded female who went crazy weeping over his grave. He doubted it. He wouldn't have known himself if Isabelle hadn't made all the boys read at least one of Shakespeare's plays.

"How about your biggest and best dinner as soon as you can get it here."

"Our biggest and best don't come on a plate," Ophelia said, rolling her shoulder.

"You look mighty tempting, but I guess I'd better settle for food."

Ophelia looked offended. "We've got lots of best dinners," she said. "You gotta say what you want."

"Beef, potatoes, vegetables, bread, and lots of hot coffee."

"Don't you want a beer?"

"Not with dinner."

"Everybody else drinks beer with anything."

"I like coffee. Now you'd better get going."

Sean smiled as she walked away, swinging her hips in an exaggerated manner. He guessed she wanted to let him know what he was missing. Sean knew what he was missing. But recently he'd become dissatisfied with such brief encounters. They might ease his body—though they didn't seem to be doing a good job of that lately—but they left an ache inside him, a restless irritability. It was getting to be less trouble to go back to the camp and take a dip in a cold stream.

Sean was surprised when Pearl brought beer and coffee herself.

"I don't want the beer," he said.

"It's on the house."

"I still don't want it."

He sensed a subtle change. She was still sexy but not blatantly so. She wasn't trying to prove anything. She seemed relaxed and friendly. He wondered if she was still being grateful, or if she might really like him.

He didn't like the effect she was having on his body. If he'd been back on the mountain, he'd have said it was tension brought on by sudden danger. Pearl didn't represent any danger to him. So why did he feel keyed up? He felt himself smiling when he didn't want to.

Pearl set his coffee down. She set the beer down as well. "You're a stubborn man. Can't a girl be nice to you without your throwing it in her face?"

Sean wished she'd go talk to somebody else. Ophelia might not stir his juices, but it was impossible to ignore what Pearl was doing to them. She wasn't a girl—it was obvious she'd passed that stage some time ago—but she was a beautiful woman. Her off-the-shoulder dress was cut low in the bodice, tight in the waist, and short in the skirt.

"You did that before."

"And you made it clear you didn't like my type. At first, it hurt my feelings. Later I started to wonder if it was my figure or my character you didn't like."

Sean had to admire a woman who could face up to

what she was without apology. And while he'd heard plenty of guesses as to what might have happened in Pearl's past, he didn't actually know anything to her discredit. She might not be as bad as he imagined.

"No man in his right mind can fail to admire your figure," he said. "After performing for these men every night, you can't doubt that."

"I'm not talking about these men. I'm talking about you." She kept smiling at him in that inexplicable way.

Sean didn't understand how she did it, but she made him feel as though he were the only man in the room. That warning voice told him he was getting into deep water.

"Why should you care about what I think when you've got all of Twisted Gulch at your feet?" He gestured to the men. "Half of them are staring at you this very moment, hoping you'll forget me and talk to them."

"But I am interested in you." Pearl settled into the chair opposite and fixed him with a wide-eyed gaze. "It's been a long time since any man has defended me as you did."

"All these—"

"They're regulars. Most strangers would've walked out. Why didn't you?"

The effect of her presence, the fact that she was focusing entirely on him, was mesmerizing. Now she had him feeling like a saint. He didn't know but what that made him more uncomfortable than being thought a crude miner. He wasn't used to feeling noble. It unsettled him.

So did having her seated across the table. A small inner voice tried to tell him she was skilled with men, that she could do this at will, but his pride rejected that. Besides, she looked too sincere.

When you added to that the smell of her perfume and her being so close he could reach out and touch her, it was no wonder he felt a little giddy. Sean prided himself on his self-control, but a man would have to be made of stone not to be flattered at being singled out this way.

"Your customers are wondering why you're ignoring them," Sean said.

"Because I want to talk to you."

"I come in every two weeks. Some of these men are here every night."

"That makes you more mysterious," Pearl said, smiling at him as though they were sharing a confidence. "No woman can resist a mysterious man."

"There's nothing mysterious about me. I'm just a miner, like everybody else. I get dirty, wet, and cold like everybody else. I spend most of my time in the gold fields like everybody else."

"It must be mighty lonely up there all by yourself."

"I have a partner, but he's laid up with a gunshot wound. That's the reason I'm here. He used to make all the trips."

"A man could get awfully lonely for female company."

He didn't know what she had in mind. It sounded as if she was leading him to her bed, but there was something about her that told him this wasn't so.

"Here comes your food," Pearl said. She stood and moved over next to him to allow Ophelia to set down a platter covered with a thick piece of beef, potatoes, and tomatoes. A bowl of peaches and a plate of bread completed the meal.

"Are you sure that's enough?" Pearl asked. "You're so big and strong." She reached out, ran her fingers along his arm from shoulder to elbow, from elbow to forearm.

Sean nearly jumped out of his chair.

"I don't want you to go away hungry."

Sean was in the grip of an appetite that had nothing to do with food. If Pearl had invited him up to her room at that moment, he wouldn't have given his dinner a second thought. Unfortunately, the piano started up right then.

"That's my cue," Pearl said. "Would you like me to sing something special for you?"

Sean nearly choked on his coffee.

"Lord-a-mercy, he's all choked up at the thought of me singing to him," Pearl said, laughter brimming in her eyes.

"Teary-eyed, too," Ophelia added.

"I guess I'd better not sing him a love song," Pearl said. "I don't want him crying in his dinner."

"How about *The Streets of Laredo?*"

"You're an Irishman," Pearl protested. "Don't you want an Irish song?"

"Do you know *Take Me Home Again, Kathleen?*"

Pearl feigned surprised. "Is there a chance our big, strong miner is a romantic at heart?"

"It's just a song I heard," Sean said, praying his treacherous skin wouldn't turn red. "Sing anything you like."

"You asked for *Take me Home Again, Kathleen,* and that's what you'll get." She pinched his muscle.

"Take good care of him, Ophelia. We don't want anything to happen to our protector."

Sean started to tell her he wasn't her protector—or anybody else's—but she had begun working her way to the front of the saloon, singing the words of her first song.

"Eat your dinner before it gets cold," Ophelia said. The sharpness of her tone implied that his preference for Pearl hurt her vanity. Sean would have explained to her—if he could have found the words—that Pearl had something few women had, that no matter who else might be in the room, Pearl would always be the center of attention. It wasn't just her beauty or her figure. It wasn't just her energy or her lust for life. There was a pure vitality inside her, something that drew people to her like deer to a salt lick.

Sean settled down to eat his meal, watch Pearl perform, and worry that he should be so affected by this woman. He had been in all-male company for two weeks, so it wasn't surprising he should be strongly affected by a woman's attentions, especially those of a woman like Pearl. That was normal, especially in a man who had so little opportunity to enjoy the company of women. It was physical, momentary, wouldn't last five minutes after he left her.

What bothered him most was that he *wanted* her to like him. He knew about women like Pearl. His own aunt had turned her back on her family obligations to be ogled by any man with the price of a drink. Women like that wanted a man only as long as he was willing to spend money on them.

But as he listened to Pearl sing, watched her tease the men with clever lyrics—slightly altered by her to make them more suggestive—and taunt one with a bit of personal attention before moving on to the next, he wondered if she might not be different. She used her body as a magnet to attract and hold the attention of every man in the room, but she was playful, offering the men a little innocent fun to help make up for the drudgery and boredom of the camp.

He was impressed, too, by her honesty. She knew he disapproved of her, but she didn't apologize for what she was. She had guts, character. She had—

Sean's muttered expletive caused several heads to turn, but he was too angry at himself to care. This was how it all began. A man started trying to make excuses for a woman, and before long he couldn't see the truth for what he wanted to see. Pearl might be better than most—he hoped she was—but she was still on the other side of the yawning divide that separated the two kinds of women in this world. Once a woman crossed that line, she couldn't go back.

Most didn't want to go back. His aunt hadn't. She'd twice refused to take him. He'd never forgotten the other kids' taunts that nobody wanted him, not even his own family. Finding her now in reduced circumstance hadn't changed his feelings about her. The more generous part of his nature told him he should forgive and forget, but he couldn't do it.

"You're mighty slow tonight. Don't you like the food?"

He looked up, startled to find Pearl standing next to his table.

Chapter Four

"Your dinner must be cold by now." Pearl gestured to Ophelia. "Have the cook warm it up for him." She picked up his plate and handed it to Ophelia. The girl threw him a disgruntled look and headed toward the kitchen.

Sean gathered his scattered thoughts. "I don't mind cold food."

"I do when it's being served in my saloon." Pearl pulled out a chair to Sean's left, sat down, put her elbows on the table, rested her face in her hands, and gave him a smile that stirred in his groin. "Now tell me what was wrong with my performance," she said. "It's not often I put a man off his food."

She was teasing him, trying to provoke him into assuring her nothing about her could possibly cause a man to lose his appetite. He stared at the white skin of her shoulders and the tops of her breasts, looked into her blue eyes, wary of their treacherous depths.

His gaze focused on her generous, bright red lips, slightly parted now.

She sure could throw a man into turmoil, set his physical nature into a pitched battle with his common sense. She could even make him sit at a table with her and not care that he was breaking a decade-long promise to himself.

"I had some serious thinking to do," Sean said.

She didn't appear to be the slightest bit upset by his reply. Another woman might have been incensed that he preferred thinking to lusting after her.

"Did you come to any conclusion?"

"No, but it's a problem I've wrestled with for a long time."

"In that case, you're not likely to solve it tonight. Why not have a few beers, loosen up, and have some fun?"

"And let my food get cold again?"

He thought he detected a twinkle in her eyes that wasn't sexual in nature.

"Ophelia can keep it warm."

"I'd better eat. She's already glared at me twice."

"She's just miffed because you've shown more interest in your food than in her. Did you like the way I sang your song?"

Sean was startled to realize he hadn't heard a single note of it.

"I have to confess I got so involved with my own thoughts, I didn't hear it."

From the momentarily arrested look on her face, he could tell that did surprise her. She got to her feet, laughing. "Boys," she called out over the hubbub, "we've got an honest man in our midst. Not a very gallant one, but honest."

"Let's hang the blighter!" somebody shouted back. "Can't have him setting a bad example."

"He just confessed he didn't listen to my song."

"Not listening to you is a worse crime than cheating on your wife," another said.

"You didn't hear it because I didn't sing it," Pearl told Sean while the men continued to toss jokes back and forth. "I don't know all the words. I came over to ask you to sing it for me."

Sean's feelings had gone from one emotional extreme to another since entering the saloon, but the idea of singing for Pearl sent him into near panic. "I don't sing."

"Sure, you do. Every Irishman sings."

"What makes you think I'm an Irishman?"

"I don't know," Pearl said, pretending to inspect him closely, "but I think it might be your red hair, fair complexion, and the freckles."

"You've got red hair, too."

"Mine comes out of a bottle. Yours is natural." She reached out and pulled one of the mass of curls that covered his head. When she let it go, it sprang back into place. "So is the curl."

Sean couldn't believe what he was hearing. He'd never known a woman to admit that anything about her wasn't Nature's own creation. Yet Pearl had just admitted, without the slightest hint of embarrassment, that she dyed and curled her hair. Maybe she *was* different. Maybe she was—

"Come on," Pearl said, taking him by the hand and pulling. "You've got to teach me the words."

Sean didn't budge.

"Don't be shy," Pearl said. "I know you know them."

"I'll write them down for you."

"No. I want to hear the tune. The piano player's not sure of it either."

"No."

Pearl turned to the other men in the saloon. "Boys, help me persuade him to teach me a new song."

"What new song, Pearl?"

"About an Irish lassie he left behind. Ought to be just the kind of song you boys like."

"As long as he finds another Irish lassie when he reaches America," one wag called out.

"He needs some persuading, boys. Want to give me a hand?"

More than two dozen men converged on Sean. He leapt to his feet, ready to fight even though he knew he was facing impossible odds. Next thing he knew, someone had rolled against the back of his knees and he was going down. Rather than jump on him and beat the life out of him, what seemed like a hundred hands lifted him off the ground. Much to his surprise, the hands moved him forward like a series of rollers. Moments later they set him on his feet on Pearl's little stage.

"Now sing that damned song," one of the men ordered. "Or next time you go down, you won't get up again."

"Take it easy, Paul. You'll scare him so badly he won't be able to sing a note."

He had to sing now. Not to do so would be an admission of cowardice.

"Okay," he said, jerking his clothes about to set them to rights, "but you've got to come up here with me. I'm not making a fool of myself alone."

"Think I ought to join him, boys?" Pearl asked.

"Hell, no. You oughta join me!"

"Let the blighter show his stuff, if he's got any!"

"Show him how it's done, Pearl!"

"Anybody got any rotten eggs?"

Pearl scampered up the steps to stand beside him. "You ready?"

"I guess so. Just don't let your piano man make it go too high." Sean looked out at the gathering of faces—some doubtful, others laughing, all expecting amusement. He'd come in here to eat dinner. Now he was standing up to sing to a bunch of miners. All because he'd let a woman he didn't even admire bamboozle him.

"This sound okay?" the piano player asked as he started.

"Sure," Sean said. He had no idea. He'd never sung to a piano in his life. Hadn't sung much at all except to the cows when he was still living at the Broken Circle. They never complained, but these men were used to Pearl. Sean doubted he could sound as good. He knew damned well he didn't look as good.

Sean figured he wouldn't come out of this with a whole skin if he tried to mumble his way through the song. These men might not have any rotten eggs, but they'd find something to throw at him. He attacked the chorus with gusto, singing as loud as his Irish tenor would allow. The sheer volume of it gave him confidence.

He finished up the chorus and started in on the verse.

He turned to Pearl and was delighted to see the look of surprise on her face. He didn't know whether she'd expected him to embarrass himself—or hoped he would. He was certain she'd expected to have to rescue him. She was mouthing the words as he sang. She knew the words, damn her hide. She'd just used that as an excuse to get him up on stage.

At the chorus, she started to sing, but her look of surprise didn't change. That made him feel even better. It had to have been a good while since any man took Pearl Belladonna by surprise. Sean was as pleased as blazes that he'd been the one to do it.

By the time he'd finished the second and third verses—Pearl improvising some harmony for the chorus in between—he was feeling rather pleased with himself.

"Everybody sing," he called out as he started into the chorus for the last time.

The noise was awful, but the men joined in with good spirits, and the song ended up with shouts of appreciation from all corners of the saloon.

"Give us a dance, Pearl," someone shouted.

"Show a little leg."

"I will if our Irish songbird will dance with me."

"We don't want to see his legs!"

"I don't dance," Sean said, panicked at the thought of having to dance in front of all these men.

"You said you didn't sing, either."

"But I really don't dance."

"Play us a jig or a reel, something Irish," Pearl called to the piano man.

"I was raised in Texas," Sean said, desperate now. "I wouldn't know an Irish jig from a French waltz."

"Play something Spanish," she said. "Our songbird says he hails from Texas."

"I can dance an Irish jig," Paul Higgins called from the floor.

"I'll dance with you next," Pearl promised. "Right now it's our songbird's time."

"I'm damned if I'll let you call me a songbird," Sean said. "You'll have every man in camp doing it. My name's Sean."

"I remember. Now shut up and dance."

Sean didn't know a thing about Spanish dances, but he'd seen a lot of them in San Antonio growing up. He was too big for the kind of quick, light movements required. Every time he stomped the floor in an imitation of the Spanish dancers he'd seen, the stage sounded as if it was about to collapse under him.

"We're liable to end up under a pile of splintered lumber," Pearl said, laughter in her eyes.

"Why don't you stop?"

"I haven't had so much fun in weeks. You can't dance a lick."

That wasn't news to Sean, but it piqued his vanity. Maybe he couldn't dance—hell, he *knew* he couldn't—but he could give his tormentor an evening she'd remember for a long time.

He grabbed Pearl around the waist and whirled her in a circle until she was dizzy.

"This isn't a Spanish dance," she protested, breathless.

"I know. But since I can't dance a lick, it doesn't matter."

He lifted her off her feet and swung her in a circle above the heads of some of the startled onlookers. Shouts of encouragement from others egged him on.

Pearl's eyes widened in appreciative surprise. "I'll bet you can't do that again."

"Lady, you just asked for it."

The Spanish dance was a shambles. Now it was a

contest to see what startling maneuvers he could do next. After whirling her through the air a couple more times, he swung her around his hips.

"Put me down," Pearl said, laughing so hard she could hardly talk. "I'll have bruises all over me tomorrow."

"I'm not done yet," Sean said.

"Oh, yes, you are." Pearl tried to break his hold on her.

"One more."

"No."

Sean lifted Pearl, swung her high in the air, and brought her down over his shoulder. Pearl landed on her feet with a small shriek. He turned, and they faced each other, both panting from their exertions.

"Never challenge me again if you're not ready to follow through." Sean had to shout to be heard over the clamor of the men's noisy appreciation.

"I'm ready for anything you can give, but not tonight. I've got to save enough breath to sing another set of songs." She started off the stage. "And you've got to finish your dinner."

Sean shouldered his way through the crowd without difficulty. Pearl followed him. After telling Ophelia to heat Sean's plate—again—she seated herself at his table.

"Aren't you going to circulate?" Maybe knowing she'd gotten him up on stage to embarrass him caused the edge in his voice, but he didn't really feel upset about it.

"Right now you're the only man in this place who *doesn't* want to dance with me. This is the only place I'm safe."

"If you don't like it, why do you do it?"

"Who said I didn't like it?"

"You said—"

"I said I wanted a rest. I've got to perform again tonight. And tomorrow night. And every night after that. I can't keep it up unless I pace myself."

"You don't strike me as a woman to worry about pacing herself."

Pearl smiled so knowingly that he felt almost foolish. "That's the trick, to hold back without letting the customers know you are."

Sean's food arrived and he dug in. Dancing had made him hungry again.

"Why don't you let some of the other girls take over?"

Pearl sat up tall in her chair. "These men don't come here to see the other girls. They come to see me."

"You don't mind?"

She looked at him as if he were crazy. "If they didn't come, I'd have to find some other line of business."

"Would that be so bad?"

"What would you have me do? Take in washing?"

His aunt did. He wondered what Pearl would be doing ten years from now. He found himself hoping she'd manage to escape this life before it was too late. But escape to where? There was no other place for a woman like her. She was trapped.

"We've talked enough about me," Pearl said. "Tell me about yourself."

Sean shrugged. "I'm a miner."

"So are more than half the men in Colorado, but they all had different mothers. What about you?"

"I didn't know my mother. She died when I was a baby."

"Sorry. I guess I shouldn't have asked."

"It's okay." But it wasn't. He didn't like to be reminded of it.

"It must have been hard on you and your pa. I hope you had a lot of brothers and sisters."

"My pa died at the same time. I was their only child."

"It's a good thing you Irish have big families, aunts and uncles to take you in."

"I had only one aunt in America. She refused to take me because it would ruin her career. She used to sing and dance. Now she takes in laundry."

For the first time, Pearl looked disconcerted, even embarrassed. He thought he detected something akin to sympathy in her eyes.

"I am sorry."

"Don't be," he said, wondering why he should want to tell this woman about himself. "I drifted in and out of orphanages and foster homes until I was adopted by Jake and Isabelle." He smiled at the memory. "They weren't even married when they decided to adopt eleven of us."

"Eleven!"

He'd succeeded in surprising Pearl for a second time. "Ten boys and one girl. All of us as wild as antelope and angry as a longhorn bull with a thorn in his nose."

"They had to be crazy."

"They probably were, but you'd understand if you knew Isabelle."

"You think a lot of her."

"She was perfect, the mother I never had. She and

Jake were hard on us sometimes—she was always insisting we not neglect our schooling—but they gave us pride and confidence in ourselves."

"Why did you leave?"

"It was time to strike out on my own."

"So why does an educated man come to the gold fields?"

"Why not? Knowing Ophelia was named after Hamlet's girlfriend doesn't keep me from knowing how to work with my hands."

Pearl chuckled. "How did you come to know something like that?"

"Isabelle insisted we all read a play by Shakespeare. I kept putting it off until after the other boys picked the good ones about wars and killing."

"What a surprising fella you've turned out to be."

"I'm nothing out of the way. There are lawyers, bankers, even university professors up in the gold fields."

Pearl reached out and touched the muscle in his arm. "But how many of them are as big and strong as you? Or can sing all the verses of *Take Me Home Again, Kathleen?*"

"You forgot to mention I dance, too."

"How could I forget that?" Pearl tried to grimace, but a smile broke through. "I've never been that far off the ground in my life."

"I could have thrown you higher."

"Is that an offer?"

Why was he showing off? If he wasn't careful, he'd get himself tangled up with a woman who wasn't worthy to stand in Isabelle's shadow. She was only paying attention to him out of thankfulness. He was a fool to let himself think her attention meant anything more than an evening's amusement for a woman who was probably bored with seeing the same faces night after night.

"I've got to get back to camp," Sean said.

For a moment he thought he saw fear—or panic—in her eyes. But it was so brief, her expression so natural and relaxed, he decided he must have been mistaken.

"You don't get into town very often," she said. "Finish your dinner, drink your beer, play a little cards. You may as well make a night of it while you're here."

"I can't. My friend is laid up and can't take care of himself very well."

Now he was certain. She was tense and trying to hide it. Surely she couldn't like him that much. She must have met lots of men who were more interesting, richer, better-looking. Besides, she wasn't the kind to let herself get attached to a customer.

"Have a beer, and maybe you won't feel so serious."

She was trying to sound playful, but there was an unmistakable strain in her voice.

"Not tonight."

"Is your claim so good you can't leave it for two days?"

He didn't know why that question bothered him. It's what anyone would ask. "Good enough, I guess."

"Do you get any gold out of it?"

"Enough."

"Most men celebrate when they have a good week. They come in, have a good meal, drink a little, play a little cards. You eat and disappear."

"I want my own ranch back in Texas. When I get enough gold to buy it, I'm leaving."

"You don't want to become rich? These men do."

"I'm not depending on luck to give me what I want. I'm willing to work for it."

"What is it you want besides that ranch?"

"What everybody wants, I imagine. Maybe not you, but most people. A home, kids, friends, a place to belong."

She looked as if he'd offended her. "What makes you think I don't want something like that?"

He nearly laughed. "You can't expect me to believe you'd give up all this to cook and clean for a man, bear and rear his children."

"Why not?"

He almost said something cutting. But he was starting to like Pearl. There was no need to hurt her feelings. "You'd be bored with only one man. Besides, there'd be no reason to dress up pretty every night."

"I would think looking nice for the man you loved would be the best possible reason to dress up. And if you think you can't get bored with a hundred men just as easily as one, you don't know as much as you think."

Sean had to admit that answer wasn't at all what he'd expected. The woman continued to surprise him.

"You're much too serious," Pearl said. She seemed to be forcing herself to be cheerful. "You're even making me feel gloomy. So you'll go back to your claim and work to buy your ranch, but there's no reason you can't have a little fun first. Have a few beers. Play a few games of cards, make some new friends. The fellas in here are pretty much like you.

Several of them send money back to their families every month.''

"When their gold isn't stolen.''

"I heard about that. Did you lose very much?''

"No.''

"Good. I hate to see hardworking men robbed of what they've earned.''

"Then why do you encourage them to come here?''

He hadn't meant to say that, but nothing could be more calculated to separate a man from his money than women, liquor, and cards.

"I don't make anybody enter my saloon,'' Pearl snapped at him. "They come here because they want to. The liquor is the best in town, and the card games are straight.''

He ought to leave right now. This kind of talk was going to get him in trouble. Besides, he didn't need an older sister or another aunt. He already had one he didn't want.

"You're a beautiful woman,'' Sean said, getting to his feet, "but you're not the woman for me.''

Pearl jumped to her feet. "Why should I want a big, hulking Irishman who thinks dancing is throwing a woman around like a sack of flour? I was just trying to be nice, help you have a good time, forget the gold fields and the tent you live in. Go back. Stay if you like. You're right. I'm not the woman for you. I'm too good!''

She turned and stalked off. He took some money from his pocket and put it down on the table. He glanced back as he reached the door. The piano was playing a fast jig. Pearl was dancing with Paul. They looked good together. She threw Sean a triumphant look, then turned and gave her partner a brilliant smile.

Sean stepped into the dark street. There was nothing for him in the Silken Lady. There never had been. He'd been a fool to come back.

"Why didn't you keep him here?" Rock demanded angrily. He had dragged Pearl into her office less than ten minutes after Sean walked out of the saloon.

"He wanted to go home," Pearl said. "I didn't see how I could stop him."

"You can hold any man when you set your mind to it."

"Not this one. He doesn't think much of me."

It had hurt to be told she was good enough for a night's fun but not the kind of woman decent men married.

"I don't believe you," Rock said.

"Next time he comes in, if he does come in again, you ask him what he thinks of women who work in saloons. While you're at it, ask him about his aunt refusing to take him in because it would interfere with her career."

"What does he do with his money?"

"I tried to ask, but he dried up like a mud puddle in the summer sun. You'll have to get somebody else to do your dirty work."

"There's not a man in Colorado you can't get around if you try."

"I told you—"

"I've got two men trying to find where you've hidden that daughter of yours. I'm going to find her. If you don't help me—"

"I didn't say I wouldn't, Rock. I said I couldn't."

"Try harder. He's up on that mountain for weeks on end. He's got to weaken sometime."

"What if he doesn't come back?"

"Go after him."

"Rock, I—"

"I mean it, Pearl. You bring that man to the card table, or I'll bring your kid here and show her where you work."

Pearl fought back panic. "What makes you think she'll come?" she asked, fighting to preserve an indifferent attitude.

"She'll want to know what you do."

"What makes you think she doesn't already know, that she isn't ashamed of me, that I haven't already asked and she's refused?"

Pearl could tell Rock hadn't expected that response. She doubted he believed her, but he had to wonder if she might not be telling the truth.

"I'll bring her anyway."

"Look, Rock, I've said I'll do what I can to help. But if you bring Elise within ten miles of this place, I won't lift a finger. I've already told you she'd be bad for business."

Pearl walked out of the office. She was shaking so hard that she had to grip her hands together to keep them still. Everything she'd ever wanted for her daughter was in jeopardy, and she didn't know what to do about it. There was no one she could turn to. Calico Tom would do anything for her, but he couldn't help her with this. She had to find a way out of this mess on her own.

In the meantime, she had to go after Sean. He was

a grown man. He could take care of himself. Rock said he won all the time. Elise was still a child. Pearl couldn't take chances with her future, not even for a man like Sean O'Ryan.

Chapter Five

"What's it like dancing with her?" one of the men asked Sean as a group of miners walked down the mountain from the diggings to their camp.

Sean could never make this trek without being aware of how their coming had changed the landscape forever. The steep mountainsides had been stripped of trees to build cabins and provide fuel for cooking and heat. Already erosion had deepened canyons and carved gullies where there had been none before. Game had been wiped out, the constant tramping of booted feet had shorn the soil of its thin, protective cover of decaying leaves and pine needles, and placer mining had silted the streams. The landscape looked barren, forsaken, as if some tremendous storm had come through, destroying all before it. Only a few scattered trees remained to reseed the mountain after the men had taken their riches and left.

"Is holding her in your arms like holding a soft cloud?" another wanted to know.

"It can't be," Pete said, plainly disgusted with the conversation. "With all that red hair, it must be like dancing with yourself."

"Not quite," Sean said with a laugh. "She's light as a feather on her feet."

"That's because you're a giant," Pete said.

Sean and Pete had been friends from the time Sean was thirteen and Pete nine. Sean had used his size to protect Pete, and Pete had used his sharp tongue to attack anyone who made fun of Sean's overgrown body. Even after Sean's coordination caught up with his size and Pete had a growth spurt, they remained the best of friends. But today there was an edge to Pete's words. The way he talked, you'd never know he had practically begged Sean to go see Pearl. The green-eyed monster of jealousy had him wriggling painfully in its grasp.

"I'm sick of hearing about her," Pete said. "You'd think she was the only woman in the world."

"She's certainly the best-looking woman in Twisted Gulch."

"I can't imagine why she's interested in you. It's not your looks. Big as you are, she's liable to mistake you for a grizzly bear."

"She's not interested in me," Sean said. "She just tries to make sure everybody in the saloon has a good time. It's good for business."

"When did you become an expert on what's good business for a saloon?"

"Forget it, Pete. I don't know why you're so upset."

"Because it's all you've talked about for a week."

"It's all the *other men* have talked about."

"Well, you haven't been slow to elaborate."

"Why should I? It was fun. She said I was a pretty decent singer. She even invited me back."

"You're letting this attention go to your head. If she gets a notion how much gold we've taken out of this claim, she'll—"

"She won't learn anything from me."

"You know what kind of woman she is. I heard you say—"

"I know what I said," Sean said, tired of the conversation. "I said she was just like my aunt, didn't care about anybody but herself, and was interested only in men and having a good time. But when I go there, that's exactly what I want. Like you told me, she's a *real* woman, not a girl."

"So you get a swelled head because she showed you a little attention. You think it's going to last?"

"Of course not."

"Then go someplace else."

"No."

"You sure you aren't going back hoping she'll dance with you again?"

"Hell, yes," Sean said, and laughed. "Her attention was nothing but gratitude, and people tire quickly of feeling grateful. But until then, I intend to snatch every bit of fun I can. After spending two weeks looking at your ugly face, I deserve a few hours with a pretty woman."

Pete didn't look convinced.

"Now what's worrying you?" Sean asked.

"You've changed. You used to avoid women like her. I had to badger you to even look at her. Now she's all you think about. I've heard it said she can make a man forget his mother. His wife."

"I don't have either."

"His common sense."

"Our gold is safe, Pete. I worked too hard for my share to let anybody get their hands on it."

Sean didn't know why Pete should be so certain Pearl was after their gold, but since the robbery he'd been jumpy and irritable. His wound pained him, and he felt he wasn't doing his share of the mining. But mainly Pete felt responsible for the robbery. He'd offered to drive the wagon, had promised the men he would make it safely into town. He knew the men who'd lost gold, knew how hard they worked for what little they had.

"Tell us again what it was like to dance with her," Teddy Pickens asked. Tall, thin, and beardless, he was the youngest of the miners.

"Oh, for God's sake," Pete groaned. "I can't stand to listen to that again."

"I've already told you a dozen times," Sean said as he watched Pete hurry ahead until he was out of hearing range.

"I want to hear it again," the boy said. "She never so much as talked to me."

"Maybe it's because you smell worse than stagnant water," a friend said.

"Come on, tell us," the boy said.

"It was like dancing with an angel," Sean began. He'd embroidered the story so much already, it didn't matter what else he said. The men weren't after the truth. They wanted something to dream about. "No matter how fast I moved, she kept up with me, pressing her body against me until I was so wrought up I could hardly breathe."

One of the men groaned. "What does she smell like?" he asked.

"Like roses. I never smelled anything so sweet. It was like I was back in my mother's garden when I was a baby, all the blooming flowers making me dizzy with their fragrance."

One of the men had talked about his mother's garden. The others liked it. It reminded them of their own childhoods, a time of safety and innocence, a far cry from their lives now. Sean liked it, too, especially when he described his mother and her garden as he imagined they might have been in Ireland. He found bits of Isabelle and her garden sneaking into this description.

"What was her smile like?"

"If you could find words to describe the sun as it sets over the Arizona desert or describe the beauty of a mountain covered in spring flowers dewy from a gentle rain, then maybe you could find words to describe a smile that would put both these pictures to shame."

"Did she smile at you like that?"

"That she did," Sean assured him.

"You're killing me," Teddy moaned. "I wouldn't be surprised if my heart stopped and I died right here."

"Don't stop!" came a voice of dissent. "We don't care about Teddy's heart."

"She can't be all that wonderful," one man said. "She's nothing but a saloon girl."

While a chorus of voices threatened to batter him into bear bait if he slandered Pearl again, Sean tried to decide what she was really like. He could describe the outside of her until he had the men panting, but he didn't know what was inside Pearl Belladonna.

"I don't know," he admitted.

"But you ate dinner with her, danced with her," Teddy protested.

"I know, but—"

"Then tell us what you *think* she's like."

Sean opened his mouth to say she was a woman of doubtful reputation who had probably done a good deal worse than any of them knew, but he changed his mind. "She seems like a real nice lady," he began, "one who's got something nice to say to everybody." He hated to give these men a false picture—at least a picture he was certain in his own mind was false—but he didn't *know* anything to Pearl's discredit. "She's never in a bad mood, laughs at everybody's jokes, and sings the songs her customers request. She even gives a meal to some of the men when they're down on their luck."

"She's an angel," Teddy sighed. "I want to marry her."

"She'd make you give up panning, take a bath regularly, and live in town," a friend warned.

"If you wouldn't do that and more for a woman like Pearl Belladonna, there's something wrong with your head," Teddy retorted.

"I'd say it's something else that's not working," another man said.

While the men indulged in a bit of roughhousing, Sean wondered what Pearl was like under her charming exterior. Her life couldn't be without its tragedies. Nobody's was, especially not a woman who'd had to take up working in a saloon.

Did she have the same feelings as ordinary people? His aunt didn't seem to care about anything, not the drudgery of her present life, not even her lost career. He remembered Pearl's brief moment of fear, the attempts to hide her anxiety.

He told himself not to be a fool, that Pearl was exactly what she seemed, a woman who wanted only fun, who wouldn't care about the things that mattered to ordinary people.

Yet his instincts told him that wasn't true. Isabelle used to say he ought to think things through more. He had tried, but he always came back to his instincts. Maybe that meant his brain didn't work too well—that was what Pete said—but an Irishman had to go with his feelings.

Still, he couldn't believe Pearl had any of the feelings and sense of duty that had led Jake and Isabelle to adopt eleven orphans and come to love them as their own children. Maybe women of her type couldn't appreciate love of family, loyalty, responsibility, the ability to take pleasure in helping others. Maybe they were so totally involved with their careers and looks that they were unable to see anything but their own wants.

That was sad. When they lost their looks—the only thing about themselves they or anyone else valued—they would be cast aside, forgotten. He was certain that if every man who'd ever seen his aunt perform passed by her door now, not a dozen would recognize her. Even fewer would care.

They reached camp. Sean was the first man to strip to the waist. He washed every day before he and Pete had supper. It was his turn to cook tonight. He'd better get rolling. His stomach was already growling.

He made so much noise splashing water all over himself, dunking his head, he was slow to notice that the noise in the camp had suddenly ceased. He dunked his head one last time, brought it up dripping, and reached for the towel he had placed on the bench.

"Use this. It's a lot softer than that rag."

Sean froze, eyes closed, water dripping from his hair and chin. That voice belonged to Pearl Belladonna.

What in hell was she doing in their camp?

He reached blindly for the towel. His fingers closed around something soft. When he brought it to his face to dry the rivulets that dripped from his nose and chin, the fragrance put him strongly in mind of the night he had held Pearl in his arms. He dried his face—hardly aware that water from his dripping hair ran down his back—and looked up.

Pearl stood before him, even more beautiful in the daylight than in the flickering lamplight of the saloon. "What are you doing here?"

Women never came to the mining camp. It was a bachelor kingdom where men lived free of all the rules and restraints normally imposed by female society. Most of its denizens lived like dirty animals. They were only there until they had enough gold to leave.

"You didn't come back to the Silken Lady, so I brought the Silken Lady to you." Sean's stunned gaze landed on four girls, all dressed as they would have been in the saloon.

"I couldn't bring the piano," Pearl said, "but Elliot plays the banjo. It ought to do just as well."

The men stood in a bemused circle around the girls, who looked decidedly uncomfortable with their quiet, almost reverent admiration.

"You planning to dance for us?" Sean asked.

Nothing like this had *ever* happened. He had only to look at the men's faces to know that.

"I'm putting on a whole evening's entertainment. Get yourselves cleaned up, fellas," Pearl said to the gaping onlookers. "The beer and the liquor will cost you twice as much, but you can dance with the girls for free."

A moment of stunned silence was followed by a volley of shouts and whistles as the men, realizing the extent of their good fortune, ran off to their own tents or cabins.

"You'd better get something to eat as well," Pearl called after them. "I didn't bring the kitchen."

"Then what's this?" Pete demanded.

Sean turned to see that a table with several baskets on it had been set up in a small flat area next to their tent.

"It's a sort of picnic," Pearl said, giving Sean a wink as she sashayed over to Pete, turning on the charm full force. "I couldn't let my girls starve and expect them to do their best for the men. I haven't seen you in town lately."

"You wouldn't know if I was around," Pete growled.

"Sure I would. I always notice a good-looking man. I thought you had deserted me for another saloon."

Pete's bad mood melted before Pearl's charm. "I wouldn't go anywhere else. I don't trust the women."

"He thought he was in love once," Sean explained. "The girl's boyfriend knocked him out and they robbed him. He hasn't seen many women since he didn't want to spit on."

"Just a certain kind of women," Pete said.

"Untrustworthy ones," Sean said quickly. He had seen Pearl flinch at Pete's words.

"I'm very trustworthy," Pearl said. "So are my girls." She glanced at Sean, and a smile spread over her face. She lowered her lashes, her voice sank a pitch, and her lips parted slightly. "I'm not a stickler for formality, but I don't think I'd be able to concentrate on my food with you sitting across from me like that."

Sean looked down at his naked chest. Red hair curled in an unruly mass in the center; a faint trail headed south and disappeared under his belt. Water still dripped from his body. His pants were damp.

Sean knew he was blushing. He cursed audibly. He was certain it made him look like a naive fool in Pearl's eyes. He could tell himself he didn't care what a woman like Pearl thought of him, but he knew it wasn't true.

"We're not fixed to entertain females," he muttered as he dried his torso. "We pretty much do as little as we can except eat, sleep, and dig for gold."

"I don't want to interfere with any of that," Pearl said. "I just want to make some of it a little more fun."

Sean thought it was a good thing women didn't usually come to the camp. The men wouldn't be able keep their minds on their work long enough to find sufficient gold to buy food. "You'll have to excuse me a minute while I finish washing."

"Aren't you done?"

"I still have the lower half to go."

"Do you do this often?"

"Every night," Pete said. "I have to sleep in the

same tent with him. I don't want him smelling like a hog."

"And what do you smell like?" Pearl asked, her voice as soft and caressing as silk.

Pete blushed.

"He smells worse than a bear," Sean said, laughing at Pete's reaction. "I threatened to toss him in the creek a couple of days ago."

"Then you'd better go with Sean. I don't like bears very much."

"Come on," Sean said, grabbing Pete and pushing him ahead.

"You're not going to let those women stay, are you?" Pete asked.

"If I tried to run them back down that mountain, the men would probably shoot me on the spot. She's offered to give them a chance to sing and dance with her and the girls. They're not going to let that slip away, not for you or for me."

"I'm not taking my eyes off them," Pete said as they reached a spot screened from the camp by the foliage of several bushes.

"I thought you liked Pearl and her girls," Sean said as he started stripping off his pants.

"I do—in town where they belong. I don't trust them up here."

Sean shed the last of his clothes and waded into the icy stream. He shivered as he splashed water on the lower half of his body.

"No women ever came here before," Pete said as he waded into the water. "Why did they come now?"

"I don't know," Sean said, equally baffled. "But I do know they're not after our gold." He wondered how her regular customers were taking her absence.

"Now hurry up. Every man in the place is going to bolt his dinner and be at our tent before you know it. At the rate you're going, you'll still be standing here naked with nothing to keep you warm but hot suspicion."

Sean ignored Pete's steady stream of complaints. He didn't know what Pearl was after—he was certain she was after something—but he had every intention of enjoying the fun. He'd pay for it tomorrow when the lack of sleep made the long hours at the diggings seem nearly intolerable, but he'd let tomorrow take care of itself.

"Hurry up," he said, dragging Pete out of the water and tossing his clothes at him. "My stomach is growling."

Pete started to complain again.

"Nobody's going to roll you and steal your money. You can't go through life distrusting women just because one turned on you."

"It's just women of that type."

"It's the only type of woman we've got." He grabbed Pete by the back of his pants. "Come on. You can finish dressing on the way."

Pete cussed and Sean laughed all the way back to their tent. Pete's attitude changed when he saw the food Pearl had brought.

"Have a seat, gentlemen," Pearl said. "Just tell us what you want."

"Everything," Sean said, sitting himself down.

"I like to see a man with a good appetite," Pearl said.

"Then you'll love Sean," Pete said. "He can eat enough for three men."

"I'm half in love with him already," Pearl said.

Sean looked up, startled. Pete looked from one to the other.

"He's my guardian angel," Pearl said. "He stopped a fight that could have ruined my place." There was nothing coquettish about her manner, nothing flirtatious. It was just a statement.

Sean felt himself relax, but he thought it was about time Pearl stopped putting so much importance on his part in the fight. He'd tell her, too, but not tonight.

"You boys look mighty nice," Pearl said as she passed a succession of dishes down the table. "Who does your wash?"

"A woman comes by once a week." Pete answered for Sean, who was busy stripping a drumstick of its meat.

"It must be expensive."

"It's better than going to bed in clothes stiff with dirt."

"And here I was all ready to offer to take some of your things back to town for you."

Sean noticed Pearl wasn't eating. "You not hungry?"

"I can't eat when I'm excited."

"What are you exited about?"

"I've never seen a mining camp."

"It's a cesspool, not fit for a woman."

"Maybe if you had a few women up here, it wouldn't be so bad."

"We'd never get any work done. See those men over there?" A ring of men had begun to gather about twenty feet from where Sean and Pearl were sitting.

Pearl nodded and flashed a smile, which made the men squirm with eagerness.

"Usually they'd be eating. In about thirty minutes,

most of them would be asleep. A few would be drinking, some gambling, but this place would be dark in an hour.''

"That's awfully early."

"Half of them haven't had a bite to eat," Sean continued. "Some are wearing wet clothes because they didn't have anything to change into after they washed in the creek. Not one of them is thinking of anything but you and your girls.''

"I can't see what's so bad about that."

"Nothing. In Twisted Gulch. Up here, it can cause trouble.''

Pearl puckered her lips in a pout that was as false as it was provocative. "Do you want us to go away?''

"Not on your life. Every man here may be cussing himself tomorrow morning, but tonight we're going to have a shindig unlike anything that's ever happened in these hills. Tell your girls to get their legs limbered up. Once we get going, there won't be any stopping for hours.''

Four hours later, Sean's respect for Pearl and her girls had risen several notches. He'd been certain they'd pack up their picnic baskets and their banjo player and head back to Twisted Gulch after a couple of hours. Pearl hadn't stopped singing, and her girls had danced with one miner after another. Occasionally a man's foot would start tapping so hard he couldn't wait for his turn. He'd tie an apron around a friend, and they'd dance together.

Despite the steep prices, the miners kept Pearl's barman busy. Pete even managed to pry open his purse strings for a couple of drinks.

"Okay, why did you do it?" Sean asked Pearl when she took a break to sit down at the table and catch her breath. He motioned Teddy Pickens away. He wanted to have Pearl all to himself for a few minutes.

"What do you mean?" Her expression was one of innocent curiosity. But her act was too perfect. Nobody could be this relentlessly cheerful, this thoughtful, and still be a successful businesswoman.

"Why did you go to all the trouble of coming up here?"

"I thought it would be fun. I've never seen a mining camp."

"What other reason?"

"Do I have to have one?"

"Yes. You're a shrewd businesswoman. You didn't come up here for nothing."

Pearl looked injured. "I'm still a woman. I thought you'd noticed."

"I'm certain even the coyotes noticed. You haven't covered up too much of yourself."

Now she did look injured. "You don't like what you see, or you don't approve?"

"I just want to know why you came."

"Partly because I thought it would be fun. Partly to say thanks for helping me out."

She looked so sincere, so hurt, he was tempted to believe her. Almost.

"And what else?"

Now she really did pout. "You're cruel. You don't believe a girl—"

"You haven't been a girl in a long time," Sean said, brutally pushing aside her charming pretense. "Neither have you been foolish or innocent. I doubt you've even been curious."

Pearl's eyes snapped. "I have. I was curious about

you. I thought there might be a scrap of decency somewhere in that great hulk. You didn't have to help me out. When you seemed to have such a good time singing, I decided you were fun, that I wouldn't mind seeing you again. I may not be a *girl* any longer, but I'm certainly a foolish woman for thinking there's anything human inside you.''

"I did have fun," Sean admitted, stung by her words. "I was planning to come by next time I was in Twisted Gulch."

Now why did he have to admit that? He had no intention of becoming entangled with Pearl. Seeing her was dangerous, but it was just for a short while. He wouldn't believe anything she said.

"Were you really?" Her lightened mood seemed fragile, as if it would shatter if he said no. He couldn't. He'd be a liar if he did. "Sure. I had fun. Besides, you do have good food."

Pearl's broad smile set his insides turning somersaults.

"I knew you were having fun, even though you pretended not to. That's really why I came. The whole town is having a big party in three nights."

"What are you celebrating?"

"We've gone a year without burning down the place."

Sean couldn't help laughing. "That's something to celebrate?"

Pearl grinned. "It is when the whole town is made of wood. Last time something like this happened, I had to dance with every man in town. My feet were so swollen, I couldn't get them into my shoes for a week. This time I decided to limit myself to one partner. I want it to be you."

Sean had expected almost anything but this. He was flattered Pearl would choose him. He wasn't rich, he wasn't important, and he wasn't more than average-looking. Other than his size, there was nothing to make him stand out.

"Why not Paul? He dances better."

"I know, but I'm a sucker for an Irish tenor."

Pearl was the first living creature besides the cows to appreciate his voice. Isabelle defended him, but his adopted brothers howled in protest every time he opened his mouth.

"I won't sing. Just dance."

"Okay. You're big, but there's a lightness in your step."

Sean wasn't immune to flattery, but he wasn't going to be taken in just yet. "There must be fifty men you know better than me. Some of them are bound to feel they have a stronger claim on you than I do."

"Maybe, but none of them are as big as you. When I wear my favorite dancing shoes, I'm taller than they are. A girl just naturally likes to look up to a man."

There she went with that "girl" business again. He guessed that in her profession one had to think young. The time would come soon enough when she'd have to face the truth.

Pete wasn't at all happy when Pearl told everyone she'd invited Sean to be her escort. "You'll lose a whole day at the diggings," he told Sean, "Two, if you drink so much you have to spend the next day recovering."

"Who the hell cares!" Teddy exclaimed. "I'd give Pearl my whole dad-blasted claim if she'd ask me."

When Pearl pinched his cheek, Teddy turned pink and cradled his cheek reverently.

"Yeah, you gotta go," another said. "You gotta uphold the honor of our camp."

"I never heard anything so ridiculous in my life," Pete fumed. "There's not a single one of you galoots with enough honor to make a show in the bottom of an empty bucket."

"I'd go, no matter what," a third man said. "Besides, he's got you to watch his claim. With that face of yours looking like you just bit into a green persimmon, sure as hell nobody could get close enough to rob it without feeling downright queasy."

"Now, boys," Pearl said, treating them all to a dazzling smile, "you shouldn't be so hard on Pete. I can't say I'm happy he doesn't like women, but he has a right to be peculiar if he wants."

"I'm not peculiar," Pete snarled when the men laughed. "I've got my reasons for not trusting women."

"I trust you," Teddy said to Pearl. "Take me. I can dance all night."

"On her feet," another said. "Take me. I'll show you steps you never saw before."

"You can all stop your jawing," Sean said. "Miss Belladonna has invited me, and I'm taking her up on her offer."

He was probably crazy, but the temptation to spend the entire evening with his arms around Pearl was too much.

But he wasn't going to let a little flattery and an evening of dancing change his mind about Pearl. She was a damned fine-looking woman and he liked her, but he was going to remember what she was. When he finally left Twisted Gulch, he would leave all thoughts of her behind.

Chapter Six

Sean was kneeling in front of the small shaving mirror outside the tent when he heard Kathleen's voice.

"I heard you were going to the celebration with Pearl Belladonna."

"Who told you?"

He had almost finished dressing, but he was having trouble with the tie. He hadn't worn a suit in so long, he was out of practice.

"It's all over Twisted Gulch," Kathleen said.

"Why should you care?" He didn't like having to talk to her. He still got angry every time he did.

"I was just surprised, you looking down your nose at saloon women the way you do," she said as she unloaded the clean clothes from her wagon. Her tone was sarcastic.

"I'm just out for a little fun," Sean said. "Isn't that what women of your type offer—fun and laughs with no rules and no responsibilities?"

"I loved each one of the men I was with."

"Then you were hankering to settle down, get married, start a family, maybe even send for me?"

His aunt ducked her eyes. "I was never much on that sort of thing, not like Gwenda. She was the one wanted a husband and a house full of babies."

"How could two sisters be so different?" He could find no resemblance between this tired, lined face and the full-cheeked beauty his mother had been at nineteen. When he left the orphanage, Mrs. Grasty had given him a small picture of his parents on their wedding day. It was the only memento he had of them.

"I took after my father's side of the family. He ran off. None of the Kelly men were any good."

"You ran off, too. Now you've got what follows, so you've no reason to complain."

"I'm not complaining," Kathleen insisted. "But I'll be warning you. Watch out for Pearl. She doesn't do anything for no reason. She's clever. She's hard, too. She doesn't like any man except that Chinaman of hers."

"I thought she'd had lots of lovers," Pete said.

"She just puts that about to get everybody's hopes up. She don't have nothing to do with nobody."

That was a surprise to Sean, one he wasn't sure he believed.

"If she's picked you out," Kathleen said, "it's because you got something she wants."

Sean laughed. "What have I got that a woman like her could want?"

"Gold. Everybody knows you got a rich claim. Everybody knows you're tighter than a Scotsman."

"Then everybody knows I don't carry it around in my pockets."

"If you did, she'd have it by now."

"She seems to be doing right well with her saloon. What makes you think she's after more?"

"What else could she be wanting with you?"

"That's what I told him," Pete said.

Sean had ignored Pete, but Kathleen's remarks struck him differently. She looked at him through the eyes of a woman. Despite the fact that she was his aunt, she would see him pretty much as Pearl saw him. It was a blow to his vanity to know he had made such a poor impression that she thought Pearl could only be interested in him for his gold. Other women had wanted him. He was generally considered serious and responsible, but he wasn't above having a little fun.

He wasn't fool enough to think Pearl had fallen in love with him, but he had his pride. "She likes the way I sing."

Kathleen's scornful laugh was like a dipper of cold water in his face. "And I'm sure you think the little people are going to keep your gold safe while your back is turned."

"I'll do that," Pete said.

Kathleen's reaction to that was nearly as scornful. "It takes more than a wounded dab of a man to stop a thief."

"Just because I'm not the size of a mountain doesn't mean I can't defend myself," Pete said.

At six feet, Pete wasn't little, but everybody looked short standing next to Sean.

"Then you'd better be watching what she puts in your drink," Kathleen said. "And stay away from the card table. Pearl doesn't play herself—not that she can't handle the cards as well as any man, mind you—but she's got them as does it for her.''

"Collect the clothes and get on home," Sean said. "I'm not going to lose my gold—or my head—in one evening."

Kathleen tossed the last of the clothes into her basket and hefted it on her hip. "Smarter men than you have lost everything they had in less time than that." She turned and walked away, speaking over her shoulder. "Can't nobody say I didn't warn you. Can't nobody say I don't look out for my relations."

"You don't look out for anybody but yourself. You never have!" Sean shouted after her. "Don't start pretending you're doing it now."

Kathleen didn't bother to respond.

"Look at her," Sean said, "sashaying about like she was somebody, tossing her head like it wasn't covered with gray hair crammed under a battered hat. She's got bruises all over, probably from falling down drunk. A man starved for the sight of a woman wouldn't touch her, yet she walks like she owns the Earth."

"She's got pride," Pete said.

"In what? Being a used-up old hag?"

"I sort of like her. She's got spirit."

"She didn't leave you in an orphanage."

"No, but I still like her."

"You two can entertain yourselves thinking of all the horrible things Pearl is going to do to me when she gets me in her hidden room, or wherever she hides miners while she tortures them until they tell her where they've hidden their gold. With your combined imaginations, it ought to keep you busy for the entire evening."

"I admit that's kind of farfetched, but I wish you'd—"

"I've heard more than enough. What can possibly happen to me in one evening?"

"Look, Rock, I went after him, didn't I? Have you seen that place? Somebody ought to take a stick of dynamite and blow it off the mountain. I could hardly take a deep breath." She was in no mood to deal with Rock. It had been two days, and she still hadn't recovered from the trip to the mining camp.

"I don't give a damn about your sensibilities. I want you to get that man drunk and at my card table."

They were shouting loudly enough to be heard outside the office, Rock thinking Pearl was dragging her feet and Pearl trying to make him understand he'd latched onto somebody unique when he set his sights on Sean O'Ryan.

"If you think you can find somebody else who can do it faster, be my guest," Pearl snapped. "You may think every man falls at my feet—I don't know why when you didn't!—but his opinion of women like me is only slightly higher than the toe of his boot."

Pearl struggled with her conscience every time she thought of what she was doing.

Odd. For years she'd sailed along, doing what had to be done, never thinking too much about it one way or the other. She didn't cheat people, but she figured that folks who entered a saloon or sat down to a card game knew what they were doing. If they didn't, they ought to find out so they'd know better next time. Besides, they were all grown men. She wasn't their mother. She was there to offer a bit of fun. That's what they wanted from her, and that's all she meant to give.

But things had been different with Sean from the first. Sure, he wanted his fun like any other man, but he never let her forget it was temporary, that he was marking time until he could get back to his *real* life.

A lot of men wanted to forget their former lives. There was a great deal Pearl wanted to forget, too. Rock for one. The sound of dirt falling on her mother's casket. Her husband's death. The loneliness of the years since. The times she'd been so scared she couldn't think. The time a gambler almost killed her.

Right now she wanted to forget what Sean thought of her kind of woman. For years she'd told herself she really wasn't one of them, that she was only doing this until she got enough money to sell out, go where people had never heard of her, make a decent life for her and Elise. Sean had forced her to open her eyes, to look at herself, and she didn't like what she saw. She particularly didn't like what she was doing now.

"Don't go getting moral on me, Pearl. I told you what I'd do to your daughter if you back out."

Pearl refused to succumb to the fear that had haunted her since Rock told her he knew about Elise. She hadn't let him beat her fifteen years ago when she had nothing. Now she had her daughter to fight for. No matter what, she wouldn't let Rock ruin Elise's life.

"I thought you were clever. Why can't *you* get him to the table?"

Rock didn't answer, and Pearl began to wonder if there wasn't something personal about this, if Sean hadn't possibly beaten Rock at cards sometime. No, that couldn't be it. Rock never lost. He made sure of it by cheating.

"All you have to do is get O'Ryan to the table," Rock said.

"I'm trying. He'd still be on that mountain if I hadn't gone after him. Do you know what that trip cost me?"

"I don't care."

"Fine. I'll send you the bill."

"Now look here, Pearl—"

"I said I'd get him here for you. I didn't agree to ruin myself."

"We'll talk about that later."

"We'll talk about it now. I want you to call off your bloodhounds. I don't want them upsetting the people at Elise's school. If the headmistress finds out what I do for a living, she's liable to kick her out. If that happens, I'll send her to you."

"I don't want your daughter on my hands," Rock said. "I never did. But I want O'Ryan at the gambling table."

Pearl breathed a sigh of relief. As long as Rock wanted nothing to do with Elise, she was okay. He'd have no reason to look for her because finding her would put an end to Pearl's willingness to help him.

But she would have to move Elise. The first chance she got, she'd slip out of town and go to Denver. She needed to see her banker, maybe ask him to sell the saloon sooner than she'd planned. If Rock could discover she had a daughter, so could others. She'd never be safe from her past as long as she owned the saloon.

Sean wanted to go far away from here, too, but for a different reason.

Thinking of Sean, her conscience started to bother her again. What right had she to double-cross this innocent man? How could she look herself in the mirror after that?

She didn't know, but she'd sacrifice anybody in the world for her daughter.

Hardly anybody ever got the better of Rock at cards, but somehow she didn't think Sean was going to be easy prey, not even if he had too much to drink. He had refused to drink or gamble so far. He might keep on refusing. What would Rock do then? Probably try to find Elise and bring her to Twisted Gulch just for meanness. That was exactly the kind of thing he would do.

Pearl didn't know how she was going to get out of this mess. She hadn't felt this scared since she was fifteen and walked out on Rock. To her amazement, the wild idea of asking Sean for help flashed through her mind. She nearly laughed out loud. Him, help a woman of her type! He'd be more likely to say her daughter would be better off if she was taken away and given to some decent family. He'd certainly tell her she'd gotten exactly what she deserved.

No. It was very inviting to think of resting her troubles on those broad shoulders. There was something about that man that inspired confidence. She even liked him. But he was one man beyond her power to entrap.

At first she had tried to see him just as a way out of a bad situation. But the minute he'd opened his mouth and started to sing, things had begun to change. She couldn't say why the lilting sound of an Irish tenor coming out of a body the size of a small mountain should entrance her, but it had. Then his dancing had ruined any chance she had of remaining impersonal. He was a terrible dancer, but he had great fun trying.

"What that man say to upset you?" Calico Tom asked after Pearl escorted Rock out of her office.

"Nothing."

"I know you long time. No hide things from me. It about big miner?"

"Yes, but you don't have to worry. I'll handle it."

"I catch him in alley, break neck. Nobody know."

She smiled at Calico Tom. He was the only true friend she had ever had, but murder was a desperate alternative.

"I've handled Rock before. It might take me a little while, but I'll do it again."

"You watch," Calico Tom said. "I no trust."

"Neither do I." She brightened her face. "It's time for me to sing a drinking song. Tell the barman to set up the bottles. The men are always thirsty afterwards."

"Where did you get that dress?" Ophelia asked. "I've never seen you wear anything like that before." Pearl had called Ophelia into her room to help her dress for the celebration that evening.

"What's wrong with it?" Pearl asked. She'd bought the dress the last time she was in Denver.

"Nothing if you like being covered up from top to bottom. It makes you look like somebody's wife." The dress was made of ruby-red satin with long sleeves, a high collar, and no slit down the side of the skirt. Only her face, neck, and hands were uncovered. She'd wanted the dress the minute she saw it. She made up her mind to buy it when she tried it on.

109

It was tight enough to show every curve of her figure, but it covered enough of her body to make her feel respectable. She liked that.

"There must be some attractive wives somewhere," Pearl said.

"Probably, but I doubt anybody in Twisted Gulch ever saw one. You'll make them think of their female relations. That'll cool them right off."

Pearl's mother had been pretty once, but hard work on a Missouri farm and ten children in as many years had destroyed her youth and her beauty. Pearl had been determined her life wouldn't turn out like her mother's. It hadn't, but she had worked about as hard as a human could for these last fifteen years, and she might still end up broke. It wasn't surprising that a lot of women were willing to trade their youth and beauty for the security of a home and family.

"I don't want to be the center of attention tonight," Pearl said. "I'm with one man. The rest of them can wait until I'm back in the saloon."

"You sweet on him?" Ophelia asked.

Pearl laughed, but her laughter didn't feel easy or spontaneous. "No, just relieved. After having to please a hundred men a night, one's going to feel like a vacation."

Funny, she hadn't thought of pleasing a man in years. Entertaining them, yes. Pleasing them, no. Why should that thought come to her with Sean? She hardly knew him. He wasn't her type. Too sober. And she certainly wasn't his type. She didn't want to be entombed in respectability for the rest of her life. Any woman Sean married would be expected to be so good she might as well become a nun.

What on earth was she thinking about marriage for! Had she lost her mind completely?

"Why did you pick him?" Ophelia asked. "He's not much fun."

"He can be," Pearl replied. "Besides, he's got very strict ideas about how a gentleman should treat a lady. I know he doesn't think I'm a lady, but he won't be trying to kiss me all the time, making my stomach churn with his beer breath."

"Isn't he going to expect to spend the night in your bed?"

"Maybe, but he'll soon learn otherwise."

She wouldn't mind a kiss or two. The idea of being held in Sean's arms was rather appealing—though she doubted he could forget his disapproval long enough to get that far—but that didn't mean she was looking for anything more. No man had been in her bed since her husband, and it could stay that way.

"He's the first man you've ever let take you anywhere," Ophelia pointed out. "If he doesn't know that, others do."

"Good. He'll realize how lucky he is and not expect more."

"He doesn't look like a man to be satisfied with what's handed to him. He looks like he's used to taking what he wants."

Nearly all men were like that, but there was a difference with Sean. It didn't make her afraid of him. It made her afraid of herself. Which was really stupid. He was just another in a long string of men who'd paraded through her life. He wouldn't be any different from the others.

If that was true, why had she chosen to wear this dress?

"If I had your skin and shoulders I'd never cover them up," Ophelia said, doing up the buttons on the back of Pearl's dress.

"There's a lot more to life than nice skin and shoulders," Pearl said.

"You're beautiful."

"There's more than that, too."

Now where had that thought come from? She hadn't stopped thinking about her looks in fifteen years. Everything she had depended on them.

"Well, maybe not," Pearl said with a laugh when Ophelia gave her an odd look. "But sometimes I get tired of worrying about how I look. Tonight I want to relax and enjoy myself."

"And you think covering yourself with this red dress is going to cause anybody to ignore you?"

Pearl looked at herself in the full-length mirror, an extravagance that had cost her dearly. The dress might cover her arms, shoulders, and legs, but there was nothing modest about the way it clung to every curve. She could take pride in the fact that no woman in Twisted Gulch had a comparable figure. The bodice might not be cut low, but it did nothing to disguise the fact that Nature had been very generous. Her neck was long and slim, without wrinkles. Even without the skillfully applied makeup, her skin would have drawn attention. Then there were her enormous blue eyes, deftly outlined in black. Everything was topped off by a huge mane of hair so vibrantly red that everyone took a second and third look when she passed by.

"I don't want to be mobbed," Pearl said, "but I don't want to be ignored, either."

"No man has ever been able to ignore you."

Pearl felt an urge to tell Ophelia that being the center of attention wasn't as much fun as it might appear, but the girl wouldn't understand. Or believe her. Pearl wouldn't have at the same age.

A few weeks ago she'd have been quite content to be in Sean's company, but it wouldn't have taken more than five minutes to decide what to wear. It worried her that Sean had caused so many changes in her thinking.

She'd thought at first it was Rock's threat that kept him in her thoughts. Then she decided she couldn't forget Sean because he was the first man in years who hadn't fallen at her feet. Maybe she wanted to bring him to his knees just to prove she could. That wouldn't have bothered her if it hadn't meant letting Rock rob him of his money as well. But there was no point in worrying herself about that.

For years Pearl had divided her world neatly in half—the saloon, her looks, and the parade of men on one side, Elise and the life she wanted for the two of them on the other. She'd been determined no one would ever connect the two.

Now Rock threatened to entangle them forever. Helping him with Sean was the only means of preventing that. She wished there had been another solution, even had the vague feeling there was, if she could only think of it. But she couldn't.

"It's time to go down," Pearl said, giving herself one last look in the mirror. "How do I look?"

"Beautiful." Ophelia sighed. "Like a real lady. Do you think I'll look like you when I get old?"

Pearl bit her tongue, telling herself the child didn't realize her words had sharp edges that cut like razors. She wasn't a lady. And though she didn't feel old, she knew her age was forcing her toward a crossroad.

"I'm sure you will," Pearl said, forcing herself to smile, "if I let you live that long."

Ophelia blushed. "I didn't mean—"

"I know you didn't." Pearl took a deep breath, swirled her skirts, and did a tiny dance step across the room. "Now open the door. This old lady is going to kick up her heels and have some fun."

"They'll mob you the minute you appear on the landing," Ophelia warned.

Sean felt like a fool. There wasn't a man in the saloon dressed in a suit, white shirt, and black tie. He'd even polished a pair of shoes he hadn't worn more than three times in his life. With the help of some expensive hair cream, he'd managed to comb his rebellious hair into some semblance of order. He stuck out like a sore thumb. He was already tired of men looking at him as though he was some tenderfoot. He was also tired of the glowering, angry looks Paul Higgins was shooting his way.

"Can't I get you something, handsome?" one of the girls asked.

Sean didn't remember having seen her before. Apparently no one had told her he was only here to pick up Pearl.

"I'm fine like I am. I'm waiting for Pearl."

The girl nearly jumped back. "You the man who's showing her around tonight?"

"Yes. Do you think you could run up and see how much longer she's going to be? I'd just as soon get out of here before—"

The words died in this throat. A vision in scarlet had just appeared on the landing above the stairs that led down into the saloon. He swallowed a huge lump in his throat, a lump big enough to contain all his prejudices and preconceived notions about Pearl Belladonna.

She was beautiful. There was no question about that. But there was something different about her tonight. He didn't know what it was, but he felt it immediately. It was as though he was seeing her—really *seeing* her—for the first time. Everything he'd seen before was still there, but she seemed changed.

"She's beautiful," Sean murmured.

"I know. You think it would show by now."

"What?" Sean asked, half in a daze.

"The way she's lived," the girl said.

Reality tried to force its way back into Sean's thinking, but he wasn't having any of it. Reality told him Pearl was older than he was, that she couldn't be trusted, that she was unworthy of his regard. His eyes and emotions told him something else entirely. He liked the second message better, so he resolutely pushed the first from his mind. He'd face reality when he was back at the diggings, struggling to separate the tiny flakes of gold from the tons of dirt that hid them.

He'd just seen a vein of gold. It might be fool's gold, but it glowed as brightly as the genuine article. It couldn't hurt to believe in it for the next few hours. Tomorrow would be plenty soon to wrestle with the truth. Tonight was for having a good time. If the beauty of his companion was any measure of the pleasure of the evening, he was in for a memorable experience.

Chapter Seven

One look at Sean, and Pearl knew she ought to go back upstairs and lock herself in her room. There was no controlling the runaway beating of her heart when he stood up and walked toward the bottom of the stairs. She could hardly believe he was the same man who'd once come to her saloon dressed in worn pants and a heavy checked shirt. Nothing about him looked the same.

He looked magnificently huge, as always, but tonight he seemed somehow more handsome than big. His hair, usually an unmanageable tangle of red, had been ruthlessly combed into place. His eyes, as blue as ever, sparkled with the vitality that filled the man. His rough beard had been shaved. When his lips parted in a welcoming smile, she felt something tighten inside her.

This man was no impersonal victim to be baited and dragged into Rock's trap. He was a man with feelings, a man who apparently appreciated her appearance, who liked her enough to dress for her, who looked to her for a good time without having to watch his back. She saw him once again, wading through the tangle of fighting men, effortlessly tossing Rock's bullies from her saloon. He'd had no reason to help her except a sense of fairness, maybe even goodness. She'd seen too little of either in her life. How could she justify turning her back on that?

But then images of her daughter flooded her mind. She recalled the joy she felt every time her arrival wreathed Elise's face with smiles. She had her mother's blue eyes and blond hair, her father's lanky frame, ready smile, and love of horses. She was a sweet, gentle, idealistic child who adored her mother. At the end of every visit, she begged to come live with her. Pearl could never forget the tears in Elise's eyes, never forget her own promise that she would come for her very soon, that they would never be separated again. She'd spent nearly every minute of the last twelve years working toward that goal. She couldn't let it go now, not even for Sean O'Ryan.

"Aren't you tired yet?" Sean asked.

"No," Pearl replied, looking as vibrant and full of energy as when she'd come down the stairs three hours earlier.

"Come on, tell the truth."

"Truly I'm not. I've only performed twice tonight. The rest of the time I've spent wandering about, talking and dancing."

Bonfires, built in the middle of the street and carefully monitored, illuminated the night. The local businessmen had hired a band from Denver to play for the whole evening. People thronged the boardwalk, going from one place to another, or simply enjoying themselves on the two dance floors constructed at opposite ends of the town. Sean and Pearl had been inside nearly every saloon in town. They'd sung all the songs, danced all the dances, and drunk enough beer to make them light-headed.

"Isabelle said men always underestimate a woman's strength," Sean said. "Looks like I'm no better than anybody else. I'm worn out."

"But you work in the gold fields all day."

"Apparently it's easier than keeping up with you all night."

Pearl's laughter turned heads. Just about everything about her caused men to stare. Especially the dress. Though entirely respectable, it heated Sean's blood to a boil. Apparently the man who said a little mystery enhanced a woman's appeal knew what he was talking about. The effect appeared to be equally strong on other men. Seemingly every one who'd ever been to Pearl's saloon expected her to dance with him. Sean liked feeling Pearl was his for the evening, and he didn't want anyone horning in on his time. He had come close to starting a fight several times, but the message had finally made it around the town that for tonight, Pearl wasn't giving her attention to anybody but Sean.

"I thought all you miners were so much bigger and stronger than we poor, insignificant women."

"The man who called you insignificant had to be drunk, blind, and a misogynist."

"What on earth is that?" Pearl asked, turning to stare at him.

"It's one's of Isabelle's favorite words," Sean explained with a chuckle. "It means a man who dislikes or distrusts women."

"That could be just about any man, especially the distrust part."

"That's what Isabelle said."

"Who's Isabelle?"

"My adopted mother. Let any man dare to express a similar opinion about women, however, and she immediately orders him off the place."

"She gets away with it?" Pearl asked in disbelief.

"Isabelle does just about anything she wants."

"How?"

"She rescued us when nobody else wanted us. Then she practically forced Jake to adopt us. We all adore her."

Pearl stopped and turned to face him. "You obviously love your family very much. Why did you leave Texas?"

"They're not my real family."

"Where's your real family?"

"Back in Ireland." He didn't want to talk about Kathleen. "What about your family?"

It was polite to ask after a person's family after they'd shown interest in yours, but he was sorry the moment the words left his mouth. Pearl recoiled, actually backed away. Her face showed pain rather than horror or anger.

"I didn't mean to bring up unhappy memories."

She seemed to struggle to get her feelings under control. The familiar smile came back, but it was clearly there by force of will.

"You couldn't know. I haven't seen my family in quite a long time. After my mother died, I guess I felt a little bit like you, that I ought to get out and make my own way.''

He didn't know what to say next.

''I've got to get back to the saloon. It's about time to go on again.'' She turned and started back.

''Can't you leave this show to your girls?''

''No.''

''Not even during a night of celebration?''

''Especially during a night of celebration. I'm my own best draw. I'm taking a chance not being there this evening.''

''You've been there twice already. Last time I thought I'd never get you out again.''

Sean knew what to expect the minute Pearl entered the saloon. A cheer went up, and instantly she was transformed into a different woman, one who no longer belonged just to him.

He didn't exactly want her to *belong* to him, but he resented the presence of every other man in the saloon. Even more he resented the change in her. He must have been dense not to have noticed it before. Many of the saloon girls acted like mechanical dolls wound up to sing and dance until they ran down.

There was nothing mechanical about Pearl. Her genuine pleasure in her work made every man in the place feel as if she was excited to be with *him*, that *he* was special. Sean had had a chance to see a different side of Pearl, even if for only a short length of time. He knew that no matter how much she might genuinely enjoy her work, what the men were seeing was her public face. There was a different Pearl Belladonna inside. He'd only caught a glimpse—no, it was more of a feeling—but he was sure it was there.

Pearl turned back to him. "Why don't you find yourself a card game while I'm busy?"

He hadn't gotten dressed up to play cards. "I'd rather—"

"Here's a table just finishing a hand," Pearl said, "and there's an empty chair. Mind if my friend joins you?" Pearl asked the men at the table.

Two men looked up with little interest. A third, a handsome, well-dressed man, stood and extended his hand. "Rock Gregson," he said. "Make yourself at home."

"I'm just waiting for Pearl to finish her numbers."

"No matter," Rock said. "We've got an empty chair."

"Go ahead," Pearl said. "Have a few drinks. I won't be done for half an hour."

Why not? If he had to waste thirty minutes, it would be better to spend it playing cards than being jealous of every man enjoying Pearl's attention. "I don't have much money on me."

"The stakes aren't very high."

From the piles of coins before Rock and one other man, they must have been high at some point.

"Okay, but I'm dropping out as soon as Pearl finishes her numbers." He turned back to Pearl. "Don't be so long this time." He leaned closer and whispered, "Most of them have had so much to drink, they won't know if you cut a couple of songs."

"I'll think about it," Pearl said with one of her most brilliant smiles.

But something wasn't the same. He supposed it was part of the transformation that had taken place the moment she walked into the saloon, but he had the feeling there was something more. The connection between them had been broken. She was treating him with the distant familiarity she used for her regulars. He didn't like that. He liked feeling special.

Maybe he was imagining things. In all fairness, he had to remember that Pearl had told him she'd invited him to save her feet. Now that she wasn't focusing on him, he could see he'd been trying to read too much into the evening.

But as he sat down to the table, he felt absolutely certain Pearl hadn't been acting tonight, that the way she'd behaved when she was alone with him was the closest she'd come to being herself in a long time.

"How much you got?" one of the players asked.

"Enough for a five-dollar opening bid," Sean replied.

The man turned to Rock, his mouth open to speak.

"That's fine," Rock said. "I'm sure if he wins, Ira, he'll bet more."

Sean didn't like sour-faced Ira. He clearly didn't want Sean in the game. Or maybe he didn't want to play for such small stakes. Sean didn't care if he played or not, but he wasn't going to bet just to please this man.

Sean couldn't say he thought much of the third man at the table, either. He hadn't said a word. He looked at Sean out of expressionless eyes, then turned his attention back to shuffling the cards in his hands. In contrast, Rock seemed like a likable, good-natured fella, not one to keep a stranger out of a friendly game just because his pockets weren't lined with gold.

"I heard you have a good claim," Rock said.

"I'd be happier if it were better," Sean replied as

he watched Rock shuffle and deal from what appeared to be a new deck.

"Wouldn't everybody? Still, it must be good enough if it keeps you up at the camp all the time."

"How would you know that?" Sean asked, beginning to wonder at the questions.

"A big man with a head of hair like yours can't go anywhere without being noticed, especially after what you did for Pearl."

Pete had said the same thing. "I won't make anything if I don't work my claim," Sean said as he picked up his cards.

"True," Rock replied.

Sean looked at his cards. They were worth a five-dollar bet, but Pearl had just started to sing. "I'm out," he said, throwing down his hand and settling back to listen.

"But you hardly looked at your cards," Ira protested.

"That's all the time it took."

Ira looked like he wanted to say more. Even Rock didn't look happy. Sean ignored them and the play of the hand. It went quickly, and the silent man won a small pot.

"Maybe you'll get better cards this time," Ira said.

"Hope so." Ira was beginning to irritate Sean. He felt a momentary desire to concentrate on the game and see if he could move a few of Ira's gold coins into a pile of his own. Then Pearl started to do a dance number with her girls, and he lost the urge.

His second hand was better. He asked for one card, and it got so much better that he bet his five dollars. He got distracted by Pearl and was surprised when Ira's irritable voice cut through the sound.

"Are you going to bet?"

Sean wasn't interested in playing cards, but this hand was too good to waste. Besides, he didn't want to lose the money he'd already bet. At the same time, he didn't want to get in over his head. Pearl might have thought she was settling him into a friendly game, but these men looked like serious gamblers to him. In Sean's mind, anybody who sat down at a table with a couple of thousand dollars on it was in a serious game. He bet another five and watched it go around the table. The silent man dropped out, but Ira and Rock matched his bet.

When the bet came to him again, he stopped to consider. Either he could get serious and settle down to play, or he could decide to lose a few dollars while he waited for Pearl. It was an easy decision. "I'll raise you ten and call," he said.

Ira looked startled. Even the silent man seemed to come out of his trance long enough to open his eyes a little before retreating into his shell.

"That all?" Rock asked.

"On this hand," Sean said.

Even though Rock seemed friendly, Sean was getting the sense he'd missed something that was going on. They clearly wanted him to do some serious wagering, but he'd told them when he sat down he wasn't interested. If they didn't like it, they should have said so then.

Sean's full house won the hand. The pot was less than a hundred dollars.

"You could have ridden that hand around several more times," Ira said.

"That would take concentration," Sean said. "I'm just waiting until Pearl's done."

"She always stays to talk to the men when she's through singing," Rock said.

"Not tonight."

Again Ira directed a silent look at Rock. This time Sean got the distinct feeling that something had been said, and Rock understood it.

"If you deal before Pearl starts to sing again, I might be able to pay some attention."

The hand came quickly. Sean had another good hand.

Pearl took a break. Instead of resting at the bar as she often did, she worked her way over to the table and around to Sean. "How are you doing?" she asked.

"He'd do a lot better if he'd pay attention to his cards," Ira said.

"I'm ready to go," Sean said to Pearl. "You're more fun than a deck of cards."

Mild as it was, Pearl seemed to have been caught off guard by the compliment. He didn't understand why.

"I told him you'd want to stay and mix with the customers," Rock said.

"I always do," Pearl said.

"Tonight's different," Sean said.

"All nights are the same," Pearl said. "That's how I keep the men coming here."

Pearl and Rock exchanged looks. Now Sean was certain something was going on. His instincts were telling him Rock had some kind of hold over Pearl. The man appeared too relaxed and friendly as far as Sean was concerned. Most gamblers he'd met were more like Ira, intense and short-tempered. But it was

Pearl's reaction that made him certain something was up.

He hadn't known her long, but he'd been sensitive to her changes in mood from the beginning. Most of the time she was relaxed and easygoing. Even when she was tired or the miners were being difficult, she never lost her enjoyment of being in their company.

Earlier tonight he'd sensed a different Pearl. As they walked through the town—looking into one saloon after another, dancing with dozens of other couples, or looking at the full moon that shone through the gap in the mountain walls that towered over each side of the town—she had gradually shed some of the attitudes and mannerisms that were Pearl Belladonna. Some little bit of the woman she might have been had shown through. The difference fascinated him.

He couldn't be certain, but he thought she might be more comfortable out of the limelight. In the dark of the street, she seemed to relax, her smile and laughter to become more natural. Sean had started to believe she really liked being with him.

The Pearl who stood next to him now, however, had nothing in common with either Pearl he'd seen before. She was stiff. Her smile never reached her eyes. It was as if her vitality had been dulled.

"It looks like the men are ready for your next number," Rock said to Pearl.

Her smile grew so artificial that it almost looked like the painted-on face of a circus clown. She glanced down at the jumble of gold coins in front of Sean. "Did you win any of that?"

"Most of it," Ira informed her.

"Don't tell me you're a card shark." She turned from Sean to Rock. "I guess it's a good thing he wanted to play for small stakes.'' Despite her words, she didn't sound amused. She sounded worried.

"I had a good hand," Sean said.

"You'd better hurry back," Rock said. "The men are getting restless."

Pearl flashed Sean an artificial smile. "Don't take too much of Rock's money. It's expensive to dress like he does."

As Sean watched Pearl make her way back to the stage, the feeling that Rock had some hold over her grew stronger. But that shouldn't have surprised him. Any woman with a past—and every saloon woman had a past—had something she didn't want known.

Sean didn't like to see a man take advantage of a woman. Isabelle had beat it into the heads of all the boys that women deserved as much consideration as men. Just because they were physically weaker and often unable to defend themselves didn't change that. A gentleman, Isabelle had informed them, would go to the assistance of a woman without hesitation. Any woman! In Isabelle's mind, there were no qualifying factors.

Rock failed to qualify as a gentleman on several scores. Sean decided to see if he could separate him from a few more gold coins. It wouldn't hurt him to live a little less expensively for a week or so.

Being careful not to let his opponents sense the change in his attitude, Sean settled down to do some serious playing. By now he had formed the suspicion that Ira and Rock—maybe the silent man as well— had formed an unspoken partnership in an attempt to sucker him into losing his money. Once his blood was up, they would close for the kill. He didn't intend to stay long enough to fall into their trap. But he might be able to do a little damage before they sprang it.

His first hand was quite good. He suspected that they intended him to win no matter what cards he held. Okay, but he wouldn't appear too eager. When it came his turn to bid, he raised the pot by only a few dollars each time. When he had to match a bid, he appeared to agonize over whether to keep going. Finally, when he'd pushed the pot to the expected limit, he raised by a hundred dollars. All three players showed surprise. They either had to equal his bid or drop out. Sean was certain they'd intended to let him win this pot, but they planned to limit the money they lost. All three men folded. Sean threw his cards into the pile and drew the pot toward him.

"What were you holding?" Ira asked.

"If you'd wanted to know, you should have called," Sean said.

Ira's hand reached out to pick up Sean's discarded hand. Sean's powerful fingers closed around his wrist. "It'll cost you a hundred dollars to see those cards."

Ira looked startled. Then furious. "The game's over."

"It'll still cost you a hundred."

"Forget it," Rock said, smiling with strained affability. "My deal."

He shuffled and dealt the cards with the speed and efficiency of an experienced gambler. Sean's cards weren't great, but they were good enough to make him think he had a chance to win a reasonable pot. Without hesitation he threw his hand in.

"What the hell?" Ira muttered.

"Bad hand," Sean said. "I'll wait for the next one."

It amused him to see stunned looks on the faces of

all three men, but he didn't let it show. "I'll listen to Pearl until you're done."

The hand was played quickly. Rock took a small pot and dealt again. Once again Sean gave his hand only a brief glance. "My luck must have run out," he said as he tossed it aside.

From the depth of the crimson color that flooded Ira's complexion, Sean judged it was all the man could do to keep from exploding. "What the hell do you mean throwing down your cards all the time? You're supposed to play, dammit."

"Nothing says a man has to play bad cards," Sean said.

"But your cards weren't—"

Ira stopped himself just in time.

"They weren't good enough for our friend," Rock said, his affability stretched thin. "Apparently he's a very careful player."

"No point in playing to lose," Sean said.

Rock tossed his cards in. "Mine weren't very good, either. Your deal, Ira."

Ira glared angrily at Sean while he shuffled the cards with the same quick, practiced movements Rock had shown. "What's the point? He won't play unless he's got at least a full house."

"Then give him a full house."

Rock laughed, as if giving any player a specific hand was impossible and everybody knew it. Yet when Sean picked up his hand, it was even better than a full house. He studied his hand carefully, trying to guess their strategy.

"Don't tell me you're going to throw in that hand, too," Ira said.

"I've got to think," Sean said.

"Well, make it snappy," the silent man spoke up. "My cards aren't great. I want to get on to the next hand." He tossed his cards aside and took a large swallow from his drink.

Sean pondered a moment longer before placing his bet on the table. Five dollars. A hiss of air escaped from between Ira's teeth. Rock's expression seemed to freeze. Sean chuckled to himself.

They'd dealt him a flush, queen high.

Making small bets and taking his time mulling them over, Sean managed to drag out the game through Pearl's last two numbers. Just as she sang her last note and started down from the stage, he said, "I guess I'd better not go any higher. I'm betting fifty dollars and calling."

"You did that last time," Rock said. "What if we want to go higher?"

"Can't stand the tension," Sean said as Pearl began to make her way toward them. "Gotta know."

Both men tossed two twenty-five-dollar gold pieces into the pot. "What have you got?" Rock snapped.

"A flush," Sean said, beaming as he laid down his cards and drew the money toward himself.

"How do you know you've won?" Ira demanded.

"Can you beat his hand?" Rock asked, all trace of affability gone.

"No, but—"

"Then he's won."

Surprise and a little bit of shock showed in Pearl's expression when she saw the money piled in front of Sean. She looked from Rock to Ira. Neither man returned her glance.

"You seem to have been doing very well," she said. "I'll let you keep on."

Sean stood. "I'm done."

"You can't quit now," Rock said, his voice low and harsh. "You can't walk away a winner."

"Somebody has to," Sean said.

"Maybe a few dollars," Rock said. "But not a thousand."

Sean let his gaze travel from one man to the next. Rock gave back his look in full measure. Ira looked furious and didn't care who knew it. The silent man refused to meet Sean's gaze.

Sean turned back to Rock. "I only agreed to play because you were so insistent. It's cowardly to complain now that you've lost."

Rock's expression remained as stern and unyielding as ever, but Ira's face flushed purple with fury.

"I'll give you back a little of your money," Sean said as he motioned to Ophelia to come over. He took a twenty-five-dollar gold piece from the pile.

"You finally going to order something to drink?" Ophelia asked when she came up.

"Give this to the barman," he said, handing her the coin. "Tell him to give free drinks to everybody." Sean took another coin from the pile. "This is for a bottle of your best whiskey. Bring it to these men."

"You think a bottle of whiskey makes up for the money you took?" Ira exploded.

"I *won* it." He scooped up the rest of the money and stuffed it into his pockets.

"What are you going to do with—"

Sean shushed Pearl's question. "Free drinks on the house," he shouted.

The customers moved toward the bar like snow in an avalanche.

"Let's leave before anybody notices we're going," Sean said to Pearl.

"Pearl can't leave now," Rock said. It sounded like a command.

"Nobody will miss her for at least a half hour," Sean said.

"I really can't go," Pearl said. "I've got to—"

Without warning, Sean reached down and swept Pearl off the ground. "You promised me an evening I would never forget. I'm calling in your promise."

Without a backward glance, he started though the crowd, Pearl still held firmly in his arms.

Chapter Eight

"Are you crazy?" Pearl protested. "Put me down."

"Not until we're out of sight of the saloon. I mean to keep you all to myself for the next half hour."

Pearl didn't know what to think. No one had ever carried her off. Her first inclination was to fight, to call for help. She was a woman who had to stand on her own, take care of herself in a harsh and unforgiving world that had crushed stronger women than her. Loss of control, even for a moment, threatened everything she had worked for since the day she'd walked out on Rock.

But hard on the heels of that thought came an entirely different feeling, a new realization. Men never picked her up because she'd let them know she wouldn't like it. And because she was neither small nor light. She was an armful few men could handle.

The feeling of being in the arms of a man strong enough to take care of her was so unfamiliar, she'd actually forgotten what it was like. She hadn't felt that way about her husband. Looking back on it now, she wasn't sure she'd felt that way about Rock, not even in those first few euphoric days. Had she ever felt that way about her father? She couldn't remember. She only knew that settled in Sean's strong embrace, she felt safe and protected.

It was a wonderful feeling, so enticing, so comforting, so bewitching, Pearl had to struggle not to yield to its seductive power. What woman wouldn't want to settle her cares on the shoulders of a strong man, secure in the knowledge that he would take care of her? The lure was all the greater because she had never fully allowed herself to feel this yearning before.

"I don't want to know what my customers are thinking now," Pearl said, unable to resist waving to them as Sean whisked her through the door.

"They're probably wishing they'd had the foresight to do the same thing."

"Aren't you going to put me down?" Pearl asked when Sean didn't immediately set her down on the boardwalk.

"No."

"You can't carry me through the streets like a trophy. People will think—"

"That I've got the most beautiful woman in Twisted Gulch all to myself."

"If they do, it won't be their first thought," Pearl observed dryly. "Do put me down. My reputation won't survive much more of this."

Sean stopped in the light flooding through the open doorway of a competing saloon. "Why should you care about your reputation?"

His expression—honest surprise—destroyed all the pleasure Pearl had taken in being swept off her feet.

"Put me down at once." She fortified her command by pounding on Sean's chest with the only arm she could get free.

"What did I say?"

"It's even worse that you don't know."

"Tell me."

"Just put me down."

"I will, after you tell me what I said to make you so angry."

Pearl tried to force him to release her, but pushing on his arms was like pushing against a tree trunk.

"Stop wiggling," he said. "You'll tear your dress."

"That won't make any difference since I don't care about my reputation."

"So that's it," he said as he set her carefully on her feet.

"Yes, that's it." She swung at him in frustration. He caught her wrist. "Let me go."

"Not until you tell me what's turned you into a wildcat."

Pearl jerked hard, and Sean released her. She started back toward the saloon, but he blocked her path. "We're going to have this out right here. It can be quiet, it can be noisy, but we're doing it."

"Why do you care?" Much to her surprise, she wanted to cry. She hadn't felt that way since her young, idealistic husband died defending her reputation, the one Sean was surprised she cared about.

"I said something to upset you. I didn't mean to do that."

"Are you stupid when it comes to women?"

"Sometimes."

His honesty took some of the steam out of Pearl's anger. She'd never known a man to make such an admission.

"Isabelle says no man understands a woman, not even a smart man. I never pretended to be smart."

But he was clever. He'd neatly cut the ground out from under her feet. He had done something unforgivable, didn't even know it, and *she* was feeling sorry for *him*.

She smoothed her hair with agitated hands. "Every woman cares about her reputation," she said, "even if she doesn't have much of one. Do you think those men would come to see me every night if they thought I was ready to jump into bed with the first man to carry me off?"

"I didn't mean that," Sean said, his fair skin turning delightfully red.

"Then what did you mean?"

"I don't know. I suppose I was thinking of respectable women who wouldn't be seen out on a night like this, who—"

"So now I'm not respectable." She knew she wasn't, knew it was none of his doing, but she longed to have somebody to take her frustration out on.

"I didn't mean it like that."

She faced him squarely, ready to indulge in a fight loud enough to relieve years of pent-up anger. "Then what did you mean?" She could see him searching for an answer, trying to find words that wouldn't make her more furious. She wanted him to say all the wrong things so she could scream and yell at him with a clean conscience.

"I spoke without thinking," he said. "I'm sorry."

No! It wasn't fair! He couldn't get her all worked up and then apologize. She felt like a locomotive with a full head of steam and no track ahead.

"Some things you can't take back." She tried to sound furious, but the effort fell flat.

He looked so unhappy that she couldn't stay angry. Besides, after practically forcing him into a card game with Rock, she was the one who ought to be apologizing. If she did, he'd probably walk away and never speak to her again. And as stupid and futile and dangerous as it was, she very much wanted him to like her.

"I haven't had much practice in taking things back," Sean said.

"What kind of women have you been hanging around? Don't answer that. You tell me it was women who'd as soon steal your money as hop into bed with you, and I'm going to be mighty put out."

They stood there, facing each other like a cat and a dog, not sure whether to settle in for a real fight or make up and be friends again.

"I shouldn't have worn this dress," Pearl said. "No woman worried about her reputation parades about the streets after dark in a bright red dress."

"I like that dress," Sean said. "You look real nice."

"It's too tight."

A gleam of amusement appeared in Sean's eyes. "I think it's just right."

"You'd never see anybody wear a dress like this to Sunday School."

A smile split his face. "I don't know. It covers a good deal more of you than that pink dress you were wearing the last time I saw you."

"That's the kind of dress I work in."

"That's why I was suggesting this would be a better choice for church."

The sound of a chuckle escaping from him despite his obvious effort to keep a straight face caused her temper to flare. "Are you laughing at me?"

"No." An even bigger chuckle rumbled forth.

"Yes, you are."

"No, I'm not." He managed to wipe the smile off his face, but his control was tenuous. "Your mentioning Sunday School made me think of somebody."

"Who?"

"Miss Honoria Lonetree."

"Who was she?"

"A maiden lady of generous endowment. She worked at the orphanage. She wore extremely tight dresses and was always getting us boys in trouble for staring at her. All she had to do was look at me, and I'd blush. She said it was because I was thinking lewd thoughts. She got me beaten regularly."

"What was she doing around young boys if she didn't want to be stared at?"

"She enjoyed it. She just didn't want to admit it. One day, when she was in the bath, all the other boys lined up down the hall like they were supposed to, waiting their turn. I climbed on the roof and down to a trap door in the ceiling. I dropped a bag full of snakes into her bath. They were nothing but gopher snakes, but she ran out stark naked, screaming like a crazy woman. She ran by half the boys lined up against the wall before she realized there was anybody there."

Pearl felt a bubble of laughter start to build inside her.

"She started screaming that they were filthy boys, that they shouldn't be staring at her, that they were responsible for the snakes. She couldn't go back into the bath for her clothes, and she couldn't go out into the main hall. She just stood there screaming."

"What happened?"

"The head of the orphanage came in, saw what was happening, and told the boys to leave. He sent one of the women in to take her away and get her dressed. She screamed all the way upstairs. She left that night and never came back."

"What happened to you?"

"I got a beating and was kicked out of the orphanage, but it turned out to be the best thing that ever happened to me. Isabelle heard about me. That's how I ended up being adopted."

"And your well-endowed volunteer?"

"I heard she left town." He smiled. "Am I forgiven?"

"No." She knew she didn't sound convincing, but she couldn't stay mad at him. Despite his size and obvious strength, there was something of the little boy about him that disarmed her. Maybe it was the freckles. Maybe it was the curly red hair that had begun to rebel against discipline.

"Please."

That did it. Nobody said please to her. They threatened, tried to bribe, seduce, manipulate, or overpower her, but they never asked as though they truly meant it. It wasn't fair for this overgrown Irishman to have so much charm.

Pearl suddenly felt dangerously vulnerable. "I shouldn't," she said.

"Yes, you should. We can still have that night to

remember. If you don't forgive me, I'll go back to camp ready to fight any man who wants to know how the evening went. And they're *all* going to want to know. You'll have to go back in there and sing and dance for the same men you've sung for and danced with for the last I don't know how many months. Now what's worse—a few hours with a charming Irishman with a nice voice and a promising lightness to his step, or the same old drunks?''

Pearl couldn't resist his good humor. Besides, it wasn't his fault she wasn't a respectable woman. ''What do I get if I forgive you?''

Sean cocked a quizzical eye. ''If I were to give you something, what would you want?''

''Something of immense value.'' She saw some of the fun drain from his expression. ''Not gold,'' she said quickly. ''I'd want something more personal.'' She was relieved to see the sparkle reappear in his eyes.

''Like what?''

She pretended to think. ''Let me see. I can do without your undying allegiance. That sounds too much like you'd be on my payroll for the rest of your life. I'd rather not have your heart. Continual protestations of your eternal love probably wouldn't be good for business.''

''Especially if I started hanging around looking depressed and downtrodden.''

''Definitely no hearts or eternal devotion.''

''So what would you want?''

''How about a curl of your hair?''

She could tell immediately her request had surprised him. More than that, it had completely changed his mood. Even more surprising was the change in her own. Suddenly everything felt too serious. Every word implied more than she wanted to say, every glance carried too much meaning, every thought contained too many unspoken wishes.

"I don't have any scissors."

"And I don't have a locket to put it in." She'd said the wrong thing again. These were the things lovers said to each other. There could never be anything like that between them. He'd already told her what he thought of women like her. His weren't thoughts that kindled love affairs.

"Then I guess you'll just have to forgive me for free," he said, attempting to restore the conversation to its previous level of banter.

"Looks like it," she said, relieved. "But I'm going to remember you owe me something. Women always do, you know. Now, what are we going to do first?"

"I thought we'd try dancing again. That fella with the banjo promised to play something slow so you could show me what to do with my feet."

"If you had any consideration for my toes, you'd put them under a table and leave them there."

Unexpectedly Sean picked her up and swung her off her feet. Pearl couldn't get used to being treated like a wisp of a thing. She was a businesswoman who expected people to listen to her and do what she said. That seemed to make no difference to Sean.

He set her down. "Is that easier on your feet?"

"Yes," she said, laughing. "But now I'm so dizzy, I can hardly stand up."

"That's no problem. I'll hold you up." He put his arm around her waist and drew her close to him. "I can't have you staggering down the boardwalk. People will swear I got you drunk."

Pearl felt intoxicated. From the moment Sean picked her up, events had moved well beyond her control. One thing after another had served to reinforce the fact that Sean was in control. He was bigger than she was and, much to her surprise, more determined. It was frightening.

But it was very nice.

She couldn't explain it. She'd been on her own so long, she didn't remember what it felt like to depend on someone else. She felt the yank of fear as well as the tug of attraction and didn't know which way to go.

Sean didn't give her any choice. "I hear the banjo now," he said as he turned, his arm still around her, and started toward the music. "If we don't hurry, he won't play any requests."

"What are you going to request?"

"Take Me Home Again, Kathleen."

"That's a ballad, not a dance."

"It's the first song you ever sang for me."

Pearl didn't understand her sudden difficulty in swallowing. She felt perfectly well. Why should her throat close up on her?

"You have memorized the words, haven't you?"

"Yes." She'd never forget the words to that song.

"Good. You can sing it to me while we dance. I'll be dancing on air. So if I step on your toes, it won't hurt."

Pearl knew he was joking, saying silly things to please her. She didn't know what it was about Sean that was turning her into a sentimental idiot, but she had to get over it quickly. He was rekindling hopes and dreams she hadn't thought of in ten years.

Yet he hadn't done anything except joke around,

be a pleasant escort—exactly what she'd hoped for but had no right to expect when she'd meant all the while to sacrifice him to Rock's greed.

"I'd better teach you how to dance," she said. "It would take a tornado to make you dance on air."

Sean grabbed her hand and they ran toward the music. Afterward, Pearl decided that was all that had saved them from being hit by the hail of bullets.

Pearl had lived in boom towns for fifteen years. She instantly recognized the sounds as pistol shots. The *whap! whap!* as the bullets buried themselves in the walls of the building behind them were unmistakable. The only questions were who was doing the shooting and which one of them was the target.

These thoughts had barely flashed through her mind before Sean picked her up and, breaking the lock on the nearest doorway, carried her inside the building. People in the street ducked into doorways, escaped down alleys, dropped to the boardwalk.

The burst of gunfire ended as suddenly as it had begun.

Pearl found herself pushed up against the wall inside a lawyer's office, Sean's considerable bulk between her and any danger from the street.

"Who could be shooting at you?" she asked.

"Nobody," Sean said. "I think it's the people who tried to break up your place. You must have made a powerful enemy."

Pearl started to tell him he was wrong, that the last thing Rock wanted was her death. It occurred to her that Ira might still be mad about losing so much money, but she couldn't say anything to Sean. He might go hunting for him. That would be the worst possible thing he could do. If Ira was willing to shoot at them once, he was perfectly willing to do it again. She had to find a way to get Sean off the street, somewhere safe, until daylight.

"I want you to stay here," Sean said.

"Why?"

"I'm going to find out who fired those shots."

"No," Pearl said, petrified he would get himself shot.

"You'll be safe enough in here."

"I'm afraid."

"You!"

He didn't have to sound like it was so unlikely. "Maybe people shoot at you all the time, but nobody's ever shot at me before."

"Sorry. It's just that you act like you can handle anything or anybody," he said.

That sounded almost like a compliment. "I want to go back to the saloon."

"I don't think we ought to go back into the street just yet."

"We can go behind the buildings."

"It'll ruin your dress," Sean said.

"Better to ruin my dress than my hide." She was willing to sacrifice any number of dresses to get Sean out of danger. She had felt guilty about drawing him into Rock's net, but she felt even worse that she might have done something to endanger his life.

"I'll carry you," Sean said.

"You can't carry me that far," Pearl said, unsettled at the thought of being in Sean's arms again.

"Why not? You're a little thing."

Nobody had ever called her a *little thing*. It wasn't an appellation she would have expected to like, but she liked it a lot.

"I haven't been little since I was ten," Pearl said. She would have given anything to see Sean's expression, but it was lost in the dark.

"Neither have I," Sean said. "Now let's see if we can get out of here without a light."

The building was small, only one long room. All they had to do was head toward the back. They bumped into a desk and stumbled over chairs, but the light coming in from the street was enough to enable them to find their way to the back door. The fact that it was locked didn't stop Sean.

"Now I'll have to pay for two doors," he said as he broke it open by slamming the door with his foot. Outside, steep canyon walls came right up to the back of the building. Sean nearly ran into a hand-operated pump and a large tank filled with water.

"What's this for?" he asked.

"After the last fire, I tried to get everybody to build tanks to store water in case we had another fire. Most didn't want to, but I didn't stop until I got every building owner on this side of the street to build a tank and buy a pump."

"Probably a good idea. Which way do we go?"

"To the right."

He scooped her up in his arms.

"Are you sure you're strong enough to carry me?" She realized immediately that she'd said the wrong thing. He'd carry her all the way to Denver to prove he could.

"Jake always said it was a waste of time for me to use a rope at roundup," Sean said with a deep, rumbling laugh. "He said I ought to just wrestle the steers to the ground."

Pearl laughed. She felt so good she almost forgot the gunshots. But not quite.

"Once I get you back to the saloon, I intend to find out who did this," Sean said.

"You can't leave me alone."

"Calico Tom can stay with you."

"He's got to stay in the saloon."

"Aren't you going downstairs?"

"No. I'm too upset. Take me to my room." They'd gone past half a dozen buildings, each with its pump and barrel of water, and Sean wasn't even breathing hard. "It's the next building," Pearl said. "You can hear Ophelia singing."

The light soprano didn't have the appeal of Pearl's darker, warmer voice. Sean set Pearl on her feet. "You'll be all right now."

"You've got to come in with me."

"Call one of the girls."

"I don't want anybody to know what happened. It'll upset them, and they won't be able to work." She reached out, took him by the hand. "You won't have to stay long, just until I stop shaking."

He hesitated, and she wished she could see his expression. Despite her years of taking care of herself, of thinking on her feet, she'd never had to face anything like this. She didn't know what he was thinking, feeling, even wanting. But she couldn't allow him to go back out on the street.

"You sure you want me?" he asked.

He sounded different, uncertain, unlike himself. More than ever she wished she could see his expression, but even the moon had forsaken her tonight.

"Haven't you ever had to help a lady in distress?"

146

she asked, trying to ignore a quality in his voice she hadn't heard before.

"Not when I've been invited into her bedroom," he replied.

"I've got nowhere else to go." She drew him inside the building.

The Silken Lady was one of the largest buildings in Twisted Gulch. In addition to the saloon itself, there were the kitchen and a series of storage rooms. A staircase at the back allowed them to go upstairs without having to go into the saloon.

"Do you take men up these stairs often?" Sean asked. She recognized that tone of voice. She'd heard it all too often.

"You're the first." She could tell he didn't believe her, but that couldn't be helped. His safety came first.

"What are all these rooms up here used for?" Sean asked when they reached the upper hall.

"My girls live here."

"Why?"

"It's not safe for them to live anywhere else."

"You worry about their safety?"

"Of course. They work for me. I'm responsible for them." He looked at her in amazement. "I've been in their shoes. I know what it's like."

Again he gave her a look of disbelief, but she had reached her bedroom. She opened the door, went in, and lit four lamps.

Pearl enjoyed watching Sean's eyes grow wide with surprise. She doubted he'd ever seen a room quite like this one.

The only extravagance Pearl allowed herself was her private suite. She had the only suite in the saloon—a sitting room, bedroom, bath, and storage room for her clothes. Parisian wallpaper set off the Italian furniture, and a profusion of crystal chandeliers and plush crimson velvet dazzled the eye. A velvet perfume box sat next to an ornate red-and-silver lamp on a dresser covered with bottles and canisters, most hand painted with pastoral scenes. A hand-painted dressing screen covered the door to the bathroom. Everything was covered or decorated with lace, embroidery, or appliqué. Pearl closed the door, smiling at Sean's look of wonder.

"I wish Isabelle could see this," he said in an awed voice.

"I thought your father was rich."

"Jake put all his money into land, hoping we'd all come back." Sean walked around, inspected several items. "Isabelle was brought up by a rich aunt. She'd know what all this stuff is." He turned, standing near the bed. "Where did you find it all? Not in Twisted Gulch."

"You can buy anything if you have the money to pay for it. I have to work hard when I'm downstairs. I like to pamper myself when I'm done."

"Do you pamper the men you invite to share it with you?"

Sean believed she'd used the excuse of the gunshots to get him up to her room. He thought she was trying to seduce him. If she knew anything about men—and she knew enough to fill several volumes—he would never believe she'd gotten him up here to protect him. He'd think she was just pretending to protect her modesty, playing hard to get.

She sighed. She hoped she wouldn't have to use the knockout drops on him.

Chapter Nine

"I don't invite men to my room," Pearl said.

Sean smiled. "That's a very good policy."

He didn't believe her, but why should he? She'd just invited him, insisted when he'd hesitated. "No one has ever shot at me before."

He walked toward her. "Are you still shaking?"

"A little."

"Let me see."

She held out her hands. She couldn't hold them steady, but it had nothing to do with the shooting. It had everything to do with Sean's presence in her room. And his nearness.

He took her hands in his. Pearl was used to thinking of herself as a big woman, but her hands disappeared in Sean's grasp. It was a novel feeling—another one she wouldn't have thought she'd like, but found she liked very much.

"You don't have to be frightened. I'm here, and I'll stay as long as you need me."

The weakness that attacked Pearl was so severe, she thought she was going to faint. Her legs gave out from under her, and she felt herself sinking to the floor. Her husband had said almost exactly the same thing the very morning he was killed.

She didn't fall. Sean's arms closed around her like a protective barrier.

"Are you all right?" Sean asked.

"Just a momentary weakness. It happens when I get too tired or forget to eat. I'll be all right in a minute."

He picked her up, carried her over to the bed, and laid her down. "How long has it been since you ate?"

"I don't know. Probably since morning."

"Have you been in that saloon all day?"

"Of course."

"So you don't get enough sleep either."

"I imagine I get as much as you do."

"We can't work after dark. That's when you're the busiest. I'll be back in a minute."

"Where are you going?" The men who had shot at him could be waiting outside. Even downstairs. Besides, she didn't want him to leave her.

"I'm going to get you something to eat."

"We don't serve food after nine o'clock."

"I'll fix it myself if I have to, but you're going to eat something."

"If you're going to bring food, you might as well bring something to drink."

"What?"

"Beer or whiskey for yourself. Ask Calico Tom to give you some of my special stock."

"I'll be back in a minute," he said and disappeared through the door.

She could hardly believe Sean was worried because she hadn't eaten dinner. Nobody except Calico Tom worried about her. Everyone expected her to worry about them. And for years she had.

She knew she ought to tell Sean she was too tired to eat, that she needed to rest. She could call Calico Tom to stand guard over her. She could even get under the covers and pretend to be asleep when he returned.

She also knew she wouldn't do any of those things. It had been too long since anyone had wanted to take care of her. It felt wonderful. She doubted she'd get a chance to experience it again. She couldn't resist the temptation to settle back and let Sean take over. Just for the evening. Just for a few hours.

She didn't have to wait long before Sean returned with a plate piled high with cold ham and buttered bread. And a bowl of cold peach cobbler. Calico Tom followed with a pitcher of beer and one of her special drink.

"You okay?" Calico Tom asked.

"I just felt faint," Pearl replied. "Sean insisted I eat, but I'll never be able to eat all that."

Sean grinned a little guiltily. "I got hungry just looking at all that food. Besides, Isabelle says it's rude to let a lady eat alone."

That word hurt because she knew he didn't mean her. She forced herself to smile. "Pull that table over here, and we can share."

Calico Tom's look asked her what she wanted him to do about this unusual situation. "You'd better go

151

back downstairs now," she told him. "I'll be down before long."

"She's staying here the rest of the evening," Sean said as he set the table down next to the bed. "She's tired, and she's hungry."

"They asking for you," Calico Tom said.

"They'll have to make do with Ophelia," Sean said. "Someone shot at Pearl. I don't want you to let her outside the saloon until I find out who did it."

Calico Tom turned his inquiring gaze on Pearl, his mouth open to speak. Pearl shook her head. When Sean turned away to get the food, she signaled that the gunman was actually trying to shoot Sean, not her. "Tell Ophelia to take my place tonight."

Pearl issued more orders before Calico Tom left. When she turned back to Sean, he was already eating a sandwich made of a thick slice of ham and two pieces of bread.

"I don't know how you can talk when there's food sitting in front of you," Sean said around a mouthful of sandwich.

"I learned long ago that if you don't take care of business first, there might not be any food." Pearl picked up a piece of ham and took a small bite out of it.

"Is that all you're going to eat?" Sean asked, a look of disbelief on his face.

Pearl couldn't help laughing. When she compared the size of her bite to the portion of Sean's sandwich that had already disappeared, she could see how he might wonder how she managed to stay alive.

"I nibble during the day. I guess I just forgot today."

"I'm going to see that you eat more than that tiny

bite," he said. "You're not a skinny girl. You've got a body to keep up."

"Nobody ever complained about it before."

"Who's complaining? I want it to stay just the way it is. Eat."

"Okay, but you'll have to entertain me. Tell me something about yourself."

"There's nothing to tell."

"There's always something to tell. How did you get here from Texas?"

She had to prompt him several times, but slowly she got the story from him. She smiled and nodded, asked questions as she munched her way through three slices of ham and a little bit of cobbler, but her thoughts weren't on what Sean was saying. Maybe he didn't realize it, but he kept referring to Isabelle as though she were the pinnacle of womanhood. He mentioned his aunt only once. Pearl had no doubt that as far as he was concerned, the gulf that separated Isabelle and his aunt was too wide to be bridged.

Though he didn't actually say so, it soon became clear that he was looking for a woman like Isabelle to take back to the Texas ranch he was going to buy when he found enough gold. Pearl didn't entertain thoughts of marrying again, but she couldn't help being a little regretful that she hadn't found a man like Sean before she let Rock seduce her with promises of what life would be like when she became his wife.

Wife! That word was a curse to men like Rock. Women were something to enjoy, like a bottle of wine or a favorite horse. When the bottle was empty or the horse went lame, they simply abandoned them. Sean wanted someone to stay with him for the rest of his life.

"What will you do on your ranch?"

"I want to raise horses as well as cows." He launched into his plans for the future.

Pearl hadn't thought much about her future beyond making enough money to get out of the saloon business and find a place where she could bring up her daughter as a lady. Sean made her realize that she'd left all thoughts of herself out of her plans. How did she want to spend the rest of her life?

She knew without a doubt that she didn't want to live it alone, but her decision to cut herself off from everyone she knew after she sold the saloon would guarantee a lonely old age. By the time Elise married, Pearl would be close to forty. Men didn't marry women that old. They wanted them young enough to bear children, young enough to be pretty for a long time to come.

"Is that all you're going to eat?"

Pearl came out of her reverie to see Sean pointing to her plate with a disapproving look. "Yes."

Sean took the last piece of ham, popped it into his mouth, and grinned. "Now there's nothing to take back to the kitchen."

He had finished off the cobbler and his pitcher of beer. Pearl didn't know how he could hold so much and still have room for more. Sean placed the empty dishes outside the door and moved the table and chair back against the wall. He came and sat on the bed.

"Do you feel better now?"

"Yes." Actually, after hearing what he wanted out of life and knowing she could never have anything similar, she felt a little depressed. "We don't have to stay here any longer. I need to go back downstairs. Why don't you come and play some cards?"

She started to get up, but Sean took her by the shoulders. "You're not going anywhere, especially not back downstairs."

"Why not?"

"If you feel up to going downstairs, you feel up to dancing."

"I always dance with the men."

"I'm talking about dancing with me."

Pearl hadn't expected it to be so easy to get him out of her room. She was a little disappointed. "I'll be glad to save you a dance or two."

"I mean all of them."

"I couldn't do that. The men wouldn't like it."

"They won't know."

"Of course they will. I'll be right in front of them."

"You won't be."

"Then how—"

He got up and opened the window to the street. Music from the band poured in. "We're going to dance right here." He came back to the bed and held out his hand to her. "Come on, you promised me an evening I would remember. I'm not counting the gunshots."

"I can't dance a jig above the saloon. They'll be up here demanding to know what's going on."

"This is a slow dance." He tugged on her hand. "We'll think of something else to do when they play a jig."

Pearl was good at resisting temptation because she got a lot of practice, but she never enjoyed it. She decided it wouldn't hurt to give in just this once. She liked the way he made her feel—important, valued, fragile, needful of his protection.

"Okay, one dance."

Sean didn't say anything. He took her in his arms and started to move slowly about the room.

He had the makings of a good dancer. Maybe his perfect, ideal, ladylike wife would teach him. But maybe she wouldn't like dancing. She certainly wouldn't let him eat ham sandwiches in the bedroom or carry her though the streets in his arms. Or sing Irish ballads in a saloon.

His lady wife would miss a lot, but then, she would have a lot Pearl would never have.

The music changed to a slightly faster tune. Sean continued to hold her tightly against his chest and dance silently around the room, his chin resting on the top of her head. She smiled when she realized he was trying very hard not to make any noise that might be heard downstairs. She didn't tell him she'd been exaggerating. They would practically have to come through the floor before they could be heard over the din in the saloon. When the tune ended, the band was silent. Sean kept on dancing.

"What's that tune you're humming?" she asked.

"I don't know."

"It's pretty."

"I heard it in Santa Fe. It's about a man who went away and never came back. The girl knows he would have come back if he were still alive. She swears to remain faithful to his memory."

Songs about lost love and missed opportunities were only for the very young or the very old—those too young to have suffered pain or old enough to be well past the worst of it.

Pearl's hip brushed lightly across Sean's groin, and she became instantly aware that he wasn't thinking about lost loves. He was thinking about the woman in his arms, and his thoughts had taken a very definite direction.

She became extremely sensitive to the pressure of Sean's hand in the small of her back. She'd danced with thousands of men. Being held by them, touched by them, was something she did because it was her job. It had been years since she'd felt anything in a physical way.

But now she was acutely aware of nearly every sensation—Sean towering over her with his chin resting on the top of her head, his huge body a comforting presence, the physical and emotional warmth that radiated from him, the vague scent of cedar, probably from the chips he'd used to keep his seldom-worn suit safe from moths, the feel of his work-roughened palm against her own soft, scented hand, the slight vibration of his chest as he continued to hum with a soft tenor sound that cloaked her like a warm blanket.

She was equally aware of the changes in herself— the relaxation that came from knowing that for the moment she had nothing to worry about, the feeling of physical safety that came from being in his arms. But these were counterbalanced by more disturbing feelings—that she liked where she was, that she didn't want him to leave.

Just as unnerving, however, was her body's response to knowing he desired her. Over the last several years Pearl had occasionally wondered at her lack of response to the men who wanted her. She had been relieved to be spared the constant tug of war that afflicted so many of her girls, but she worried that there was something wrong with her. If tonight was any indication, she'd just been waiting for the proper stimulus. She'd never expected to find it in Sean O'Ryan.

"I really need to go back downstairs," she said.

Sean's arms closed around her, enfolding her in his huge embrace, pulling her close to him until their bodies met from breast to thigh.

Instinctively she pulled back.

He leaned back to look at her, surprise in his expression. "Are you mad at me?" he asked.

"No." He frightened her. Rather, her response to him frightened her. She wanted to put her arms around him and press herself hard against him. It wasn't just the physical attraction. It grew from another need, one deep inside her. After so many years of taking care of herself, she hadn't even known it was there.

"Then why are you pulling away from me?"

"I told you I need to go downstairs."

His smile was slyly triumphant. "No, you don't."

"What have you done?"

"I told Calico Tom to tell everybody we'd gone for a buggy ride in the moonlight. That you wouldn't be back for another couple of hours."

Pearl tensed. She never left her saloon for such a long period of time. "And he agreed?" That wasn't like Calico Tom.

"He hasn't come back."

Sean pulled her back into his embrace. The music had started again, a really slow tune this time. The band must be getting tired. Miners weren't often nostalgic or overcome by tender moods. They tended to play with the same fierce energy they put into their work. Sean tightened his hold a little. He put his cheek against Pearl's cheek. His dancing had degenerated into barely more than rocking back and forth in place. "Relax. We have all the time we need to ourselves."

That was what was bothering Pearl. She had no doubt how Sean expected to use that time. What really worried her was that she found her thoughts turning in the same direction.

Every part of her that touched Sean burned with hot, spangled sensations that sent warmth all through her. The roughness of his cheek only made her wish to explore the softness of his lips. The fact that she hadn't been attracted to a man in so long made her anxious to explore feelings long feared dead. She was alive! She could feel again!

But she couldn't afford to risk acting on her feelings. Her brain had warned her both times she'd become involved with men, but she'd thrown caution to the winds and gone with her instincts.

Her instincts had been wrong both times.

She couldn't afford to make another mistake. She had a daughter to think of.

Sean was massaging a spot in the small of her back. A sensation of calm radiated from his touch. It made it very difficult to worry about anything as distant as tomorrow. Even a few hours seemed like a lifetime away. It was so easy to stay here for now, not worrying about anything, trying not to think about anything, just letting the pleasure of the moment seep into every part of her being.

"What are you worried about?" Sean asked.

The question startled her. How much could he guess? "Nothing. Why do you ask?"

"Your body's tense. Does the first time with a man make you nervous?"

She was disappointed that his thoughts hadn't

changed. Why? What did she want him to think?

She sidestepped his question. "Do you always romance a woman by taking her dancing, eating supper in her bedroom?"

He held her a little tighter. "It's the first time."

"Why now?"

"It feels right."

"Would you have done the same things if it had been Ophelia?"

Why did she have to ask a question like that? She wasn't a fool. She knew what it meant. She also knew what the wrong answer could do to her. She'd spent years insulating herself from being hurt by anything men said. But for some reason, Sean had made her care what he thought of her, care what he did, and why. It was foolish, but she couldn't help herself.

"I like you better than Ophelia," he said.

Then he kissed her. A light peck on the forehead, but the kiss rocked Pearl as nothing else had in more than ten years.

Many men had tried to kiss her. Quite a few had succeeded, not all of them against her wishes. None of those kisses had been as chaste, as innocent, as unassuming as the kiss Sean planted on her forehead. Yet the consequences flooded her body, heart, and mind. She felt as though everything she'd ever known had been thrown out, and she was suddenly pitched headlong into a world of chaotic emotions without the slightest idea how to understand or control them.

His gentle massaging of the place in the small of her back wasn't helping her think clearly. She had to stop being seduced by his gentle thoughtfulness and figure out what to do. She couldn't let him leave the saloon.

But she couldn't let him remain in her room without going to bed with him. It was clear he thought that was why she'd invited him there. It was equally clear he wasn't going downstairs to play cards or have a few beers. It was keep him in her room and figure out how to hold him off, or let him leave and hope the murderers weren't still waiting for him.

"Relax," Sean coaxed. "You'd think you'd never done this before."

How in hell had she gotten herself into such a mess? She couldn't explain that she didn't invite men up to her room. He wouldn't believe her. She couldn't explain that the men were shooting at him rather than at her. She'd already gone to great lengths to get him to believe she was the intended victim, that he had to protect her.

She could tell him the truth, that he wouldn't be in this position if she hadn't agreed to help Rock. Then he would hate her and leave. But she couldn't abandon Elise. No matter how much her conscience hurt, her daughter came first—over Sean, over Rock, even over Pearl.

Pearl was quick to admit she'd made a terrible miscalculation. She'd started to like Sean, to like being with him. She didn't want him to go away. More important, she didn't want him to go away hating her, distrusting her, feeling she'd confirmed his suspicions about women of her kind. She knew the end had to come, that it would be quick and brutal when it did, but she wanted to hang on to the few moments she could salvage. She didn't have many memories to fall back on in the coming years.

"I'm thirsty," Pearl said. "How about you?"

"Not yet."

"I want something to drink."

"Drink from my lips."

It was a silly thing to say. She was certain he meant nothing by it—it was a practical impossibility—but he might as well have dropped to his knees and sworn eternal devotion.

She tried for a light tone. "Then you'd be thirsty."

"We could be thirsty together," he said and kissed the top of her head.

She tried to break out of his embrace, but he wouldn't let her go.

"Not yet, my pigeon," Sean said, his voice growing husky. "You may not be thirsty for my lips, but I'm dying to taste yours."

Pearl's first thought was to fight. Her second, which followed instantly on the first, was that it would be useless. Sean had thrown grown men across the room. Her third thought, which came almost simultaneously with the second—it wasn't exactly a thought, more of a realization—was that she desperately wanted this man to kiss her, that she'd been waiting all her life for someone like him.

Her fourth thought was that she'd taken leave of her senses, and if she didn't do something quickly, a disaster so huge that even she couldn't imagine its proportions would come tumbling down on her head.

Overwhelmed by more thoughts than any self-respecting female should have at a time like this, she waited too long. Sean kissed her again, but this kiss was nothing like the first. It began respectfully enough, then quickly threw caution to the winds. He kissed her as though he meant it. She kissed him like a woman who appreciated it.

She didn't draw back when the pressure of her

breast against his chest caused her nipples to become hard and sensitive. She didn't push him away when she felt his swollen sex against her abdomen. She didn't turn away when she felt his tongue invade her mouth. She clung to him, wanting to prolong each moment, each sensation.

But when his hands covered her breasts, she broke the kiss. "Let me go," she mumbled as Sean tried to kiss her again.

"Why?"

"I'm thirsty."

"Can't it wait?"

She struggled against him. "No. I really want something to drink."

Still he wouldn't release her.

"I thought you were one man who wouldn't force himself on a woman."

He let her go. "I didn't have to force you to kiss me," he said, anger bright in his eyes.

"I didn't mean that," she said, retreating out of reach. "Now what would you like to drink?"

"Nothing."

"Don't be angry with me," she pleaded. "I'm a little nervous. You are such a *big* man."

Men were so easy. Compliment them on their size, and they were putty in your hands. Sean's smile proved he wasn't an exception, at least in this instance.

"Okay, give me some of this fancy whiskey I've been hearing about."

Pearl breathed a sigh of relief and moved behind the dressing screen. "Settle back. I'll have your drink ready in a minute."

She heard the bed springs squeak. He'd taken her literally and settled on her bed.

She opened the cabinet, took out a bottle of her finest Irish whiskey, and poured a large portion in a glass. She took out another bottle and put a few drops of clear liquid from it into the glass. She considered Sean's size and doubled it. Remembering he was already on the bed, probably half undressed by now, she added a few more drops just in case.

She came back into the room. "Here's your drink," she said, handing it to him. "And while you're up, undo these buttons I can't reach."

Sean had the buttons undone in no time. "Enjoy your drink," she said, slipping away before he could help her out of her dress. "I'll be back in a minute."

Pearl took her time changing. She wanted to give him time to finish the drink. However, when she reentered the bedroom, he didn't appear to have touched it. Sean took one look at her filmy silk wrapper and sat up straight in the bed.

"What's wrong with my whiskey?" she asked, wondering if he could somehow taste the narcotic despite the strong taste of the liquor.

"I was waiting for you."

"I had something while I changed."

"In that case—"

"I'm not coming a step closer until you've at least tasted that whiskey," Pearl said. "If I'd known you really didn't want it—"

"I want it," Sean insisted.

"Then why haven't you drunk it?"

"I am now," he said. He picked up the glass and drained its contents in one prolonged swallow. "There," he said as he set the glass down on a nearby table. "Now come here and let me get my hands on you."

"If I'd known you were going to throw it down like water, I'd have given you the cheap stuff."

But Pearl wasn't as dissatisfied as she sounded. The drug's effect wouldn't be gradual. It would hit him like a fist to the temple. She knew she had to last at least two minutes, maybe as many as five, before the drops would take effect. From the obviously aroused condition of his body, she wasn't certain she could hold him off that long. Just then the band started playing again.

"Let's dance," she said.

"I'm tired of dancing. I want to—"

She pretended to be hurt. "A woman likes it when a man is gallant."

"I don't think I can wait that long," Sean said, getting to his feet.

"Hum to me," Pearl said as Sean reached out for her. "And be careful. I don't want to rip this wrapper. It's real silk."

If Sean had known her feelings were very nearly the same as his, he probably would have ripped the fragile garment from her body and taken her right then.

"I don't know that tune," Sean said. It didn't matter. Passion was so thick in his voice that he couldn't have sung a note.

"I'll sing it."

Pearl's voice was so shaky, she had to sing it down an octave, low in her chest. Even to her own ears, the sexual overtones were blatant. Sean groaned and ground his groin against her. Fighting the passion that threatened to cut off her voice and destroy her resistance, Pearl resolutely continued to sing, to move just fast enough that the feel of Sean's body against her own didn't rob her of her last bit of resolution.

"To hell with the song," Sean said, driven beyond endurance. "I can't stand it any longer. It's driving me crazy to stand here dancing when all I can think of is making love to you."

Why did he have to say it that way? Why couldn't he have used any other word? An ugly one would have made it easier.

"It'll be over soon," Pearl said, praying at the same time that the band would play another chorus. "Then we can—"

Sean staggered.

"What's wrong?" she asked.

"I don't know. I don't feel very well."

"Hold on me to me."

Sean stumbled. "That whiskey. Something tasted funny about that whiskey."

"There was nothing wrong with the whiskey. Maybe you shouldn't have had it after the beer."

"It was the whiskey. I felt fine before. What—"

He couldn't finish the sentence, but the accusing look he directed at Pearl said it all. He knew what she'd done.

But it was too late. Pearl pushed him toward the bed. He took a few staggering steps and fell. She caught him and rolled him onto the bed. He was out cold.

She stood back. "I'm sorry," she said as a tear started down her cheek. "I'm so sorry."

Chapter Ten

"Where the hell have you been?" Rock shouted the moment Pearl reached the saloon. "Where is that miner?"

Pearl ignored his question. "Someone tried to kill him."

"What are you talking about?"

"Someone shot at him. Didn't you hear it?"

"There's always somebody shooting in this town. Nobody listens."

"Are you sure it wasn't you?"

"Why would I do that? I want his money."

"Then who did it?"

"How should I know?"

"You know about all the rotten things that have been happening in this town lately, Rock. You're behind half of them."

"I don't go in for killing."

"Who does? Who could want him dead?"

"Look, Pearl, I don't know anything about this shooting. I'll ask around, but you must be mistaken."

"I can show you where we were standing. The bullets are still in the wall. It was pure luck one of us wasn't killed."

Either Rock wasn't convinced, or he didn't care. "Where is he now? Maybe I can still get him in a game."

"He's in my room."

Rock's eyebrows rose. "When did you develop a taste for hulking miners?"

Pearl had expected Rock to act exactly like this. "I had to get him off the street before those killers tried again. I told him they were after me, that I was scared, that he had to get me to my room and stay with me."

Rock howled. "You, scared!"

"He doesn't know me. Neither do you, for that matter. Anyway, he got other ideas, so I had to give him some knockout drops."

"Why didn't you send him back down here?"

"I tried, but he wouldn't come. It was either keep him in my room or let him go after the men who shot at him."

"Oh well, at least he's still here. We can try again tomorrow."

"You can count me out."

"Now listen, Pearl—"

"I refuse to have anything to do with murder."

"I told you I had nothing to do with that."

"Maybe, but he wouldn't have been shot at if I hadn't talked him into coming into town. I'm through, Rock."

"I've warned you—"

"If you force my daughter on me, I'll seat her at

your table. That'll end any chance you have of making a living in this town.''

Pearl turned and walked away. Rock started after her, but Calico Tom stepped in front of him.

"She want be left alone," Calico Tom said.

He wasn't a big man, but there was something about Calico Tom that Rock couldn't ignore.

Even without Calico Tom, Pearl's conscience wouldn't let her help Rock any longer. She certainly wasn't the kind of lady Sean was looking for. But she had some pride, some character, and—she hoped— some courage.

She thought again of Sean's tenderness, his honest feeling for her, and wondered if there wasn't some possibility . . .

She told herself she'd already been enough of a fool where this man was concerned. Tomorrow she would put him out of her bedroom and out of her life. That shouldn't be hard. Once he realized what she'd done to him, he'd never want to see her again.

Sean felt as if someone was pounding on his head with a sledgehammer. He couldn't open his eyes for the pain. At first he couldn't figure out where he was or what might have happened to him. He remembered a few times when he'd had too much to drink, but he'd never had a hangover. He could tell he was lying in a soft bed. At least he hadn't been shot or beaten and left to die.

But what had happened?

He opened his eyes to find himself in a woman's room. But whose room? How had he gotten here, and why hadn't he left? The sun was streaming in the window. He should have been at the diggings hours ago.

Then he remembered. Someone had shot at Pearl, and he'd brought her back to her room. Where was she? He didn't have to look around to know he was alone. But that didn't explain why he had slept so late or why his head felt as though it was about to split open. Grimacing at the onslaught of pain, he sat up. Despite the knife blades that seemed determined to dice his brain into tiny pieces, he had enough presence of mind to realize he was in his underwear. He didn't remember drinking that much beer. He'd had only one whiskey. He was certain of that because—

He remembered. Something was wrong with the whiskey. Minutes after swallowing it, he'd felt weak and groggy, unable to focus his thoughts or his eyes.

Holy hell! He'd been drugged. Drugged and robbed just like Pete! Everybody had warned him against Pearl, but he hadn't paid any attention. He was too clever to be duped and robbed. Those shots had probably been fired by a confederate to give Pearl an excuse to get him to her room, knock him out, and rob him.

But even as Sean pushed himself upright and staggered across the room toward his clothes, he was already questioning his conclusion. If Pearl had robbed him, why had she left him in her room?

Because she was going to deny there'd ever been any money. Well, she'd find out Sean O'Ryan wasn't so easily duped. He grabbed his pants, struggling to keep his balance long enough to get his legs in them. That was when he noticed the bulge in his pocket. He stuck his hand in and pulled out a wad of money.

He hadn't been robbed.

The sense of moral outrage that had sustained him drained away, leaving him too weak and disoriented to stand. He sank down into the chair, unmindful that he was sitting on his coat and shirt. What the hell was going on? Nothing made sense. If he hadn't been robbed or his clothes stolen, why had Pearl given him knockout drops? She couldn't have been angry at him, or she wouldn't have let him sleep in her bed.

And she wouldn't have undressed him.

Sean blushed. He couldn't see it, but he could feel the heat in his face and neck. He didn't know why he should be embarrassed. Pearl wasn't the first woman to see him without his clothes on. But she had undressed him while he was unconscious, unable to do anything about it. That was more embarrassing than if he'd been completely naked in her bed. That would have meant they had made love. Then his being half naked would have been perfectly understandable. In fact, that was what he'd had in mind last night. Which made it all the harder to understand why . . .

Pearl had been willing. She'd changed her clothes, danced close, and . . .

She *was* willing, wasn't she? Wasn't that what women who worked in saloons did when they liked a man? But if that was what Pearl wanted, why had she drugged him?

Nothing made any sense unless he assumed Pearl *didn't* want to make love to him. But surely . . . Why shouldn't she . . . When he told her that first night what he thought of women who worked in saloons, she'd refused to speak to him again. She'd flirted at a distance, but that was to prove he wasn't immune to her attractions. But if she didn't entertain men . . .

Maybe she just wasn't interested in entertaining him. No, that didn't make sense either. She'd gone out of her way to show she *was* interested in him. Then why . . .

His head couldn't stand any more thinking. He was getting nowhere. He'd get dressed, find Pearl, and get to the bottom of this. Then he had to get back to camp. Pete was going to be fit to be tied.

Sean had just finished combing his hair when he heard the bedroom door open. He waited, but Pearl didn't come into the bathroom. Realizing that she wasn't going to come to him, he stepped out into the room. Pearl was just about to close the door behind her.

"Wait!"

The sharpness of his voice caused Pearl to stop as if frozen in place. When she turned around, her expression nearly defied interpretation. She looked frightened, guilty—and there was something else he couldn't identify.

"What's that?" he asked, pointing to the tray she had set on a table rather than asking the question that burned in his mind.

"Your breakfast."

She had obviously gotten over her first shock. Her expression had turned impersonal but friendly.

"Why did you bring me breakfast?"

"You've got to be hungry," she said. "You haven't had anything to eat since midnight." Her smile remained friendly, but she stayed close to the door.

"Are you going to eat?"

"I ate hours ago."

"Then keep me company." He didn't know why

he was standing there talking about food when he wanted to shout at her for drugging him. But her fragile expression told him that if he shouted just once, she might never talk to him again.

"I've got to go back to the saloon."

"Stay."

"Why?"

"I have several questions I want you to answer. Why did you drug me last night? Don't try to pretend you didn't. And who undressed me?"

He thought he saw a gleam of amusement flare briefly in her eyes.

"For God's sake, come sit down. I'm not going to beat you, though you probably deserve it. If I tried to move fast enough to get out of the way of a crawling baby, I'd fall on my face. What the hell did you put in that whiskey?"

She didn't answer.

He moved slowly toward the table where she'd set the food. He was sure that if he could get some strong coffee in him, he'd be okay. "I know you drugged me. I just want to know why."

Still she didn't answer.

"Was it because you didn't want to sleep with me?" He didn't have to ask. Her silence was the only answer he needed. "I thought you liked me."

"I do. It had nothing to do with that."

He eased himself down in the chair. "You're going to have to explain that one. My head's not working too well."

His hand shook when he tried to pour the coffee. She left the doorway quickly, took the coffeepot from him, and poured the hot, black liquid into a heavy mug. He picked it up with both hands and took a swallow. He didn't mind that it burned him.

"I feel like a mule kicked me," he said.

"Sorry. I used too much."

"Sit down. Why can't you stand me?"

She sat, still eyeing him warily. "Those men last night—the ones who fired the shots—they weren't trying to kill me. It was you they were after."

"How do you know?"

"Nobody shoots a woman in a mining town."

"But why should anybody want to kill me?"

"I don't know, but I couldn't let you go back into the street. They could have been waiting."

"So you convinced me they were shooting at you so I'd stay safely in your room."

"Yes."

"But then I got ideas you didn't like, so you—"

"You wanted to go after them. I couldn't let you."

"You know you could have kept me here without that."

Her look didn't waver.

"Why didn't you?"

"I can't afford to confine my favors to one man. Others will get jealous. They'll go—"

"You know that's not the reason. The men don't expect you to make love as freely as you hand out dances. I thought you wanted me to stay. Was I wrong?"

She looked very uncomfortable. "I know what you think of women like me, but not all of us are like that."

She was holding back. It was clear she wasn't going to say any more.

"Okay. While I eat my breakfast, tell me what women like you are like."

She seemed willing enough at first, but Sean soon realized she wasn't giving him any personal information. She talked about the difficulties of operating a business in boomtowns, the problems of finding and keeping good help, of finding dependable suppliers, quality merchandise, capable performers. The person she talked about could have been male or female, Pearl or anyone else. He could admire her ability as a manager and businesswoman, but she hadn't told him why she'd behaved the way she did last night.

Sean finished his breakfast and got to his feet carefully. He still wasn't as steady as he'd have liked to be.

"You've given me a wonderful lesson in saloon management, but you haven't told me a thing about yourself. I mean to find out, but right now I've got to get back to the camp. Pete's probably ready to shoot anybody who comes within a hundred yards of the claim. And if I don't show up soon, there'll be plenty of them trying."

"Why do you risk it if it's so dangerous?"

"Because it's the only way I can get the money I need to have the kind of ranch I want without letting Jake give it to me. The only other choice is to spend the rest of my life working on a hardscrabble ranch hoping I can make something of it, probably never having enough money to set myself up properly."

"Then let me warn you to—"

Sean pulled Pearl to him. He felt her stiffen, then relax when he kissed her on the forehead. "Tell me when I get back." He grabbed his coat. "Next time I want a straight answer."

Pearl's smile was wintry. "Maybe."

175

Sean opened the door to leave. But just as the words of good-bye rose to his lips, he changed his mind. Crossing the room with quick, determined strides, he took Pearl in his arms and kissed her without mercy. At first she placed both hands on his chest and pushed, but her resistance collapsed in a moment. She slipped her arms around his neck and melted into his embrace.

Sean had meant the kiss to be as short as it was ruthless, but Pearl's coming into his embrace changed all that. Beneath the hunger that attacked his body, he felt a tenderness toward her that hadn't been there before. The pressure of his mouth on her lips lessened, and he tried to gauge her response to him. She came to him freely and willingly, her participation in the kiss fully equal to his, her arms around his neck pulling him down to her.

Sean felt more confused than ever. That wasn't the kiss of an uninterested woman any more than her behavior the night before had been that of a loose woman. He didn't consider himself an expert in kisses, but he *did* know when a woman kissed him because she liked him.

But if she liked him that much, why had she drugged him rather than let him spend the night with her? She owed him a lot of answers.

"You never did tell me how you got me out of that suit," he said, deciding to save the more difficult questions until later.

"Calico Tom did it. I couldn't move you."

"He must have wondered what I was doing here."

"I told him. He's the one man I can trust."

Much to Sean's surprise, that cut deep. He wanted her trust. He was surprised to realize that he'd assumed he already had it. He didn't know when he'd started to take for granted that kind of relationship existed between them.

"You can trust me," he said.

She smiled in response, but he could tell she was still wary of him.

"You'd better get back to your claim," she said. "I wouldn't want to be responsible for anyone trying to jump it."

Before he thought, he laughed and said, "I don't think anyone was expecting me back right away."

Her expression told him what he'd said even before his brain registered the meaning of his words. It wasn't hurt or anger, just a stilling of her reaction, like putting on a mask, cutting off her emotions so she couldn't feel anything.

"The celebration went on most of the night," he added. "They'd expect me to stay and come up late."

They both knew what he had been thinking, what everybody else was bound to think now. He cursed his thoughtless tongue, but it was too late. He could apologize for his words, but he could never unspeak them.

"I've got to go," he said, deciding to leave before he said anything else to hurt her. "I'll be back in two weeks, maybe sooner."

He went out the door and came face to face with a maze of twisting halls. "Which way are the stairs?" he asked.

"I'll show you."

She was wearing a simple yellow dress this morning, nothing like what she usually wore in the saloon. A ribbon gathered her hair at the nape of her neck and let it cascade down her back. She wore no makeup. She looked like an ordinary woman—particularly lovely, to be sure, and more tired than she ought to be—but exactly the kind of woman a man dreamed of coming home to at night.

Sean jerked his thoughts back to reality. His brain still wasn't working right. Pearl wasn't that kind of woman. He was sure she didn't want to be.

"Are all the girls still asleep?" he asked as he followed her around one corner after another. The man who'd designed this building must have been drunk.

"Some of them are. They work different shifts."

Even before they reached the steps, he could hear voices coming from downstairs.

The first person Sean saw when he reached the landing was Rock. The man's gaze grew wide with speculation as he watched them descend the stairs.

"Doesn't he ever go home?" Sean asked.

"Rock's a gambler," Pearl answered. "He couldn't make a living if he stayed home."

"Is he always here?"

"No. He's just showed up recently. He'll stay here for a few weeks, then move on."

"I could move him along for you."

The smile Pearl gave Sean was as wooden as a totem pole. "One thing a saloon owner learns very quickly is not to make enemies of the gamblers."

"I thought you didn't want professional gamblers in your saloon."

"I wouldn't let anybody set up a roulette wheel or a hazard table, but I don't stop my customers from getting up a game among themselves. If the men want to gamble with Rock, I can't stop them. Men like to drink more than gamble, but not by much. Women come in a distant third."

"Not in your saloon."

"Maybe," she replied, then turned to Rock. "You're starting early today. Business that good or that slow?"

"A little slow, but I expect it'll pick up." He turned to Sean. "I see you've managed to do what nobody else in Twisted Gulch has."

"What's that?" Sean asked, only half paying attention. He didn't like the familiarity he sensed between Pearl and Rock, didn't like the idea of Pearl knowing him so well.

"Spend the night in Pearl's bed."

Sean's fist shot forward. It was instinctive. He wasn't even aware of what he was doing until he saw Rock lying on the floor. The murmur of talk in the saloon, the rustle of activity, ceased instantly. Sean sensed rather than saw that every eye was on him, every ear straining to hear what he would say.

"I did spend the night in Pearl's bed," he said, "but I was out cold. I drank too much and made a fool of myself. Pearl was kind enough to have Calico Tom put me to bed." He turned to Calico Tom, who was never more than a few steps from the bar.

"I take off clothes," Calico Tom said. "You sleep like bear in winter. Pearl no can move. You heavy as bear in winter."

One of the girls giggled, but that only served to underscore the tension in the room.

"I won't have anybody slandering Pearl because of me," Sean said to Rock. "She's always acted like a real lady. If you say otherwise, I'll knock you down again."

"That won't be necessary," Rock said, slowly getting to his feet. But his gaze was on Pearl rather than

Sean. "I'm sure you understand how I could make such a mistake."

Blood trickled from a cut in Rock's lip. Sean itched to hit him again.

"I judge a person by what they do, not by what other people would have done in the same situation. I suggest you do the same."

"Certainly," Rock said, appearing to recover some of his easygoing mood. "Why don't we have a drink and forget it, play a few hands of cards?"

"Some other time. I've got to get back to my claim. My partner's going to be mad as a caged bob-cat as it is. Remember what I said about next time," he said, turning back to Pearl. Then he headed out the door.

Pearl watched him go, his back looking as big as a mountain. She was amazed at the sense of loss she experienced when he left. It was as though she got all her energy from him, as though nothing mattered except his return. She knew that wasn't so, but the feeling of biding her time wouldn't go away.

"What have you done to him?" Rock demanded, all the easygoing humor he'd shown to Sean gone, the old black anger Pearl remembered from so long ago in full evidence. "I thought you said you gave him knockout drops, not some mind-altering drug."

"You wouldn't understand."

"Try me, Pearl. Try me."

"He's got ideals," she said, talking more to herself than to Rock, "standards, some real nice notions of what women are like."

"Well, he certainly didn't get them from you."

"No, he got them from his mother."

"He told you about his mother! You must be slipping."

"You don't know anything about good men," Pearl said scornfully, "men who want to marry a woman, not use her, then toss her aside. You only know about rats like yourself."

"Watch it, Pearl. You keep talking like this and—"

"Lots of men talk about their homes, the girls they left behind, their dreams. They're lonely. They feel forgotten even though they're the ones most likely doing the forgetting. They appreciate being with a woman who'll listen to them."

"Allow me to remain skeptical," Rock said.

"Remain what you want, but Sean O'Ryan is a man of principles. I don't say you won't get him into another poker game. I don't say you won't beat him. But you'd better not let him catch you cheating. If you do—"

"You let me worry about that. You just get him in here."

"I already told you, I'm through. I won't stop you, but I won't help you. Now I've got to get dressed."

Rock looked her over, and a mocking smile crossed his face. "I would think so. You look more like somebody's wife than a dance-hall girl."

But once Pearl reached her room, she didn't change her dress or put on her makeup. She went to her window. To the right, she could look between the mountains that enclosed Twisted Gulch. Somewhere up there, Sean was returning to his claim. But in Pearl's mind, he wasn't the same man who'd come down that mountain yesterday. She wasn't sure just who he was or how she felt about him.

He'd defended her reputation. Nobody had done

that since her husband all those years ago. Men had said things, assumed things, tried to do things, and nobody had stood up for her. Sean hadn't hesitated. What's more, he'd done so at the risk of his own reputation.

Some women might not think much of what he'd done, especially the kind of woman he wanted to marry, but no man wanted to admit he couldn't hold his liquor, that he'd had to be put to bed by a woman and a Chinaman. It wouldn't add to his status in a place like Twisted Gulch. People might talk about him, laugh at him, even drive him away. He could fight one or two but not the whole town.

Then there was the kiss. Never in her whole life had anyone kissed her like that. It wasn't the kind of kiss a man gave his fancy woman after spending the night with her. Pearl knew instinctively it was the kind of kiss a man gave a woman he liked very much, one he might even fall in love with. There was nothing of lust or duty about it. It burned with a passion Pearl realized she'd never experienced in her life, not with Rock, not with her husband.

It excited her that she could inspire such a passion in a man like Sean. It frightened her as well. There was no possibility that anything could develop between them. She was the wrong kind of woman for him. She was too old. She already had a daughter. Besides, any passion he might feel for her would burn hot and die quickly. Men confused a woman's being near and available with a love that would last forever. As soon as the man left, he forgot that woman for another who was nearer.

Pearl didn't want it to happen to her. Not that she thought she would fall in love with Sean. She was far too sensible. Besides, she didn't intend to marry. She had never met a man who would give her the kind of life she wanted, one who could forget the kind of life she'd led. Being alone was a haunting reality, but one she'd already faced.

She turned away from the window and seated herself at her dresser. She hadn't realized she'd stood at the window so long. The men were waiting for her. They expected her to sing songs of gaiety and good times.

But how could she? Everything she'd ever wanted had just walked out of town.

Chapter Eleven

"I want to see Pearl," Rock barked at Calico Tom the next morning. "She hasn't been down all day."

The Chinaman stood at Pearl's door with the erect alertness of a military guard. "She sick."

"That's what I heard," Rock said, attempting to push past Calico Tom. "But Pearl's never sick. She's just trying to hide from me."

Despite Calico Tom's age, he stood firm. Rock backed off. He had figured Calico Tom was barely smart enough to attach himself to a woman who would take care of him. The rock-hard muscles that had effortlessly pushed him back from Pearl's door forced him to reassess that impression. The unwavering determination in those black eyes was accompanied by open dislike. It irritated Rock that this foreigner who could barely speak English would have the arrogance to dislike him.

Even scorn him.

Rock's temper urged him to use his fists, but Calico Tom seemed as immovable as a man twice his size. The long, curved knife at his side was a weapon Rock had never doubted Calico Tom would use. He might be a hanger-on, but he wasn't useless. More than one visitor to the Silken Lady had found it preferable to take his business elsewhere rather than face Calico Tom.

"When is she going to be up and about again?" Rock asked, making no attempt to hide his rising temper.

"She no say."

"Then ask her."

"No wake."

"Then ask her when she does wake up."

"Me no go in bedroom."

"Then who does?" Rock demanded, losing what was left of his temper.

"Pretty girl."

"Hell, you damned crazy Chinaman, all of Pearl's girls are pretty. What's her name?"

"Calico Tom too crazy to remember."

The thought that Calico Tom was making fun of him crossed Rock's mind, only to be dismissed. The Chinaman wasn't smart enough.

"Well, she'd better get well soon. The men weren't too pleased when they found out she wasn't going to be here."

That wasn't exactly true, but Rock had been thoroughly out of temper ever since Sean O'Ryan had cheated him out of his money. It didn't matter that Sean hadn't, in fact, cheated. Rock considered Sean's money his own. And when he didn't get it—when he actually lost some of his own—he felt cheated.

"Pearl sick," Calico Tom repeated.

"I know, you fool, you already said that. Tell Pearl I'll be back tomorrow, and every day after that until she gets out of bed. Tell her I said we still have a deal. If she tries to back out of it, she knows what will happen."

"Pearl sick," Calico Tom repeated.

Rock lost his temper. He raised his arm to knock Calico Tom from his path. In the next instant, he found himself clutching his cheek, a searing pain burning one whole side of his face. He pulled his hand away and stared at it, amazed to see it covered with blood.

"I'll kill you for this!" Rock shouted.

"Pearl sick," Calico Tom said, his expression as bland as always. "No bother."

"Stop here," Pearl said.

The cab rolled to a stop in front of a bow-fronted brick house in an affluent Denver neighborhood near Brown's Bluff. Gaslight from the recently installed street lamps gave the evening a soft glow. At this hour of the night, the neighborhood was quiet. Light glimmering through windows provided the only sign of people within.

"Please come back for me in an hour," Pearl said as she paid the driver.

Pearl ascended the steps and rang the bell. It was only nine o'clock, but no light came from the windows of the house. She hoped Mrs. Hodges hadn't gone to bed.

Only a stroke of luck had enabled Pearl to board her daughter in the home of a widow connected by marriage to one of Denver's elite. The same connection had enabled Pearl to enroll Elise in an exclusive school reserved for daughters of the wealthy. She shuddered to think what these people would do if they discovered their daughters had been going to school with the child of a saloon chanteuse.

Pearl rang the bell again. If they were in the back of the house, they might not have heard the first ring. She nervously smoothed the folds of her dove-gray traveling dress. She had parted her mousy brown wig in the middle and tucked the hair under an expensive feathered hat. She was trying to look like an unremarkable woman of means. A gray cloak modestly covered a body that would have been considered remarkable anywhere. No one in Denver would have guessed that Mrs. Albert Warren could have heard of such a woman as Pearl Belladonna, far less been her. They knew her as the widow of a wealthy Wyoming rancher who sent her daughter to Denver to be educated. They admired the devotion that caused her to come twice a year to spend a few days with her only child. Pearl kept her trips to a minimum to lessen the chance she'd run into someone who knew her.

Pearl breathed a sigh of relief when she saw a light appear behind the glass panel in the door. ''Mrs. Warren!'' the maid exclaimed when she opened the door. ''Nobody was expecting you.''

''It was an unexpected trip,'' Pearl explained as she stepped inside.

''Mrs. Hodges is in the back sitting room. She'll be pleased to see you. She was just saying the other day you'd be surprised to see how much Elise has grown.''

It had been nearly nine months since Pearl had last seen her daughter. She'd felt guilty for waiting so long, but the saloon made far more money when she was present. The more money she made, the sooner she and Elise could be together.

"I wasn't able to get away until now."

"I'm surprised you come as often as you do. The trip must be dreadful."

"It is rather."

The lamplight cast strange shadows on the walls of the narrow hall and into the doorway of the front parlor. Pearl remembered the room and disliked the heavy, dark furniture that filled it. It was a relief to enter the small sitting room at the back.

"Mrs. Warren," Mrs. Hodges exclaimed, surging to her feet. "Why didn't you write you were coming? I've already sent Elise to bed. You'll have to get her up again, Donice. It won't do to have her mother here and her sound asleep."

Mrs. Hodges, a pink-cheeked, short, stocky woman, wore a black bombazine gown which failed to mute the bright twinkle of the hazel eyes that gazed out at the world with a cheerfulness that never waned.

"It was an unexpected visit," Pearl said, embracing the vivacious woman.

"Hurry along, Donice," Mrs. Hodges said to her maid. "I'm sure Mrs. Warren is anxious to see her daughter."

"How is she?" Pearl said as Donice left the room and Mrs. Hodges resumed her seat. "Donice said she's changed."

"Grown up right before my eyes," Mrs. Hodges declared. "Sit down. She'll be here in a minute. You'll hardly recognize her."

Pearl felt a bitter pang. She had already missed so much of her daughter's life. It seemed cruel that she should have to miss still more. She would have given all she owned to be able to keep Elise with her, but she'd decided long ago that she couldn't sacrifice Elise's future to her own selfishness. The mistakes were hers. She should be the one to pay the price.

"Is she still liking school?" Pearl asked, as she settled into a deep armchair.

Mrs. Hodges's merry smile faded. "I don't think so. We have a new headmistress, an old crab named Eleanor Settle. She's more strict than the girls are used to. Elise is very intelligent for a female, but she doesn't have the same enthusiasm for her studies she once had."

"Is she getting along with the other girls?" It was essential for Elise's future that she have the right friends. If her schoolmates liked her, she'd be accepted by society for the rest of her life.

"Of course. A girl as pretty and bright as Elise would get on anywhere. She's got a sweet disposition, but she's turning into a very determined young lady. Very much, I imagine, like her mama."

Pearl was thankful for Mrs. Hodges's sincere interest in Elise. Mrs. Hodges's only child, a son, was advancing rapidly in a bank owned by Jefferson Randolph, Pearl's banker. It had been Mr. Randolph who'd told Pearl about Mrs. Hodges.

"It's not hard to be determined when you're left on your own." Pearl had told Mrs. Hodges that her husband had died in a blizzard. "But I don't want my daughter to have the kind of life I've endured."

Mrs. Hodges reached over and patted the hands Pearl had clenched in her lap. "She won't. Already the boys have begun to single her out for attention. She doesn't encourage them," Mrs. Hodges hastened

189

to assure Pearl, "but you can't help but see where they're looking. Makes me as proud as if she were my own daughter."

Mrs. Hodges wiped away a tear, and Pearl remembered she'd lost two infant daughters.

Pearl's purpose in bringing Elise to live with Mrs. Hodges and attend the Wolfe School had been for Elise to win acceptance in society so she could make a marriage that would assure her of a respectable future. Though her plans were working just as she'd hoped, Pearl could see the beginnings of a gulf that might eventually separate her permanently from her only child. But that was a decision Pearl had already made, and she wouldn't change it.

"She has been wondering when you'd find time to visit," Mrs. Hodges said.

"I know it's been longer than usual, but the press of business . . ."

"She understands," Mrs. Hodges assured her, "but she misses you. I do my best, but I can't take your place. She loves you very much."

Pearl told herself she wasn't going to cry. She'd cried enough in the past to last a lifetime. She wondered how Elise could love a mother she saw so seldom. Pearl wondered if her daughter knew her well enough to truly love her. Elise had spent nearly all of her life living with someone else. She undoubtedly had an idealized picture of her mother that would never fit with the reality. Even as the time when Pearl could have her daughter with her drew closer, she wondered if it might not be best to continue as they always had.

A knock on the door and Mrs. Hodges's invitation to enter interrupted Pearl's gloomy thoughts. Elise stood in the doorway. One glance, and Pearl forgot everything else.

She hardly knew her daughter. She was only twelve, but it seemed that almost overnight she had been transformed from a little girl into a young lady of promising beauty. She had grown tall and slim. Her thin nightgown and robe didn't disguise the fact that her body was on the verge of becoming that of a woman. Cheeks of delicate pink and lips of pale rose gave her a porcelain beauty that caused Pearl's heart to ache. Flaxen hair hung almost straight to her waist.

She looked uncannily like a girl on a Missouri farm who had looked into the mirror one day and decided that her face would be her ticket out of poverty and misery.

"Mama!" Elise flew across the room and threw herself into Pearl's outstretched arms.

The tears Pearl had struggled to keep at bay poured forth.

"I thought you would never come back," Elise said as she hugged her mother with fierce energy. "I almost got into a fight with one of the girls when she said you didn't want me back."

"You don't have to worry about that, not ever," Pearl managed to say through her tears. "I'll always want you."

Elise pulled out of her embrace. "Then take me back with you. Right now. Tonight."

Elise looked at her mother out of brilliant blue eyes glistening with tears. Pearl couldn't doubt her daughter meant what she said.

"You can't live on a remote ranch," Pearl said, falling back on the piece of fiction she had used so often. "There'd be nothing for you to do."

"I could help you run it."

"You don't know anything about ranching. Besides, I have a foreman to do that."

"Then why can't you live in Denver with me?"

"Even though I don't do the actual work, my presence is necessary to see it's done properly." She'd thought of leaving the saloon, but she couldn't bring herself to trust anybody else with her business. It meant too much to her future. "Besides, there's your education to be thought of. You can't go to school in Wyoming."

"Mrs. Hodges can send me books. Would you do that for me?" she said, turning to Mrs. Hodges.

"I'd be more than glad to," Mrs. Hodges said.

"See, we can—"

"That's out of the question," Pearl said firmly. "You have to stay here and finish your education. When you do, I'll sell the ranch and we can be together."

"But that'll be four more years."

"Maybe I'll sell up in a couple of years."

"That still seems such a long time."

"You'd still be too young to leave school. I'd have to take a room with Mrs. Hodges until you finish."

Elise laughed happily. "That would be fun. You could meet all my friends. They'd like you ever so much." Elise dropped her voice into a confidential whisper. "You're much prettier than any of *their* mamas."

"You shouldn't even think such a thing," Pearl said, warm with happiness that her daughter thought her pretty. "I can't be pretty in this old gray dress, and my hair gives me a fright every time I look into a mirror. You get your lovely hair from your father, not from me." Another fabrication. Her life was so full of them.

"You're still the prettiest mama in my school—isn't she, Mrs. Hodges?"

"She certainly is, my dear." Mrs. Hodges's eyes twinkled with merriment. "If she decides to take up rooms here, they'll have to put my address on the city map to save all those poor bachelors from wandering around lost looking for her."

Elise clapped her hands happily. "Mama would marry the handsomest man of all," she declared, "and the kindest. Then we could all live together like a real family."

Pearl couldn't tell Elise she could never marry again, that they could never live together as a normal family. This was all the harder because it was something Pearl wanted so much for herself, as well as for her daughter. She didn't know why Sean O'Ryan should have to be the one to make her realize that.

She forced herself to keep smiling. "I just might do that," she said, trying to sound as cheerful as Elise and Mrs. Hodges. "Of course, he'll have to be very rich. I plan to be a very expensive wife."

"Not Mr. Randolph," Elise said. "He scares me."

"Certainly not Mr. Randolph," Pearl agreed. "He scares me, too."

"My son says half of Denver is scared of him," Mrs. Hodges added.

"I'm not surprised," Pearl said. "If he didn't take such good care of my money, I wouldn't have the courage to enter his bank."

They talked and laughed for another ten minutes, imagining all the ways they could spend the money of the rich, handsome husband Pearl was going to find after she sold her ranch.

Suddenly Elise turned very serious. "I don't think you should marry anybody rich at all."

"Why?" Mrs. Hodges asked.

"The fathers of all the girls who go to the Wolfe school are very rich, but they're mean. They hardly ever come to see their daughters. And when they do, they make them cry. The girls say they make their mamas cry, too. I want Mama to marry a nice man. I don't care if he's handsome or rich. I just want him to make her laugh and be happy."

Vivid images of Sean flashed though her mind— Sean singing, throwing her over his shoulders, carrying her bodily out of the saloon, dancing in the middle of the street. No one had made her laugh more often.

Pearl had to hug her daughter once more to hide the tears that seemed to be flowing tonight with unfamiliar frequency. Elise had truly grown up. Already she had more sense than Pearl at that age.

"I'm sure your mama is pretty enough to marry any man she wants," Mrs. Hodges said.

Not the one man who did make her happy, the man she was beginning to love.

"Enough talk about my getting married," Pearl said. "You'll turn my head, and I won't want to go back to the ranch."

"Don't," Elise cried. "Please don't."

"I have to," Pearl said, forcing herself to face reality. "It's how I make our living. Now it's time for you to go back to bed. I'm going to be here first thing in the morning. I'll take you out of school, and we'll spend the whole day together. We'll do anything you want, so be thinking about it."

"I don't care as long as I'm with you," Elise said.

"Then I guess we'll have to ask Mrs. Hodges for suggestions. Now give me a kiss, and jump back in bed. I want you bright-eyed and bushy-tailed tomorrow."

"Miss Settle says a proper young lady is never bushy-tailed," Elise said.

"Then it's a good thing you're going to be with me instead of Miss Settle," Pearl said, mentally chastising herself for using language that was certain to betray her origins. She hugged her daughter and watched her reluctantly leave the room.

"She adores you," Mrs. Hodges said. "She'd give anything to be with you."

"I can't. If only . . ."

"I understand. I had to give up society when I took in boarders, but I did if for my son. I'm not sure I really mind very much. Tell me about your plans for tomorrow."

Pearl spent the next few minutes going over her ideas with Mrs. Hodges, listening to suggestions, not really caring what she did as long as she and Elise were together.

"You'd better have Donice bring my cloak," she said finally. "The cab will return for me soon." She paused, unsure of how to begin. "Have you noticed any strange men lurking in the vicinity?"

"Goodness me, no. Why should anyone do that?"

"It's a neighbor of mine," Pearl explained, weary of the need to fabricate yet another lie. "We're having a dispute about some land. He believes he can take it from me because I'm a woman."

"I hope you've told the sheriff," Mrs. Hodges said, incensed enough for both of them.

"We don't have a sheriff," Pearl said. "It's up to me. He's threatened to kidnap Elise. It's a foolish threat, one I don't take seriously, but I thought it best to ask you to be careful of any strangers about."

"I certainly will. We do have officers of the law in Denver, and I wouldn't hesitate to call them immediately."

"I don't expect he'll bother Elise. I doubt he knows where to find her. I just thought I'd mention it."

"You did right," Mrs. Hodges assured her. "It's always best to be on the lookout for trouble before it finds you."

But it had already found Pearl, and in far more than the person of Rock Gregson.

The maid entered the room. "A cab is at the door, Mrs. Warren. He said you called for it."

"I did," Pearl said, getting to her feet.

"How long are you staying this time?" Mrs. Hodges asked.

"I have to go back day after tomorrow."

"Elise is going to be upset."

"No more than I will be."

"I heard Pearl was sick," Sean said to Ophelia.

"Took to her bed after you left and hasn't been seen since," the girl said. "But I'm not sick, and I'll be back in a few minutes."

Ophelia smiled coquettishly at him, gave her derriere a little extra wiggle as she left to take a customer a beer. She was undeniably pretty. But despite the long flaxen hair and girlish innocence, Sean couldn't remember why he'd thought she was so beautiful when he first saw her. Being with her didn't give him the same sense of excitement and heightened perception he experienced every time he was with Pearl.

"Is Pearl likely to be in bed much longer?" he asked the barman. Despite Pete's taunts, he'd come into town a week early when he heard she'd taken to her bed and hadn't been seen for days.

"Can't say," the barman said without taking his eyes off his work. "I ain't seen her."

"Who has?"

"Calico Tom."

"Where's he?"

"Upstairs. Hasn't left her door since she took to her bed. She won't let anybody in but him."

Sean turned toward the stairs.

"You'd better not go up there," the barman warned. "That crazy Chinaman's liable to stick a knife in you. He's worse than a mama grizzly when it comes to Pearl."

"I just want to see her to know she's all right."

"That Rock fella tried to force his way in yesterday. Calico Tom cut open his cheek faster'n a bullfrog can swallow a fly."

"I'll be careful," Sean said, pleased at the thought of Rock coming off worse in an encounter with the old Chinaman.

Calico Tom stood outside Pearl's door like a sentinel. Sean was pleased to know Pearl had such a faithful friend looking after her.

"How's Pearl getting along?" Sean asked Calico Tom.

"She sick," he replied.

His posture didn't relax by the slightest degree, but Sean was certain he sensed a change in the man. There was a feeling of heightened tension, but Sean couldn't tell if it was positive or negative. He remembered that Calico Tom had been the one to undress him the previous Saturday. It hadn't occurred to him then to wonder what Calico Tom thought of his being in Pearl's room.

"Is she well enough to see me?"

"Pearl see nobody."

Sean studied the expressionless brown face. He would have given a lot to know what the man was really thinking, but he didn't believe for a moment that Calico Tom was going to divulge even the tiniest bit of information about Pearl.

"What would you do if I tried to see Pearl anyway?"

The Chinaman's expression didn't change. "You no try."

"You think I'm afraid of your knife?"

"Pearl say you gentleman. Gentleman no be bad to lady."

That unexpected answer left Sean momentarily without a reply. What could have prompted Pearl to call him a gentleman? He hadn't behaved differently from the other miners, especially when it came to trying to insinuate himself into her bed. Isabelle wouldn't call that gentlemanly behavior.

"Do you have any idea when she might be better?"

Sean thought Calico Tom seemed angry at Sean's continued interest in Pearl. Maybe he was afraid of being replaced. Sean didn't want to take over. He just wanted to see for himself that Pearl was okay. He felt responsible. It wasn't logical, but he did.

"She be better you go back to camp," Calico Tom said.

Sean was sure Pearl hadn't said that. He hadn't

forgotten the way she responded to his kiss. That memory had ruined several nights' sleep. He wanted to try it again, to see if he had imagined any of it.

Why was he trying to convince himself Pearl liked him, might even love him? He didn't want that. He was sure Pearl didn't either. He was reading too much into one kiss.

"Tell her I asked about her," Sean said. "I'll probably see her when I come to town next time."

"You stay at camp," Calico Tom said. "You no good for Pearl."

Pete didn't think Pearl was good for Sean, either. Sean couldn't figure out why no one was able to understand they were just friends. After all, what did they expect to happen between him and a woman five years older than he? Pete said a man and a woman couldn't be friends. Kathleen said the same thing, but neither of them understood the relationship that had developed between him and Pearl. He liked her. She was fun. She liked him, probably because he wasn't always trying to get into her bed.

And it all stemmed from his itching to get into a fight and her being thankful for his help. That's all it was. Just friendship. They had nothing to worry about.

The road through the mountains to Twisted Gulch seemed more lonely and menacing than usual. Pearl didn't like traveling it alone, especially at night, but it was the only way she could be certain no one knew when she left and returned to the saloon. No one knew about her trips to Denver except Calico Tom.

Towering pines rose up against the night sky, obscuring the moon and casting inky shadows across the road. Pearl trusted her horse and allowed him to pick his way through stones and fallen rocks, but she kept a wary eye and an attentive ear alert to danger. Cougars and grizzly bears lived in these mountains, but she was more wary of human danger. She traveled with a rifle and a pistol.

But she hadn't been as watchful as usual. She'd left Denver with her mind burdened by worry. She was certain she was falling in love with Sean O'Ryan, and nothing she'd been able to say to herself seemed to change her feelings.

She'd gone through the usual objections so often that she didn't bother to remember them any longer. Any woman who could ignore simple facts was beyond rational thought. It was clear that Sean wasn't in love with her, that he never would be. If she let anyone know how she felt, she'd make a fool of herself. Even if she didn't mind being embarrassed, such a rumor was bound to hurt her business. Not even miners wanted to know the woman they idolized was an idiot. Besides, her being unattached was part of her mystery.

She'd talked and reasoned and warned and fussed at herself, but she couldn't keep herself from falling in love with Sean. Now she would have to keep on seeing him whenever he came in, dance with him, sing with him, eat dinner with him, pretend he didn't mean any more to her than any of the other miners. She was a good actress, but she didn't know if she could pull this one off, especially in front of the girls. Women were very astute when it came to knowing what another woman was feeling, especially if they liked the same man. Ophelia was already suspicious.

She should have sold the saloon and run as fast and

as far from Twisted Gulch as she could. She couldn't put Sean out of her thoughts, and she didn't feel safe from Rock. She was afraid that if she stayed in Twisted Gulch for two more years—or any other mining town where Rock decided to ply his trade—he would try to force her to help him again, and that if she didn't, he would start looking for Elise again. The possibility gave her chills.

But she couldn't afford to run now. Too much of her money was tied up in the saloon. She had gambled that Twisted Gulch would be a bonanza, that she would be able to stay there for three years, that if she had the best saloon in town with the best food and entertainment, she'd make enough money for her future. She had been right. She needed only two more years before she'd be able to sell up and never have to set foot in a saloon again. She wouldn't go into Denver society herself, but she could support Elise there until she got married. After that she'd gradually fade into the distance.

Deep in thought, Pearl had allowed her horse to slow nearly to a walk. That was when she heard the hoofbeats on the trail behind her. Despite the weapons she carried, she didn't want to meet anyone in the dark. She turned her horse into the shadows of the forest.

A man rode by minutes later, but Pearl didn't recognize him. It made her feel better. Strangers she could trust. It was people she knew who frightened her.

She pulled back onto the trail, glad to be reaching the outskirts of town. She'd had enough of riding about in the dark. Even in disguise, there was always the danger of being recognized.

She turned her mount into the narrow alley that separated the buildings from the mountain. As much as she missed Elise, it would be good to be back in her familiar world where she didn't have to watch everything she did or said, to remember the lies and fabrications, to feel like a thief waiting to be discovered.

Chapter Twelve

"You've got no business going back to that place again tonight," Pete said. "You've been there every night for a week. People are beginning to look at you funny. I'm beginning to think you've let this woman get her claws into you."

They were riding down the mountain to Twisted Gulch, a trip Sean had made every evening since Pearl had taken sick.

"And don't scowl at me. You think everything is just the way it's always been, but it's not. You haven't been the same since that night you spent in her room. And nobody believes you didn't make love to her. I know what you said. I know what that crazy Chinaman said, but nobody believes either of you. You made love to her, and she's bewitched you. Look at you. You run back to her place every night like a calf mooning after its ma. You haven't done half the work you're supposed to, and there's no one here to guard our claim or our tent.''

"You could have stayed,'' Sean said to Pete.

"And do nothing to keep you from falling into the clutches of this woman? What would I say to Isabelle and Jake?''

Pete went on with his tirade, but Sean didn't listen. He'd heard the same arguments every evening. It bothered him that Pearl had been sick for a week. It bothered him even more that no one except Calico Tom had seen her. He had complete faith in Calico Tom's devotion to Pearl, but he didn't have any in the old man's ability to render medical attention. Calico Tom had said Pearl didn't need a doctor. When Sean called one anyway, Calico Tom had sent him away, saying Pearl wouldn't allow him in her bedroom.

Sean had considered forcing Calico Tom aside until Ophelia told him Pearl got sick at least twice a year, that she always emerged from the sickbed looking healthier than when she disappeared. Ophelia thought Pearl wasn't sick at all, that she was just pretending so she could rest up. Sean hoped Ophelia was right, but he'd reached his limit. He had to *know* Pearl was all right.

"The way you carry on, you'd think she was some simpering little miss who couldn't take care of herself,'' Pete was saying. "She's a grown woman. She knows more than the two of us put together. If I didn't know you had some sense, I'd say you were in love with her.''

"I'm not.''

"So you say, but how is anybody to know with

you hanging around her door like some lovesick Romeo?''

Pete had read *Romeo and Juliet*. He insisted he hadn't liked it, but he was always making some allusion to it.

"What I do is nobody else's business."

"It's mine, especially with me getting poorer by the minute because you're running into town instead of working the claim."

"Then you do it."

"I can't with this arm."

Pete was better, but the wound still kept him from hard work.

"Then stay home and watch over the gold we do have."

"I've got to make sure you don't fall in love with this woman for real. Wouldn't Isabelle just love that?"

"Both of you can stop worrying. I'm not in love with anybody."

But he did like her a lot more than he'd ever thought possible. Something had happened that night she took him to her room. He wasn't certain just what it was about that evening that had made such a difference. He should still be mad about her putting knockout drops in his whiskey, but he couldn't forget that she'd risked her reputation to help him. He hadn't thought much about her reputation, but it was obvious she took it very seriously. Pearl considered herself a cut above the women of her class. Sean had to admit he hadn't found any reason not to accept her evaluation. She obviously hadn't been handing out favors. Men weren't usually ready to boast about their failures, but everybody was willing to admit they'd tried and failed with Pearl. It was almost a badge of honor. Sean was upset that people believed he'd succeeded.

Or maybe it was his failure that bothered him most. Nothing would have been more natural than for them to jump into bed after their evening together. But though Pearl had gone to a lot of trouble to protect him from whoever was shooting at him, she'd been just as determined he wouldn't spend the night in her arms.

He didn't know exactly what he did feel about Pearl, but he intended to get it straightened out. Going to see her was the only way he knew to do that.

"There wasn't any point in your falling in love with her anyway," Pete said. "She's not the type to settle down on a cow ranch and raise a bunch of red-headed brats."

That thought had never occurred to Sean. But now that Pete mentioned it, the image wouldn't leave his mind.

He really had to get things figured out. He was beginning to think like a crazy person.

Pearl knew Sean had entered the Silken Lady before she saw him. Such a thing had never happened before, but she actually felt his presence. She turned to see him looking for her. Their gazes met, and the strangest feeling spread through her. He smiled, and the feeling grew even more intense. It felt like a fever chill, racing all over her body, making her scalp tingle. Ironic if, after pretending to be sick, she should actually become ill.

"That man no good for you," Calico Tom said.

The sound of his voice, the meaning of his words, struck Pearl like a blow.

"He's just a miner looking for a little fun," Pearl said. "He's no different from the rest."

"Maybe not. But you hope he is."

"Even if I did, it wouldn't make any difference to him. He can hardly take his eyes off the younger girls, especially Ophelia."

"He no like Ophelia."

"Nonsense. Don't you remember that first night he came here?"

"He come by every day you sick."

Pearl hadn't known that. She'd gone straight to her room when she came in the previous night and hadn't seen anyone until this morning. No one could talk of anything except Calico Tom cutting Rock.

"How do you know?"

"I at your door. I see him."

It had never occurred to her that Sean might actually care about her well-being. Only her cowboy husband ever had. She'd known thousands of men in her life, but she'd never known one to smile at her the way he was smiling just now, straightforward, as if he were simply happy to see her. Not as if he wanted anything from her, just that he was glad she was well.

"He was probably just looking for an excuse to get away from working his claim," Pearl said. "Or maybe he wants to learn to dance."

"He no good for you," Calico Tom insisted. "You no good for him."

"I thought you were my friend," she said, turning angrily on Calico Tom.

"Friend always tell truth."

"Maybe I don't want to hear the truth," Pearl said, wondering why the truth was always so unpalatable. "Maybe I'd like to hear a lie for a change."

"Lie no good."

"Don't tell me about lies," she said, more angry still. "I've heard more than you ever will. Told more, too." She had to get her emotions under control before someone other than Calico Tom guessed what was in her mind. "Sorry, I'm still upset about leaving Elise. I'm not fool enough to think anything can come of this, but it feels good to have a man want to be nice to me for a change."

"Nice dangerous."

Yes, it was. Very dangerous. It had seduced her into thinking the impossible might be possible after all. But Sean had reached her, and any remaining inclination for rational thought went out of her mind. He grabbed her around the waist and swung her in the air. The moment he set her on her feet, he kissed her smack on the lips.

"You're looking great," he said. "I thought after being in bed nearly a week you'd look pale and washed out."

Pearl couldn't tell him that sleeping twelve hours a day had done wonders to restore her looks and energy.

"I'm very good with cosmetics," she said.

Pete came hurrying up. "You never let me whirl you around and kiss you," he complained. "Why can he do it?"

"Because I'm so big she can't stop me," Sean said.

"She won't let me, either," Paul Higgins said. "And I'm here every night."

"I won't let Sean do it again," Pearl said. "If he decides to take advantage of his size, I'll get Calico Tom to give him a talking to."

Pearl decided things were about to get out of hand.

The three men seemed to be about to square off with each other. Normally Pearl would be flattered. She'd turn the whole situation into a game where she played one man off against another, but she didn't feel like doing that tonight. Besides, after doping Sean's whiskey, she wouldn't be surprised if he never took another drink in her place.

"It's time for me to sing," Pearl said. "Go have a drink, play cards, take a stroll in the moonlight. It'll do you good."

"I'll sing with you," Sean offered.

"Nobody wants to hear you," Pete said.

"I know I don't," Paul added.

"You're going to hear me whether you like it or not," Sean said. "Come on, Pearl, what'll we ask Elliot to play tonight?"

"I ought to do this one by myself."

"This is the first evening you're well. We're going to celebrate." He took a coin from his pocket and handed it to Calico Tom. "Tell the barman drinks are on me. Now let's not keep them waiting."

Pearl couldn't see anything to do but go along with Sean. Besides, as long as he was paying for the drinks, the men wouldn't mind him singing.

"You shouldn't waste your money buying drinks," she said, not sure why she was so irritated with him.

"You said I didn't have enough fun. Consider this making up for lost time."

"Then go dance with some of the other girls."

"None of them can sing as well as you. Have I ever told you that your voice is like liquid honey?"

Pearl forced a spurt of laughter to cover the quiver of pleasure. "You mean it's sweet and sticky."

"No, warm and golden."

"I'm twenty-nine, Sean. Nothing about me is warm and golden any longer. Go find a younger girl."

"They're cool and green. Not what I'm looking for."

"And just what are you looking for?"

Sean wasn't ready to answer that question, certainly not while getting ready to sing. "A good time," he replied. "That's enough for the moment." But he wasn't interested in just moments. Something about Pearl made him think of years, and he had to find out what that was.

They sang a fast song. They sang a funny song. They even did a dance that got the men to laughing and banging their feet in rhythm. As they left the stage, the mood of everyone in the saloon seemed to be one of unbridled hilarity, but Sean didn't feel that way in the least. He didn't believe Pearl did, either.

The tension between them seemed to escalate with every passing minute, every time they stared into each other's eyes, every time they touched. Her question— *What are you looking for?*—had burned itself into his brain, repeating itself like a litany.

What did he want? He knew he'd passed well beyond merely looking for a good time. If that had been his objective, he could have gone to any one of two dozen saloons or taken up with Ophelia. He wanted more than relief from the physical demands of his body. There were lots of women who would have been willing to provide that.

He felt a need in him that was as unexpected as it was impossible to interpret. He knew it had something to do with Pearl. That made it all the more confusing.

The piano player began a slow number. Saloons

were famous for their loud, fast songs with high kicks and suggestive lyrics. It was almost unheard of to play a ballad, especially when the customers were dancing. There weren't enough girls to go around. Sean wasn't about to take a chance on anyone cutting in on him and Pearl. He maneuvered her over to the hallway leading upstairs and away from the saloon.

"Don't let anybody follow us," he said to Calico Tom as he passed.

"Don't be ridiculous," Pearl protested, trying to pull back. "We can't leave the saloon."

"That's exactly what we're going to do."

Pearl tried to pull away, but Sean didn't release her. He was sure she didn't really want to go back into the saloon. He had seen the excitement in her eyes when they were singing.

"Don't think you can start singing and convince me to stay out here," Pearl said. "I'm on to your tricks, Sean O'Ryan."

Sean figured being on to his tricks and being immune to them weren't necessarily the same thing. Only Pearl's words protested against being alone with him. Her body and the warmth in her eyes told him she wanted to be with him just as much as he wanted to be with her.

Sean sang a few lines of the song, a sad ballad about a man going away because his girl favored another man.

"What do you mean by singing in my ear about an unfaithful hussy?" she demanded, not fighting when he pulled her closer.

"I'm just singing the words," he whispered in her ear. "Blame Elliot for the choice of song."

"I most certainly will."

Sean felt her resistance soften and gradually disappear as she let her body gently mold itself to his.

Pearl let herself relax against Sean. His huge arms formed a cage she couldn't escape, didn't want to escape. As silly as it sounded, she wanted to melt into his arms and let him take care of everything, including Rock. She felt certain he could. All she had to do was tell him about Rock, and . . . But that was impossible. If he ever learned what she had done, he'd never trust her again.

She was in love with him, regardless of how foolish it was, how dangerous, how pointless, how much it would hurt when it came to an end, as it inevitably would. For the first time in her life, she was truly, deeply in love. And she had to choose a man who had no respect for saloon women.

"You're mighty quiet," Sean said. "What are you thinking?"

Wouldn't he love to know what she was really thinking. It would give him a big laugh. "I was trying to figure out why you are so determined to get me to yourself," Pearl said.

"I thought that was obvious. I think I'm in love with you. I know I want to make love to you."

For a moment Pearl thought she wasn't going to be able to move or breath or think. Her heart skipped a beat, then kicked into double time. He didn't mean it. He didn't know what he was saying. He *couldn't* mean that.

Yet every fiber of her being ached to believe him. Her cowboy husband had said he loved her. He had been sweet and kind, would have done anything for her, but she had known it was just infatuation. That must be what Sean meant. Both men were cowboys reared in Texas, brought up by mothers who filled their heads with visions of the ideal woman. They confused beauty with virtue. It had cost one his life. She was determined that wouldn't happen a second time. She pulled back so she could look him in the eye.

"You're just flattered by the attention of a pretty woman," she said. "Don't look shocked. I know I'm pretty. I work very hard at it."

"You're not pretty," Sean said with the earnestness of youth. "You're the most beautiful woman I've ever seen."

After all these years, Pearl had thought she was invulnerable to flattery. She was stunned to discover that she desperately wanted to be beautiful in Sean's eyes. Not just physically beautiful, but *deeply* beautiful, the kind of beautiful that lasts after the physical beauty has given way to the ravages of time.

"It's probably fascination," she said, smiling with as much saucy impertinence as she could muster. "You're flattered that a racy woman finds you nearly irresistible. I'm the devil on young men. Your own friend—"

"Stop it!" Sean said, his voice harsh, his gaze hard enough to pin her to the wall. "I won't let you run yourself down. You're not a loose woman. You had me in your room. I was hot to spend the night in your bed, but you dared to use the knockout drops rather than give yourself to a man you didn't truly care for."

"That's not it. I told you I was afraid—"

"I know you believe those shots were meant for me, but I've asked around. There was some talk of a gunman who left town, but nobody knows his name

213

or anything about him. I think it was high spirits, some fella feeling his oats. We just happened to be in his way."

"Sean—"

"It's no use trying to make me believe you're like all those other women. I know better. That's why I think I love you."

All her life Pearl had been looking for a man who'd believe she was good despite her mistakes. Now she had finally found one, a man she could trust, one she could love, and he was the one person she couldn't tell the truth—the truth that would prove her to be everything he'd thought her to be in the beginning.

She tried to escape his embrace, but he pulled her to him and kissed her hard.

"I've been wanting to do that all evening," he said. "Hell, I've been wanting to do it ever since I woke up that morning and realized what had really happened. I nearly went nuts when you got sick. I was about to force my way in until Ophelia said she thought you were pretending so you could get some rest." He grinned broadly. "I think she was right. You look more beautiful than ever."

Pearl knew she ought to persist in trying to get him to recognize the true nature of his feelings, but she didn't. She wanted to be loved. She wanted to be treated as somebody special, a woman to be protected and cherished.

It wouldn't hurt Sean any more to learn the truth a few days or weeks from now. And she was certain he would learn it. Sooner or later things like that came out. He would hate her then. But in the meantime, she would keep him close for as long as she could.

"Why won't you look at me?" he asked.

She looked up and smiled. "It gives me a crick in my neck."

"I can fix that."

His arm tightened around her waist, and he lifted her off the ground, raising her until her eyes could look directly into his, until the tip of her nose brushed his.

"Is this better?" he asked.

"No," she gasped. "I can hardly breathe."

But it wasn't his arm around her waist that inhibited her breathing. It was her body being pressed tightly against his—her breasts against his chest, her loins suspended only a hair's breath away from his groin. Pearl hadn't been in such intimate contact with a man in nearly thirteen years. She had thought herself beyond the youthful explosion of sexual energy.

She was wrong.

Her whole body felt foreign to her. Everything tingled and ached and seemed beyond her control. Especially her brain. Millions of thoughts sparked, only to fade before her mind could grasp them. She felt helpless to do or say anything.

"Do you want me to put you down?"

"No."

She didn't know where that answer came from. Certainly not from her. Surely she'd never have said anything so insane. Yet her lips had moved. It had sounded like her voice, but she couldn't have spoken. Her heart was in her throat. It should have been impossible for any sound to escape.

Sean started to hum again. He looked directly into her eyes and ever so softly sang the final line to the verse:

"They carved just one line on his tombstone.

Here lies half a heart. The rest is somewhere in Texas."

His kiss was feather-light. A gentle brushing of his lips against hers. It felt sweet, caring, but something inside her craved more. Something wanted to be overcome by brute force.

He moved his cheek against hers. She felt the roughness of his beard, the heat of his skin. Both sensations were sent into eclipse when he nibbled her earlobe. A shiver raced through her from top to bottom. She doubted she could have remained standing if Sean hadn't been holding her up. Then the tip of his tongue dipped into the curve of her ear, and frissons of energy arced through her body until she felt like a glowing ember. No one had ever touched her like this. She hadn't known that anything so gentle, so seemingly innocent, could have such a powerful effect on her.

She put her arms around Sean's neck, then laid her head on his shoulder. Yet there was nothing restful inside her body. Her breasts seemed to be on fire. She pressed against his chest until her nipples grew hard and achingly sensitive. Almost unconsciously, she pushed harder against him, rubbing, pushing herself against him in an attempt to ease the ache that seemed to grow more insistent by the moment.

The piano stopped, then shifted to a sprightly tune, but Sean continued to hum softly as he kissed the side of her neck. Pearl moaned, grew rigid when she realized that sound had come from her, and moaned again when Sean started to suck gently on the side on her neck. She would never have thought she would like anything like that. The moist heat of his mouth seemed to flood into her like a liquid, melting every bone as it went.

Pearl slipped lower, felt her belly rub against Sean's groin, and heat rush through her. Sean tensed as his body began to swell from the friction, and she felt hotter. Before she could decide whether to draw attention to the situation or try to ignore it, she felt Sean shudder and press against her. His humming faltered. His voice lost some of its sweetness. If he'd been a fiddle, she'd have said his strings were being wound too tight.

That was how Pearl felt. "Let me down," she managed to say with a shaking voice.

Sean let her slide a little further until the tips of her toes came to rest on the floor.

"All the way," she said. "I still can't take a deep breath."

Sean set her on her feet, but he immediately turned her face up and kissed her, deeply and hungrily. His arms closed around her with some of the roughness she'd longed for earlier. She felt his strength, the latent power, experienced the feeling of its being safe to surrender to his embrace. She knew·she shouldn't be standing there, letting him kiss her. Anybody might walk up and see them. But she couldn't make herself stop. The well of need was so deep, she felt as though it could never be filled.

"I want you," he whispered.

The words galvanized her. She wanted him, too, more than she'd ever wanted anyone in her entire life. For a moment she didn't see any reason why she shouldn't have him.

Then she knew exactly why she couldn't. She had

lied to him. She had tried to rope him into losing his money to Rock.

She couldn't give herself to him, couldn't let her true, genuine, honest feeling for him be defiled by association with her lies. She loved him as she had never loved anyone, but once he learned the truth, she'd never be able to make him believe that. Her love was pure, unsullied even by her own actions. She would keep it that way.

One day soon it would be all that remained.

"I have to go back to the saloon," she said. "I've been gone too long already."

"Let the other girls take over," he said, pressing his kisses over her eyes.

"I told you before, the men come to see me."

"Then I'll wait until you close."

"It'll be too late to get back to your camp. You'll be too tired to work tomorrow."

"I don't care."

"I do." She tried to pull herself loose from his hold, but it was useless. He was too strong. Her feelings were too divided. She probably wouldn't have been able to free herself at all if Calico Tom hadn't come out at that moment.

"They waiting," he announced. "They bang glass on table."

Pearl didn't know how she'd missed the regular beat. It sounded like an army of giants marching through her saloon.

"I have to go," she said, tearing herself away from Sean.

"I'll wait."

"Go home, Sean. It's late."

"I'll wait," he said stubbornly as he followed her inside.

"Then you might as well have a drink and find a card game."

Chapter Thirteen

"You no good for Pearl," Calico Tom said when Sean followed Pearl back inside the saloon.

Sean was irritable enough to fight anyone who crossed him. Being told he was no good for Pearl qualified. "Why not?" he barked. "Don't you think I love her, or do you think I said that just to get into her bed?"

"When you get gold, you go, leave Pearl behind."

Sean hadn't considered what would happen when it came time to leave. Right now he wanted Pearl, and that was all that mattered.

"That's between me and Pearl," he said.

"Go Naked Dragon," Calico Tom said. "They got plenty girls. They go camp with you. You no have come here bother Pearl."

"I don't want any of the girls at the Naked Dragon or anywhere else," Sean snapped. "I want Pearl."

"Pearl no want you."

"Yes, she does," Sean said, remembering how she'd kissed him, how she'd pressed her body hard against him.

"I ask."

"You do that, and after she answers, stay out of my way."

Pete met Sean before he'd gone twelve feet. "What do you mean taking Pearl off with you?" he demanded. "You didn't go to her room, did you?"

"It's none of your business what I did," Sean said.

Sean started to walk past Pete, but his friend grabbed him by the arm. "I'm your partner. Remember?"

"Not when it comes to women."

"Especially when it comes to this woman."

The jealousy in Pete's eyes caused Sean to swallow a brutal answer. "Look, Pete, you've got to make up your mind whether you want Pearl for yourself, or whether you're afraid she'll get me drunk and find out all my secrets."

"I like Pearl a lot, but not the way you do."

"Just how is that?"

"You're acting like you're in love with her."

"Is that so crazy? Half the men in this place are in love with her. Ask any one of them."

"But it's not like it is with you. You mean it."

"Pete, you're talking like a fool, and right now I've had all I can take of people telling me I'm not good for Pearl."

"Who said that?"

"Her damned tame Chinaman."

"There. What did I tell you?"

"If you think I'm taking the word of any yellow-skinned foreigner—or a white-skinned one for that

221

matter—that bullet must have affected something besides your shoulder. Now if you want to hear her sing, you'd better get yourself up front, or you won't be able to get within twenty feet of her.''

Pete looked torn between getting as close to Pearl as possible and trying to convince Sean of the danger of his attachment. "I've got more to say to you later.''

"I don't want to hear it," Sean said as Pete hurried away.

Sean didn't know why everybody thought they had a right—no, a duty—to tell him what they thought of his interest in Pearl. It was nobody's business but his own. He stalked toward the back of the saloon. Someone reached out, touching his arm as he passed. Sean whirled, an evil-tempered snarl rising in his throat.

"You look like you could use a drink," Rock said. His ever-present smile was broader than ever.

"I want whiskey," Sean said.

"Have a drink from my bottle," Rock said. "It's one of Pearl's best.''

Sean didn't want to drink with Rock and his friends, but he recognized the name on the bottle. It was the most expensive whiskey you could buy in Twisted Gulch. He'd drink Rock's whiskey. He might even have several glasses. It would serve Rock right for being so irritating.

"Thanks for the offer," Sean said and seated himself at the table. A tray held three extra glasses. Rock poured out a generous amount of whiskey, and Sean downed it in one swallow.

Rock's eyebrows arched. "One usually savors his drink when he's offered a whiskey as fine as this."

"I'll savor the next one," he said and slid his glass across the table.

Rock filled and returned it. Sean sipped the amber liquid, rolled it around on his tongue before swallowing. The taste was strong and biting, just the way he liked it. "Very nice," he said. "Do you always drink the most expensive whiskey?"

"Only when it's the best to be had."

Rock's genial smile would have taken the edge off anyone's temper. "That's fine if you can afford it," Sean said.

"I can."

Sean wasn't in the mood to bandy words with Rock. Most of the men in the saloon had gathered at the front when Pearl started to sing. Sean had never paid any attention to it before, but there was nothing polite about the way they stared at her. Every man in the place was busy undressing her with his eyes. Several tried to grab hold of her dress as she passed by. One was even foolhardy enough to take hold of her ankle when she executed a dance step.

Sean rose to his feet, determined to teach that young idiot to keep his hands to himself. He felt a restraining hand on his sleeve and turned angrily to throw it off.

"Sit down," Rock advised. "Pearl knows how to handle these men. She won't thank you for interfering."

A mix of emotions churned in Sean's gut. He didn't know where they'd come from, why they'd chosen this moment to appear, or what they were all about. And that made him all the more irritable.

"They've got no business bothering Pearl while she's trying to sing."

"If the men didn't fight to get as close as possible, she'd be worried," Rock said. "She's having as much fun as they are."

Sean had to admit that if Pearl wasn't enjoying herself, she was doing a masterful job of hiding it. The more unruly the men, the more fun she seemed to be having.

Sean sank back into his chair and tossed off the rest of his whiskey in a single gulp. He didn't want Pearl enjoying the adoration of all those men. He wanted her impatient to be with him. She didn't so much as look in his direction. He might as well not be in the room.

"You need something to take your mind off Pearl," Rock said. "How about joining us in a game of cards?"

Sean wasn't interested in playing cards, not even in the possibility of winning. It was on his lips to refuse.

"If you keep fretting about Pearl, you're going to do something to cause a ruckus, and she won't like that."

Sean didn't like Rock telling him what to do, especially since he knew he was right. He imagined Calico Tom would have even more to say. Though what right that damned Chinaman thought he had to decide things for Pearl, Sean would like to know. And where the hell had he gotten a name like Calico Tom?

"Why not?" Sean said. "I've got some money this time."

"I hear you win pretty much all the time at the mining camp."

"I do all right." Sean realized it was irrational, but he didn't like having people know things about him.

He liked to feel they only knew what he wanted them to know.

"You going to throw your cards down half the time?" Ira asked.

"I never play a hand I don't like," Sean said.

"It's no fun playing if you know you're going to win," Rock said. "The pleasure comes in matching wits."

"For some people," Sean said, irritated that one of the men was trying to take advantage of Pete's wounded arm to muscle him out of his position in the front row. He was pleased to see that Pete's good arm was more than enough to convince the man Pete intended to stay right where he was. Sean turned back to find Ira already shuffling the cards.

"I'm not lifting a card until I know who I'm playing with," Sean said.

"I'm Rock Gregson."

"I know you and Ira," Sean said, irritably. "I was talking about this fella over here. He's never said a word I've heard."

"His name's Clive Britton," Rock said.

"With a name that fancy, why can't he talk for himself?"

"He doesn't much like talking," Rock said.

"Well, I don't much like people who sit and stare at me," Sean responded. He didn't know why the man should irritate him so much, though probably anything would irritate him given the mood he was in.

"I don't have nothing to say," Clive said. "Besides, I can't hear Pearl if you're always talking."

"I thought you wanted to play cards."

"I can do both," Clive said.

225

Sean doubted it. He picked up his cards and looked at them. Decent. He discarded one, got a better card. He decided to play the hand. It would give him something to do to keep his mind off Pearl.

Sean played his hand and managed to win a modest pot, but not for one moment did he cease to be aware of Pearl. At any given moment he could have described what she was doing, the words of the song she was singing, the distance of every man in the front row from the hem of her gown.

Ira's irate voice broke through his abstraction. "Are you going to bet or not?"

Sean tossed ten dollars on the pile. It was obvious that playing cards wasn't going to help him put Pearl out of his mind.

Rock raised twenty dollars, and Sean dropped out when it came to him. He noticed the look of irritation on Ira's face, but Ira seemed perpetually irritated about something.

The minute Pearl finished her song, the men started begging her for a dance. She surprised Sean when she selected Pete from the group. Pete was a terrible dancer, especially with one arm still stiff from his wound. Sean allowed himself to become so engrossed watching Pearl and Pete that he continually forgot to bet.

"You going to play cards or watch that dame dance?" Ira demanded, angrily.

"Both," Sean replied without taking his eyes off Pearl.

"I never know when you're going to play or throw down."

Sean turned his attention to Ira. "Why should you care?"

"Because I want to win back the money I lost."

Pearl had finished her dance with Pete and started another song. It would be a while before she finished.

"Deal," Sean said.

"Think you can keep you mind on the cards this time?" Ira asked.

"Don't keep nagging him," Rock said. "The man's in love."

"What do you mean?" Sean demanded of Rock. It stunned him that anyone would think such a thing, particularly a man who hardly knew him.

"It's written all over your face," Rock said. "Like half the poor slobs in this place, you can't see anything but Pearl."

"That doesn't mean I'm in love," Sean said, picking up his cards. "I'm not a eunuch."

"None of us are," Rock said. "It makes living in this place all that much more difficult."

Sean wasn't interested in Rock's philosophical thoughts about men living in isolated places or the strains on his self-control. Being a bachelor wasn't easy, but it gave him the freedom to form an emotional liaison without feeling he was cheating on anyone. That was what he'd done with Pearl. They liked each other better than they liked anyone else.

"Two cards," Sean said. He got a king of clubs and an eight of spades. That gave him two pairs. He bet twenty dollars. The pot rose quickly, and Sean kept betting. His two pairs lost to Rock's three of a kind. Sean lost more than half his money. He was angry at losing, but he was most angry at himself for letting Ira's taunts cause him to bet so much on a weak hand.

He grabbed his drink and tossed it down, surprised to find the glass still full. He was certain he'd already drunk most of it. Then he remembered it had been full every time he took a drink. But that couldn't be true. He'd been taking drinks all during the game. When he tried to think back, he found he couldn't remember the evening as well as he'd expected. His mind wouldn't focus properly, and he couldn't concentrate on anything.

He pushed his empty glass away and picked up his cards. He'd been dealt a full house, two aces and three sixes. He decided to stand pat. When it was his turn to bet, he matched and raised the bet. The betting moved slowly but steadily until Clive dropped out. Ira soon followed. The pot had reached several hundred dollars, and Sean was nearing the end of his resources. He looked at his cards, studied Rock's expression, found no clue to the gambler's thoughts. Sean had never played with a man who showed so little emotion. His expression was always pleasant, even when he lost.

Sean wasn't used to that. It bothered him. It also bothered him he couldn't concentrate. It wasn't like him to drink without realizing Rock was continually refilling his glass. That was what he got for paying too much attention to Pearl and too little to everything else. If he was going to drink and play cards, he should stick to playing for matchsticks. But it was too late now for good advice.

He looked at his cards and calculated his chances. If he won, he'd win back everything he'd lost in the last hand. If he lost, he would have lost the thousand dollars he'd had when he entered the saloon. It represented all the gold he and Pete had dug out of the ground during the past week. If he was fool enough to lose his money, he deserved to suffer for it. But he had no right to lose Pete's share.

In his befuddled state, he studied his cards, absently fingering a rough mark on the back of one of them. It went through his mind as a fleeting thought that two cards had rough spots. He'd have to tell Pearl it was time to replace her cards. He raised and looked to see what Rock would do. Sean was almost out of money.

Rock equaled Sean's bet. "And I'll raise you the fifty dollars you've got left," he said.

Sean had a sinking feeling that he'd let himself be suckered, but dropping out would mean he had only fifty dollars left. That was hardly better than losing everything.

"I'll raise you fifty and call," Sean said.

Rock's expression didn't change as he laid down his own cards. He held four queens.

Sean had a cold, bitter feeling in the pit of his stomach, a rancid, cottony feeling in his mouth. Worse than the loss of the money and the certain knowledge that Pete would never let him forget it, was knowing he'd let himself be taken for a fool. He'd let himself get so caught up in being jealous of every man who came near Pearl, angry at every smile she directed at someone else, that he'd acted like an idiot.

He rubbed the rough spots on the backs of the two cards, unwilling to lay his hand down, unwilling to admit defeat.

"You called," Ira said impatiently. "You got to show your hand."

"A full house," Sean said, laying down his cards.

"It's not enough," Ira said, gloating over Sean's loss. "You cleaned out?"

"Yeah."

"We'll let you play on credit."

"No," Sean replied. He'd been a fool. No need to compound his mistake by being a *stupid* fool.

"Shuffle the cards and think about it," Rock suggested as he pushed the deck toward Sean.

"I don't bet money I don't have." Sean reached out to push the cards away, and his hand froze in position. He pulled them back.

"I'm glad you changed you mind," Rock said with his ever-present smile. "How much credit do you want? Five hundred? A thousand?"

Sean hardly heard a word Rock said. His fingers had encountered a rough place on one of the cards. Even though his brain wasn't functioning at its best, it made the connection between that and the rough places on the backs of the cards in his hand. He reached for his cards, turned them over, and felt the backs until he found the one with the rough place. He turned them over. Both were kings. He reached for the card in the deck and turned it over. An ace, but the mark felt different. He pulled Rock's discarded hand toward him.

"Looking at his hand won't do you a bit of good now," an onlooker commented.

Sean ignored the man. He stared at the four queens as he let his fingers run over the backs of the cards.

"What are you doing?" Ira asked.

Sean thought he detected a note of anxiety in Ira's voice, but he concentrated on the queens in his hand. He hadn't found any rough places on any of them. If someone had marked the cards, it wouldn't do him any good if he'd been the only one holding the marked cards. He'd almost given up when his fingers encountered a tiny scratch on the upper right corner of one of the cards. A quick check revealed that all the cards had been marked similarly.

Sean began to search through the deck.

"If you're not going to deal, give me the cards," Rock said. His words were spoken as deliberately as always, but there was a new quality in his voice. Uneasiness.

Sean didn't respond. He'd turned up an ace. He located the mark almost immediately.

"These cards are marked," Sean announced in a steely voice. He started sorting through the deck, pulling out the rest of the face cards as he came to them.

"Don't be a fool," Ira snapped. "Just because—"

"The cards are marked," Sean said louder. "Somebody is cheating."

"Marked cards!" shouted the man who'd been looking over Sean's shoulder. "This man says somebody's been cheating!"

Men stopped what they were doing, fell silent, and then rushed to surround Sean's table.

"Are you accusing me of cheating?" Ira asked. The anger had changed to a vicious glare.

"I am if you marked these cards," Sean replied.

"Who says they're marked?" Rock asked.

"I do," Sean said.

"Who's been winning?"

"The same man," Sean said, fixing his gaze on Rock.

Sean had to give Rock credit. His expression didn't change. He seemed to find the whole proceedings faintly amusing.

"I won the last two hands," Rock said, "but I defy anybody to prove I cheated."

"There are scratches on the backs of these cards," Sean said.

"I have nothing to scratch them with." Rock held out his hands. "I have no rings. Not even a cigar knife."

"One of you marked those cards," Sean said. "I don't know how you did it, but you did."

"They must have been marked already," Rock said. "We used house cards."

"Pearl!" somebody shouted, "this man says you're supplying marked cards."

Anger hot enough to match his red hair rose within Sean. An accusation like that could ruin Pearl. He reached across the table and pulled Rock up by the front of his clothes until he was halfway across the table. "Pearl would never used marked cards. She runs a clean place."

Before anybody could reply, Clive and Ira had produced guns, each pointing them at Sean.

"Let him go!" Ira barked. "You're drunk."

"Those cards are marked," Sean said. "Ask anybody."

Ira turned his pistol on the crowd. "Anybody say these cards are marked?"

Nobody said a word.

"Like I said," Ira said, turning his pistol back on Sean, "you're drunk."

Sean slung Rock from him. "Look at those cards," he said. "Any one of you. Run your fingers over the backs of the face cards."

But Sean knew the moment he looked down at the scattered cards that someone had exchanged the decks. He didn't know how it had been done, but they weren't the same cards. It was soon clear from their expressions that the men checking the cards found no incriminating scratches.

Hot fury seized him. He wanted to fight, to curse, to shout that Rock and his friends were liars and cheats, that they ought to be driven out of town. But one look at the grim faces around him convinced him nobody would believe him. He'd made a serious accusation—one that could have ended in a killing—and he hadn't been able to back it up.

They were all against him. It was all right to cheat and get away with it, but making a false claim of cheating was a violation of the male code of ethics.

"You'd better go home and sleep it off," Paul Higgins said.

"I'm not leaving until I find out what happened to the real deck, the one we used."

"He's drunk," Ira said.

"I watched him down more than half that bottle," one onlooker said. "He threw the stuff down like it was water."

The mood of the crowd started to turn ugly. Most men were quick to turn on a cheater. But they were equally ready to turn on anyone who attempted to get his money back by accusing an innocent person of cheating. Frontier justice wasn't always logical, but it was quick. It allowed little room for extenuating circumstances or reasonable doubt.

"What's going on here?" It was Pete. He'd managed to force his way into the center of the mob.

"Move aside," Sean heard Pearl say. "Let me through."

"He accused Rock of cheating at cards," one man said.

233

"He said the cards were marked, but they ain't," another explained.

"They switched the decks when I wasn't looking," Sean told Pete.

"Put those guns away," Pearl ordered. "I won't have them in my saloon."

Ira pointed his gun at Sean's temple. "He accused us of cheating. We ought to—"

"Pearl say put gun down," Calico Tom said. "Do like she say."

Calico Tom stood just behind Ira, a knife poised less than an inch from his jugular vein.

"You too, Clive," Pearl said as she positioned herself between him and Sean, "or you'll never set foot in this saloon again."

Neither man seemed willing, but Ira eyed Calico Tom's knife fearfully. Pete twisted Clive's gun out of his hand and laid it on the table.

"Now what's this about cheating?" Pearl asked.

"If Sean says they were cheating, they were cheating," Pete said. "He doesn't lie."

"Neither do we," Rock said.

"Search them," Sean said. "One of them has the marked deck on him."

"I'll be damned if anybody's searching me," Ira shouted. "And tell your damned Chinaman to put up his knife, or I'll cut him open from chest to navel the first chance I get."

"Put it up," Pearl said to Calico Tom before turning to Ira. "If you didn't cheat, why would you object to showing us what's in your pockets?"

"You're welcome to search every inch of me," Rock said. "If you'll do it, Pearl, I'll take it as an honor."

"I'll do it," Pete said. "Pearl's too much of a lady."

"That's too bad. I was looking forward to it."

It was said with a smile, but Sean was certain Rock was mocking Pearl.

A thorough search of all three men failed to turn up cards of any kind. Sean didn't care about the men or their angry murmurs. He only cared about Pearl. He couldn't stand for her to think him a liar. Except for a quick glance when she broke through the circle, she hadn't looked at him. She busied herself talking to the crowd, calming them to prevent a free-for-all.

When she finally did turn to him, she looked like a stranger. "You'd better leave," she said. "I can't have anything like this in my saloon."

It was cruel and unfair of her to say that to him, especially after he'd told her less than an hour earlier that he loved her, but she couldn't have done anything else. Still, he had to talk to her. He had to know she believed he was telling the truth.

"I want to talk to you."

"Pearl's got nothing to say to a liar," one of the men said.

"Watch who you're calling a liar," Pete said, squaring up to the man. "He's my partner."

"Then you'd better keep him in camp. He'll get you killed one of these days."

"Pearl, I need to talk to you," Sean said again. He didn't care about her saloon now. He reached out to her, but she backed away.

"Pearl's not going anywhere with you," Rock said.

That was the wrong thing to say. Whatever Pearl had meant to do, she changed her mind.

"I believe in giving every man a chance to speak for himself."

She'd already judged him. He could see it in her eyes. He might as well give up and go home, but he couldn't. No matter what anybody else thought, Pearl had to believe him.

"Outside. I want to talk with you alone."

"He's just going to tell you more lies," Ira said.

"This really isn't necessary," Rock said. "You've already given the man more consideration than he deserves."

Sean watched Pearl's face, hoping for some indication that she believed him. He got none.

"I'll give you five minutes," she said

Chapter Fourteen

Sean hardly knew what to say. Five minutes was too much and too little. Pearl acted as though she couldn't wait to get away from him and back to the people she trusted.

"What's this all about?" Pete asked when they got outside.

"I'll tell you on the way back to camp," Sean said. "I want to talk to Pearl now."

"You'll talk to me, dammit," Pete shouted. "One of those men said you lost a thousand dollars. I told him he was a fool, that you never lost that much money in your whole life."

"I'll tell you about it in a minute."

"A thousand dollars—half of it my money!" Pete shouted. "And you want me to go sit in a corner while you talk to a woman?"

"I never blamed you when you lost that gold shipment," Sean said.

"That was different. They had guns."

"I'll get the money back. Just let me talk to Pearl."

"How?"

"I don't know. I'll figure something out. *Now go away and leave me alone!*"

Pete looked as though he was about to explode. "Five minutes," he said. "That's all you get. Then I want to hear your plans for getting that money back—*in detail!*"

Sean's gaze hadn't left Pearl. "I didn't lie," he said. "I felt the marks on the backs of the two kings in my hand but didn't think anything about it."

"Why not?" Pete demanded from twenty feet away. "Any fool should have known there was something wrong. Why didn't you?"

"Because I wasn't paying attention," Sean admitted.

"Why weren't you?" Pete shouted. "You had a thousand dollars in your pocket. I'd think that ought to be enough to hold anyone's attention."

"I was listening to Pearl, watching the two of you dance."

"Now you're trying to blame it on me," Pete said.

"No, it was my fault."

"What about that whiskey?" Pete asked, not letting up. "I never knew you to drink so much, not when you were playing cards."

"Same reason," Sean said. "I was watching Pearl."

"Dammit to hell, man, you don't swill whiskey and pay attention to everything in the room except the cards in your hand."

"I know that, but it's done now." He wasn't about to tell Pete that the cause of his uncharacteristic be-

238

havior was jealousy. He didn't know what he was
going to do about it, but he couldn't continue like
this.

"You believe I'm telling the truth, don't you?" he
asked Pearl.

Her behavior throughout this whole episode had
confused him. She was usually very outspoken. Other
than telling him he had to leave the saloon, she hadn't
said a word. Now she looked as if all she wanted to
do was forget the whole thing. That wasn't like the
Pearl he knew, the woman who'd fascinated him so
much he'd just lost a thousand dollars.

Pearl didn't answer, wouldn't look at him.

"Answer him," Pete said. "This is your fault. Tell
him you think he's a fool. Maybe he'll get over you
then."

"Shut up, Pete, or I'll break your neck."

"No, you won't. You won't be able to take your
eyes off Pearl long enough to find it."

Sean forced himself to ignore Pete. "I wouldn't
lie," he told Pearl. "If I'd lost that money fair and
square, I'd never have said a word."

"He's telling the truth there," Pete said. "He's a
crazy Irish fool, but he's a truthful one."

"You know I can't have you accusing people of
cheating," Pearl said, still refusing to look at Sean.
"It could ruin me."

"I'm not blaming you," Sean said. He put his finger under Pearl's chin and forced her to look at him.
"I'm only asking if you believe me."

"Tell him," Pete prompted. "I'm waiting to see
how he plans to get my money back."

"Shut up, Pete," Sean barked savagely.

Pearl kept her eyes averted. "I believe you," she

said, but her voice didn't sound right. Nothing about her was like her usual self.

"Good. Now we can be going." Pete said.

"You say one more word before I'm finished, and I'm going to break your other arm," Sean thundered. "Go get the horses."

Pete stormed off, muttering curses.

"You don't act like you believe me," Sean said to Pearl.

She finally looked at him. "I do. I've suspected for some time that Rock didn't always play fair."

"Why don't you throw him out?"

"For the same reason the men were ready to throw you out. I don't have any proof, and the men like to gamble with him. If they like losing their money, there's nothing I can do to stop them."

Things still didn't feel right "I'll get the proof," Sean said. "I'll come back every night until I catch them."

Pearl's cold disinterest vanished. "You can't come back here again."

"Of course I'm coming back to see you. Nothing can keep me away, not even Rock and his thieving friends."

"You've got to stay away!" Pearl said. There was nothing cold or distant about her now. She reached out to him, grabbed his arm, and held on tight. "There's no telling what the men might do."

"I'm not worried about them."

"I am. You don't know what a crowd like that can do when they get angry. I've seen it before. They can kill a man, beat him to death, hang him—without listening to anything he says."

He smiled with relief. He didn't know what had

bothered Pearl, but he was relieved she hadn't stopped caring for him. "I won't make a fuss. I'll stay in the back."

"You don't understand," she said, openly upset now. "Rock might forget about it. Sometimes I don't think he cares about anything. Clive might even overlook it, but Ira won't. He'll stir up the men the minute he sees you."

"Why do you put up with these men? What are they holding over you?"

"Nothing. They're just here looking for a friendly game, exactly what my customers want. If I didn't let them stay, the men would complain."

Sean was certain there was more to it than that. He didn't know why Pearl was afraid of Rock, but he didn't like it.

"Everybody will have forgotten all about it by the time I come back next week," Sean said.

"Don't you understand?"

"I understand nobody is going to keep me from seeing you again. I'll be back in a week. Count the hours."

"I'll come to you."

He hadn't expected that. "I don't want you to come to the camp again. I want you to myself."

"You can have me to yourself. Just don't come back here."

"How? When? Where?"

"We can have a picnic next Sunday. I'll bring the food. You know those mountains. You find a place."

He knew the perfect spot, a tiny meadow tucked away between two ridges not far from the camp. Now that there was no game to hunt, nobody ever went there.

"I'll come get you," he said.

"No. I'll meet you at the foot of the mountain."

"Promise you won't change your mind."

"I promise. Now go. They'll be out here if I stay any longer."

"I don't like it," Sean said. "I feel like I'm running away."

"I won't meet you if you don't go now," Pearl said. "Here's Pete with the horses."

Sean still didn't like leaving things as they were, especially with Rock in the saloon, but he couldn't do anything about it now without upsetting Pearl still more. He wouldn't do that, but he intended to find out what was going on. Soon.

Pearl knew she had no business meeting Sean. All week long she'd been telling herself he'd probably break her neck when he found out she had set him up. The sensible thing to do would be to stay in the saloon, get Calico Tom and Paul Higgins to make sure Sean couldn't get near her if he did decide to come back. They'd do it, too. Paul had been after her to become his woman for nearly a year. Calico Tom had been telling her ever since she got back from Denver that she was heading for trouble, that the gods were angry and she was blowing smoke in their faces.

None of them had said half of what Ophelia had said when she found out what Pearl meant to do. And all of them together hadn't come close to matching what Pearl said to herself.

But when it was all said and done, Pearl couldn't stay away. Sean was like an addiction. She knew hanging around him could be the death of her, but she had to have every moment she could. He said he loved her. She didn't believe he felt real love, the kind that lasts for a lifetime and doesn't change no matter what. But she loved him. Desperately, stupidly, wildly. All her arguments with herself had changed nothing. She wouldn't love anybody else like this ever again.

Yet every time she thought of Sean—and she hardly had any thoughts that didn't include him—guilt weighed more and more heavily on her conscience. She knew Rock had cheated. She didn't know how, was certain she couldn't prove it, but she knew he cheated. She'd always known it. She'd led Sean right to him, practically shoved him into the trap knowing Rock planned to fleece him.

If she had any courage or integrity—any *honor*— she'd cut Sean loose. Maybe not tell him the truth. That might hurt him too much. Just make him think she considered him a silly young man whom a woman of her maturity couldn't take seriously. She'd done it before.

But she couldn't do that with Sean. Not to do it was selfish, probably cruel, but she simply couldn't.

Life had offered her very little in the way of love. Her mother might have loved her children if she hadn't had so many, if she hadn't been so poor, if she hadn't wanted so desperately for her life to be different. As far as she could tell, her father hadn't loved anybody. She had finally come to the conclusion that he didn't know how. Responsibility was as close as he could come. For a young girl desperate for affection, it wasn't close enough. She supposed her husband had loved her, but he hadn't lived long enough for her to be sure. Rock was incapable of loving anyone but himself.

Calico Tom offered her uncomplaining devotion, her daughter unqualified love, but neither of them could offer her what Sean begged her to take. She was twenty-nine, the mother of a twelve-year-old daughter, the owner of a saloon, its premier attraction. She should have been strong enough to resist the temptation to take advantage of Sean's innocence.

But she wasn't. Later, when he knew what she'd done and hated her for it, she'd ask his forgiveness. He wouldn't give it, but that would make separation easier.

Permanent.

When she reached the fork in the road and saw Sean waiting for her, she knew a moment of remorse, felt the prick of her conscience telling her to go back before she hurt this man any more.

Then he smiled at her, and it was too late.

He came toward her at a run. She brought her horse to a halt and fell into his arms. He kissed and hugged her with a youthful abandon she'd almost forgotten. It was good to be reminded that a man could still think the world worth losing for love. Even if it was only for a few hours.

"I thought you'd never come," Sean said when he finally set her on her feet.

"I'm early."

"I know, but I've been here for nearly an hour."

"I thought you were going to work on your claim," she said as she let him lift her back into the saddle.

"Pete complained so much about my being gone all day I decided to *really* be gone all day."

He brought up his own horse and mounted.

"There's no way to get there except by a game trail, but it's an easy ride."

The tiny scar in the earth Sean indicated didn't encourage Pearl to have much faith it would be easy. It didn't look wide enough for a medium-sized deer, much less a thousand-pound horse.

The trail followed every dip and twist of the mountainside. On her right the mountain rose up to a height of more than thirteen thousand feet. On her left, it fell away abruptly until it joined an adjacent mountain that rose even higher. Below, a narrow chasm carried a stream that wound its way between peaks until it reached Twisted Gulch. The mountainsides were covered with thick stands of pine, fir, and spruce, their narrow silhouettes stretching against the sky in millions of individual peaks. An occasional lodgepole pine rose high above the rest, as though proud to show off its additional height. Occasional patches of bright green signified stands of aspen that would turn golden in the fall.

"It's a perfect day for a picnic," Sean called back to her.

At an elevation of more than eight thousand feet, even summer days could be cool, the nights cold, but with the warmth of the bright sun on her back, it was hard to imagine that it occasionally snowed at some of the higher elevations all year round. Bird calls filled the limitless expanse of sky. An eagle soared above, its wings motionless, seemingly suspended in the sky by invisible strings. Though she'd often worked in mountain towns, she could never recall finding herself where there were no signs of human habitation. She felt as though she and Sean were the first two human beings to wander this trail. It was exciting. It also made her slightly uneasy. It was strange to feel cut off from civilization.

They came to a series of deep gorges, where a stream fell more than a thousand feet to join the creek below. At the head of the gorges, the land suddenly opened out into a flat, treeless meadow that stretched several miles to distant mountains, which formed a ring around this secluded corner of paradise. A stream flowed leisurely along an erratic path from a distant slope to the thundering gorges.

Their horses waded across the shallow stream, their hooves striking the stones in the gravel bed with dull thuds, leaving deep imprints in the coarse, wet sand. Thick grass crowded the stream on all sides, even growing in patches of earth that had collected between rocks in the streambed. In the distance Pearl could barely make out a small herd of bighorn sheep.

They passed a beaver dam. It was hard to believe such a tangled mass of sticks could hold back the large pond behind it. She could see only one beaver lodge, but it must have required several beavers to build such a large structure. Large masses of blue and white columbine were scattered in great profusion across the meadow. Some yellow flower she didn't recognize and the flame-colored blossoms of fireweed added splashes of vivid color.

Millions of insects filled the air, darting from flower to flower, hovering over the still waters of the beaver pond. Pearl wondered how she could have been in Colorado for so long and never seen such beauty.

"Where are you taking me?" she asked when Sean kept riding through grass that reached his horse's belly.

"You'll see," he said as he paused and waited for her to come alongside. "It's a good thing there's no gold here, or all of this would have been destroyed by now."

Pearl felt that the loss of such a sanctuary of peace and solitude would be a great tragedy. If she could find a place like this to spend the rest of her life, she might not mind being alone. She told herself she was just running away, but she felt a liking for this solitude. After so many years spent in rooms lighted by lamps, the air filled with smoke and the aroma of whiskey and human bodies, the sound of music, laughter, and voices so loud she could hardly hear people talk, being here was like coming out of the dark into the light. Being here made her feel as though the past might not be a brand burned in her skin for all time.

A covey of quail exploded from the grass a few feet in front of her. They startled her more than her horse. She laughed. She didn't know why. She just felt like it.

Sean looked at her and smiled, and she wanted to laugh all over again. She couldn't remember feeling so carefree, so young, so beautiful, so cared for. Somewhere during the past nineteen years she'd lost her way. She'd looked for happiness, for fulfillment, in the hectic world of men rushing to make easy fortunes. She'd subscribed to their practice of hurrying from one place to another, always on the lookout for an opportunity for a quick buck, never satisfied with where they were. She'd been working harder and harder every year and ending up in the same place.

Odd that it should take something as simple as riding into this mountain meadow to show her that.

She vowed from that moment to begin doing things differently. She was going to be with her daughter as soon as she could arrange it. She'd have to work to support them, but she'd missed too much already. If she kept waiting, hoping to earn a little more money, get a little more comfortable, she might lose out altogether.

Her time with Sean was an undeserved gift.

"Here it is," Sean said, pointing to a grassy knoll at the edge of a grove of alders growing beside a tiny stream where it emerged from the pine forest that blanketed the lower slopes of the mountain.

Sean lifted her from the saddle. He stole a kiss, then set her on the ground. "Can I help you with anything?" he asked.

"No. I'll see about the food while you see to the horses."

The grass was spongy and damp under her feet, but a flat shelf of rock was warm and dry. A thin covering of moss and pine needles made it easy to sit on. She had spread out the blankets and put the beer in the stream to keep cool by the time Sean came back from picketing the horses.

"What did you bring to eat?" he asked.

Pearl chuckled. "Worried about your stomach?"

"Just hungry. Your cook does a lot better than Pete or I can."

"I fixed this myself. Don't look so surprised. I learned to cook as soon as I was tall enough to see over the stove."

"You'll have to tell me about the time when you were a little girl," Sean said. "I can't imagine you in pigtails and barefooted."

Pearl hoped she could get him to talk about something else. She didn't want to think of her childhood.

"Why don't you have freckles? Your skin is flawless."

"That's the reward for spending the last fifteen years indoors. No burning sun or drying winds. Here, go fill this pitcher with beer. It's in that small pool there."

She had the rest of the food laid out by the time he got back. Cold chicken, bread, cheese, and a can of peaches. It wasn't elegant, but then she'd never before been called upon to make up a picnic.

"Tell me what you do at your mine," she said as she invited Sean to help himself. "I've never seen one. I don't even know how you get the gold out of the ground."

That started Sean talking about himself rather than wanting to know about her. After he explained the whole laborious process, she asked about Pete and how they came to be partners. That started him talking about the time before he lived with Jake and Isabelle. She could hear the anger in his voice when he spoke of his aunt refusing to take him when he was a baby. She was certain he would feel the same way about her if he knew she lived apart from her daughter.

"What was it like living on a ranch?" Pearl asked.

She'd hated her father's farm, the long hours of hard work, the poverty, the loneliness, her father's cold condemnation, her mother's desperation. But the life Sean described bore no resemblance to hers. It was full of people, some angry, some distrustful, but all working together. As far as she could tell, there was a great deal of love as well. She laughed at his stories of Will and Drew, got misty-eyed over Isabelle's determination to give the boys a decent home and their fierce devotion to her.

Through it all, she sensed Sean's love for Jake's valley and understood that he couldn't wait to go back. She didn't understand why he and Pete had left. Maybe his pride wouldn't let him take anything from Jake because he wasn't a blood relative. After so many years of being considered a failure and unlovable, maybe he'd left to prove he could succeed on his own.

She knew all about feeling unloved.

"Now tell me about yourself."

Pearl came out of her abstraction with a jolt. "There's nothing to tell."

"Of course there is," Sean said, settling back against a small boulder. He put his arms around Pearl and pulled her back against him. "I want to know everything about you, even the tiniest thing. I don't feel as if I could ever know too much."

The unsuspected danger that lay beyond that statement made Pearl shudder.

"Are you cold?"

"No. The sun is warm."

"Good. Start from the moment you were born, and don't leave out anything until this very minute."

"How many days—no, weeks—do you plan to stay here?"

He chuckled and nuzzled her. "Okay, leave out all the men. Just tell me about yourself."

He probably didn't realize it, but he couldn't have said anything that more boldly underscored the differences between them. His life was full of cows and orphans and a couple who loved him. Her life started with a family that didn't care about her and ended with men who wanted to use her.

"I was born on a farm in Missouri," Pearl began. "My mother hated it, but not as much as she hated my father for dragging her out there, or her children for keeping her there."

"Where is your family now?"

"I don't know."

"Don't you keep in touch with them?"

He sounded surprised. "My mother's dead. My father told me never to come back."

"What did you do?"

"I ran off with a man who promised to marry me. When I realized he wasn't going to honor his promise, I left him. I went to work in a saloon because there wasn't anything else I could do."

"Did you ever get married?"

Why should he want to know that? "Once."

He seemed to tense. "What happened to your husband?"

"He died a long time ago." She wasn't going to tell him how. That was something else he didn't need to know. "Ever since then I've been working so I could have enough money to get out of the business. I'm almost there."

He relaxed and pulled her even more deeply into his embrace. "And what are you going to do then?"

"I haven't made up my mind," she said.

"Maybe I can give you some ideas," he said.

Chapter Fifteen

Sean kissed her. She figured that was as good a beginning as any. She pushed her guilt out of her mind. For the rest of this afternoon she was going to pretend she was a young girl of unblemished reputation on an outing with her beau.

"Let's eat," Sean said. "It's hard for me to think on an empty stomach."

That response disappointed Pearl. She often skipped meals because she was too busy to eat, but she should have known Sean would feel differently. He was a big man. Besides, you were supposed to eat on a picnic.

"Here," she said, handing him the plate of chicken. "Start with this."

Grinning broadly, Sean took a slice of cold chicken in his fingers and popped it into his mouth. He took a second piece and held it out to Pearl. "Open up," he said.

"Are you going to feed me?" The smile she flashed couldn't convey the excitement that suddenly coursed through her.

"Of course."

Pearl opened her mouth, and he placed the chicken on her tongue.

"I've never been fed by a man before," she said between bites.

"Do you like it?"

"I don't know yet."

"Maybe this will be an improvement." He took another slice of chicken, put one end in his mouth, and brought the other close to her.

A gurgle of laughter escaped her. "You want me to take it from your mouth?"

"Bite off a piece, and I'll eat the rest."

It wasn't really any different from feeding her with his fingers, but just the thought of taking food from his mouth made her feel deliciously decadent.

She leaned forward and took the end of the piece of chicken between her teeth. It made her giggle when their noses touched. She bit off a small piece, and the rest disappeared into Sean's mouth. They sat there like mischievous children watching each other chew, a silly grin on Sean's face, probably an even sillier one on hers. He finished before she swallowed the last of hers.

"Hurry up," he said. "I could starve waiting for you."

"You don't have to wait."

"I want to."

He placed a second piece of chicken between his teeth. She took hold of the other end, but she couldn't bite it in two as easily as she had before. Their noses rubbed together as she pulled harder. She started to giggle. Once she got started, she couldn't stop. Sean started to laugh as well. They continued to pull at the piece of chicken like two puppies fighting over a bone. The more she thought about the picture they must present, the harder she laughed. When she finally broke off a piece, she fell backward, still laughing.

"You did that on purpose."

Sean's tongue wrapped around his piece of the meat, and it disappeared into his mouth. Pearl didn't understand why, but it was one of the most sensual things she'd ever seen. Her laughter dried up. She swallowed hard, then began to chew. Sean seemed to have sensed her mood. His gaze locked with hers, intense and unwavering.

"I want something to drink," she said.

Sean poured beer into two glasses. He held one out to her. "You drink from my glass, and I'll drink from yours."

"Are you going to feed me everything I eat?" She'd never heard of anybody doing such a thing.

"It's more fun that way."

They linked arms and drank from each other's glass. Pearl wondered where he had learned this. He'd obviously done more in his life than herd cows and dig gold out of a crack in the mountain.

Next he fed her pieces of cheese. It seemed he devoured a slab for each mouthful she swallowed. He picked up a long, slender piece of chicken. "I'll eat from one end, you from the other."

"You'll get more than I will," she said with a laugh.

"Not if you eat faster."

"It's not ladylike."

"Forget you're a lady and pretend you're starving."

Pearl was almost too shocked to eat. After all the things he'd said about her and women like her, *he'd called her a lady!* Was he just saying words, or did he really mean it?

Pearl told herself to stop trying to think, reason, or worry over the meaning of his words. This was her day to just be. She was alone with Sean in a beautiful mountain meadow. They had the whole afternoon to themselves. She didn't need to think. She didn't want to. She intended to let the afternoon roll over her, absorb her, carry her away. She'd think tomorrow . . . or some day after that.

She started eating from her end of the piece of chicken. Sean deliberately ate very slowly. So did she. She wanted to make this last as long as possible. She looked into his eyes, wondered what he was thinking. His eyes looked like highly polished sapphires shining with his excitement, his sheer love of life.

Their noses met. They tilted their heads in opposite directions and kept eating until their lips met. It was the strangest feeling. The taste of chicken in her mouth, the smell of pine in the air, the feel of his lips against hers, no sound except birds calling to each other across the meadow.

She bit off her piece of chicken, then pulled back just far enough to look him full in the face as they chewed.

A smile spread slowly over his face. "I like eating this way," he said.

"This is a long way to come just to eat."

"I didn't come here just to eat."

Pearl's throat constricted. It was a moment before she was able to swallow the last of her chicken. "What did you come here for?" Her voice was hardly more than a whisper.

"To be with you."

She experienced a twinge of disappointment. She had hoped for more. She knew she didn't deserve it, but she wanted it.

"And to tell you I love you."

Her throat constricted again and her stomach rolled into a tight knot. He said it so simply, as though there couldn't possibly be any doubt about what he meant. Yet she was certain he didn't think of love the way she did. He was young, still on the threshold of life. He probably couldn't see beyond the moment, the woman at his side as opposed to the woman of his dreams. He couldn't tell infatuation or lust from a passion that burned with steady intensity.

Yet that was more than she deserved, more than she could have hoped for. It would be better that way. For both of them.

"You say that often enough, and one of these days I'm going to believe you." She tried to act coquettish, to sound like she was teasing, but the deep need to be loved sounded in her voice.

He leaned forward until their foreheads touched. "I want you to believe it," he said.

"I bet you say that to every girl who lets you eat chicken from between her lips."

He pulled back, a serious expression on his face. "I've never done that before."

Pearl felt her throat tighten even more. "I haven't either," she managed to say.

They stared at each other for a moment; then Sean smiled and said, "There's more chicken."

They ate most of the chicken, some of the cheese, and one piece of bread. Pearl groaned and settled back. "I can't eat another bite."

"You can't stop now. We haven't tried the berries."

"You eat them. I'll watch."

"Feed me," Sean said, a wicked gleam in his eye.

He grinned, and Pearl couldn't help grinning back. The Irish in him was impossible to resist. He put her in mind of a devilish imp. She didn't know how, considering his size.

"Okay, but you bite my fingers and you'll go hungry."

"Don't tempt me. You must taste better than food."

Pearl fed him the berries, which he promptly devoured.

"I'm stuffed," he said when they were all gone.

"At last. I was beginning to wonder if I was going to have to roast one of those bighorn sheep to keep you from eating me as well."

"I thought you'd never ask," Sean said and pounced on her. He nibbled her neck, ears, nose, and lips until she collapsed with laughter.

"If Pete could see you now, he'd think you were crazy."

"How dare you think of another man when you're with me," he growled. "I'll just have to make you forget him."

He nibbled, nipped, tickled, and teased until she was shrieking with laughter.

"I forgot!" she pleaded.

He continued to torture her. "I've got to be sure."

"Honestly, I forgot. I've never known any man but you in my whole life. I've never thought of anyone else. I never will."

"That's better," Sean said as he settled down next to her, "but just to make sure . . ."

He started nuzzling the side of her neck again, but this time he dipped lower until his lips found her shoulder.

"Sean."

He didn't respond, just kept kissing her neck and shoulders.

"Sean."

He seemed deaf to the increased urgency of her entreaties. In an attempt to escape his marauding lips, she slipped down until she was lying flat on the blanket. He took shameless advantage of her position to undo the top button of her gown and cluster hot kisses on the tops of her breasts.

Pearl thought she would stop breathing. After years of dancing with thousands of men, she'd been touched and handled until she thought she was numb to the touch of any man. Everything was different with Sean. There was no question that she loved him, that his touch had the power to reduce her to helplessness.

Yet she pulled away from him, rebuttoned her dress, and sat up.

Sean didn't seem the least bit rattled. He pulled her close until she leaned against him. "Sometimes I think I'd like to live here."

His remark was totally unexpected. "There'd be snow on the ground nine months out of the year," she pointed out.

Mountains rose as far as she could see, one ridge behind another. Despite the heat of midsummer, snow covered the peaks, filled shaded hollows tucked into the folds of mountainsides. The tree line was only a few thousand feet above them. The beauty and grandeur were awe-inspiring. The thought of being alone up there during the winter was frightening.

"There'd be no miners demanding dances or songs, nothing to do and nobody to worry about but each other," he said.

Usually a practical cowboy, he was beginning to sound like a dreamer with no understanding of the real world. But it was wonderful that he wanted to be up here with her.

"You'd get bored with nothing to do."

He nuzzled her neck. "I could think of a lot of things."

"You'd get cabin fever."

He nibbled her ear. It tickled. She pulled away from him, but his teeth managed to grasp her ear lobe. A shiver went through her body that left her momentarily weak, helpless to move.

He whispered into her hair, his breath hot against her ear, "Not if I never wanted to go outside."

He was trying to entice her into wanting to make love to him. Many men had wanted her. Many had tried to overcome her resistance in dozens of different ways, but no one had tried to make her *want* to make love to him. They had thought of little beyond their own needs, if indeed they thought of anything at all. Sean was willing to consider her needs as well as her wants. It made her love him that much more.

"You'd get tired of me before a month passed."

"I'd never tire of you," Sean assured her. "No man would."

Pearl had seen too many men tire of women to believe anyone but the most dull and unimaginative man could remain faithful to the same woman for more than a few years. Rock had cheated on her after a few months.

"We could sing songs all winter," Sean whispered. "You could teach me to dance."

"That *would* take all winter," she replied. But the laugh in her throat changed to a whispery sigh when his tongue traced the outline of her ear. She twisted in his arms until she faced him. "That's driving me crazy. You know that, don't you?"

He grinned. She didn't understand how he could look so much like a man and still have so much boyish appeal.

"I just want to make sure you're not thinking of anybody but me."

She hadn't thought of anyone else for days. "I'm just thinking about this little valley," she said. "I never knew it could be so beautiful up here."

"Everything was beautiful before we came with our shovels, you with your towns. It'll be beautiful again after we leave."

She wondered if she'd ever *feel* beautiful after Sean left. She'd always thought her customers made her feel beautiful, but she realized now that was an entirely different feeling from the one Sean inspired in her. They made her feel beautiful like an object to be possessed, owned, used. There was heat in their admiration but no lingering warmth. They saw only the beauty that age would soon alter.

Sean made her feel truly beautiful, inside, where

everything got better with age, where warmth lingered like the heat of a summer day, where the spirit that filled one's soul was more important than the body that surrounded it.

Suddenly her need of him was so great, she could hardly stand it. She turned in his arms and pulled him to her. "Kiss me. Make me feel as beautiful as this place."

He pressed his lips to hers, caressing her mouth more than kissing it. "You're far more beautiful than anything in Colorado, even the gold everybody works too hard to pry from the earth."

Pearl knew it wasn't so, that every man she knew would willingly forget her in exchange for a promising claim, but the words were sweet to her ears.

His next kiss was as tender and light as the summer breeze, but Pearl didn't trust kind and gentle. Nothing gentle in her life had had the strength to survive. She needed something tough, demanding, harsh. She had a burning desire, an aching need to be possessed, owned.

"Kiss me hard," she begged. "I don't want to think of tomorrow or yesterday. Make me think of nothing but today."

His lips recaptured hers, more demanding this time, but that only fueled her need to feel she'd been so thoroughly possessed, so inescapably captured, she'd never feel vulnerable or uncared for ever again. Her mouth covered his hungrily, devouring the strong hardness of his lips, drinking his power.

It was as though she'd uncapped some inner fire. He moved his mouth over hers, consuming its softness, leaving her lips burning with fire. He pulled her against him until their bodies met along their entire length. His arms closed around her like bands of steel, pulling her closer until she felt crushed against him. She felt the hardness of his desire as it pressed against her.

She returned his kiss with reckless abandon. It was divine ecstasy to be held like this, kissed like this, wanted like this. Years of heart-hardening experience fell away, leaving her feeling as innocent as a teenager experiencing her first love, convinced this was a love meant to last. She longed to tell somebody, to shout it to the skies, to sing and dance and do all the foolish things she hadn't done in so many years.

"Do you love me?"

The question caught her by surprise. He had stopped kissing her. He was watching her closely, their faces only inches apart, his anxiety plain to see.

She longed to cry out that she loved him more than life itself, that she'd never thought she could love anybody so deeply, that she could never want more from life than to be his wife and never leave his side. She wanted to tell him that when her time came to leave this earth, she could go happily if he would only sit beside her, hold her hand, and sing softly. She wanted to tell him she wanted to have his children before she became too old to have the sons he deserved, the daughters who would be near to his heart.

She wanted to tell him all that and so much more.

But the lies she'd told, the deceit she'd practiced, choked off her voice and stood ready to destroy her. It was only a matter of time before he learned the truth. Then he wouldn't believe anything she'd told him.

In the end, her answer was a simple nod.

For it was true. No matter what she'd done, no matter what she might do in the future, she loved him.

"When did you begin to love me?" he asked.

She was certain he had no idea how much it hurt to have him ask that question. It only served to remind her even more forcefully of her deceit.

"I was grateful when you broke up the fight," she said, retreating to the safest point. "You caught my interest when you insisted you wanted Ophelia to serve you rather than an old woman like me."

"I didn't mean that. I was a fool to—"

She put her fingers to his lips. "I started to like you when you sang."

"Nobody's ever liked my singing."

"But I think I fell in love with you when you started to dance."

"I can't dance."

"I know, but you looked so adorable trying."

Sean turned pink. She guessed nobody had ever called him adorable.

"When did you start to love me?" she asked.

He grinned and the flush faded. "Probably before I ever saw you. Pete had been describing you in great detail for weeks. I knew if I ever found a woman who looked like I thought you looked, I'd fall in love immediately."

"But you didn't like me. You told me so."

"I was wrong. I thought I shouldn't like you."

"And neither one of us knew how the other felt."

"I tried to show you that night you put the knock-out drops in my whiskey."

"You wanted me out of lust."

"I still want you out of lust, but I've got enough love to last forever."

Pearl knew nothing was forever when you were twenty-four. If she didn't take what he offered today,

she might never get a second chance. She couldn't
say yes. The word wouldn't cross her lips, but she
could signal her surrender with a kiss.

She drew his face to hers in a renewed embrace.
There was an extra measure of warmth in his kisses.
They were more insistent, demanding rather than asking. His lips parted hers, and his tongue invaded her
mouth. Again she marveled that he should know so
much when she, supposedly the experienced woman,
knew so little.

His tongue searched her mouth, sought out her
tongue, circled, then darted about as in a graceful
dance, prodding, encircling, twisting and turning until
she felt dizzy with the swirling tide of sensations
building up inside her. She felt pursued, cornered,
breathless.

So she attacked.

Pearl wasn't as good at strategy as Sean. His
tongue foiled her every assault, but she soon discovered her strikes were having a pronounced effect on
his body and on his ability to concentrate. Soon his
breath came in noisy rushes, his invasions more blind
assaults than a sensuous dance. After a particularly
vigorous exchange, he broke their kiss and fell back,
breathing heavily. He rested his head in the curve of
her neck.

"Where did you learn to kiss like that?" she asked.

His laugh was raspy. "I didn't have to practice a
lot, if that's what you're asking."

"You seem to have a natural aptitude."

"You bring out the beast in me," he said and
growled menacingly. He bared his teeth and attacked
the top of her breasts. Laughing, she tried to roll
away, but his arms captured her; the weight of his

body pinned her to the spot. He quickly undid the buttons at the top of her gown. She struggled against him, but her heart wasn't in it. She wanted him to make love to her. She only struggled because some instinct told her the prize would be all the sweeter for the struggle to attain it.

His lips descended on her mouth once more, smothering her with the heat of his hunger. The eagerness of her response still had the power to surprise her. She wanted him as desperately as he wanted her. Her body arched, rising, pressing against his hand on her breasts. The feel of his fingers through the material of her dress caused her breasts to become more sensitive. Tendrils of sensation spiraled away to other parts of her body, lighting smoldering fires wherever they landed. Her nipples, already sensitive from being pressed against his chest, became hard and began to ache.

Heat began to build deep in her belly, warming her all over, causing feelings that were utterly new to her.

He opened her dress down to the waist, even as he kissed her chin, her eyelids, her cheeks, and the end of her nose. Pearl sighed with pleasure as he nibbled his way down the side of her throat, out over her shoulder, back in by way of her collarbone. But when his hands closed over her breasts, she forgot about his lips.

The rough skin of his work-coarsened hands felt like abrasive cloth to the tender skin. Yet his touch was so gentle, the pressure so slight, it heightened the pleasure. Soon she wanted him to do more rather than less. Yet when Sean took her nipple into his hot, wet mouth, she wasn't sure she could stand any more. A groan escaped her as her body arched against him.

Never had she experienced anything so exquisitely delicious, so agonizingly wonderful. He suckled gently and she felt like a star-burst. She was certain she was about to disintegrate, to dissolve, to simply vanish into thin air.

But not only did she not vanish, Sean compounded her ecstasy by gently rubbing the pebble-hard nipple of her other breast with the moistened tip of his finger. Pearl began to squirm under the dual assault, constantly pushing against him, unsure she could endure it but wanting more. She wanted to touch him, to caress his body as he caressed her, but she couldn't concentrate on anything but what Sean was doing to her.

He sucked hard on her nipple. She reached up, clasped her hands behind his neck, and pulled him hard against her. He responded by using his teeth on her nipple with a gentle, rhythmic motion. She gasped and tried to push him away, but Sean held her down, punishing her until her moans reached a crescendo of tiny screams. She pounded on his chest with her fists, begging him to let her go. When she was certain she could stand it no longer, that she would either pass out or go crazy, he released her nipple.

He loved her breasts with his tongue, creating trails of moisture that tingled as they cooled and evaporated in the warm sun. He started to slide her dress off her shoulders, down her torso, and under her hips. She tried to remove his shirt, but she couldn't without interfering with what he was doing.

"Take it off."

"In a minute." Sean sat up and slipped her dress off completely. He quickly unlaced her shoes and set them aside. "Let me remove your stockings, and you'll be able to run your feet through the grass.''

But it wasn't grass Pearl thought about when Sean's hands moved under her chemise and up her thigh to unhook and remove her stockings. The feel of his hands on her thigh sent her temperature soaring. For a moment she couldn't breathe; her heart refused to beat. Then the dam broke, and both her breath and heart started racing. She could do nothing to calm them. She would have sworn Sean took his time rolling the stocking down her thigh, over her knee, down her calf until he finally reached her ankle. Then he did it all over again with the other stocking.

By the time he had finished, Pearl felt too weak to move. The moments he took to unbutton his shirt and remove it gave her a small period of calm. But the respite was short-lived. Sean's lips returned to their exploration of her breasts. His hand began an odyssey that took it down her side, across her abdomen, down and around her hip, and up and over her thigh. By the time he reached the inside of her knee, she'd completely forgotten about her desire to run her hand over his broad, powerful chest. She could think of nothing beyond what he was doing to her.

When his hand moved up her thigh, the heat that had been building in her belly spread in a wider and wider pool until it engulfed all of her. She followed the movement of his hand with hypnotic helplessness. When he reached the juncture between her legs, she stiffened. When he parted her flesh and entered her, she gasped.

Pearl's perception of exactly what was happening to her—in sequence and degree—began to lose focus. Sean had found a magical spot within her body that reduced her to a state of mindless ecstasy. As he gently rubbed, she felt pressure begin to build inside her. She moved against his hand, against his body, wanting more but not knowing of what. The pressure mounted steadily, driving moan after agonized moan from her until they all ran together into a single wail that came from the bottom of her soul.

"Please!" she begged without knowing whether she wanted him to stop or drive her beyond the reaches of sanity.

He increased the intensity of his attentions until Pearl felt a scream begin to form within her, felt it begin to work its way toward her throat and utterance. Then the floodgates seemed to open, and all the tension flowed from her like water from the beaver dam.

She didn't know how it happened, but somehow Sean had managed to remove her chemise and his own clothes. Even as the world about her began to come back into focus, his body moved to cover her. She felt a pressure between her legs, felt him enter. With the grunt of a primitive male animal, he plunged deep inside her. She felt filled, stretched wide to encompass him.

Sean began to move within her, and very soon she felt the pressure begin to build once again. Even as the whirlpool of desire threatened to sweep her away, she heard herself begin to moan, heard Sean groan in concert. The waves of rushing desire encompassed them, swept them into the same rushing, incoming wave. She felt pounded, hurled about, robbed of the ability to move or think. Nothing but feeling remained, feeling that swirled and crested, filling every part of her, stretching her stamina, straining her control, until she couldn't hold back the scream that burst from the very depths of her being.

Sean's mouth covered hers, swallowing her scream as their union swallowed them both, propelled them to impossible heights, then opened the floodgates of release.

Chapter Sixteen

As they lay together, their bodies slick with the moisture of their lovemaking, their breath coming in halting gasps, Pearl was too filled with emotion to speak. Everything about this day had exceeded her wildest expectations. She had expected Sean to make love to her—she had hoped he would—but she'd never expected to feel transformed, purified by it. She couldn't explain it—it was such an incredible feeling—but she felt as if she'd been created anew, as if the past had been exorcised, that she was as pure and innocent as she had been the day she left the farm.

And he'd call her a lady. She'd never expected that. He was the first man she'd ever known who could look past the songs and the laughter and see the woman behind the makeup. He was the first man since her husband to love her for herself, not what she could do for him. No matter what happened in the future, she would always love him for that.

Despite the coolness of the air, the sun beat down on her, heating her skin. She stretched, luxuriating in the warmth and her sense of contentment.

Sean sat up without warning. "Let's go for a swim," he said.

"You're crazy," she replied, looking up at him and shading her eyes from the sun. "That water comes straight from melting snow. Besides, it's only a few inches deep."

Sean took her by the hands and pulled her into a sitting position. Her breasts, free of restraint, rose firm and resilient. She might be twenty-nine, but she was proud to be able to say she still had the body of a young woman.

"There's a pool in the middle of that clump of reeds and antelope bushes," Sean said, pointing to a place they'd passed a short distance below. "The sun heats the water each day."

Pearl didn't move. She knew how long it took to heat water for a bath. She wasn't convinced the sun could do it faster.

"Are you afraid?" Sean asked, teasing.

"Yes. You may be used to bathing in ice water, but I'm not."

Sean jumped to his feet. Pearl was too mesmerized by the sight of his naked body to guess what he intended to do. He knelt down, scooped her up, and headed toward the pool.

"Put me down!"

"Not until you've had a swim."

"No."

"I promise you'll love it."

"No, I won't. I'll catch my death of cold, it'll develop into pneumonia, and I'll die a horrible death."

But it was difficult to focus her thoughts on anything horrible when she was being carried, naked, in Sean's arms. Everything about what was happening was unique in her experience. She was acutely aware of her bare skin rubbing against his body, her breasts against the roughness of the tangled red hair on his chest. But it was knowing Sean was naked, that her hip touched the red hair at his groin, that threatened to cause her entire being to melt into a puddle of liquid desire. Her womanly heat had not been roused from its slumber for a long time. Now that it was awake, it seemed unwilling to take even a short nap. The bouncing, jolting, and rubbing as Sean carried her through the tall grass guaranteed that her body would be a seething mass of sensations within seconds.

Some small creatures scampered out of Sean's way.

"Marmots," he said.

As Sean pushed his way through the tangle of tall grass and small bushes that surrounded the pond, a small flock of ducks took to the air, noisily squawking their resentment at being disturbed. Pearl suddenly wondered how many creatures had been silent witnesses to their lovemaking. The idea of being watched by dozens of pairs of animal eyes struck her as utterly laughable, and she started to giggle.

"What's so funny?" Sean asked.

"Nothing." It would be impossible to explain.

"Tell me, or I'll drop you in the water."

"You wouldn't dare."

She should have known never to dare Sean to do anything. The man knew no fear, no hesitation. She went into the water with a splash and a scream she was certain sent half the birds and animals for miles scurrying for cover. After the heat of the sun, the water felt ice-cold. She came to the surface sputtering and gasping for air.

Sean dived in after her, sending waves of water crashing against the stones at the pond's edge. She attacked, tried to wrestle him down, but it was an impossible task. He was too big and strong. Besides, the water came to just under her breasts, making it difficult to move quickly. She stumbled on the stones at the bottom of the pool and resorted to splashing water at him.

He didn't seem to have any trouble moving through the water. He captured her effortlessly.

"That's not fair, you big ox." She struggled to break away from him.

"Why isn't it?" he asked, wrapping his arms around her, holding her helpless against him.

She could have objected to their naked bodies touching for her entire length. She could have argued against his holding her so tight that her breasts tingled. She could have complained about the feeling of his sex, half erect, nudging against her inner thigh. Instead she took the easy way out.

"I can't throw *you* down in the water. I push and push, but you're like a big old tree stump."

"Do you like this better?"

Before she had any notion what he was going to do, Sean fell backward into the pool, pulling her down on top of him. They hit the water with such a tremendous splash, she was certain the water level dropped several inches. The ducks were going to be really upset when they got it back.

She found herself lying atop Sean, their bodies in even more intimate contact.

"No, I don't like it better," she said as she pulled free and struggled to get to her feet. Seeing that Sean was letting his body float as though he didn't have a care in the world, she yielded to temptation. She dunked him, turned, and ran for the edge of the pool as fast as she could go. She made it out of the water and a few yards across the meadow before he caught her.

"You shouldn't have done that," he whispered in her ear as he hoisted her off the ground, her arms and legs flailing.

"I couldn't resist," she replied, giggling.

She couldn't believe this was happening. Here she and Sean were, naked as the day they were born—though considerably altered over the intervening years—playing in an open meadow like Adam and Eve. Sean acted as though he were totally unaware of his nakedness—no, as though it was totally natural to him. She didn't feel the same degree of ease, but she didn't feel embarrassed, either.

She twisted around and saw the light of deviltry in his eyes. He had started back toward the pool. "What are you going to do?" He lifted her higher. "It had better not be something terrible." He lifted her still higher until she was almost above his head. "Put me down," she squealed. "This isn't fair. You're bigger than I am."

"You shouldn't have dunked me," Sean said in a singsong voice. "You're going to be sorry."

"You're not going to throw me in, are you?"

He was walking toward the pool with long, swinging strides. Any moment now they would reach the water.

"No!" she cried as he lifted her higher. He waded

into the pool. Pearl screamed when he dropped her.

He caught her just before she hit the water.

Pearl clung to him, oblivious to the fact that their nakedness brought their bodies into contact that at any other time would have been highly suggestive as well as stimulating.

"Let go of me," he said.

"No, you'll drop me."

"I'll drop you if you don't."

She loosened her hold on him and he immediately tossed her into the air. She screamed as he caught her once again before she hit the water.

"You're a devil," she said, caught between laughter and being scared half to death. "Let a poor, defenseless woman dunk you, and your manly pride is wounded. You're doing this to prove you're bigger and stronger than I am."

"No, I'm not." Despite his protests, she could see a faint tinge of color as he set her on her feet. He blushed so delightfully easily.

He looked absolutely magnificent standing there, his body half out of the pool, drops of water on his skin glistening in the sun like diamonds, his blue eyes sparking with mischief, his hair a riot of curls. He looked so astonishingly like some pagan gods she'd seen on a set of cards Rock once showed her—all muscles, brawn, pride, and confidence in his splendid youth—that she could only stand and stare at him. It was hard to believe such a perfect man was in love with her.

In a flash, all the excitement, the energy, and the fun turned to hot, churning, sexual energy. She wanted him all over again, even more desperately than she'd wanted him when they'd made love just a little while ago. But she had spent nearly all of her life keeping men at a distance. Now that she didn't want to keep Sean away, she didn't know how to tell him.

"What's wrong?" he asked.

"I'm cold." The water evaporating from her skin was stealing the heat from her body. But that had nothing to do with her chattering teeth. Her entire body was shaking with desire. She couldn't even keep her hands still.

"Let me dry you off," Sean said.

He led her back to their blankets, picked up a linen towel, and began to dry her skin. He dried her back and arms first. A sharp breeze had sprung up. Despite the bright sun and the brisk rubbing, Pearl still shivered. Then he started to dry her breasts, and her temperature soared.

Sean gently patted each breast dry, lifted it, and dried underneath. She stood absolutely still, unable to move, her limbs paralyzed with the aching need boiling through her like flood waters through a narrow, rock-walled channel. He finished with her second breast and slowly dried her abdomen, moved toward her thighs. Her muscles tightened, and her body turned rigid in anticipation.

He skipped down to her feet.

He lifted each foot to brush away the bits of grass and gravel stuck to her moist skin, then dried each foot with painstaking carefulness, the toes, the instep, the heel. Pearl had to lean on his shoulders to keep her balance. The moisture had beaded on his skin, but the droplets had been reduced to tiny points of sparkling light. They seemed to be boiling away from the heat of his body. She trembled. She knew it had nothing to do with being unbalanced because she was standing on one foot.

Then he moved to the ankle of one leg, the calf, the knee, the thigh. Anticipation was creating so much tension, her muscles ached. He paused at her upper thigh—she held her breath—before dropping to the ankle of her other leg.

Again the slow, agonizing wait as he moved up her leg. This time he didn't stop. She released her breath when his hands moved to her buttocks. She was certain any remaining drops had sizzled away long ago. She was certain Sean knew that, too. Still, he started to dry her bottom with the same care he'd lavished on her feet.

Then Pearl forgot all about her derriere.

Sean started by placing kisses on her belly. Then he traced designs around her navel with the tip of his tongue. She started to tremble so violently she feared she would collapse. She held onto Sean, praying he'd soon stop, praying he wouldn't.

The moist heat within her seemed to turn to a river of molten desire. The more Sean fondled her bottom, laved her abdomen, the more turbulent the river, until Pearl thought she couldn't stand.

"Please," she moaned. She pushed hard against him, the need deep within her driving her relentlessly. "You're driving me crazy."

Sean slowly rose to a standing position, his hands moving up her back, his body rubbing against her nipples. It was all she could do to keep a tortured scream from ripping out of her throat. "Now!" she begged. "I can't stand it any longer."

Sean kissed her, and she grabbed him, her arms around his chest, pulling him to her as tightly as she could. She pushed her breasts so hard against him they hurt. But the pain didn't make a dent in the erotic spell that had her completely in its grasp. She ground her body against him, felt his erection between them, pushed even harder against him, trying to quell the tremors that made her shake like an aspen in a storm.

"You're cold," Sean said.

"No."

He didn't heed her. He laid her down on the blanket and covered them both with a sheet. Impatiently Pearl threw the sheet aside. She was burning with a fire that only Sean could quench.

"If you care anything for me," she gasped, "if you feel even a tenth of the love you profess for me, you won't make me wait any longer."

She pushed against him, maneuvering her body to try to force him to enter her. He wanted to make love to her breasts. Using all her strength, Pearl rolled Sean over on his back and straddled him.

She took hold of him. It was the first time she'd ever touched a man in the throes of passion. He felt so hot, so hard and soft at the same time. Lifting herself, Pearl settled over Sean, gradually taking him into her body until he was buried deep within her. In her impatience to put out the fire that threatened to consume her, she hadn't realized that by sitting astride Sean, she could control the speed and extent of her gratification.

But there was little room in her thoughts to celebrate her triumph. She had to quench the need that had set her brain and body on fire. Moving her hips from instinct rather than experience, Pearl drove Sean deeper and deeper within her, seeking, reaching for relief from the fire that threatened to consume her whole being, that endangered her reason as well as her control. No matter what she did, it only seemed to make her hotter, make her desire more intense, until she felt desperate for release.

Sean had begun to move with her, withdrawing and thrusting to meet her. But Pearl could think of nothing but her own relief. She cried out as she felt the coils tighten within her. Her movements became more frantic, less controlled, until she felt she was entirely at the mercy of the forces that had taken control of her body. They moved her above Sean in a gradually increasing rhythm, pulling her, driving her until unseen bands threatened to cut off her breathing.

Just when she thought she couldn't last a moment longer, she opened and all the tension and need flowed from her in a rushing stream. Barely aware of Sean's desperate plunges as he reached his own climax, Pearl stiffened, shuddered, and collapsed as Sean erupted with his own shout of release.

Pearl slid down to Sean's side, empty, drained, sated. She had never guessed being with a man could be so intense, so shattering, so life-altering.

She would never again think of love in the same way. Nothing else could have transformed the simple act of physical union into a benediction. She felt reborn, inside and out. The fire of love had burned away the old, complacent Pearl and made her into a woman trembling on the threshold of rebirth. Until today she'd never know how powerful love could be, how consuming, how utterly wonderful and beautiful.

Knowing that, feeling it was almost within her grasp, she feared she would never have the courage to give it up.

"We can't stay here much longer," Pearl said after

a long silence. They lay side by side, the sheet drawn over them after the heat of their lovemaking had died away. The breeze from the mountains was growing cooler. Though the sky remained clear, she feared one of the sudden storms so frequent in the Rocky Mountains.

Still, she didn't move. A glorious lassitude filled her. She propped herself up against a boulder. Sean turned to her, then laid his head in her lap. She looked out over the meadow. The ducks had returned to their pond. She'd heard some kinds mated for life. She wondered what they thought of the goings-on in their meadow. A pair of bald eagles soared high above the meadow, their wings motionless as they floated, appearing weightless in the sky. The bighorn sheep hadn't returned. She smiled. She guessed they didn't trust people who made such unusual noises.

Even though she knew they ought to move, ought to return before anyone started to wonder where they were, she couldn't force herself to bring this magical afternoon to an end. The fear was never far from her mind that each moment with Sean might be the last. For that very reason she held on, not wanting to let go.

But she didn't want anybody to know about this afternoon. It was for her alone. Sharing it with the outside world would destroy it. She wouldn't even tell Calico Tom.

"We have to go."

"Why?"

Nothing seemed unnatural to him—singing and dancing, lying naked beneath a sheet in a meadow in the Rocky Mountains eight thousand feet up. Playing in a pool, making love on a blanket—he approached each new experience with the relish of a child. Yet no man could possibly be more unchildlike than Sean O'Ryan.

"The wind is picking up. We have to go."

She had to push him before he would move. He sat up, sleepy and lethargic. "I don't see why."

"Have you forgotten you want to own your own ranch?"

"I can work tomorrow."

"People who put off everything until tomorrow never get anything done."

"You sound like Isabelle."

"I consider that a compliment."

"It is." He leaned over and kissed her. It wasn't a compliment-type kiss. His tongue forced its way between her teeth and plunged deeply into her mouth, searching, playful, threatening to reignite the passion that had twice ravaged her. Pearl didn't think she could stand a third time, not today. Sean seemed to have no such doubts. Maybe that was what came of being so young

She broke off the kiss. "We've got to get dressed. I've got to get back."

"Let me dress you."

"No." She wouldn't be able to withstand him if he did that.

"Then you dress me."

"No." That wouldn't be much better.

Doubt clouded his expression. "Are you angry with me?"

"No." She leaned forward, took his face in her hands, and kissed him. "How could I be angry after such a wonderful afternoon? But we can't stay in this meadow forever."

"Why not?"

Pearl stood. "We've driven the bighorn sheep off. If they don't come back, they'll starve."

"There are other meadows."

"We still have to go."

"I can't find my clothes."

She caught up his pants and tossed them at him. "There. Put them on."

Pearl had expected the magic would fade as they got dressed. But even after they had gathered up their things and prepared to leave, the happy glow lingered. Maybe part of her brain had decided there was a chance her love could have a happy ending. She wanted to prolong this happiness. If that meant lying to herself, she would.

"When can we do this again?" Sean asked when he returned with the horses.

"I don't know. I can't just leave whenever I want."

"Why not?"

Why indeed? Why not take advantage of every opportunity to be together? Soon she would have nothing but her memories. She wanted as many as possible.

"I'll have to see," she said.

"Forget your business just once. I've forgotten my gold."

But she couldn't. Everything she'd worked for depended on it. After Sean left, it would be all she had.

"A lot of people depend on me," she said. "But I'll see what I can do."

Sean had taken her in his arms and was kissing her again. The temptation to give in, to stay a little longer, to make love just one more time, was nearly overwhelming, but she'd pushed her luck about as far as she dared.

She broke their kiss.

Sean grumbled, but he lifted her into the saddle. It always gave her a thrill to see how easily he lifted her. It made her feel feminine and vulnerable, not at all the tough owner of a saloon. But that was a dangerous feeling, one she could grow to like too much.

"Don't come to the saloon," she said. "I'll let you know if I can get away."

"Are you ashamed of me?"

"No. But the men haven't forgotten you accused Rock of cheating. I don't want any trouble. Besides, this is just for us. Having other people know would ruin it."

"They'll have to know before long."

She didn't ask him what he meant by that. "Let's not tell anybody now, okay?"

He reached out and took her hand. "I want everybody to know I'm in love with the most beautiful woman in Colorado. I'll stay away a few days, but don't make me wait too long."

"It won't be that much longer," she told him, squeezing his hand in return.

When they reached the edge of the meadow, she stopped her horse and turned back to look.

"What's wrong?" he asked.

"Nothing. I just wanted one last look."

"Why? We'll be back here lots of times."

But something warned Pearl that she would never see this meadow again.

Chapter Seventeen

Some of the afterglow faded when Sean reached his tent to find his aunt inside. "What are you doing in here?"

"I had to straighten it up just to find the dirty clothes."

Sean knew neither he nor Pete would win a prize for housekeeping, but their place was neat by camp standards. "You never straightened up before."

"Somebody was always here to give me the stuff."

"Have you been snooping?"

She looked insulted. "What would I be looking for in this place? Rats?"

"Gold."

"If I cared about gold," she said, drawing her faded dignity about her, "I could have held on to what I earned."

She was such a disgraceful wreck that Sean didn't know whether to believe her.

"Why aren't you at the diggings?" she asked.

"I took the day off." It was none of her business what he'd been doing, and he'd be damned if he was going to tell her.

"I thought you never took time off. You said—"

"It doesn't matter what I said," Sean snapped.

He couldn't explain it, but her presence made him feel guilty. Anger he could understand. He could never forgive her for what she'd done to him, but how did he explain the guilt?

She didn't move. "You were with that woman, weren't you?"

"What woman?" He didn't know why he should have thought he could keep a secret in a place like Twisted Gulch.

She picked up a shirt and threw it into her basket. "I never met an Irishman who didn't make a fool of himself over a woman sooner or later. Pearl Belladonna is just an invitation to do it sooner and be a bigger fool."

"What makes you think I've been anywhere with Pearl?"

"Because there's nothing in this place to keep a man from his work but a woman. Everybody knows you've been making a fool of yourself over her. Spending the night in her room, then announcing that nothing happened!" She hooted derisively.

"She was afraid somebody would shoot me if I came back to camp before dawn, so she doped me to keep me there."

Kathleen picked up a pair of Pete's pants, shook them vigorously, and tossed them into the basket. "I don't doubt you were a dope. All men are. I never doubted she kept you there, though I doubt she had to resort to powders and such to do it.''

Sean knew it was pointless to try to convince his aunt that Pearl wasn't like all the other women who worked in saloons. ''Believe what you want.''

''Where did you go?'' she asked.

''Why do you want to know?''

''I'm just curious to know how tightly she's got you wrapped around her little finger. After the way you fell into Rock's little trap, I hope Pete has his share of the gold safely hidden.''

There were so many accusations in that one statement, Sean didn't attempt to answer. ''I was stupid that night, but I won't be caught again. He cheated.''

''Of course he cheated. He makes his money robbing unwary miners. Everybody knows about his setup with Pearl.''

''That's a lie!'' Anger swept through him. ''I don't know why you're saying these things unless it's jealousy because Pearl has managed to be more successful than you. She won't end up taking in washing. She's a lady.''

Kathleen's nearly hysterical laughter was tinged with bitterness that started a chill of doubt churning in Sean's stomach. ''Stop it,'' he said. ''I won't have you laughing at Pearl.''

In a flash her laughter turned into scowling anger. ''I'm laughing at you, you blind fool. Pearl has known Rock Gregson for fifteen years. She ran away with him when she was fourteen. She was his mistress until he threw her out.''

Sean's anger turned to fury. He knocked the basket of clothes from her grasp, grabbed her by the shoulders and lifted her off the ground. ''If you say anything like that ever again, you'd better be headed out of Colorado before I hear about it.''

If he'd thought his size and the violence of his anger would frighten his aunt, he was mistaken.

''You can do anything you want to me,'' she threw back at him, defiance in her eyes, ''but you can't change the truth.''

''It's your lies I'm mad about.''

''I've done many things in my time I'm ashamed of, but I never told lies. Not to nobody. Why do you think I ended up with nothing?''

The sick feeling in his stomach wouldn't go away. ''Because you were a fool to trust all those men,'' he growled.

''No more a fool than you are to trust Pearl.''

''I love her, and she loves me. There are no secrets between us.''

''There's no help for you!'' his aunt moaned. ''Has the red of your hair destroyed all your reason?''

''Even Pete agrees with me.''

''Pete thinks she's beautiful, but he hasn't forgotten what she is. Rock taught her everything she knows. When he threw her out, she set out on her own. I'll give Pearl her due. She's a clever woman, but she's hand in glove with Rock. She never used to let a real gambler near her place. Now you stumble over Rock every time you go near it.''

Sean couldn't prove anything, but he had a feeling Rock was involved in a lot more than gambling. Maybe he had something on Pearl and was threatening to expose her if she threw him out. She had always seemed uneasy around him.

''She doesn't want Rock in her saloon,'' he said.

''Then why is he still there?''

He stared at his aunt's rebellious features. He was furious that she could go around telling lies about Pearl. He was helpless to stop her. But he was honest enough to admit the source of his real fury was a nagging worry that somewhere in this tangle of lies was a fragment of truth, that Pearl was no better than hundreds of other women who prowled the saloons of the Colorado gold country, living off the loneliness and desperation of the men attempting to wrest wealth and dreams from the hard-fisted grasp of Mother Earth.

Despite the ravages of age and the life his aunt had led, he could see the remains of the beauty that had once been the foundation of her success. Now her hair was faded, dry, and stringy. Wrinkles fanned out from her eyes like rivulets in a mountain canyon. Her skin was dry as a desert, bruised and discolored—

He stopped. "Where did you get those bruises?" he asked.

Her defiance fell away like a discarded mask. "I stumbled on a rotten floorboard. They'll go away in a few days."

She tried to pull away from him, but Sean didn't release her. Seeing the bruises had triggered a memory. He had seen her bruised like this once before. He hadn't asked because he'd figured she'd fallen down in a drunken stupor. But he knew his aunt better now, and he'd never known her to be drunk or even to show any interest in whiskey.

Kathleen pulled away from his grasp, bent, and picked up the dropped basket of laundry. "You're lucky I don't stop coming by," she grumbled. "You rough me about like this again, and I won't."

Sean watched silently as she finished gathering up

the laundry. Her clothes were hardly more than rags, her horse and wagon the poorest to be had. It didn't add up. She made good money doing laundry. Besides, Pearl had told him the last fire destroyed Twisted Gulch. No building in the town was more than a year old, far too new to have rotting floorboards.

"You're lying about those bruises," Sean said. "Where did you get them?"

"I got them from a man," his aunt said. "He was cheating on me. I hit him, and he hit me back." She glared at him. "Well, that is what you think of me, isn't it—a drunken whore going from one man to the next?"

Maybe he'd thought that before he stumbled across her at this camp. But though he hadn't been aware of it, his opinion had changed. He didn't know when, and he didn't know why, but it had.

"No, I don't think that."

"You used to." She didn't try to hide her surprise. "You sure I haven't come up so much as you've lowered your sights?"

"I don't believe what you said about Pearl."

"Ask her. I'll be interested to know what she tells you."

"I'm more interested in knowing how you got those bruises."

"I told you. Now get out of my way. I've got other customers to see, ones who won't be throwing me about."

Pearl noticed Sean the moment he barreled his way through the doors of the Silken Lady. Her initial surge of joy at seeing him changed to cold fear as soon as she saw his expression. He looked angry enough to fight every man in the saloon. He didn't appear to notice the unfriendly looks that came from all parts of the room. He headed straight to where she was leaning against the bar, her special drink in her hand, a cluster of men around her.

He unceremoniously pushed the men aside. "I've got to talk to you," he said as he took her by the arm and started to pull her toward the office.

"Take your hands off her," Paul Higgins growled. "She was talking to us, and we ain't finished."

Sean ignored him.

"What's wrong?" Pearl asked. She was afraid the time for truth had come much sooner than she'd expected.

"That's what I want you to tell me," Sean said. He turned to Calico Tom, who had materialized out of nowhere. "Make sure nobody comes in here until we're finished. If Paul still wants a fight, tell him I'll be happy to oblige as soon as I'm done."

Calico Tom looked at Pearl. She nodded. Sean didn't slow down until he had dragged her into her office and closed the door.

"Did you know Rock Gregson before you came here?" Sean asked, coming straight to the point. "Did you know he was a cheater?"

He knew! Pearl felt the color drain from her face. Apparently interpreting that as a confession of guilt, Sean turned to leave. He had his hand on the doorknob before Pearl could get any words past the constriction in her throat.

"Are you going to give me a chance to answer?" she asked.

Sean stopped, but he didn't turn around.

Pearl knew she ought to let him go, that as much as his leaving now would hurt, it would hurt even more later. There was absolutely nothing about what she had done that was honorable.

But she couldn't give up while there was any chance that she could hold on to a few days, hours, even minutes more of the love he had for her. The hunger in her was so deep, so overwhelming, it swamped her common sense, her honor, her sense of fair play. He couldn't hate her any more when he finally discovered the truth. She couldn't despise herself any more for putting it off a little longer.

"I thought what you said up in that meadow meant something," Pearl said, "but I guess I was a fool to think love means something to you."

"It's because it does mean something that I'm here," Sean said, nearly choking on the words.

He turned as he spoke, and the pain in his eyes nearly caused Pearl to change her mind. "I'll tell you anything you want to know, but first you've got to promise to listen to my whole story."

"I can't promise to believe it."

She could tell he wanted to. At that point the good angel in her lost the battle completely. "Sit down. It's not a short story."

"How long does it take to say yes or no?"

"I'm not going to say either." When he didn't move, she said, "You promised to listen."

He stood still a moment longer, then abruptly pulled out a chair and dropped into it. "Okay, talk."

"Would you like a whiskey? I've got several—"

"You going to knock me out again?"

She guessed she deserved that. "No. Next time I'll let them shoot you."

She didn't mean that, and she knew he knew it.

He relented a little. "Maybe that was unfair."

She started to tell him she'd never do anything to hurt him, but the words wouldn't pass her throat. There were some lies that were simply too big to say.

"I grew up on a poor dirt farm in Missouri," she began. "My mother was beautiful, but work and too many children turned her into an old woman. She used to tell me I had to get out before some man got me pregnant, married me, and turned me into a hag like her. She died one summer of scarlet fever. I don't think she minded. She had escaped the farm at last."

Sean's expression didn't change. She didn't know whether he didn't believe her story or he didn't care.

"I don't know what would have happened if my father had been different," Pearl continued. "I don't know if he disliked me, but I thought he did. He kept saying I was like my mother, that I'd leave, that if I did I could never come back. Since I was the oldest, all her work fell to me. He drove me harder every day. It was almost as though, having decided I would leave, he was trying to force me to do it sooner than later."

"At least you had parents," Sean said.

She supposed a man who'd been an orphan since birth would think parents were more important that anything else in the world, but Pearl wasn't sure. She'd have traded hers for his Jake and Isabelle.

"I might have stayed if Rock hadn't come along."

Sean jumped as though prodded in the ribs.

"I was fourteen and very pretty. Boys came from miles away to court me," Pearl said, refusing to respond to Sean. She was afraid that if he distracted her, she'd never finish her story. "Papa tried to drive them off. With them he acted like I was his greatest treasure. But as soon as they were gone, he accused me of trying to ruin myself.''

She thought he was going to interrupt, but he didn't.

"Papa went to St. Louis and took me. We stayed in a cheap hotel down by the river. That's where I met Rock. He was the most handsome man I'd ever seen.''

"Was he a gambler then?'' Sean asked.

"He said he worked for the riverboat company. He said we could live on board, travel up and down the river, see all the sights. He said he'd buy me the prettiest clothes in stores from New Orleans to Chicago. When Papa caught me with him a second time, he hit me, threatened to beat me. I made up my mind right then I wasn't going back home. I went looking for Rock. The riverboat was pulling out, so we had to talk on the gangplank. When I told him what had happened, he said he'd fight my father. No one had ever done that before. When he said he'd marry me at the first town up the river, I jumped on the boat and put my whole life behind me.''

Pearl decided Sean's life must have been worse than he'd let on. She'd seen girls with less affecting stories reduce grown men to tears. Sean sat dry-eyed, unmoved.

"For six months, Rock kept all his promises except one. We lived in a spacious cabin, I had more beautiful clothes than I had ever imagined possible, we danced and enjoyed ourselves every night, and I was never expected to do a lick of work.''

"But he didn't marry you,'' Sean said.

"No. I soon found out his occupation was gambling. Since a new town meant new gamblers, he continually found reasons to postpone marriage.''

"Men like him always do."

"I didn't know that then. I was too dazzled by the world I'd entered, too afraid I might be forced back into the one I'd left. I might have stayed with him much longer if I hadn't found him with one of the girls who ran a monte table. I knew then he wasn't going to marry me, that he didn't love me, and probably never would. So I left him."

It would have been so much easier if Sean said something instead of sitting there like a black-robed judge, condemnation written in his scowl.

"I didn't know how to do anything except attract men. The riverboat owner let me run a table until he discovered I was better at singing. For the next few months I worked my way up and down the Mississippi."

"How did you end up in Colorado?"

"One day I realized I'd been working for years and didn't have more than a few dollars. I also realized someday I'd lose my voice and my looks. Unless I started working for myself, I'd end up broke. So I borrowed money from Rock—he was the only one who'd lend money to a woman—and opened my own saloon. I did so well, I was able to pay him back in three years."

"So for old time's sake, you let him rob your customers."

"I know Rock cheats. At least, I've always suspected he does, but no one can prove anything against him. He made you look a fool when you tried. People *want* to gamble."

"You could bar him from the saloon."

"Not and stay in business. There's an unspoken law around here. Nobody bars anybody from a saloon unless he can prove cheating. After what happened to you, nobody's going to try."

He hadn't heard of any such rule. "Are you sure he's not blackmailing you into letting him stay?"

"I don't want him here, but my customers ask for him."

"What other dealings did you have with him?"

"None. I never wanted to see him again after he cheated on me, but I didn't have any choice. He helped me get my first job. He lent me money after everybody else had turned me down. I asked him to leave when he showed up here, but he just laughed at me."

"Is he here now?"

"I haven't seen him here tonight."

"If he is, I'll make him leave," Sean said, getting to his feet. "If he won't leave on his own, I'll throw him out."

As much as Pearl would have loved to let Sean get rid of Rock, she didn't dare for fear Rock would retaliate through Elise.

She reached out to take Sean by the arm. "Forget about him. You've already told everybody he cheats. If they play with him now, they know what they're getting into."

"That's the same as protecting him, Pearl. You can't keep doing that."

"I'm not protecting him. I'm thinking of you. I wouldn't put it past Rock to have somebody try to shoot you if you make trouble."

"I'm not running from him."

"Sean, you don't understand. He's dangerous.

You've got to promise to leave him alone."

"I won't have him forcing himself on you."

"He's not. Forget him. He's not important."

Pearl really didn't know if Rock would go so far as to kill someone, but she did know nobody had ever stood in his way. Something always happened to anyone who tried. He lived extravagantly. She knew he couldn't win that much money by fair means, but she'd always refused to think about it. It hadn't concerned her. Now, if she couldn't convince Sean to ignore Rock, it might. She hadn't forgotten that someone had already tried to kill Sean. She had a gut feeling it had something to do with Rock.

"I'm worried about you," Sean said. "I won't have him coming in here frightening you. I saw how you reacted that day."

"I've never had reason to be afraid of him."

"Promise?"

"Promise."

"Why didn't you tell me all this before now?"

"I never expected things to turn out like they have. After that, telling you would have made it appear as if I was hiding something."

"That's how it did appear."

"Are you still mad at me?"

There was no hesitation this time. His ready smile appeared quickly, without uncertainty. He held out his arms and she walked into them.

"Don't you know I could never stay mad at you?"

"Nobody's ever felt about me the way you do. I didn't know what to think."

"Think that I love you and that I don't intend to let anybody hurt you." He kissed her possessively.

Pearl clubbed her screaming conscience into obliv-

ion. She was fighting for every minute she could have
of Sean's love. She'd have plenty of time to do pen-
ance later.

Sean paused on the boardwalk outside the Silken
Lady and took a deep breath. He hadn't realized until
now just how tense he'd been. He didn't like parts of
Pearl's story, but he realized that a woman with her
history must have known quite a few unsavory characters. But he was going to make certain Rock wasn't
blackmailing Pearl. She probably felt indebted to him
for helping her, but Sean was sure Rock didn't help
anybody without helping himself even more.

As far as Sean was concerned, the man was a liar
and a cheat. Sean had every intention of getting his
money back. He just didn't know how yet.

He left the boardwalk and mounted his horse. He
had to get back to the mine. Now, more than ever, he
wanted to find lots of gold. He had decided to get
Pearl out of the saloon business.

Only now did he stop to think what that said about
his plans for the future. Somehow now and the future
had always remained separate in his mind, but that
wasn't true any longer. He couldn't think of his future
without thinking of Pearl. That meant marrying her.
Much to his shock, Sean had never even considered
the possibility before. In his mind he'd put Pearl and
all women like her into one category, Isabelle and the
woman he hoped to marry into another. The two had
nothing in common.

He'd fallen in love with Pearl anyway.

If he couldn't marry her, the only solution was to
live with her for as long as their passion lasted. When
it ended . . . well, he didn't know. He'd never consid-

ered this kind of relationship. He wasn't a prude, but he wanted a marriage like Jake and Isabelle's.

He did love Pearl, didn't he? It sure felt like it. If this wasn't real love, how was it different from what he'd feel for any other woman? How could he tell which was which? It would be pointless to ask Pete or his aunt, and Isabelle was a thousand miles away. He'd have to decide for himself.

Everything he knew told him he loved Pearl as deeply as he could ever love any woman. But everything he knew also told him he couldn't want to marry a woman who would prefer the adoration of many men to the love of one, who wouldn't want to be the mother of his children because it would get in the way of having fun.

He didn't think Pearl was like that, but she had run away from her home. She'd never known anything except saloons. She'd never said she wanted to leave. She gave every sign of enjoying what she did.

What the hell was he going to do?

In frustration he turned off the road and headed toward the small shack just outside town where his aunt did her washing.

As he approached, he wondered, not for the first time, why his aunt chose to work in such a hovel. He had thought she might be putting her money away, but tossed that idea aside. If she'd gone through this much of her life with nothing to show for it, there was no reason to expect she'd suddenly learned to save money. She'd be poor until the day she died.

Sean couldn't figure out what she did with her money. She didn't gamble as far as he knew. She wasn't drinking it all up. Considering the way she looked, it was unlikely she had a fancy man she was keeping on the side. Despite his anger toward her, he felt guilty about letting her work in such a place. Somehow it reflected badly on him.

The wash shack was pushed back up alongside the creek to give her access to plenty of water. The inside was dark and steamy. Kathleen was leaning over a deep tub, stirring its contents with a big wooden paddle.

"I thought you'd be up on that mountain making yourself a rich man," she said when she saw him.

"What you said about Pearl got to working inside me until I couldn't concentrate."

"It ought to."

"So I came down to ask her about it."

His aunt stopped her work and turned to look at him. "And what did she say?"

"She said she ran away with Rock years ago, but she doesn't work with him now. She knows he cheats, but she can't prove it."

"And you believed her?"

"Why shouldn't I?"

"You're just as stupid as all the rest of them," she said, turning back to her pot, "falling for a pretty face, believing anything she tells you because you don't want to believe anything else."

"Why shouldn't I believe her? It sounded perfectly logical."

"Of course it does. She's had years to work it out."

"She doesn't even like Rock. She said in her business they have to work together."

"She's right about that. She's forced her way into a man's world. Some are for getting rid of her because she's too successful. Sometimes I think Rock is the only reason they let her stay."

His aunt was making him mad. It was bad enough she'd turned against him years ago. There was no excuse for her to do it again. "She said—"

"I don't want to hear anything she said. It makes me sick to think of the men she's fooled." Kathleen snatched up a bucket and headed out to the creek.

Sean followed her. "I'm going to make you listen," he said. He grabbed her by the arm and spun her around. "I'm going—" He stopped. His aunt's face and arms were covered with fresh bruises.

"Where did these come from?"

"I told you." She dropped her gaze. "I fell down."

"Tell me what really happened."

"Nothing."

"You're lying."

"You believe everything that hussy tells you. Why can't you believe me?"

"Because Pearl was telling me the truth."

"I am too."

"Stop stalling."

"Leave me alone," she said, trying to pull away from him. "I have work to do. Men expect their clothes on time. If I'm late, they may find another washwoman."

"Let them."

"That's okay for you to say. You don't have to support me."

"You make enough money to support us both," Sean said. "But something's happening to it. What?"

"Nothing."

"You're lying."

"So what if I am?"

"I'm not leaving here until I know the truth. If it takes the rest of the day, I'll stay here."

For some reason that panicked his aunt. "You can't. I've got to finish these clothes and get my money."

"Why?"

"I like to get paid, that's why."

"No, it's not." She tried to escape him, but he wouldn't let her.

"Tell me, or I'm going to take all those clothes off the fire and dump them out on the ground. You won't get your money for a couple of days."

Kathleen tried to run around him, but he caught her easily. She seemed thin. Too thin.

"You're not eating." His tone had changed. Something was seriously wrong. "Tell me what's going on."

Again his aunt tried to escape. Again he caught her.

"You haven't cared about me before," she said, almost crying. "Why should you start now?"

"I'd care about anybody who didn't get enough to eat and who looked like she got beaten up all the time." As soon as the words were out of his mouth, Sean knew that was the answer. "Somebody's beating you and taking your money. Don't lie to me again," he said when she shook her head. "Tell me who it is."

"Nobody."

"And he's expecting you to pay him today, isn't he? That's why you're so afraid of not finishing your work on time."

"Leave me alone. Go back to your mine."

"If you don't tell me now, I'll wait until he shows up."

"He'll kill you," Kathleen wailed. "He'll kill us both."

"No, he won't."

"You don't know him. He's got partners. They take money from everybody in Twisted Gulch."

"What's his name?"

His aunt refused to answer.

"Okay, let's go have a beer. We'll go to the Silken Lady. You can tell Pearl why you don't believe a word she told me."

"I'm never going in that place. He might be in there."

"Who?"

"Clive Britton. He's the man who takes my money."

Sean grabbed his aunt by the arm and started toward the street.

"Where are you going?" she asked, frightened.

"To find Clive Britton. I'm going to get your money back. Then I'm going to kill him one little piece at a time."

Chapter Eighteen

Clive Britton wasn't in the Silken Lady. Sean forced his aunt to tell him where Britton had his office. He headed there without hesitation.

"You can't just go busting in on him," his aunt warned. "He'll have a gun. You're unarmed."

Sean hadn't thought of that when he set out. "I'll keep that in mind," he said and kept walking.

"What do you plan to do, ask him if he would please stop taking my money?"

"I will if you want."

"You're crazy," his aunt said. "Just like Shamus. He'd have done something just as daft."

Sean stopped so abruptly that Kathleen stumbled. For years he'd been aware of this huge void inside himself, an ache that wouldn't go away. But until now he'd never been able to name it. Now, in one sudden burst of realization, he knew exactly what it was. His parents! He didn't know anything about them. He thought he'd accepted that as something he couldn't change, that he'd have to get used to.

But he'd been wrong. Knowing about them was an endless appetite, one that he could probably never fully satisfy, but his aunt could help him. He turned on her. "When I'm done with Britton, you'll tell me about my ma and pa."

Kathleen looked a little startled by his unexpected request, but recovered quickly. "If you don't do some thinking before you step into that office, I'll be worrying about how to bury you."

Sean headed off once more. "That shouldn't cause you to lose any sleep."

"I don't want you dead," she said.

"I wish I could believe you."

She tried unsuccessfully to jerk her arm free. "If you hate me so much, why do you care whether Britton takes my money?"

Sean turned on his aunt. "I don't hate you." He thought he had. But the minute the words were out of his mouth, he knew they were true. "I was angry, I'll probably never forgive you, but I don't hate you."

"It sounds like the same thing to me."

He resumed walking. "There's a difference."

"I don't see it."

"I didn't myself at first." They had reached the building. Sean stopped. "What happens when you go inside?"

"I give him the money, and I leave."

"Is there anybody else with him?"

"No."

"What does he do with the money?"

"Puts it in a locked box he keeps in a cupboard behind him."

"Will he have to turn his back to get it?"

"Yes."

Sean thought he knew what to do. "Do you have any money?"

"You dragged me away too fast."

Sean dug in his pocket and took out a bill.

"He won't take paper money," his aunt said when he held it out to her.

"Tell him it's all you have, that a customer refused to pay you coin."

"It's a hundred dollars. I don't pay him that much."

"Tell him you need change."

His aunt looked doubtful.

"Don't close the door all the way when you go in. Stand so he can't see through the crack. Signal me when he turns to his cupboard."

"It'll never work."

"Let's go."

They entered a narrow hall. Sean counted three doors. "Anybody in those other offices?"

"Not that I ever noticed."

Kathleen walked to the last door, knocked, and entered. She left the door ajar about an inch. He couldn't see Britton, but he could hear him complaining about the bill, and his aunt explaining she'd had to take it or not get paid. Britton said he'd deduct the shortfall of her last two payments. His aunt argued, but Britton insisted. She fluttered her hands behind her back. Sean opened the door and rushed into the room.

Sean had about a second to see the layout of the room, Britton's and his aunt's positions, and decide what he was going to do. He went straight ahead, pushing Kathleen to one side as he did. He was on

Britton almost immediately, but not before the man's fingers closed around a gun he kept in the cupboard. Sean's fingers closed around his forearm.

"Drop it, or I'll break your wrist."

Britton struggled to break out of Sean's grasp, but he was a foot shorter and a hundred pounds lighter. Sean knocked his hand against the corner of the desk. The gun fell to the floor.

"Pick it up," he said to his aunt. "Now get that box out of the cupboard," he said when she had laid the gun on the top of the desk.

"It's locked," she said.

"I expect you'll find the key in Britton's vest pocket."

"That's my money," Britton growled. "I'll kill anybody who touches it."

"We're not interested in your money," Sean said. "We've just come for the money you've been *keeping* for my aunt. How much would you say it is?"

"I don't know what you're talking about," Britton said.

"It's three thousand, six hundred and forty-eight dollars," Kathleen announced. "I've been paying him every month since he set foot in this town."

"How many times has he beat you?" Sean asked.

"About a dozen."

"Add an extra thousand for doctor's fees."

"I didn't see a doctor."

"You should have. Take it."

Britton struck at Kathleen when she started to search his pockets. When Sean's hold on him kept him from touching her, he struck out with his booted foot. Sean's fist in his face brought that to a halt.

"Your mama should have taught you better manners," Sean said.

"I'll kill you," Britton shouted. "You'll be dead before midnight."

"Good God Almighty!" Kathleen gasped. "There must be forty or fifty thousand dollars in here. Where could he have got that much money?"

"There are a lot of women in Twisted Gulch," Sean said. "Count out your money."

"This is robbery," Britton shouted. "I'll have you arrested."

"He's been taking it from two other washerwomen longer than me," Kathleen told Sean. "They told me after he beat me the first time, when I wouldn't pay. They're the ones took care of me."

"Take out five thousand for each of them," Sean said.

Britton fought hard, but a ferocious growl was the only sound he uttered.

"Now write out a note saying you're accepting the money he's been keeping for the three of you."

"But he's not—"

"This is like a receipt," Sean said. "Once he signs it, he can't get the law on you."

Kathleen looked doubtful, but she wrote the note.

"Now sign it," Sean told her.

She did.

"Now it's your turn," he said to Britton.

"You can't make me sign that."

Sean took hold of the man's left wrist and smashed it into the desk. The cracking of bones was clearly audible before Britton's scream of pain filled the small, dark room.

"That's for the times you beat my aunt," Sean

307

said. "Now unless you want me to break your other wrist for the beatings you gave the other women, you'll sign that paper."

"No." He sounded less determined.

"Sign it, or I'll break your wrist and sign it myself. It's not something I brag about, but I can copy anybody's handwriting. I used to do it just for fun," he said to his aunt. "Isabelle used to tell me I'd end up in jail because of a prank. I'm all out of patience," he said, turning back to Britton.

The man sagged against his chair in defeat, but hatred and defiance still blazed in his eyes. "You'll die for his." He turned to Kathleen. "And when I get my hand on you—*eeeeaahhh!*" The man's face turned white from the pain.

"It takes a pretty sorry man to cheat at cards," Sean said. "But you must be more rotten than buzzard bait to steal from women. Those miners would tear you to pieces if my aunt stood up in the Silken Lady and told them what you've been doing to her."

Some of the defiance turned to fear.

"They'll put up with being cheated, but they won't put up with your beating women and taking their money, not when it's the miners giving them the money. Sign that paper, or I'll drag you over there right now."

Britton signed the paper. Sean picked up the gun before he let him go. "Check to make sure he doesn't have another one," he said to his aunt. "I don't want to be shot in the back."

They couldn't find a second gun.

"You come near my aunt again," Sean said after Kathleen had left the office, "and I'll kill you." He pointed to Britton's wrist. "Tell people you broke it when you tripped over something. A loose floorboard maybe.''

His aunt was waiting for him when he reached the street.

"You know he's going to try to kill you, don't you?"

"I didn't figure he'd be too happy about what I've done."

"He's got friends."

"I know about Rock and Ira. The connection was obvious. Anybody else?"

"He doesn't need anybody else. They're behind just about everything evil in this place."

"If you know anything, tell me."

"I got no proof, but—"

"Then you've got nothing," Sean said, "just like I had nothing when that marked deck disappeared. Now you take that money to those other women. And get a receipt for it. That paper Britton signed makes you responsible for it until then."

"Why did you risk your life to get my money back?"

"It wasn't much of a risk."

"I wouldn't take you when your parents died. I left you in that orphanage. You ought to hate me."

"I did for a long time, but somehow it doesn't matter anymore. I had Jake and Isabelle. That was pretty good."

"I'd like to meet them someday."

"You can tell me about my parents, but stay out of my life."

His aunt's back stiffened, and the pride he'd noticed before shone in her eyes. "Are you saying I'm not good enough for your friends?"

"We got along without each other before," Sean said, angry at somehow being put in the wrong after what he'd done for her. "No use changing things now."

"Then why did you bother to get my money back?"

"Dammit, you're my own flesh and blood. What kind of coward would I be if I let coyote bait like Britton beat you and take your money?"

Her attitude seemed to soften. She stared at him so long that he started to feel uncomfortable.

"I think I made a big mistake," she said at last. "I'd have been a terrible mother, but I wish I'd taken you all those years ago."

Sean hated it when things seemed to go all mushy inside him. There was no point in getting sentimental over his aunt. Nothing had changed.

"It was just as well," he said, his voice gruff. "I can't wait until I'm back in Texas. I'd hate living the way you do."

"You hate everything about me." She sighed. "Guess I shouldn't expect anything different. Gwenda was so pure and virtuous it'd turn your stomach. Shamus thought I was a strumpet, just like you do."

Sean was tired of having his every thought seem like an accusation. "I've got to go. I won't get my ranch standing about in the street." He turned and headed to where he'd left his horse.

"Thanks."

The word surprised him so much, he stopped and turned.

"For my money," Kathleen said. "For the others, too."

310

"Forget it," Sean said, turning quickly. He didn't like his aunt being grateful to him.

Pearl read the letter for a second time, then a third, but the message remained the same. Elise had disappeared. She'd left for school one morning and never come back. No one at the school had seen her. As far as everybody in Denver was concerned, she had disappeared into thin air.

Pearl stumbled to a chair and dropped into it, gripped the armrest to keep from fainting. She couldn't lose control. She had to think.

Rock! That had to be it. He was cruel and heartless. He might . . . but he didn't know where Elise was. Pearl had always been extremely careful to keep her trips to Denver secret.

A thousand other explanations flashed through her mind. Elise had been run over by a carriage and was this very minute lying in some hospital crying for her mother. Elise had somehow found out where Pearl had gone and had left Denver to find her way to Twisted Gulch. Elise had discovered her mother was a saloon dancer and had run away rather than face the humiliation.

Pearl blocked those thoughts from her mind. She wouldn't know until she got to Denver. Speculation would drive her crazy. She would *do* something rather than quiver and quake like a silly female. But she didn't know how to begin. She needed someone to advise her.

Instinctively she thought of Sean. She would find him, tell him what had happened. He would know what to do.

She actually rose out of the chair before she sank

back again. She was letting her heart overrule her head. Sean was big, strong, and kind, but that didn't qualify him to be a Pinkerton agent. Besides, if she told Sean about Elise, her two lives wouldn't be separate any longer.

She hadn't lied to him about Elise, but after not telling him about Rock, he was bound to start wondering what else lay hidden in her past. No, she would go to Denver alone. She would hire a detective if necessary, but she would find her daughter. She jumped up to begin packing. While she was turning out drawers, trying to think what she needed to take, a knock sounded at the door.

"Come in," she called, expecting it to be one of the girls. She would have to tell them she was going away.

"Are you planning a trip?"

The sound of Rock's voice was an unpleasant shock. She didn't want to see him. She didn't want to talk to him. She didn't even want to *think* about him.

"Since I'm packing, I'd think that would be obvious."

"It looks more like you're throwing your clothes around the room."

She hadn't realized it, but in her frantic rush to pack, she'd tossed aside everything she didn't mean to take. The floor was covered with discarded garments.

"I'm in a hurry."

"Before you go, I've got something to tell you."

"This is an emergency. I've got to leave for Denver right away."

"It wouldn't have something to do with your daughter, would it?"

She froze. How could Rock have guessed that unless he knew something about what had happened? She whirled around, started toward him, stumbled over the clothes tangled around her feet, and nearly lost her balance. "What do you know about Elise?"

His lips curved in the smile she hated, the one that meant he'd done something that pleased him very much.

"I know she's disappeared because I had her kidnapped."

Pearl fought hard against the blackness that threatened to consume her. She would *not* faint. She would *not* lose control. She didn't know how Rock knew Elise had disappeared, but he had to be lying.

"I don't believe you," Pearl said, fighting to try to remain calm.

"Let me tell you what you have to do to get her back."

"You can't have her," Pearl nearly screamed. "You don't know where she is."

"She was living with Mrs. Hodges in Denver, going to the Wolfe School for Girls. You visited her during that week you told everybody you were sick."

"Why . . . How . . . ?" Pearl's brain hardly worked. Rock *had* kidnapped Elise.

"You nearly fooled me with that act, telling me Elise was ashamed of you, that her being here would be bad for business. I believed you until I remembered the time we lived together. You wanted to leave the gambling circuit, get married, and have a bunch of children. I remember you saying *We can go where nobody's ever heard of us. We can live respectable then.*

"I didn't believe you were sick. You're the healthiest woman I ever knew. I knew you wouldn't leave the saloon unless it was really important, so I hired a man to follow you. You disguised yourself well, but it's impossible to hide a face as beautiful as yours."

"Where is she?" Pearl asked. "If you've hurt her, I'll kill you."

"She's perfectly safe. Probably quite happy now that she's spared all those boring school lessons."

"She *likes* school. She's very good at those lessons."

"How unlike either one of us."

"She's not your daughter."

"Don't you want to know why I kidnapped her?"

"No. I just want her back."

"First you have to do something for me."

"I've done everything you asked of me."

"Not quite."

"What more could you want?" Rock frightened her. She didn't want to have anything more to do with him, but she had to get Elise back.

"I've got a little problem with your friend, Sean. I think you're just the person to help me work it out."

"I got him into the saloon. I got him to your table," she cried, desperate to be freed of Rock's incessant demands. "What more do you want?"

"Revenge," Rock said, his amiable smile replaced by naked fury. "He's ruined things for me in Twisted Gulch. This was the perfect mining town, hundreds of gullible miners willing to work all day grubbing gold from the earth, then turn around and lose it to me in the evening. I had planned to stay here a lot longer. Now I can't.''

"Why?" She couldn't imagine what Sean could have done that would force Rock to leave Twisted Gulch.

"He broke Clive's hand. Just walked in, broke his hand, and stole his money."

Pearl didn't believe that. She saw no reason for Sean to break anybody's hand, but she was certain he wouldn't steal.

"I don't care about Clive," she said, worry for her daughter making her nearly hysterical. "Just tell me what you've done with Elise."

"In due time," Rock said, regaining some of his composure. "First, we have to discuss business."

Wild thoughts raced through her mind of having Calico Tom cut Rock's throat, of shooting him with the gun she kept in her bureau drawer. She discarded all of these. If Rock had Elise—and she felt a sickening certainty he did—she had to know where he'd taken her.

"Where is she?" Pearl asked.

"I figure Sean O'Ryan owes me fifty thousand dollars," Rock said.

"Fifty thousand!" Pearl exclaimed with a gulp of shock. "He can't possibly have that much."

"I fear you're right. I'll be lucky if he's got ten."

"Does anybody have that much?" It was still a huge amount of money.

"I don't know, but I mean to find out."

"How? He won't tell me how much money he has or where it is. I've already tried to find out."

"You were too subtle. Besides, things have

changed. We have a new weapon, a much better one.''

Rock was smiling again. She hated it when he smiled.

"He's in love with you," Rock said.

Pearl's heart leapt into her throat. "He's only intrigued with me. At the most, infatuated."

"It's enough."

"Enough for what?"

"To get him to bring his money to town."

"He's not going to play cards with you. He——"

"I know, dammit. And neither is anybody else."

"But none of the men believed you marked those cards."

"That's what they said. Apparently you've had your head too far in the clouds to see what they're *doing*. Nobody will sit down with us."

Rock hadn't been at the saloon much lately. Pearl had been relieved, hoping he'd found a place he liked better. Now that she thought of it, she realized she hadn't seen anybody at the table with him but Ira and Clive.

"I still don't see what that has to do with me," Pearl said.

"You're going to get him into town with his money."

"How?"

"Tell him you need ten thousand dollars, that you'll pay him back in a few weeks."

She laughed. It had a bitter sound to it. "You overestimate my powers. He's perfectly willing to dally with me while he's here, but his interest is only temporary."

"Then you'd better see about making it permanent."

"Rock, I don't want—"

"If you want to see your daughter again, you'll get that man in here with his gold!"

Heat seemed to drain from her body. "What do you mean, if I want to see my daughter again?"

"She's got your looks, Pearl. I swear she looks enough like you to make me think it's fifteen years ago. She'd make a fine partner. In a few years, there's not a man in Colorado who'd be able to resist her. I could teach her what I know. She could make us both rich."

"She won't do it," Pearl said, panic and disgust filling her. "She doesn't know a thing about saloons or gambling."

"Neither did you, but look how well you've done."

"She may look like me, but she's like her father. She wouldn't know how to live like I do. She needs a respectable life."

"Then you'd better send for your lover right away."

Rock couldn't know! Surely he didn't. But she hadn't thought he could find Elise either.

"What if I manage to get him to come to town? What are you going to do?"

"I'll have men waiting for him along the road."

"I can't send him into a trap. It'd be the same as robbing him myself."

"Don't bore me with your morals, Pearl. Get him here. I don't care how you do it. Let me know when you've figured it out."

"Where are you going to be?"

"I think I'll get better acquainted with Elise. Maybe see what kind of talents she could develop."

Pearl's fists balled. "You leave her alone."

"You afraid she might actually like cards?"

"No, I'm not. I just don't want her bullied. Now tell me where she is. I've got to see her."

Rock's smile was more false than ever. "Not until I've got Sean's gold in my hands."

Pearl's control broke. "Give me back my daughter," she cried as she flew at Rock, attacking his face with her nails. "I've got to see Elise."

Rock's fist landed her a stunning blow, knocking her to the floor. She looked up. Her vision wasn't clear, but she could see red streaks down one of Rock's cheeks. He put his hand to his face. It came away bloody.

"If you ever do that again, I'll kill you."

"If you so much as lay a hand on Elise—"

"Bring me O'Ryan, and you can have your daughter back, none the worse. You've got twenty-four hours. Fail, and you'll never see her again."

"When will I see her? When will I get her back?"

"Go to Denver and wait. As soon as Sean's gold is in my pocket, I'll send her to you."

He left the room, still cursing.

Pearl lay on the floor for a long time, too weak to rise. She ought to be crying, screaming, cursing, shouting her fury at the world for treating her so unfairly. After so many years, so much hard work, why should everything fall apart now?

She was a pragmatist. She always had been. That was how she'd survived. Crying and ranting wasn't going to get her daughter back. No one in Twisted Gulch would care. Nobody in Denver was interested in anything this far away. There was no one to help her but herself. It was Sean or Elise.

She had to choose between the two people she loved most in the world.

How could she do such a thing? How could she betray Sean and still live with herself?

She lay on the floor for a long time, her eyes dry, her heart cold. It was gone now, the hope that had grown inside her despite the harsh glare of reality, the warmth that came from knowing someone loved her, the feeling of being young and full of hope for the first time in years. Saving her daughter would destroy her slim chance for love.

She sat up. She knew what she had to do. She would love Sean for the rest of her life—there was no possibility she could do anything else—but he would hate her so completely, even she couldn't harbor any hope he might someday change his mind. As soon as this was over, she would sell the saloon and take Elise far away.

Chapter Nineteen

Sean took no notice of the now familiar trail as he traveled from camp into town. Anticipation had built inside him until he thought he would burst. He'd stayed away a week. He'd needed time to think, to search his head and heart, to make certain he was doing the right thing. He was going against everything he'd ever thought and believed.

He was going to marry Pearl.

"You're crazy," Pete had said. "You're going to wake up one morning, realize what you've done, and hate yourself forever."

Sean hadn't wanted Pete to accompany him, but he had come anyway. Sean hadn't planned to tell anyone of his decision until he had talked to Pearl, but Pete had found out about their picnic in the meadow. All week long he'd badgered Sean, wanting to know how he'd managed to get Pearl to agree to leave the saloon. Pete made no secret of the fact that he hoped to do the same. Sean had been unable to convince him Pearl wasn't one to spread her favors around. Pete had stated rather loudly that if she went with Sean, there was no reason she wouldn't go with him.

Feeling he had no choice, Sean had told Pete he and Pearl were in love and he planned to marry her. After a few moments of stunned silence, Pete had done his best to convince Sean he was making a terrible mistake. He still hadn't stopped trying to convince him.

"Sounds to me like you're just jealous she likes me better than you," Sean said.

"Of course I am," Pete said, not the least embarrassed. "No woman in her right mind could prefer you to me. Look at you! You're a mountain of a man. You'd crush a woman in bed. You've got all that tangle of red hair. On top of that you sing."

"She likes my singing."

"She can't. No one does."

"She likes my dancing, too."

"If I believed that, I'd swear she had to be nuts about you."

"Confess it, Pete, this is nothing but jealousy."

Pete twisted in the saddle to look at Sean, who was riding behind because of the narrowness of the road as it doubled back on itself. "Who's had to listen to you falling into a fit every time anyone said a saloon woman could be a decent female? Me," Pete said when Sean didn't respond. "I listened to you eight years ago when we were trailing herds to Kansas. I thought I'd never hear the end of it when you discovered your aunt in that dive in Fort Worth."

"My aunt left me as a kid."

"I know that. So does half the western world. The

321

point is, she left you because she preferred life in a saloon.''

"What's your point? And you'd better be careful what you say about Pearl. You may be my best friend, but she's going to be my wife.''

"You don't know that. You haven't asked her yet.''

"She loves me, I know she does.''

"I love her, too,'' Pete shouted, "but I don't want to marry her.''

"You don't know what you're talking about.''

"You think she's going to want to give up being adored by hundreds of men? Singing and dancing every night, being her own boss, doing what she pleases whenever she wants? You think she'd going to turn her money over to you?''

"I don't want her money.''

"Fine, but you'll expect her to hide herself away in some dusty corner of Texas and think only of you.''

"Pearl's tired of working in a saloon. She wants a home, peace, someone to love her.''

"Did she tell you that?''

"No, but I know it's true.''

"Maybe you're right. Maybe she will prefer cooking your dinner, working herself thin on a hot Texas ranch, getting up in the middle of the night with your babies. Of course, that may not be a problem. She's probably too old to have babies.''

"She's not too old,'' Sean said. He made no attempt to keep the anger from his voice.

But he was worried Pearl might not be able to have children. Being an orphan and an only child, he'd always wanted a big family. He'd enjoyed his time on Jake's ranch when all eleven of them were still there—working, playing, and fighting together like brothers. It had been wonderful, but it wasn't the same as family. They weren't related to him by blood. He wanted to go back to Texas, to return to Jake's valley—he'd never really be able to think of any other place as home—but this time he wanted children of his own.

Yet he'd made up his mind to marry Pearl. He'd be disappointed if they didn't have children, but that wouldn't change the way he felt about her.

"You sure she loves you enough to give up her way of life for yours?"

"I think so, but I haven't talked to her."

"What if she doesn't? Are you ready to work in a saloon for the rest of your life?"

He'd never considered that option, but he knew immediately he couldn't to that. "It won't come to that."

"What if it does?"

"We'll think of something."

"You should have thought of that beforehand. If you'd let me know what was going on instead of keeping everything a secret, I could have—"

"Pete, have you ever been in love?"

"Sure. I'm in love with Pearl."

"I don't mean like that. I mean so in love you wanted to get married right then."

"No. And seeing what it's done to you, I'm not sure I want to."

"Well, it doesn't happen to you because you want it to. It doesn't ask when, where, or who. It just lands on your back, sinks its claws in deeper than a cougar, and rides you until you can't do anything but give in.

What's more, you don't want to fight it.''

"You sound like you've got a brain fever."

"It's probably something like that. But it's the best feeling in the world, too."

Pete jerked his horse up in the middle of the road. "Hell, if that's the way you feel, there's no point in my going along."

"I told you that back at camp." Sean rode by. "I'll be back tomorrow."

Pete paused, then started his horse forward. "I've come this far. No point in turning around now."

"There is if you expect to sit next to me while I talk to Pearl. You say what you've got to say before we get to town. Once we do, I'm going one way and you're going another."

"If you're dead set on making a fool of yourself, there's nobody can stop you except Isabelle, and she's too far away to do any good."

"Isabelle would be on my side."

"She probably would," Pete admitted, "but that still doesn't make it a smart thing to do. What are you going to do after you get married? Have you ever asked Pearl what she thinks about being a rancher's wife?"

"How could I when I haven't even asked her to marry me?" But that worried him. He was certain Pearl loved him, but he remembered what she had said about running away from her father's farm. She might not think a ranch was any different. He supposed it really wasn't, especially if you hated dirt, heat, and the smell of cows. Pearl was used to working hard, but it was a completely different kind of work.

He told himself to stop worrying. When two people

loved each other as much as they did, they could figure out something.

It always gave him a jolt to drop out of the wilderness of the mountains and within a hundred yards find himself in a bustling town.

"Why don't you go see about rounding up some supplies?" Sean said to Pete.

"You're serious about not having me around when you talk to Pearl."

"Would you want me around if you were about to ask a woman to marry you?"

"Hell, yeah. I'd need you to catch me when I fainted after she said yes."

"Go buy the supplies, and don't forget to buy extra bacon. I never got enough to eat this last week."

"That's because you've been working like a madman."

"The faster I find the gold I need, the sooner Pearl and I can get married."

Pete clearly wanted to make one last argument.

"Don't say anything more," Sean said. "I've made up my mind."

Pete left, and Sean headed for the Silken Lady. He hoped Pearl wasn't in the middle of one of her numbers. He didn't want to have to wait.

She was.

"She just start," Calico Tom said.

She wouldn't be done for half an hour.

"Tell her I've got to talk to her about something very important." Calico Tom just stared at him as if he hadn't heard a word. Sean walked over to the bar, asked for a beer, took it, and seated himself at the only empty table, which was in the far corner of the room.

He enjoyed watching Pearl. She was a fine singer, a good dancer, a marvelous entertainer. No wonder half the men in Colorado were in love with her. Pearl saw him, winked, threw him a kiss. It didn't bother Sean that half the men in the saloon thought the kiss and wink had been meant for them.

But as he watched, he found his attention straying to the men in the audience. They'd call out for a little kiss, ask her to show some shoulder, to kick a little higher next time. One young miner even climbed on her little stage and danced with her. Paul Higgins pulled him down. Only then did Sean realize he was on his feet, his beer knocked over, his fists in a tight ball.

He had been ready to drag the man from the stage himself.

Things got worse. Sean could see nothing but men clamoring for her favor, hear nothing but their calls for her to share what he now considered his own. He felt that if he didn't do something, he was going to tear somebody limb from limb.

He surged to his feet and headed for the back of the building. "Tell Pearl I'm in her office," he said to Calico Tom as he hurried past.

But waiting in her office was worse. He could hear music and voices, but he couldn't see what was happening. His imagination filled in the blanks with pictures that had his blood boiling.

Pearl would have to leave the saloon immediately. This would have to be her last night in the Silken Lady.

That decision made him feel so much better, he was able to endure the rest of her program without rushing out and strangling the first man he came to.

The moment Pearl entered the office he knew something was wrong. He crossed the room in a few strides, enfolded her in an impatient embrace, and kissed her unceasingly, trying to fill up the well of need that had grown to a yawning chasm since their picnic.

"What's wrong?" he asked when she failed to respond.

"Nothing."

She wouldn't meet his gaze. He tipped her face up until she was forced to look at him.

"You don't have to worry about things on your own. You've got me to share them with now."

"Until you leave to find your Texas ranch."

That caught him by surprise. She expected him to leave her behind.

"Is that all you're worried about?"

She moved out of his embrace, walked to the desk, and pulled out a bottle of whiskey. She poured a large drink and swallowed half of it in one gulp. "Do you want some?"

Surprise imprisoned Sean's tongue. He'd never seen Pearl drink. He'd never even suspected she could throw back whiskey with a nonchalance that implied she'd done it a thousand times before. "I just had a beer."

"No reason you can't have some whiskey." She swallowed the rest.

"Something is wrong," Sean said. "I've never seen you like this."

"I'm just tired."

She did look tired, but there was something about her that made him uneasy. He didn't like the empty look in her eyes. It was almost as though she'd lost something terribly important and could never get it back. Then there was the fact that her body hadn't melted into his embrace. In fact, she had seemed to stiffen. Now she moved away from him and dropped into a chair. Not very far in terms of feet and inches, but miles away emotionally.

He reached out to her, took hold of both her hands, tried to pull her to her feet.

"Don't," she said. "I'm worn out."

Sean knelt on the floor in front of her chair. "Please tell me what's wrong. Maybe I can help."

"I told you there's nothing wrong."

Her words said one thing, but the rest of her said something else. Maybe after he asked her to marry him, she'd feel more like letting him help with whatever it was.

"Are you sure you don't want some whiskey?" she asked. She reached for the bottle, handed it to him.

"No," he said, taking the bottle and setting it aside. "I've got something I want to ask you."

A wary expression entered her eyes.

"It's something you'll like," he said. "I want you to marry me."

Pearl sat as still as a statue. Sean couldn't tell if she was stunned or horrified.

"Say something," he said when he couldn't stand the silence any longer. She looked devastated, as though someone had killed her soul. If he hadn't known better, he'd have sworn he'd said the most cruel thing possible.

"I'm not in the mood for jokes." She looked ravaged by pain rather than angry.

"I'd never joke about something like this. I'm serious."

"How can you be? I know what you think of women who work in saloons. You told me that first night, remember?"

He couldn't remember what he'd said, but considering what he'd said to his aunt, he was certain it was rude and unfeeling.

"None of it applies to you. You're different."

"No, I'm not. I'm just like every one of my girls out there. We're saloon dancers, women with pasts, and nothing is going to change that."

"I don't know what's in your past, but I'm sure it's nothing terrible."

"How can you say that when I've already told you about Rock?"

"Anybody can make a mistake. It doesn't matter anymore."

This time she looked him full in the face. "You're serious, aren't you?"

"Of course I am. Any man who asks a woman to marry him had better be serious."

She stared at him a moment longer. "You're infatuated. That has to be it."

He felt himself getting angry. Why couldn't anybody believe he knew his own mind? "I'm not infatuated. I'm in love. I thought you felt the same. You said you did."

She withdrew from him again. Her eyelids lowered slightly, as though guarding her inner thoughts.

"I thought you meant you loved me today, here, now. A lot of men love me, but they never mean for it to last after they leave the gold fields."

"I don't know what I thought at first—I probably didn't think at all—but I know what I want now, and I want you to be my wife."

329

She looked doubtful. "I never expected anything like this."

He couldn't tell her he hadn't expected it either, had actually fought against it at first.

"There's so much to consider."

"You love me, and I love you. What else is there to think about?"

"Sean, you're younger than I am. You probably want lots of children. No, let me finish. You want me to live on a ranch somewhere in Texas to cook and raise babies. I've never even thought about doing anything like that. I don't know if I can."

"You can do anything you want."

"There's the problem of my reputation."

"I don't care about that."

"Other people will, probably your Isabelle most of all."

It bothered him that she wouldn't look at him. It also bothered him that she was discussing everything so calmly, as though this wasn't the most important discussion he'd had in his whole life.

"Isabelle won't care."

"Then there's the question of whether your love will last."

Now she really had hurt him. "I've never loved anybody but you. I can't imagine loving anybody else."

"You're young. You haven't met many respectable young women. You'll see plenty once you own a ranch. You may see things quite differently then."

"I'll never stop loving you. Why can't you understand that?" Why didn't she say she wanted to believe him, that she'd always dreamed of marrying somebody like him, that she was only waiting to be convinced?

"I guess because it's such a surprise," she said.

"But we made love. Surely that meant something to you. It meant everything to me. I've never told a woman I loved her."

"It meant a lot to me. I've never felt about a man the way I feel about you."

For a moment he thought she was coming out of whatever shell she was hiding in. Passion vibrated in her voice, her eyes turned luminous, and she reached out to touch him.

Then, as though she remembered something she'd momentarily forgotten, everything changed. Again, she separated herself from him.

"We've only known each other a short time. I think it would be wise to wait for a time to see if our feelings remain the same. What you're proposing would be a radical change for both of us."

"There's no need to wait. Don't you think I know my own mind?"

"We'll get a chance to find out. I'm going to leave Twisted Gulch."

She could hardly have said anything that would have surprised him more. "What's happened? Where are you going?"

"It's nothing for you to worry about."

"Pearl, haven't you heard anything I've been saying? I love you. I want you to be my wife. You can't announce that you're leaving and expect me to go back to the mining camp and forget about it."

"It's not your problem."

"It would be if I were your husband."

"You aren't."

"I'm going to be as soon as I can convince you my love isn't going to change or disappear the moment I get off this mountain. Now tell me what's wrong."

"No."

"I'll ask Calico Tom."

"He doesn't know."

He had an ugly suspicion. "It doesn't have anything to do with Rock, does it?"

"No."

He didn't believe her. She'd reacted as though he'd struck her.

"You're not telling me the truth."

She still wouldn't look at him; if possible, she withdrew further into herself.

"Pearl, don't push me away. I want to help you. I want to be with you when you have trouble as well as when you don't. Please tell me what Rock has done before I go find him and break his neck."

"It's not Rock."

"Then who is it?"

"Somebody you don't know."

"Who?"

"A business acquaintance."

"What has he done?"

"Nothing."

"Pearl, stop playing! Tell me what's going on!"

"I owe some money, and I can't pay it."

"How? This place is making a fortune."

"It's not the whiskey bill, if that's what you're thinking. It's the mortgage on the saloon."

"I thought you said you owned the saloon."

"That's how I think of it, but I had to borrow money to rebuild after the last fire. I thought I'd earn more money faster. I didn't. I've fallen behind, and he wants his money. If I can't pay him, he's going to take the saloon.''

"Ask for more time."

"I have. That's what I did when I told everybody I was sick. I went to Denver to plead with him, but he wouldn't listen. Either he gets his money, or I lose the saloon.''

"How much do you owe?"

"Ten thousand dollars."

That seemed like a lot to him. But the Silken Lady was the nicest saloon in Twisted Gulch. He guessed it cost a lot to buy all the clothes the girls wore and provide high quality whiskey.

"How long do you have to pay it?"

"Another week."

It would be impossible for her to raise that much in such a short space of time. She would lose the saloon.

"I can't say I'm sorry," he said. "I didn't want you to work in the saloon anymore anyway."

The look of panic in her eyes caused his heart to sink. If keeping the saloon meant that much to her, how could he ever expect her to leave it for a ranch?

"How can you say something like that? I've worked like a dog to have a place of my own, to be able to stand on my own feet, to be beholden to nobody. This place represents fifteen years of my life."

"But you'll have to leave it when you marry me."

"Leaving it and losing it are two different things. I'm not going to marry you because I'm a failure. I'll go to Denver, get another loan, open another saloon, try to—"

"No!"

"I don't have any other choice. You can stay here and finish finding your gold. When you've got all you want, if you still think you love me, you can find me."

"I'm not letting you leave me. I'd go crazy worrying what was happening to you. Working for somebody else is different from owning your own place. You don't know what they'll expect you to do."

"I know a lot better than you."

He didn't like the sound of that. He knew what women did in other saloons. He couldn't stand the thought of Pearl being forced to do the same things.

"I've got that much money," he said. "I can pay off the debt for you."

"No."

"Why not? You could stay here, we could get married, and Ophelia could take over the dancing and singing. You could just run the place."

"I couldn't do that. It would take you months to find that much gold again."

"While I'm finding it, you can be looking for a buyer for the saloon. Then you could pay me back. I'd have the money for the ranch, and you'd have sold your saloon rather than having to give it up."

He could see her fighting with herself. He couldn't imagine why she didn't jump at his offer right away. Couldn't she see that such a debt between husband and wife wasn't a debt at all? What was his was hers. He didn't care. All he wanted was to marry her.

"You've worked hard for that gold," she said finally. "I can't ask you to give it to me."

"You're not asking me. I'm offering," Sean said, getting to his feet. He had a cramp in his calf muscles from kneeling so long. "I'll get it right now. You start packing for that trip to Denver. I'll go with you.''

He pulled her to her feet. She looked defeated rather than elated. He figured she was still wondering if he loved her. They'd have about a week on the road to Denver and back. That ought to be enough time to convince even the most doubtful woman he would never be able to love anybody else as long as he lived.

"What happened?" Rock asked.

"He just left to get his gold. He'll be back tonight."

"I'll get the men in place. They can—"

"I don't want to know what you're going to do," Pearl said. "I feel like the most contemptible, despicable, conniving female in the world. I don't want to ever see or hear from you again."

"I thought you'd had enough of dirt and poverty when you left Missouri. But it seems you're anxious to trade all this for a dusty ranch with your overgrown Irishman."

"This has nothing to do with Sean. I've never helped cheat and rob a man. You've made me as vile as you are."

Rock looked amused. How she hated him. It was impossible for her to believe she could have lived with him even for one day without being aware of the depth of his evil.

"I'm leaving immediately for Denver," she told Rock. "I'll expect my daughter to be there within twenty-four hours. I don't want you in my saloon when I get back."

"Now, Pearl—"

"Don't think you're going to change my mind.

335

You've forced me to help you for the last time. Now get out.''

"And to think I was going to offer you a portion of the gold.''

"I wouldn't touch it,'' Pearl said, horrified.

Rock burst out laughing. He was still laughing when he left her office.

Pearl dropped into a chair and reached for a bottle of whiskey. She'd needed it to get through the scene with Sean, but that was nothing compared to her need now.

Too late! His declaration of love had come too late. Why hadn't she known he loved her enough to marry her? Even now she found that hard to believe—nearly impossible to believe that such a union could work— but she would have given it a try. By God, she would have tried!

She poured a generous portion of whiskey into her glass, then paused in the act of bringing the glass to her mouth. Something about the pale brown liquid mocked her. She'd never liked whiskey much, only learning to drink it to please the customers—and Rock. But now it seemed to beckon her, to say they belonged together, that whiskey and men and smoky saloons were where she belonged, that she had nothing to offer young men like Sean, that she was too old, too jaded and worn out to love with their enthusiasm and abandon.

She wanted to cry out that twenty-nine wasn't old, that she could love all that much more deeply because she knew how rare true love was, how desperately one must hold on to it when she found it.

But as she stared into the glass, she saw the reflection of herself, the life she'd led, the deception she'd helped perpetrate on Sean. No one would believe in her honesty, her ability to love, to be true to one man. She'd done everything she could to prove she was exactly the kind of woman she appeared to be.

But it wasn't true. She'd trade the entire saloon, every penny she had in the bank, for a chance to be Sean's wife. Her lips curved, the only outward sign of the bitter inner laugh that said she was a fool to believe any decent man would want her. She thought of a hundred things she could say to bring him back. Her body even tensed, for one moment on the verge of running after him. There was always a chance he might believe her. It was frighteningly thin, but it existed. She would do anything, endure any embarrassment, risk anything—

She couldn't risk her daughter. She didn't know what Rock had done with Elise, but she knew that if she did anything to stop the robbery, he would make certain she never saw her child again.

She could endure anything as long as she got her daughter back.

She should have stayed in Denver, let Mr. Randolph sell the saloon for her. It didn't matter that she would have taken a loss. She should have taken her daughter and gone so far away that Rock would never have found them. They couldn't have lived the way she wanted, but she would have worked. She would have washed clothes, done anything to keep her daughter safe.

Maybe there was another man in the world like Sean, one who might be able to look at her and see something besides the woman who sang and danced for the pleasure of men she didn't know. Maybe if . . .

But she was being foolish, and she'd done that too

much lately. She looked at the glass of whiskey once more, then set it down untouched. She'd been running from herself for years. It was time to stop. Time to stop everything.

This time when she went to Denver, she wouldn't come back. If she was lucky, she'd build a life that would give her a fraction of the happiness she could have found with Sean.

She left her office and headed upstairs. Several of the men spoke to her when she passed. "Tell Calico Tom I want to see him," she said. She wanted to pack and leave as quickly as possible. She couldn't wait to get out of Twisted Gulch. Just being in the same place where she and Sean had been together was too painful to endure.

She felt a strange sense of relief. Only now that she'd decided to sell the saloon, to never do anything like this again, did she realize what a burden it had been. She had always felt trapped because it was the only way she could find to gain the life she wanted for her daughter. Now it was over, and she was glad. She was sorry for the girls, but they'd get along. Somebody would buy the place. It was a good deal, especially since she didn't intend to haggle over the price. She just wanted to sell the saloon, take her daughter, and get so far away no one would ever find her again.

She knew she wouldn't be able to outrun the memories. They would be with her forever.

"Come in," she said when she heard the knock on the door. Calico Tom entered. She hated to leave him, but he ought to stay with the saloon. The new owner would find him invaluable.

"You want?" Calico Tom asked.

"I want you to give Sean O'Ryan something for me," she said. She went to the safe she kept in the back of her clothes closet. She opened it, counted out several stacks of bills, and put them in a small paper sack. She handed the sack to Calico Tom.

"Mr. O'Ryan will be coming here in a couple of days. I want you to give this to him."

Calico Tom looked inside the sack. "Lotta money."

"Ten thousand dollars. It's partial payment for a debt I owe him. It's the only part I can pay."

"What I say to him?"

"Nothing. He'll understand."

"Calico Tom no understand."

She couldn't leave him without an explanation. "I've done something awful, more terrible than I've ever done in my life. I've got to leave."

"Mr. Sean know?"

"No."

"He go after you."

"Not now. Not ever again."

"Why? You love Mr. Sean."

A racking sob escaped her. "With all my heart, but after today he'll hate me. I can't stand to see that." She turned away. "I'm selling the saloon. I won't be back."

"You leaving Calico Tom?"

She turned back to him. "I don't know where I'm going, what I'll do, how I'll live. I can't take you away from here. This place can't run without you. The new owners will probably pay you twice what I do."

"That man take your child. You want me kill him?"

339

She hugged her old friend. "I can take care of everything. You just make sure Sean gets that money. Now I've got to pack."

"Calico Tom pay Mr. Sean. Then I find you."

"No. You ought to stay here."

"I follow," Calico Tom repeated. "Mr. Sean follow, too."

A moment of panic seized Pearl. She didn't think Sean would follow her—unless it was to get revenge—but she could never face him again, not after what she'd done.

"You make sure he doesn't," Pearl said. "I don't care what he threatens, what he promises, don't tell him where I've gone."

"I no have to tell. He find out."

She'd leave Denver as soon as Rock returned Elise. She couldn't take a chance on Sean following her. She didn't think she could stand to come face-to-face with what she'd thrown away.

Chapter Twenty

Sean could hear his aunt's voice. It sounded distant and unclear, but it was Kathleen's voice. That Irish lilt was unmistakable. But it didn't make sense. He was on his way to Twisted Gulch. It was night. She would be at home. But something else was wrong. He was lying on the ground and couldn't move. He didn't know how he knew that. He hadn't tried to move. He just knew.

"Sean, can you hear me?"

He struggled to answer, but no sound came from his lips. It was as though his body had been carved from the granite of the surrounding mountains. He lay there equally silent and immovable.

"You've been shot. You're bleeding."

That couldn't be true. He didn't feel anything. He'd been shot once before. It hurt.

"I can't move you, but you can't stay here. It's going to rain."

He thought of the flowers in the meadow where he and Pearl had made love. It would be beautiful after a rain. They'd have to go there again.

"Thank God, somebody's coming."

The faint sound of a galloping horse penetrated the fog in his brain. It was probably one of the miners who'd stayed late at the Silken Lady. He tried to move. He didn't want to be seen lying in the middle of the road.

"Don't move," Kathleen said.

He couldn't. Trying had destroyed the barrier that had prevented him from feeling the pain. Now it came crashing down on him like a thousand knives being driven into his body. He heard himself groan.

"What happened?"

Pete's voice. What was he doing here?

"I don't know. I found him like this."

He felt hands on him, pulling at his clothes.

"It knew it. The money's gone. I told him he was a fool to go off by himself with that kind of money."

"Then why didn't you go with him? He's your partner."

"We had a fight. He wanted to give the money to Pearl so she could buy off her creditors. I told him it was the same as throwing it away."

"We've got to get him to town," his aunt said. "Help me get him into the wagon. I can't lift him by myself."

Sean felt hands on him again. The pain increased until he thought he would cry out from the agony. Then it disappeared and he knew no more.

Sean awoke to find himself in a strange room. He could hear the distant sound of music and laughter.

He must be in Twisted Gulch, but where? He didn't recognize the tiny room. He pushed himself up in the bed. His head ached, and everything in the room spun madly, but after a moment it slowed and stilled. The room held little more than a chair, a table with bandages, a pitcher and basin, and a scarred and battered wardrobe. Whoever lived here was dirt poor. The bed he lay on was at least a foot too short for his body. His legs hung off the end. The thin mattress barely softened the hardness of the boards beneath. He tried to sit up, but his head spun. Tight bandages across his chest restricted his movement. He was too weak to get up. He slid back down in the bed. He would wait. Someone would come.

He was surprised when his aunt entered the room. She looked concerned when she approached the bed. Her expression changed as soon as she noticed his eyes were open.

"I see you're awake." Her voice was impersonal, edgy.

"What happened? What am I doing here?"

"Somebody shot and robbed you. I found you on the road to the mining camp."

He couldn't remember an attack. He had gone back to camp to get the money for Pearl. He was riding back to town. He didn't remember anything after that.

"Where am I?"

"In my room. I didn't know where else to take you."

He could tell she was ashamed to have him see the miserable place where she lived. He knew of the years she'd spent living in the finest hotels, enjoying the finest food and whiskey, wearing gowns that could have fed a family for months. This room was proof

343

of all the things he'd said about her, and she knew that.

"You could have left me in the road," he said. "After some of the things I've said to you, I wouldn't have expected you to do anything else."

Her discomfort seemed to increase. "I couldn't, not after what you did to Britton."

He'd almost forgotten that. "He hasn't bothered you again, has he?"

"He's gone. Disappeared." She looked around the room again. "I would have moved, but—"

"You don't have to explain anything to me."

"Yes, I do. I put the money in the bank. I'm going to save enough to get out of this town."

Now he felt guilty. He'd made her feel ashamed of her life. The lack of reproach in her eyes made him feel even worse.

"Why didn't you tell Pearl what happened? She'd have taken care of me."

Kathleen looked away. "I tried, but she wasn't there."

"You should have tried again or left a message with Calico Tom. How long have I been here?"

"Since morning."

"What time is it now?"

"The middle of the afternoon."

"She's always downstairs by this time. Go tell her—"

His aunt's expression turned angry. "I told you she's not there. She's gone, left town. She's selling the saloon."

Blood pounded in Sean's head. Stabbing pain shot through his chest. He felt as though his whole body was on fire. Could he have been too late with the money? He couldn't think clearly, but he was sure he'd gone for it right away. Still, even if he had been too late, she would have waited for him. She would never have left town without telling him first.

"Something must have happened." He sat up in the bed and threw his legs on the floor. "I've got to get up. I've got to see her."

"Get back in that bed. You'll break open your wound. It's only the luck of the Irish you're alive as it is."

"I've got to see Pearl."

"You can't see her. She's gone, I told you."

"I'm getting up," he said. "There's no use trying to stop me."

"When are you going to understand?" his aunt shouted at him. "She's just as bad as the rest of us."

"No, she's not. She needed money to pay off the debt on the saloon."

"You fool! She lied to you. She's been lying to you from the start. Everybody in Twisted Gulch knows Pearl Belladonna owns that saloon. She paid for it with cash money. Turned her back and took it out of her garter belt right there in the bank. People talked about it for weeks."

None of this made any sense to Sean. With his head about to split and his body feeling as though it was filled with a dozen bullet wounds, he couldn't reason anything out. He just knew he had to see Pearl. She could explain everything.

"Her and Rock Gregson teamed up to milk this town of every cent they could. Would have, too, if your accusing him of cheating hadn't messed things up."

"She doesn't like Rock," Sean said as he struggled

to get to his feet. "She's been trying to get away from him for years."

"It beats all how a man will swallow any lump of lies when it's told to him by a pretty woman."

"It's got nothing to do with Pearl's being pretty. I love her. We're going to be married when I get enough gold to buy my ranch."

"When's that going to be if you keep getting robbed?"

"Pearl will sell the saloon. We—"

"Stop!" Kathleen shrieked. "I can't stand you being such an idiot. When will you get it through your head that Pearl played you for a fool? You've been hooked, drawn in, and bilked of your money. She's a liar, a thief! She's worse than the rest of us, and God knows we're bad enough."

"I'm not going to let you talk about Pearl like that."

"How're you going to stop me when you can't even stand up without weaving like a willow in the wind?"

"I've got to see Pearl."

"Okay. If nothing but seeing her empty room will make you believe me, I'll help you over to the saloon. You can lean on me, but first you got to put some pants on. I won't have it said my nephew was chasing after a woman in his underwear."

Sean knew the moment he stepped through the doors of the saloon that something was different. It wasn't crowded. It seemed subdued, even quiet. He didn't see Pearl anywhere.

"Where's Pearl?" he asked the first man he saw.

"Gone, so I hear. They say she's not coming back."

Fear unlike anything he'd ever experienced began to close in on Sean. "Where's Calico Tom?"

"In the back somewhere."

He felt a little better. Calico Tom would know what had happened. He would never let Pearl leave by herself. He found the old man in the hall leading to Pearl's office.

"Come," Calico Tom said. "I give you something."

"I want to know what's happened to Pearl," Sean insisted, close to the end of his strength. "Why isn't she here?"

"You sit down. I tell."

Sean followed Calico Tom into Pearl's office. He sank gratefully into a chair while Calico Tom closed the door. "Now tell me what's going on here."

Calico Tom didn't answer. He went to the desk, unlocked a drawer, and took out a bag. He held it out to Sean. "Pearl say you come. She say give you this."

"I don't want a bag. I want to know where Pearl is." He opened the bag.

"What is it?" Kathleen asked.

"Money."

"How much?"

"Ten thousand," Calico Tom said.

"Ten thou—"

The amount of money that had been stolen from him! Had Pearl somehow managed to get it back? If so, why wasn't she here to give it to him?

"Pearl say it her fault you robbed," Calico Tom said. "She give you back."

Sean looked at the money. It didn't make any sense. If Pearl needed money for the mortgage, where did she get the money to pay him back? Then he knew. She'd sold the saloon so she could pay him back.

He had to find her, to tell her he didn't blame her for the robbery. She couldn't have known anyone would be watching the road. He should have known better than to ride alone carrying that much money. Pete had warned him. He'd just been too sure of himself to listen.

He held out the bag to Calico Tom. "Give this back to Pearl. I don't want her to be in debt because of me."

"Pearl not in debt," Calico Tom said. "Pearl rich."

Calico Tom wasn't making any sense. "She can't be. She's selling the saloon."

"Pearl still own saloon. She go because she afraid you mad at her."

"Why would I be mad at her?"

"Pearl say she set you up. You hate her. Pearl go away where you never find her."

"What do you mean, she set me up?" Sean asked.

"She lied about the debt, didn't she?" his aunt said to Calico Tom. "She just pretended to need the money so someone could rob him. Isn't that so?"

Calico Tom nodded.

"She didn't love him at all. It was just a trick to get his money."

Calico Tom nodded again.

Sean couldn't believe this. Pearl did love him. He knew it. He remembered how she'd felt in his arms in the meadow, how she'd responded to his kisses, his lovemaking. She hadn't pretended. That was real.

She wouldn't rob anybody, especially not him.

"Who robbed him?" Kathleen asked. "Was it Rock?"

Calico Tom nodded yet again.

"I'll kill him!" Sean said, getting to his feet.

"Rock gone, too," Calico Tom said. "Pearl say she meet him in Denver."

"There," his aunt said. "Now will you believe me?"

Sean fought to hold on to his belief in Pearl's love for him, but it slipped away, vanished as though it had never existed. The only fragment left was the fact that she must have regretted so deeply what she'd done, she'd given him money to make up for it. His aunt was right. Pearl couldn't have loved him. No woman could help another man rob the man she loved.

He'd been a fool. Just as Pete and Kathleen had said. He'd gone against his own beliefs, certain he knew Pearl was different. Well, he'd been wrong, and he'd paid for it.

A tremendous anger came over him. He hefted the bag and threw it against the wall.

"I don't want her money," he shouted at Calico Tom. "I don't want anything to remind me of her."

He surged to his feet, swayed, steadied himself. His aunt held out her hand to him. "Let's go home," he said.

He was going back to the gold fields. He wouldn't leave again until he had the gold he needed to buy his ranch. Until that time, Pete could buy all the supplies. Sean didn't intend to set so much as a foot inside Twisted Gulch ever again.

But despite his anger at Pearl, the fury at himself for being so blind, he was aware of a terrible, aching void. Love had gone, but it had left a painful legacy behind.

Memories.

Pearl strode past men greeting her with welcoming smiles without a flicker of recognition. She could think of only one thing. Rock had not returned Elise as he'd promised. She'd waited in Denver for five days, praying some accident had delayed him. Finally she couldn't avoid facing the truth. Rock didn't mean to release Elise.

The journey back to Twisted Gulch had been interminable. She'd gone over what she meant to say dozens of times. It always sounded weak and pitiful. She longed to be a big man like Sean who could stomp into Rock's room and knock him through the wall.

Damn! She'd tried not to let herself think of Sean. It only made the pain worse. She had to concentrate on Rock. She had to get Elise back.

She entered the Swan Hotel, the best in town. Rock always stayed at the best hotels.

"Afternoon, Pearl," the man at the desk said.

"Is Rock Gregson in?" she asked, barely slowing down.

"Yes, ma'am. Room twelve. Just came in."

"Anybody with him?"

"Not that I know of. But you can tell him he's got a message from Ira Gibson. Something about the moon being in the ascent. Don't make sense, does it? It's broad daylight outside."

"I'll tell him," Pearl said, already halfway up the stairs. As she neared the door with the number twelve, fear and anger battled for supremacy. Once again fear won. She knocked on the door. Not waiting for permission, she opened it and went in.

Rock didn't look surprised. She was certain he'd been expecting her. He stood before the mirror adjusting his tie. His vest lay across the back of a chair next to him, his coat across the bed.

"Where's Elise?" Pearl demanded as she slammed the door shut.

"She's safe enough." He studied his tie, ignoring her.

"You promised to send her to me in Denver. Why didn't you?"

"I left town just after you with that intention, but I had an idea that made me turn back."

"I want Elise!" She put her hand on Rock's arm to pull him around to face her.

He shrugged her off, turned, and snarled, "Don't ever put your hand on me again!"

His reaction was so severe, so unexpected, it startled her. "I didn't mean to upset you. I just want Elise back."

"You can have her. All she does is whimper and cower in the corner."

"She's twelve years old. How did you expect her to act? Your bullies probably scared her to death."

"I don't care what she does as long as she doesn't do it around me."

"Give her back to me, and she won't bother you."

Rock didn't answer while he put his vest on, buttoned it up, and adjusted it until he was satisfied with the way it looked. Pearl didn't understand the difference in him. He'd always been totally selfish, but there had been an element of humanity in him, and a ton of charm. He could talk people into doing almost anything.

But now he seemed indifferent. More than that, totally unfeeling.

"Rock, answer me. Why won't you give back my child?"

He turned and said, "I will, but first we have to talk business."

"I've done everything you asked. You haven't kept your part of the bargain."

"Pearl, darling, you ought to know me well enough to know I never keep my part of the bargain if I can avoid it."

"I used to know you. I don't know you at all now."

"Don't be melodramatic. It's barely past noon. Now sit down, shut up, and listen to me."

He'd never spoken to her like that, not even when she was fourteen and nearly drove him crazy. For the first time since she'd known him, she was afraid of him.

She sat down.

"I think this business with Mr. O'Ryan worked very well, don't you?"

"It looks that way."

Rock sent her a searching look. "You reassure me. I had the feeling you'd gone soft on him."

"You wouldn't care if I had."

"I can't afford sentiment."

"Spare me your working philosophy, Rock. What do you want?"

"A partnership."

"No."

He ignored her. "Between the two of us we would

get rich. You draw them into your saloon, and I pluck them.''

''No.''

''There'd be no way anybody could tie anything to us. I'd use agents for all the rough stuff.''

''No.''

The look he gave her reminded her of a porcelain fish with glass eyes she'd once seen. Cold, unemotional, as though he was considering her as prey.

''You don't seem to understand, my dear. I'm not asking you. I'm *telling* you.''

''Just give me Elise,'' Pearl said, past caring what Rock had in mind.

''I'd like to see a little cooperation first.''

''What more do you want?''

''A willing spirit. I had to force you last time. I don't like that. It means a lot of extra trouble.'' He eyed her as though he disliked her. ''I think you fell for that overgrown miner. It's an insult that after me you could actually look at a man like that.''

It was pointless to try to explain to Rock why any woman would have fallen for Sean. ''You wouldn't understand. Please tell me where you've taken Elise.''

''In time.''

''Take me to her. I've got to see her, to know she's okay.''

He turned away again to pick up his coat. He put it on and inspected himself in the mirror. ''Do you think this cut is exactly right? I think I must have put on a little weight.''

''I don't care about your weight. Where's Elise!''

''You're too hysterical to discuss business now. We'll talk about it later. Come back about dinner time.''

"Rock, you can't leave without telling me what you've done with Elise. For God's sake, can't you understand I'm her mother? I've got to know."

He smiled that smile she'd learned to hate so much. "I understand perfectly. All this maternal feeling is a waste of energy, but it is useful to me."

"Rock—"

"You will see your daughter only when I decide you will," he snarled, abruptly turning from the urbane, sophisticated gambler to the vicious monster he really was. He recovered himself almost immediately. "I think it will be a useful way to keep you under control. I don't trust you, Pearl dear. I don't trust you at all."

He turned his attention to the fit of his coat again. In that moment Pearl realized that she and her daughter would be pawns to Rock for the rest of their lives. Even if she and Elise were reunited, Rock could use her again to force Pearl to do what he wanted. She'd already been forced to turn her back on the only man she could ever love. Now he was asking her—no, forcing her—to give up her hopes of a decent life for her daughter.

"Rock, if there is any decency in you, give me back my daughter," she begged. "She's only a child. She doesn't understand what's going on."

Rock continued to ignore her.

"Please, Rock, please."

"Be back at six o'clock. We'll talk then about what I want you to do."

"You can't leave."

"I have every intention of doing so."

"God, I could kill you! Have you no heart?"

"None. It's not good for business."

Suddenly Pearl knew that Rock never intended to return her daughter. Elise was his insurance that her mother would do exactly what he wanted. She couldn't stand that. Anything was better than that. She reached into her purse and took out the pistol she'd kept in her bureau. It held six bullets, more than enough to kill this demon who'd ruined her life.

"Rock."

He ignored her.

"Look at me!" she shouted.

He turned. "I told you—" He broke off when he saw the gun pointed at him.

"Take me to Elise now, or so help me, I'll kill you."

He didn't smile. This time he laughed, a loud, rude sound that tore at her soul. He stopped laughing when the first bullet tore through the sleeve of his coat. He ducked behind the bed when the second whizzed through his hair.

"What's wrong with you?" he shouted. "Have you gone crazy?"

"Give me my daughter!"

She ran around the side of the bed and fired at him just as he dived underneath the bed. The bullet tore into the pillows, sending a small puff of goose down into the air.

"Where is Elise?"

Pearl got down on her knees. Rock was just rolling out the other side when she fired. She heard the sound of splintering wood, but Rock scrambled up unharmed. She got up in time to see him heading for the door. She fired straight at him, saw him falter, then stumble. She fired again, and he fell down, screaming that she'd broken his arm.

Pearl ran around the bed. Rock tried to crawl away from her, but he couldn't reach the door before she pointed the gun at his head.

"I'm going to kill you, you heartless bastard. You're never going to hurt another child."

"Pearl, no, please," he begged. "I'll tell you where Elise is."

"I don't need your help. I'll find her by myself." She pointed the gun at his face.

Rock's eyes closed; his body turned rigid. The only sound in the room was the click of the hammer on an empty chamber.

She'd used all her bullets before she could kill him. Screaming in fury, she threw the gun at him. She ran across the room and was searching his desk for the gun she knew he kept there when several men burst into the room.

"Stop her," Rock yelled. "She's trying to kill me."

Pearl found the gun, a small, single-barrel derringer, and turned on Rock.

"One bullet is all it takes, Rock, and that's what I've got."

She pulled the trigger. The gun misfired.

"Grab her!" Rock shouted from where he lay on the floor, his blood staining the carpet. "Take her to jail. I'm going to see she hangs for what she did to me."

"No!" Pearl screamed as she fought with all her strength against the three men who laid hands on her. "You've got to make him give me back my daughter."

"She's crazy," Rock said. "Everybody knows she doesn't have a daughter. Take her to jail."

Pearl continued to fight, but she was powerless.

"You will hang," Rock snarled as they dragged her past where he lay. "Then what'll happen to your precious daughter?"

Pearl screamed in helpless fury.

Chapter Twenty-one

"I shouldn't have let you come with me," Pete protested. "You're hardly strong enough to hold a shovel."

"I can hold a rifle."

Sean had insisted upon riding with Pete when he made the run to the Wells Fargo office in Twisted Gulch with the gold from the diggings. It had been ten days since he'd been shot and robbed, and he was tired of doing nothing. He had to have something to occupy his mind. He was going crazy trying not to think of Pearl.

Despite knowing what she'd done, he couldn't help wondering where she was, what she was doing. He didn't know what he'd do if he found out. He told himself over and over again he was a fool for thinking about her, but he couldn't stop. His aunt hadn't wanted him to return to the mining camp, but staying in Twisted Gulch had been impossible. The sounds of music and laughter from the saloons never stopped. He couldn't hear it without thinking of Pearl. It was worse than the pain of his wound.

"Where do you think they'll strike?" Sean asked Pete.

"The bend is the best spot."

"They've already used that. They'll expect you to be prepared."

"It doesn't matter where they stop us as long as Danny lets us know what they're doing."

Two young miners had volunteered to drive the wagon. Sean and Pete were lying in the bed of the wagon under the canvas that covered the strongboxes, each armed with two rifles and two guns.

"Are you sure you're up to this?" Pete asked again.

"Stop fussing. How do you breathe under this thing?"

"I can breathe just fine," Pete said, chuckling. "I'm not as big as you. I don't need as much air."

The sound of shouts and the hoofbeats of several horses cut their conversation. They lay still and ready.

"Don't move," someone shouted, "and you won't get hurt. We just want the gold."

"Why would I move," Danny said, "with four of you surrounding us, two in front and two behind, all with rifles pointed at me?"

"Smart kid. Now get in the back and throw down that gold."

"I hurt my arm. I can't lift it. That's why they chose me to drive."

"Is it that heavy?"

"Yeah, there's a lot of it. It'll take two of you to lift it out."

Leigh Greenwood

"You can pull that tarpaulin off."

"Yeah, I can do that," Danny said. "Get those in front first," he whispered as he climbed into the back. "I'll scare the horses in back with the tarp."

"Stop muttering and hurry up," one robber called.

"My arm's stiff."

"If I put a bullet in it, it'll be a lot stiffer."

Sean recognized that voice. It was Ira Gibson, Rock's gambling partner. Sean was right. The three men had been working together to milk the town dry.

"Here goes," Danny whispered.

Sean and Pete rose up on their knees with the tarp. Using the wagon seat as a partial screen, they fired on the two men on horseback in front of the wagon, then whirled. Danny had lifted and waved the tarp like a huge banner. The robbers' horses sidled and plunged. Pete and Sean fired as one. Both of the thieves returned fire, but their bucking mounts ruined their aim. Pete and Sean's bullets knocked them out of the saddle. Pete jumped down to see about the bandits in front.

"These two are hurt bad," Pete reported.

Sean knew one of the men behind the wagon was dead before Danny reached him. The other lay on the ground groaning. Danny pulled the mask from the face of the dead man. It was Ira Gibson.

"I knew Ira had to be tied in with this," Sean said as he climbed down, being careful not to reopen his wound. "The three of them just about had this town where they wanted it."

"When can we can take the real gold shipment out?" Dusty asked.

"Anytime you want," Sean replied. "It'll be safe now. Who's your boss?" he asked the groaning man.

He was sure Rock Gregson was connected with the robberies. This time he intended to have proof. When the man didn't reply, Sean hauled him to his feet. "I asked you a question. If you don't want me to leave you here for the buzzards and the mountain lions, you'd better answer it."

"He is," the man managed to say between groans, indicating Ira.

"Who's he working with?"

"I don't know. We always get our orders from him."

The others told the same story. Ira had been their only contact. He hired them, rode with them, paid them.

"Let's take them into town to jail," Sean said. "We'll let the sheriff worry about them."

Sean had expected to have a feeling of satisfaction at having helped catch the gold thieves, a release of some of the tension that had been building up in him for days. Instead it seemed to get worse as they neared Twisted Gulch. He hadn't been in the town since he'd been wounded. He'd never be able to think of it without thinking of Pearl. According to the reports from the fellas who went into town each night, no one had heard anything of her. Ophelia and the others carried on without her, but Calico Tom had disappeared.

Each step down the mountain made him feel worse. He considered leaving Pete and Danny to turn the outlaws over to the sheriff but decided against it. He had to learn to live without Pearl. He might as well start now.

Still, the first glance of the Silken Lady caused a sharp pang.

"I hear it's not the same without Pearl," Pete said.

Nothing was the same without her.

"Everybody's still trying to figure out why she left."

"Wonder what the disturbance is at the sheriff's office?" Sean said, anxious to talk about anything but Pearl.

"I hope the jail's not full. These fellas got to go somewhere."

Something definitely out of the ordinary was happening. It seemed as though everybody in town was headed toward the jail.

"What's going on?" he called out to a man hurrying by.

"Pearl's back," the man shouted. "They've got her in jail for shooting Rock."

"Why?" Pete asked.

"She said something about Rock stealing her daughter, but that must be a sham. Nobody knows anything about her having a daughter."

Sean didn't wait to hear anything else. He jumped down from the wagon and started for the jail at a run.

"Wait!" Pete yelled.

Sean didn't slow down. He found his aunt among those gathered at the jail.

"They won't let you in," she said the moment she saw him. "Half the town's threatened to lynch the sheriff. He's barricaded in there with his deputy."

"I've got to see Pearl."

"Sean, why can't you just leave it alone?"

"Would my father have turned his back on my mother?"

"No. Shamus would have loved Gwenda no matter what she'd done. He couldn't help himself."

"That's how I feel about Pearl."

"You still want to marry her?"

"I'm not thinking about that now, just that Pearl's in trouble and she needs help."

"Well, you'll have to do it from out here."

"No, I won't. Pete's bringing my ticket in now."

Sean pushed his way through the crowd until he mounted the boardwalk in front of the jail.

"Don't come any farther," the sheriff called from inside. "I don't want to shoot you, but I will if you try to take my prisoner."

"I'm not here to take a prisoner. I'm here to deliver three more. We caught the men who've been robbing the stage."

"Where are they?"

"My partner's bringing them in the wagon. One's dead."

"I'm not opening up until those men outside are gone."

"We're not leaving until you let Pearl go," Paul Higgins shouted.

"She'll stand trial," the sheriff said. "The judge will decide."

The crowd started to move forward.

"You've got to stay back," Sean said. "Nobody's going to hurt Pearl. You've got my word on that. Now somebody tell me what happened."

"She shot Rock," Paul said. "They heard shots and broke into his hotel room. There are bullet holes everywhere, including in Rock. No question she did it, but we aren't letting her hang for shooting that thief."

"Let me go in and find out what she has to say. You've got to promise to stay right where you are until I get back."

"Why should you be the one to go in?" Paul asked.

"Because I'm the only one of you who thought enough of her to ask her to be my wife."

Sean expected some laughter, sneering looks, even scorn. Much to his surprise most of the men seemed embarrassed.

"She won't marry you," Paul said. "She wouldn't like it."

"She'll like it just fine," Sean replied. "You might have discovered that if you'd had the courage to ask her."

"I did," he said. "She turned me down."

Without protest, the crowd moved aside to allow Pete to bring the wagon up to the boardwalk. It took only a few minutes to get the men inside.

"Send someone to search Ira's room," Sean told the sheriff. "I'm sure you'll find the gold taken from the previous robbery." He looked in the jail cell, but it was empty. "They said you had Pearl in here. Where is she?"

"She's in my room upstairs. That old washer-woman said it wasn't proper to keep a lady in a place like this."

"Give me the key."

The sheriff pointed his rifle at Sean. "Make a move in the direction of those stairs, and I'll put a bullet in you."

"I'm not going to break her out. But if you don't let somebody talk to her, you're going to have a riot on your hands."

The sheriff looked undecided, then shrugged. "As long as you leave your guns down here, I'll let you see her."

Sean laid his guns on the desk and the sheriff handed him the keys. "No funny stuff. There's no way out except down these stairs."

Sean headed up the stairs two at a time.

Calico Tom stood outside the door. Sean smiled. At least something was normal.

"I tell Pearl you follow," Calico Tom said.

"How is she?"

"She upset Rock take daughter."

So Pearl *did* have a daughter. Sean didn't know what he thought about that, but it would have to wait until later. Right now he couldn't think about anybody but Pearl.

She was pacing up and down in the front of the room, looking out the window when Sean entered. She turned and froze. Except her hands. They continued their nervous movement. When she moved, it was to turn back to the window, away from him.

"Why did you come?" she asked.

"You knew I would."

"I didn't think you'd ever want to see me again, not after what I've done to you."

"I don't know what you've done. I came here so you could tell me."

She turned, and the tears in her eyes were nearly his undoing. "You don't want to know."

"I have to know."

"Leave now, Sean. You'll only hate me more."

She was pacing again, wringing her hands. Something more important than either one of them preyed on her mind.

"I hear you have a child. It is true?"

"Yes."

"Where is she?"

"I don't know."

Then the dam broke. Her control vanished, and she collapsed sobbing into a chair. All of Sean's intentions vanished, and he hurried to her side. She tried to push him away. When she couldn't, she clung to him and cried even harder.

"Rock took her," she finally managed to say.

"Don't try to talk right now," Sean said. "I'm not going away."

But Pearl couldn't stop. Between sobs, the story came pouring out.

"He said if I got you to bring your money to town, he'd give her back to me. But he lied. He's got her and won't tell me where. He wants us to work together. He says if I cooperate, I can see her. But he's lying. I know he is. He'll keep her locked away forever so I'll always have to do what he wants. He'll ruin her life the way he ruined mine."

After another burst of sobbing, Pearl made a huge effort and stopped crying. "I need to start at the beginning."

"Everything was fine until Rock showed up a few months back," she began. "He left me alone at first, but he got involved with every dirty trick in town." She had trouble concentrating—fear for her daughter kept breaking in on her thoughts—but she told him everything. "I gave you back the money," she said when she'd finished. "I know it doesn't make up for all the wrong I did, but at least I could do that. Say something," she said when he was silent.

"What do you want me to say?"

"That you hate me, that I'm worse than you thought, that I deserve what happened to me. Just don't sit there looking at me like you wish me dead."

"I'd never wish you dead. I love you. Remember?"

"You don't love me. You can't, not now. Forget me, Sean. I'm no good for you."

He grabbed her by her arms. She flinched from the strength of his grip.

"What you said in the meadow that day. Tell me the truth. Was it true?"

It was hard to tell how long they stared at each other. For him, everything hung in the balance. "I can take everything—all the lies, the deception, everything—but I can't take knowing you lied about loving me. Tell me. I must know."

"Why, Sean? It can only hurt."

"Tell me," he shouted. "Nothing can hurt me more than I'm hurting now."

"Yes, I loved you. I told you the truth about that."

"You said loved? Do you mean *loved?*"

She dropped her gaze. "No. I've never stopped loving you. I don't expect you to believe that, not after what I've done, but I never have." She looked up at him. "You were the best thing that ever happened to me. You just came too late."

Sean's emotions were in an uproar. He didn't know how he felt about anything. His brain told him it was reasonable for Pearl to choose her daughter over him, but his heart couldn't understand it. The hurt and the anger were still there, brought closer to the surface by her confession. But they were blunted by his love for this woman who had become the most important person in his life.

He took refuge in something he could do. "Do you have any idea where Rock has hidden your daughter?"

"No."

"What does she look like?"

"Like me, only she has blond hair. Like mine would be if I didn't dye it."

"How old is she?"

"Twelve. She's tall for her age."

Sean got to his feet. "I'll get her back."

Hope flared in Pearl's eyes. "How?"

"I don't know yet, but I will. You sit tight. Nobody's going to do anything right away." He started toward the door, then turned. "I'll be back. I don't know what I'll say or do, but I'll be back."

"Find my child, and I'll kiss your feet."

"That would either be too much or too little. Right now I don't know which."

"So Pearl has a daughter," Pete said to Sean as they headed toward the hotel and Rock Gregson. "That's going to take some getting used to. I can't see Pearl as a mother."

"I guess that's the difference between us. I always could."

"Don't tell me you've been thinking of Pearl swelling with your child and you sleeping in the spare bedroom."

"I never thought of sleeping in the spare bedroom," Sean confessed with a smile, "and I hadn't pictured Pearl swollen with my child, but it's something I'd like to see."

"What are you going to do now?"

"Find Pearl's daughter."

"I mean about wanting to marry Pearl."

"I don't know yet."

Pete jerked Sean to a stop. "What do you mean,

you don't know? She admitted she lied to you, set you up to be robbed. You can't still love her."

Sean shrugged off Pete's restraining hand and started walking again. "Suppose I did."

Pete hurried to catch up. "You can't believe her. If she lied to you about that, she could lie about anything."

"It was either me or her daughter. She figured I could take care of myself."

"I'll give you that. I wouldn't hold what she did against her—well, maybe I would if it had happened to me—but I can see why she'd do it. No telling what else she's done in her past, maybe even had another kid. Do you think she'd lie about that, too?"

Sean was getting angry. He'd already asked himself these questions and hadn't gotten a satisfactory answer. Common sense, pride, just about everything he'd ever believed told him to chalk Pearl up as a bad experience. How could he trust a woman who'd lied to him over and over? He couldn't even trust that she was telling him the truth when she said she loved him. She was probably only doing it in hopes he would find her daughter.

But she had asked Calico Tom to give him that ten thousand dollars. It must mean something. A guilty conscience. A sense of right and wrong that wasn't entirely dead. Still, no sensible man wanted a wife like that.

But he loved Pearl. He was certain of that. He was just as certain he would never stop loving her. Maybe he was a fool, maybe he'd fallen in love with her looks, her gaiety, her flattering attention. Maybe it didn't make any difference why he'd fallen in love with her. He had, and he couldn't do anything about it.

Getting married was another matter altogether.

"I don't know what she'll do about anything," Sean said. "Right now I'm not thinking about anything but forcing Rock to tell me where he's hidden that child."

"Do you think he'll tell?"

"Not without some encouragement."

"What do you plan to do?"

"I'm keeping all my options open."

"You could always threaten to shoot his toes off one at a time."

"I've thought of that." But even that would be too easy for a man like Rock.

The hotel was virtually empty when they entered.

"What's Mr. Gregson's room number?" Sean asked.

"He's asked me not to give it out," the clerk replied. "He's been shot."

"I'll ask you once more. What's Mr. Gregson's room number?"

"I can't tell you."

"We're friends," Pete said. "You can tell us."

"I'll be fired if I do."

Sean reached across the desk, grabbed the clerk by the front of his clothes, and hauled him over the desk. "You'll be dead if you don't."

"You don't have to kill him," Pete said. "I'll just look in the book."

"I want to kill him," Sean snarled. "I'm itching to kill somebody!"

"It's room twelve," the frightened clerk said, "but he's got people with him. They won't let you in."

Sean dropped him on the floor. "We'll get in."

"Guns aren't allowed in the hotel," the clerk called out from his position on the floor.

Sean turned. He'd actually forgotten he was carrying a rifle. "You going to take it from me?"

"It's a rule," the clerk said. "I'm required to remind everybody."

Sean thought a moment before laying his rifle on the counter. "If this ends up in somebody else's hands pointing at me, I'll make sure at least one bullet ends up in you."

"I don't want it," the clerk protested.

"Then why the hell did you mention it?" Pete asked.

Sean picked up his rifle. "Come on," he said to Pete.

It was an easy matter to find Rock's room. Sean didn't knock. He just opened the door and walked in.

At any other time the scene that met his gaze would have amused him. The room seemed full of women. A man with a very ugly expression on his face got up from the chair where he'd been sitting.

"You can't come in here," he barked. "Get out."

Sean hit him in the head with his rifle stock. The man crumpled into a heap. All three of the females started screaming at once.

Rock started to get out of the bed where he'd been lounging. Sean's hand held him firmly in place. "See if he's got a gun hidden about him," Sean said to Pete.

"You can't do this," one of the women exclaimed. "He's a sick man."

"Out!" Sean's order was sharp and curt.

"I'm not leaving," one woman said.

"Here, watch him," Sean said to Pete. He walked over to the protesting female, picked her up, ignored her squeals and attempts to scratch him, slung her under his arm, walked over to the door, opened it, and set her outside.

"Which way do you want to go?" he asked the two remaining women.

They ran from the room.

"I'm going straight to the sheriff's office," the first woman announced.

He slammed the door in her face. Then he locked it.

"Now," he said as he turned to Rock, "I've got two questions to ask you, and I intend to have answers for both."

"You'd better get out while you can," Rock warned. "Those women will bring the sheriff in less than five minutes. You'll find yourself in jail."

"You think they'd put me in the same cell as Pearl?" Sean asked Pete.

"Maybe, if you asked pretty," Pete replied.

"I've been shot!" Rock shouted. "The doctor ordered complete rest."

"I'll do my best to see you get it," Sean said, "but first I want you to answer my questions."

"I'm not answering anything for the likes of you."

Sean couldn't figure why this man thought he was invulnerable.

"Watch the hallway, Pete. I don't want any interruptions. Now, first question. Where is the gold you stole from me?"

"I have no idea what you're talking about," Rock said. "I'm not a thief. I certainly didn't steal your gold."

"Second question. Where have you hidden Pearl's daughter?"

"Pearl doesn't have a daughter," he snapped. "She's just trying to use that to get out of being hanged for shooting me."

"That's two lies, Pete. Isabelle always said it was a poor man who lied about important things. Do you think Rock's a poor man?"

"He's not even that good," Pete replied. "He's a skunk. A smelly skunk at that."

"I think he deserves some punishment," Sean said, "something to remind him not to tell lies."

Without warning, Sean reached out and grabbed Rock's hand. The man tried to pull it back, but Sean was too strong for him.

"I'm going to ask my two questions again," Sean said. "And each time I get a wrong answer I'm going to break one of your fingers."

Rock turned white, but his expression didn't change.

"A broken finger doesn't hurt too much, and it heals quickly. I broke one roping a steer one time. I hardly noticed it."

"I broke two," Pete volunteered, "and they hurt like hell."

"But you might want to consider the way you make a living," Sean continued. "Not being a professional gambler myself, I don't know all the tricks you use, but it might be that a broken finger would make it a little harder to manipulate the cards the way you do. You know, mark them and slide them into the deck where you can deal them to your partners."

"You can't intimidate me," Rock said.

"You'd better get going," Pete warned. "Those

women are stopping everybody they see. Looks like they're stirring up trouble.''

"No need to rush Mr. Gregson. I want him to consider his answers well. But just to help you, let's give you a little reminder.''

Sean bent Rock's finger back until he winced. "Where have you taken Pearl's daughter?''

"I told you, Pearl doesn't have a daughter.''

"Are you sure that's your answer?''

"Positive.''

The bone made only a small noise when it snapped. Rock screamed.

"I guess he doesn't take pain very well,'' Pete observed.

"I'll ask you again,'' Sean said.

Rock was a stubborn man. He held out until Sean broke his third finger. At that point the truth came pouring out.

"The gold is in the bottom of the cupboard,'' he managed to say between gasps of pain.

"The thousand you cheated me out of in the saloon?''

"Yes, that too.''

"Where's Pearl's daughter?''

"She's in a cabin a couple of miles up the road to the old gold diggings. You bastard! My hands will never be the same again.''

"Who's up there with her?'' Sean asked.

"A couple of men.''

"You mean she's up there without a woman to take care of her?''

"You ever try to get a female to stay in those mountains?''

Sean was tempted to break the rest of his fingers.

"If you've let anything happen to her, I'll come back and break both your hands. You'll never be able to hold a card again."

"Somebody's coming," Pete said.

"Hold them off," Sean told him.

"How?"

"Put a bullet through the door."

The report of the gunshot in the room was deafening. The shrieks and shouts from the hall were accompanied by the sound of retreating footsteps.

"They'll have to regroup before they come back," Sean told Rock.

Virulent hatred burned in Rock's eyes. "I'll kill you for this."

"I'm willing to take that chance. Now let me promise *you* a thing or two. If you ever come around Pearl again, I'll kill you. If you touch her daughter, I'll tear you apart and feed the pieces to the coyotes. You're going to forget you ever knew anybody named Pearl Belladonna. And if you ever happen to find yourself in the same place she is, you're going to leave on the first stage to anywhere. Understand?"

"Agnes," Rock said.

"What?"

"Her name's Agnes Satterwaite."

"You were right to give her a new name. Pearl suits her much better. Now where did you say that gold was hidden?"

"Hurry up," Pete said, "they're coming back, and they're armed this time."

Sean found his gold and the thousand dollars. Surprisingly it didn't mean all that much to him anymore. He started to leave, then turned back to Rock. "I'd rather you not say anything to anybody for a while."

He clipped him sharply on the side of the head with a pistol butt. Rock was out cold.

They slipped out of the room through Rock's dressing room, down the hall, and into an empty room.

"Take this to the sheriff," Sean said, handing Pete both bags. "Use the gold for evidence, the money for bail if you have to, but get Pearl out of jail."

"What are you going to do?"

"Find her daughter. Tell Pearl I'll bring her to the saloon."

Chapter Twenty-two

Pearl paced restlessly up and down the boardwalk in front of the Silken Lady.

"You might as well come back inside," Pete said. "No telling how long it's going to take him to find that cabin."

"I ought to have gone with him."

"He gave me strict instructions not to let you out of my sight. He doesn't know what he's going to find when he gets there. He felt he could handle it better having only one person to worry about."

"Do you think he'll find her?"

"Sean does what he sets his mind to do."

"He's already handled Clive, Ira, and Rock," Kathleen pointed out. "I don't see how you can still doubt him."

"I'm not doubting him. I'm just scared to death something will happen—has happened—to Elise."

"Well, worrying yourself into a nervous fit isn't

going to help. You've got to be calm when that child shows up. She's going to be scared out of her mind. It'll be up to you to help her stop being afraid.''

Pearl wondered if she herself would ever stop being afraid. Being a mother made her vulnerable. Being alone made her doubly vulnerable.

And she knew she'd always be alone now. She couldn't think of marrying anybody except Sean. She was equally certain he'd never ask her again, and she couldn't blame him. She ought to get down on her knees and offer a prayer of thanks that Sean hadn't turned his back on her. If she and Elise got out of this unharmed, it would be the doing of a man she'd wronged just about as terribly as any woman could wrong a man.

But every bone in her body ached with wanting him. Sometimes she didn't know how she could stand it for the rest of her life. But she had to live with the choices she'd made. She had to forget Sean and concentrate on Elise. The life she'd planned for the two of them was gone. Elise knew now what her mother did and who she was. But somehow, some way, Pearl would see that Elise didn't make the same mistakes she had made. If a man like Sean O'Ryan ever walked into Elise's life, Pearl vowed there would be nothing to keep them apart.

"Come on, Pearl. Sit down.''

Pearl finally let Kathleen persuade her to go inside. But she couldn't sit down. She wasn't hungry. She didn't want anything to drink.

"All right,'' Kathleen said when she'd exhausted every other possibility, ''tell me what you're going to do when you get your daughter back.''

"Leave here on the first stage.''

"Walk out on a gold mine like this?"

"I don't want to see this place ever again. This town. Or one like it."

"What are you going to do, enter a nunnery?"

"That's about the only respectable place that would want the likes of me."

"That's going too far," Pete protested. "A fine-looking woman like you would find a welcome just about anywhere."

"As long as I was willing to show a bit of leg. Isn't that right?"

Pete had the grace to blush.

"At least you were smart enough to save your money," Kathleen said. "You won't end up like me."

"You don't have to stay here, either."

"If you think people won't want you looking the way you do, what do you think they'll say to the likes of me? I never looked as good as you. Now I look like what I am, a washerwoman. At least I can make a living as long as nobody steals it from me."

Pearl couldn't stand it any longer. She got up and went back outside. She looked up and down the street, but she didn't see Sean. Where could he be? He'd been gone for hours. Surely it wouldn't take this long. Something had gone wrong. She just knew something had happened to him.

She had to stop thinking about Sean, or she'd go crazy. That was over, done, gone.

"You see her yet?" Kathleen stood at her side.

"No."

"I never had any children. Never wanted any. As far as I could see, they weren't anything but a worry."

"I wouldn't trade Elise if things were ten times this bad."

"But you didn't keep her with you. She couldn't have been any trouble, could she?"

The reproach stunned Pearl.

"If I had it to do over again, I might. I sent her way because I didn't want her to know what I did. Her father thought I was a lady. He died defending my honor. I wanted his daughter to be worthy of him."

"I had a chance to have a child once," Kathleen said. "But I thought dancing and having fun was more important. I wish now I could do it over."

"You mean you turned down marriage?"

"Several times, but I wasn't talking about that. I had a chance to take my sister's little boy when she died."

"What happened?"

"Some other woman raised him. Made a much finer man of him than I could."

"How do you know?"

"Because he's gone to rescue the daughter of the woman who lied to him and cheated him, and he doesn't even hold it against her."

"You're Sean's aunt?"

"Yes, but he won't acknowledge the relationship. He's never forgiven me for deserting him. So you see, I understand how you feel. We've both let him down."

Pearl wasn't ready to admit their cases were the same, but her attention was drawn to a woman up the street walking with a little girl. Pearl's heart jumped in her throat. The child looked so much like Elise, it was painful. She looked away. She couldn't stand it.

"Who is that woman?" Kathleen asked.

"What woman?"

"The one waving at you."

"I don't see anybody waving."

"You were just looking at her."

Pearl turned.

"See, she's waving again."

"No, she's beckoning," Pete said. Pearl hadn't heard him come out. "Looks like she wants you to go meet her."

But Pearl wasn't listening. The child was waving now, pulling at the woman to hurry her along.

"Elise!" The word was a whisper of disbelief. "It's Elise!" Pearl cried when the child broke loose and started running toward her.

Pearl suddenly realized she was running. She barely saw the people in her way or their startled and angry looks when she bumped into them. She only saw her daughter. Elise was safe.

"Mama!" Elise cried. She ran into the path of a man on horseback. His horse reared, unseating the man. Running on unheeding, Elise threw herself into her mother's arms.

Pearl hugged her daughter to her and buried her face in her hair. She was crying so hard that she could barely make out Elise's features, but her precious daughter was safe. She was unharmed.

Pearl didn't know how long she remained standing on the boardwalk, her arms locked around her daughter. The world receded. Nothing else mattered. She had her daughter back. Gradually the fear receded and her muscles relaxed. Elise emerged from her mother's embrace.

"Are you all right?"

"Yes."

"Did they hurt you?"

"No, but they scared me."

"You're safe now."

"That your kid, Pearl?" a voice asked.

Pearl looked up to see a circle of men, most of whom she knew from the saloon, staring at her.

"You mean you really are a mother?"

"Yes, I'm a mother." She hadn't been a very good one, but she meant to do her best to make up for it. "This is my daughter, Elise."

"She looks just like you, Pearl. You gonna let her sing for us when she grows up?"

"I'll bet she can't dance as good as you."

"You men let them alone," Kathleen said, pushing her way through the crowd. "You know Rock stole this child. Pearl's still not over it."

"You coming back to the saloon now you're out of jail?"

"Go on," Kathleen said. "You want to know the answer to that, you can come back tonight and see."

Pearl let Kathleen and Pete herd her back along the boardwalk. She balked when she saw they were taking her toward the saloon.

"No point in hiding things any longer," Kathleen said. "That's what got you in trouble in the first place."

So many of Pearl's plans had been ruined. She hated to give up this last one, but Kathleen was right. If she'd been honest with herself and her daughter from the very first, Rock couldn't have forced her to help him cheat Sean. She'd never have been separated from Elise, and maybe she'd have been able to marry Sean.

Sean! She'd been so overcome with her daughter's return, she had forgotten about him.

"How did you get here?" she asked Elise.

"A big man brought me. He knocked those men down the mountain, then he told me he was bringing me to you. He was a lot nicer than those other men, so I went with him."

"Where is he?"

"Gone. He stopped that lady, told her where to bring me, then left. He said I was to tell you not to send me back to Denver. He said a daughter belonged with her mother. You aren't going to send me back, are you?"

"No, darling, I'm never going to send you away again."

"Are we going in there?" Elise asked, pointing to the Silken Lady.

Pearl looked at the front of her saloon. It was a respectable looking building, with two broad windows on either side of double doors. It was the biggest and best saloon in Twisted Gulch. She should be proud she'd been the one to build it.

Even if she couldn't be proud, she couldn't deny it.

"Yes, we're going in there."

"Do you live here?"

"I used to."

"Can I see the girls' dresses? Miss Settle says ladies aren't curious about saloons, but I am."

"You can see anything you want, but first tell me about the man who brought you. Did he say anything about coming back?"

"No. Oh, he said to tell you he got his gold, so you shouldn't feel like you owe him anything."

But she owed him her daughter, a debt she could never repay.

"She's leaving tomorrow," Pete said to Sean. "You're not even going to say good-bye?"

Sean's fist balled, but he didn't answer.

"You've been sore as a grizzly all week," Pete said, "getting up before anybody else, working longer, not talking, staring off into space like you were a statue. You might as well go down and see her. You'll drive me crazy if you don't."

"No," Sean managed to say without exploding. "Stop talking about her."

"I've known you for more than ten years. You've kept me from getting killed when I lost my temper. We've been like brothers."

Sean grunted. He hated it when Pete gave him advice.

"I'm not telling you to marry her, but I am saying you've got to see her. There's something between you two that needs settling. If you don't, it'll end up driving you crazy."

"I'm not that bad off."

"Not yet. You've only had a week to work on it. Give yourself a year—what's that glow over there?"

"Where?"

"In the sky, over toward Twisted Gulch."

"I don't see any—"

It was unmistakable. He didn't know why he hadn't noticed it before. He knew immediately what it meant. He leapt to his feet and headed for the horses.

"Come on. Twisted Gulch is on fire."

Sean saddled up and hit the trail at a gallop. Every doubt, every question, every uncertainty—all were gone in an instant. Sean knew nothing in the world was more important than making certain Pearl was safe. In the face of danger, it didn't matter that she'd lied. It was something he would never forget, but he was thankful he'd never been called upon to make a choice between his child and the woman he loved.

He had to respect Pearl for having the strength to be willing to abide by the consequences. She hadn't asked his forgiveness. She hadn't pleaded or begged. She'd told him what she'd done and why. She'd left it up to him to judge her.

He had judged her harshly at first, but he now realized his anger had come primarily from a sense of personal injury. He had been furious that anyone he loved could lie to him. It had taken him several days to be able to look at the situation as Pearl must have seen it. If it had happened to him, he'd have broken Rock's head on the spot, but he was a man, twice as big and strong. And if he needed help, he had family he could call on.

Pearl was alone, struggling to survive in a man's world. He wished she had come to him, but she'd had no way of knowing he'd have helped find her daughter despite what she'd done to him. In the world she inhabited, people held grudges, always wanted something in exchange. She'd never had the chance to grow up in a family where loyalty, support, and defense of all members of the family were taken for granted.

He'd never realized how unusual the heritage he'd received from Jake and Isabelle was. He wanted to offer that heritage to Pearl and her daughter.

"There won't be much left by the time we get there," Pete said.

Sean remembered Pearl's barrels of water and wondered if they would be enough. The buildings were made entirely of wood.

The first thing that met Sean's eye when he galloped into town was a row of buildings in flame. People ran frantically about in the street, some fruitlessly throwing water in the fire, others dragging to safety the few belongings they had managed to save, or simply staring in shock at the ruin of what a few minutes before had been their homes or businesses.

But none of the buildings on Pearl's side of the street was on fire. The Silken Lady was as bright and welcoming as ever. He found Pearl and her daughter in the street with everyone else. She stared in surprise when he rode his horse practically up to the hem of her gown.

Sean threw himself from his horse and grabbed her in a bearlike hug. Her body stiffened, resisted, then went limp against him.

"I was afraid something might have happened to you."

"The fire started on the other side," Pearl said. "We had time to wet the roof down with the water from the barrels."

He looked at the smoldering remains of the buildings—Clive Britton's office, the hotel where Rock Gregson had been staying, Ira's lodging. It was almost as though the fire had destroyed the evil and left the good. Occasional stubborn flames still licked at the ribs of various structures. "At least you saved your saloon."

"It's not mine anymore." Her smile was weak. "I sold it to your Aunt Kathleen."

Sean looked from Pearl to Kathleen, unable to think of a word to say.

"Me and the other washerwomen used the money you got back from Clive," his aunt explained. "We decided if Pearl could make a lady of herself, we could, too. Calico Tom is staying on to show us how to do everything right."

Sean was glad for his aunt, but he couldn't think about anybody but Pearl. "But why would you sell your saloon?" he asked.

"I'm leaving."

A chill went through Sean. "You can't."

"There's nothing to hold me. I only stayed this long to pack my belongings. They've already been sent to Denver."

"Then you'll just have to write the freight office and have them redirected to San Antonio."

"I can't go there. Too many cowboys might remember me from Kansas."

"Not if you're tucked away on a ranch deep in a valley in the Hill Country."

"I don't know what you're talking about, but—"

"I'm asking you to be my wife."

"And not doing a very good job of it," Pete observed dryly.

"Shut up!" Sean ordered. "I mean it," he said when Pearl tried to slide out of his arms.

"Sean, I'm still the same woman I was before. I lied, I set you up, I—"

"I know all that, and I thought it mattered. But when I saw that glow in the sky and thought you might be hurt, I realized nothing mattered but you."

"And I have a daughter, another man's child."

"Isabelle and Jake adopted eleven of us. If there's

anything I can't figure out, Isabelle will beat it into my head.''

He could tell Pearl was weakening, but fear still held her back.

"I wish you'd say yes," Pete observed. "If you don't, he'll go crazy. And he'll drive me crazy with him."

A faint smile cracked the solemnity of Pearl's expression. "You mean a saloon dancer has been keeping him awake?"

"Hell, yes. And if you don't do something, he's going to dig a hole through that mountain trying to work out his frustrations."

"He's right," Sean said. "I'll go crazy without you. I know a ranch isn't much to offer a woman who's used to a life of excitement, but we could live in San Antonio if you want. I don't care where we live as long as you marry me."

"Sean, think what you're asking. People are going to turn their backs on me."

"Isabelle won't, and nobody else matters."

"If you marry him, does that mean I'll live in Texas, too?" Elise asked.

Sean released Pearl and turned to Elise. "Sure does. It also means you can have your own horse. You can have three or four of them if you decide to work the cows with me."

"Four horses of my own?" she asked, awed at the possibility.

"At least."

"Mama, can we—"

"How many horses do I get?" Pearl asked.

"You get all the rest, me included."

A slow smile curved her lips. This time she went into Sean's embrace willingly.

"What woman could refuse an offer like that?"

Epilogue

"I was beginning to worry something had happened to you," Isabelle called. She stood on the porch waiting impatiently for Sean, Pearl, and Elise to get down from the buckboard and hurry into the warmth of the house. "Jake says there's a storm coming. I was afraid you'd get snowed in and wouldn't make it for Christmas."

"I'd have found a way out," Sean said, giving Isabelle a kiss on her proffered cheek. "I've missed Christmas here more than anything else."

"It's the food," Isabelle said, putting her arm around Pearl and drawing her toward the large room occupied by the family when they were at home. It seemed to be full already. "Learn to cook a decent meal, and a man's putty in your hands."

"Mama doesn't have to cook," Elise said. "She can sing and dance. Sean asks her to do it all the time."

"So that's the reason you're late," Jake teased, giving his new daughter-in-law a kiss, "doing one of your wicked dances for my boy."

"If you must know, I was doing the books," Pearl said. "I wanted to get everything finished so I could enjoy myself."

"Sean lets you do the books?" Will Haskins asked. He got up to offer his seat to Pearl.

"He says if I could run a successful saloon all those years, I can keep the books for the ranch."

"I wouldn't trust a girl with my money," Will declared.

"I trust Pearl with everything," Sean said. "She has my heart. What's money compared to that?"

"A lot if you're trying to save up to buy a ranch," Will said.

Pearl decided being so handsome it was sinful wasn't enough to make Will understand romance. A woman would have to do that for him.

"You'll never have any money unless some woman takes care of it for you," Drew said. "I never knew anybody with so little money sense."

"If you have any doubt that our assorted brood really feels like brothers and sister, their arguments will soon convince you," Isabelle said.

"I don't mind," Pearl said. "I've been without a family for a long time. It's nice to have one at last."

"You've got a family, Mama. You've got Sean and me."

"And we're going to take very good care of her," Sean said. "Which reminds me. Is Ward here yet?" Ward had been doctoring Jake's brood since they were boys.

"I'm here," Ward said, coming in from the

kitchen, three almost identical boys trailing after him.

"I want you to look at Pearl," Sean said. "She hasn't been herself lately."

"Of course she hasn't. You want to tell him, or shall I?"

"Tell me what?" Sean asked, looking worried.

Knowing how much Sean wanted children of his own, Pearl hadn't wanted to take a chance on telling him until she was absolutely certain. But she hadn't expected Ward to give her the confirmation like this. She guessed when you were part of a family this close, you shared everything. After years of being alone against the world, it was hard to get used to belonging to a family that seemed to have no end.

"I've been a little under the weather because of morning sickness," she said. "Sometime in June, I'm going to present Elise with a little brother or sister."

She heard voices all around offering congratulations, but she had eyes only for Sean. He looked too stunned to speak, but his eyes told her she'd given him something of value far beyond words. They also told her he would have loved her just as much if she could never have borne his child.

"I didn't want to tell you until I was sure," she said. "I know how much you wanted a family."

"I've got all the family I need." His voice was husky with emotion.

"A man needs a son. I plan to keep having your babies until we get one."

"If you have an extra girl, will you trade?" Marina, Ward's wife, asked. "No woman should be saddled with five boys *and* a husband."

"We'll keep all our babies," Sean said after he'd given Pearl a kiss so passionate it elicited a whistle from Jake, "even if they're all girls. No man could miss a boy when he has a house full of daughters like Elise."

They huddled close together, the three of them holding each other, their arms tightly interlaced. For Pearl her world was complete. She had worked hard for her dream, but Fate had been kind. She had her dream and a whole lot more.

Refusing to bet her future happiness on an arranged marriage, Lily Sterling flees her Virginia home to the streets of San Francisco. In the best saloon in California, she meets handsome proprietor Zac Randolph, and when the scoundrel refuses Lily's kindness, she takes the biggest gamble of her life.

___4441-2 $5.99 US/$6.99 CAN

Dorchester Publishing Co., Inc.
P.O. Box 6640
Wayne, PA 19087-8640

Please add $1.75 for shipping and handling for the first book and $.50 for each book thereafter. NY, NYC, and PA residents, please add appropriate sales tax. No cash, stamps, or C.O.D.s. All orders shipped within 6 weeks via postal service book rate. Canadian orders require $2.00 extra postage and must be paid in U.S. dollars through a U.S. banking facility.

Name_____
Address_____
City_____ State_____ Zip_____
I have enclosed $_____ in payment for the checked book(s).
Payment <u>must</u> accompany all orders. ☐ Please send a free catalog.
    CHECK OUT OUR WEBSITE! www.dorchesterpub.com

**"I loved *Rose,* but I absolutely loved *Fern*!
She's fabulous! An incredible job!"**
—*Romantic Times*

A man of taste and culture, James Madison Randolph enjoys the refined pleasures of life in Boston. It's been years since the suave lawyer abandoned the Randolphs' ramshackle ranch—and the dark secrets that haunted him there. But he is forced to return to the hated frontier when his brother is falsely accused of murder. What he doesn't expect is a sharp-tongued vixen who wants to gun down his entire family. As tough as any cowhand in Kansas, Fern Sproull will see her cousin's killer hang for his crime, and no smooth-talking city slicker will stop her from seeing justice done. But one look at James awakens a tender longing to taste heaven in his kiss. While the townsfolk of Abilene prepare for the trial of the century, Madison and Fern ready themselves for a knock-down, drag-out battle of the sexes that might just have two winners.

__4409-9 $5.99 US/$6.99 CAN

Dorchester Publishing Co., Inc.
P.O. Box 6640
Wayne, PA 19087-8640

Please add $1.75 for shipping and handling for the first book and $.50 for each book thereafter. NY, NYC, and PA residents, please add appropriate sales tax. No cash, stamps, or C.O.D.s. All orders shipped within 6 weeks via postal service book rate. Canadian orders require $2.00 extra postage and must be paid in U.S. dollars through a U.S. banking facility.

Name_____
Address_____
City_____ State_____ Zip_____
I have enclosed $_____ in payment for the checked book(s).
Payment <u>must</u> accompany all orders. ❏ Please send a free catalog.
CHECK OUT OUR WEBSITE! www.dorchesterpub.com

SEVEN BRIDES
LEIGH GREENWOOD

Iris

Rough and ready as any of the Randolph boys, Monty bristles under his eldest brother's tight rein. All he wants is to light out from Texas for a new beginning. And Iris Richmond has to get her livestock to Wyoming's open ranges before rustlers wipe her out. Monty is heading that way, but the bullheaded wrangler flat out refuses to help her. Never one to take no for an answer, Iris saddles up to coax, rope, and tame the ornery cowboy she's always desired.

___4175-8 $5.99 US/$6.99 CAN

Dorchester Publishing Co., Inc.
P.O. Box 6640
Wayne, PA 19087-8640

Please add $1.75 for shipping and handling for the first book and $.50 for each book thereafter. NY, NYC, and PA residents, please add appropriate sales tax. No cash, stamps, or C.O.D.s. All orders shipped within 6 weeks via postal service book rate. Canadian orders require $2.00 extra postage and must be paid in U.S. dollars through a U.S. banking facility.

Name_____
Address_____
City_____State_____Zip_____
I have enclosed $_____ in payment for the checked book(s).
Payment <u>must</u> accompany all orders. ☐ Please send a free catalog.

LEIGH GREENWOOD'S
SEVEN BRIDES
Laurel

Although Hen Randolph is the perfect choice for a sheriff in the Arizona Territory, he is no one's idea of a model husband. After the trail-weary cowboy breaks free from his six rough-and-ready brothers, he isn't about to start a family of his own. Then a beauty with a tarnished reputation catches his eye and the thought of taking a wife arouses him as never before.

But Laurel Blackthorne has been hurt too often to trust any man—least of all one she considers a ruthless, coldhearted gunslinger. Not until Hen proves that drawing quickly and shooting true aren't his only assets will she give him her heart and take her place as the newest bride to tame a Randolph's heart.

_3744-0 $5.99 US/$6.99 CAN

By the Author of More Than 10 Million Books in Print!

Madeline Baker

Headstrong Elizabeth Johnson is a woman who knows her own mind. Not for her an arranged marriage with a fancy lawyer from the East. Defying her parents, she set her sights on the handsome young sheriff of Twin Rivers. But when Dusty's virile half-brother rides into town, Beth takes one look into the stormy black eyes of the Apache warrior and understands that this time she must follow her heart. But with her father forbidding him to call, Dusty engaged to another, and her erstwhile fiance due to arrive from the East, she wonders just how many weddings it will take before they can all live happily ever after....

_4069-7 $5.99 US/$6.99 CAN